CONFESSIONS TO SCARE...

Munly J Munly 32nd°

~ SCACUNINC**WORDS** ~

Denver, Colorado + Lexington, Kentucky

2021

Confessions to Scare...
Second Edition

~SCACUNINC**WORDS**~ *of*
S C A C U N I N C O R P O R A T E D
scacunincorporated.com

ISBN: 978-1-7378571-0-5 (casebound, 2nd Edition)
Library of Congress Control Number: 2021910820

Words: Munly J Munly 32nd°
Map illustration: Rebecca Vera
Design & Production: Vaughan Ashlie Fielder
Co-Production: Daniel Rose

Written & published during the pandemic of 2020-2021.

Manufactured in the United States of America.
9 8 7 6 5 4 3 2
Second Edition

CONTENTS

Epilogue

Confessions to Scare...

~*Scare...*~

Whose image am I made in? I am up on this cross after all. I have seen a few others like me come and then disappear. They were attacked by human and animal, burned by fire, drowned by nature, ravaged and raped by time; not one that I know of did any self-harm. I usually am accepting of who/what I am. If I twist it around enough, I am even flattered. Mayhap I am made in *your* image. What have I not been? A man with three crossed eyes...I am going to stop there, I need not hear my complaints. If I venture into what every teenage boy thinks they invented with myself and an aubergine, well, it is exhausting. So, I have accepted my job. My fate. There is an unusual perk — that at times can be a drawback — to this line of work, I have become a confessing pole. All come to me and whisper in my *ears*. I must takes notes to keep all the crookedness straight. The acts I have witnessed; it makes me afraid for where this land is heading. I have hatred for you all. And yet I love you as well. Though I am made by your hands, I feel protective of you. But could I parentally protect you from yourself? I suppose you could un-nail me and...mayhap Ahmen and I could switch places, though, most...uncertainly we already have. I might be unqualified for that job. While in mine I have become adept, most beasts I can frighten away when necessary — and after they have confessed to me —. But Wulf, he has no fear of me. Nor should he. I do not know if I would want to chase him off if I were able. The first time we met, I felt something approaching from behind; I thought it was weather breaking. Then the *weather* started chuffing at my behind. Then, through the periphery of my glass right eye, I saw a lifted haunch followed by the *weather* producing a river of fluid all around my cuffs and the base of my cross. Then, instead of leaving as a normal beast would do, from behind me he stood and placed his two front legs on either side of my straw head and breathed his humid breath in my confessing ear. He confessed nothing, he only uttered a sub-noise, something I felt more than heard. We have had other interactions, he never loosed on me again. He is careful that no one witness us in company. I think he might care for me. If not, I am afraid that I might be out of a job.

3

Kinnery of Lupercalia

UNDELIVERED LEGION

~Ahmen~

Scare...can you hear me? It's me again; Ahmen. Don't get confused, I'm not ending my speech, I was only giving my name to you. My Fater gave it to me. He also gave me my own people. One of my difficulties is that I am hindered in getting to my people. Physically, I cannot reach them. I have done it once before, but...I was forced to leave, well...that is another story, not meant for here. I do have this ability but I do not comprehend how it works. If I cross my eyes and cross myself and sit and breathe in the correct order, then I am able to see my people, observe their actions, and hear their thoughts. And if they do all their things in the proper order, then try to believe, sometimes I can even commune with them. I must admit, that is rare. The trick is for me to physically stand before them. But, if I do that, will they even see me? And if they see me, would they even know who I am?

~asher Asher (Censer)~

I'm not an official in Astodan, the orphanage apprenticed me out to them. Which is rare, I am the only youth on Dakhma Island. My chore is to clean. Clean after The Attendants, clean after the birds, and clean after the bodies. The easiest is the humans. I clean in the kitchen which is fairly simple, the individual chambers are mostly bare so there is not too much to keep clean. The night pots and washroom are more punishing on the senses. I deal with birds' muss and passed body offal and yet I still heave, both dry and wet, when confronting humans who are supposed to be able to care for themselves. The dead bodies, which can no longer care for themselves, are mostly picked clean. I mainly need to scrub the bits the birds regurgitate and the stains that can never completely be forgotten. The birds are wild and have no want to be involved with human hygiene. I wash their relentless guano and that is all. Well...it was supposed to be all, then I started gathering the bones after they were picked clean by the birds. The Attendants did not say no. One of them used to do this. Now I do it. Mayhap they thought I had initiative. I just wanted to get them out of the way so I could clean better. Mayhap that is initiative. So I gather them and then turn them over to The Attendants. I imagine I will learn what happens to the bones after I pass my apprenticeship. I don't know what they do with them after I hand them off. Ha! I didn't mean to joke, but...ever since I gathered the first bones I decided to keep one little piece for myself. It's usually a small one: a finger, toe, the ear is amazing. I don't want to get caught doing anything wrong. I don't think it matters, but some might feel it is wrong not being completely together even if your vessel is not being used anymore. I invented a type of board game that I can play alone in my chamber, one piece represents...well, it takes too long

to explain. It's not as good as kick-rock, but I can play quietly and alone. I thought I was going to be in trouble the other night when two Attendants came to my cell and questioned me about some recently missing *parts*. Before I confessed, says they, 'What would you want with a person's skull?' And I could honestly answer, 'Nothing.' Small bits are one thing. I think the family would even consider it a payment of sorts for attending with such care to their loved one's bodies. But a skull! Who would take a skull?

~ben Asher~

Here is how me myself got my job. I was watching them humongous wobble birds coming and going and living in the dead people's tower, taking care of their business. I thought how greatastic it would be to live up there, but I can't yet because a person has to be dead before they can live in Thee Tower. So I concluded the next best thing would be for me myself to climb up in the church steeple and make a claim on it like them wobble birds has done with Thee Tower. Within the first minute of my first assent...well...I witnessed my calling. I whipped the tongue forward and back and the bell joined me in calling out, 'They're coming!' Now I live up here, doing work upon the ground for Fater Nigrescent. I ring the bell every day. Different rings for different things. I ring it with much conviction on Sunday. That's when the people shuffle and slow their walk, trying to put off what they don't want to do. But, this is all practice while I scan Thee Mountains, Thee Sea, and Thee Wandering to welcome...and warn that they're coming!

~Bird~

Says Petr, 'Come here little bird, don't be afraid.' Says I, 'I'm not afraid,' but I still keep my distance. Says Petr, 'See this, my Grandfater made this.' And it caught my attention due to the sparkle lights pinging off the metal, but a metal not of this natural world, so I skitter back as best as I can, wary. But then Petr pulls out the clincher and says he, 'Come on, it's alright, I won't hurt you little friend.' Friend, he says, and my heart out maneuvered my tiny bird brain. I hop over to his place. There is a wham and then a bam. Petr, he slammed down and quick shut the door; he had converted one of his Grandfater's old traps into a birdcage. Says he, 'Got you! This is your new home little friend, I'll take care of everything.' After friending and loving me for I do not know how long, spitting his own mastications on my head in an ignorant attempt at parenting; my feathers began to drop from my body. Rubbing me with grease from a bear combined with Duk's droppings, more feathers fly away. Taking me to town, says Dr Stump Love, 'It's pista...satine...tacipine...psittacine? Well...his feathers are all going to drop.' Petr totes me back to his home, behind his hand-

hewn spikes, and tosses my cage onto his unmade bed inside his Mother's old bedroom. He sits on his three-legged-stool staring at me, says Petr, 'Harumph…why me?' I think he is reassessing our relationship. When he had tossed his Grandfater's trap, the door had not obeyed the hinge. If I was equipped with feathers I could have flown out the barred windows. I had to lull him with my escape. I wobbled out the propped, malfunctioning door, and what would be ten stories to Petr, I vaulted off his bed. Says Petr, 'Uh…' well says nothing. And I hop underneath the gap beneath his door, bounce and roll down his stairs, out the unclosed front door, manage the obstacles of his cloister, then out between his spikes. Everyday, I climb up your shoulder and preen your straw. You're my best friend, Scare… You've been around so long, you'll show me how to fly, right? And after I learn I'll hector Petr, flitting in and out of his cloister, home, bedroom, and traps. Though…possibly not. He only needs a friend. He has none to teach him anything. So after you teach me, how about I give my feathers to Aurelius? He needs them more than myself. I don't need anything, because I've got you.

~Cat~

I wake before the sun. I am not governed by your clocks but I will do my best to speak so you might comprehend. As I was saying…before the sun, yet, that is only to patrol inside the house and circle the perimeter once as well. Then I go to Petr's room and stare at him for — ?— until he shifts from the pressure of my gaze. After I am certain he has returned to a deep sleep, I balance on his three-legged-stool. With each leg being of differing lengths, I am able to knock each leg in a disquieting un-rhythm encouraging Petr to wake and prepare my breakfast. I lead him out of the room and down the stairs to the kitchen, knowing he will forget his mission that we have done since my birth. It is odd, yet he cannot begin his ablutions until after my breakfast is served. I sniff, circle, lick the plate three times, then cover the rest with air. Petr wipes his weariness and mumbles his un-appreciation at my thoughtfulness. At certain times my mind goes blank and moments later I find myself in another room. This morning it was the foyer, after catching my breath, un-fluffing my tail, and mewling to let Petr know everything is alright in this other room; I traipse back up to Petr's bed and burrow down in his still-warm bedding. I sleep for — ? — and wake to stare out the barred windows for — ? —. Back downstairs I antique the maple legs on the sofa where Petr is sitting. His slothfulness is boundless. He tries to interact with me by pretending to swat me away from my work, I have no interest in his games so I return upstairs to catch up on my rest. I wake and wend between the bedroom's barred windows and attend to my evening rituals. I go to Duk's pond and shake a bush on one side, waking Duk, before silently racing to the opposite shore to climb

the pine and knock free a cone to splash in the water. Duk's nightmare has come true and I slink away to groom and prepare my chutzpah for the coming evening. Patrolling the bower paths, I scent for rivals and relations alike. If it is a rival I arch and fluff and yowl better than most until he runs in fear at my peacocking. If it is a relation...well...a gentleman does not tell. Then I usually come to you, Scare.., and mark your pole. You are welcome. I return and squeeze through the spikes, spring out of the bushes saying goodnight to Duk, then back to Petr's wobbling stool. He eventually shifts, and I conclude our day by comforting him into a deep sleep by blanketing his mouth and nose with the warmth of my full weight.

~*Cowan*~

I've been so busy since last I was here. You gave me those teeth and everything is lighting up. See, I never had a prime. Now with this necklace it's all lining up. Certainly my wife left me, only death would take her. But if she ever ventured back she would no longer see me as a middle-age deflated ballon. Sure I'm not middle-aged anymore...I look older than he ever did. I was going to use these trinkets inside my sunken mouth. Use screws to keep them down. Then everything started going my way. Finally...and he will never see. That old bitty lost a five-piece, she was inside at the counter unable to pay, and moments later I found one for myself. And as I was bending over to pick up the piece that limb fell and would have cracked my head open, but since the piece was under her horse it cracked his head open. I don't mean to bang my own trumpet...well, I was doing fine. As she raced past me to grieve her horse I went inside the store she had just left. With that five-piece I bought myself the last hock and last warm loaf, I could usually only scrounge for the day-old. And there was plenty of the fiver left over. I sucked on a piece of bread as I went back out the door. If I had been eating my usual day-old then I would have asked to wet it down with her tears. She was kneeling in the mud, mounting the crushed mount. That's when Cap'n come and told her she had to get that mess out of there. She cried more. He was about to notch her out a citation when I intervened. I told her I would remove it for a fair price. She said it didn't matter what a fair price was because she had lost all her money and could only get the meat and bread on credit plus 10% because Chitty is a greedy so and so. So I said I would give her half of what I just bought, which I said cost me a five-piece, for only a five-piece tomorrow. And I would take care of her unmountable mount for a to-be-determined fair price the day after tomorrow. I could see her thank you in her face, she went to eat her half dinner. I was so used to eating so little that I was already full from those few bites of bread I ate in front of her to get her stomach heated up. So I would have another full meal the next day. And another few full meals because the to-be-determined price was inching up 10% every hour inside

my head. I borrowed a saw from Chitty and started cutting up her mount right in the street. That's when I realized, I was going to have food for a month. I made six trips home and put it in my box. I stripped his hide and took that home and am now drying it to use as a throw. A throw-horse, you ever heard of that? Then I came back and kicked the dogs away from the bits I hadn't used yet. I took some of the entrails and hauled it over to the former Women's Prison and made a two-piece. I came back and kicked the dogs away again and brought the testicles, one huge and one half-dog-chewed, inside and sold them to Chitty as a delicacy. A five-piece and a half-piece and a day-old loaf. I went and sawed the legs and arm-legs. I eventually brought those to Mull who traded me a pouch. When I come back again Cap'n was swinging at the gathered dogs and yelling that she couldn't leave this offal here. He wrote her a citation for unlawful dumping. I went and returned the saw, Chitty said it was ruined and unusable, I said to put it on her credit and worked him down to only 7% in a fee. I'm sure she will thank me. Then I come back here to tell you of the good fortune. I pulled his teeth and put them all in this pouch I traded for. I thought I would return the favor. You don't need to say thank you, I can see it in your face. When we see each other when I'm dead I can't wait to tell him that I died with a full set of teeth.

~Döder~

Fuck you, you wouldn't believe the truth if it hit you in the face. Or should I say if you hit yourself in the face?

~Dr Dolan~

Not every Sunday, but every year around this time I conduct The Mass Chorale. Yes, I have a bit more education than most of my patients. I don't wield it over them, we are all from the same place. I just had a bit more fortune and drive and the parents to achieve my wants. I try to bring a bit of my higher learning — yes, I know how that sounds — but...I can joke with some of them about their unibrow-protruding foreheads. Towards the end of our performance this year, I had been flapping my arms to help guide them through, when suddenly, they stopped. During *Though Didst Leave Thy Throne*, with my arms stuck straight out to my sides, horizontal to the floor, everyone, the players, the singers all petered out. The audience shifted in their seats. Chitty had come late to The Mass, the weather he brought in with his late arrival guttered all the light within except for those protected at my feet. Those footlights were shielded so as not to blind and distract the audience and apparently to guard against any late-comers as well. Well, they cast a shine on my now-stiff form, which, it seems, amazed all who saw. The lowbrows lifted up their foreheads in surprise. I don't know

exactly what they think they might have seen, my arthritic form caught in a moment of uncertainty. But, from that day forward, my practice has swelled with some not-so-ill people. People looking for a miracle.

~Duk~

Ahh! What was that? Oh, nothing. So loud, I am going to circle over here and just, *Blah*, that noise was certainly going to get Duk, I mean me. I know I mean me, I need not to explain it. The dangers out here are coming for me...Duk. *Oh, no, oh no no no!* Run! I can't turn around, whatever is chasing me will get me, Duk, if I slow down. My word, I am such a slow Duk. Alright, I am just going to get into the pond, he won't get me from the water. But, wait, what if the perch come and try to chew the webs from between my toes? Oh Duk, just chance it, hide your feet up in your chubby belly Duk. Here comes the turtle, *No, no*, there he goes, I'm alright. Well look at him, he just went into his home that he carries around everywhere right on his back. Would that keep me safe, could I do that? I could shave myself and make a home out of my feathers. I could even give some to little bird...no, no, Duk, think. Swimming and sleeping and loosening right in Petr's pond is certainly not my best effort. Back to a tree? Can Duk live in a tree? My girth keeps me on the ground. That is from Petr just always shoving food at me, it's as if he wants me fleshy. Is it because Duk dirties his bath tub? I need a safe place so I can finally relax like I deserve. *Ahh!* Oh, that shadow had a darkness to it. Duk, you're safe. Wait...where did everyone go? Where's turtle, where are the perch? Little bird...*Where?* Is He coming? Everyone's afraid of Him. *Oh!!!* Duk, Duk, Duk, that is it! You could have the safest home possible. Get inside of Him. No one would come near, factualying, they would all run around in circles for fear overcomes all when even His scent passes them. They all would fly, fly, fly away from me in my safe-room. I could look out His ribs and watch Petr playing his childish games, *Baa!* And bird monopolizing Scare.., and I could watch-guard while he rests and give warning for the scariest of all, Thee Three Hunters! *Bakack!* Duk, Duk, Duk, this is brilliance, way to use your bird brain. Now, if I can figure out how to get Petr to feed me less, lose a bit of my cuddly chub, then I can squeeze out between his hand-hewn spiked fence and hunt down...*Ahh! Bakack! Duk!* Oh, Duk, you'll never be safe until you nestle down in Him.

~Elihu~

I had gathered with everyone around Thee Totem. I thought Jehu might come and stop the proceedings. He stayed in the back, anxious like when we were children, though now his hair is thin when he pushes his hands through it. I saw him trade a quick look with Cap'n Constable. Once everyone gathered had

quieted down, Cap'n asked if he could have a volunteer. No one stepped right up, but I think they might not have because I was stepping forward with the help of Chitty grabbing me by the elbow. He turned my back to Thee Totem and held me in place. They said it was just a demonstration, nothing serious at all. While Cap'n Constable's new Calaboose was being erected, the place where I was standing was to be the temporary lockup for anyone who might do something...*untoward*. Says someone, 'No walls, no bars?' Lessing walked out from behind my Brother and paces up to me, says she, 'You never got to wear this one. I created it myself.' She smiled the whole time she was putting the horse brace on me. But it was more than that. It was an elegantly shaped five-holed woodpiece. My head was put in the first hole; my hands stuck straight out horizontally through the second and third; and my feet were stuck through the fourth and fifth, though my ankles were touching. My neck was so tight I could only change my view by moving my eyes, my ankles and wrists were already chaffing. The only way I might have moved would be by falling. She had metal links attached to the vertical portion that was the spine of the cross. She hooked the lower link to Thee Totem by attaching it to the teeth of the lowest beast, she ran the higher link through the nostrils of the bull-beast. Almost everyone gathered was looking at me, comprehending the display. Cap'n looked at me, Chitty looked at me, Lessing looked at me and smirked. After how many years, and my Brother would still not look at me. The demonstration lasted three days. No wonder people here have a hard time getting anyone to volunteer for anything. So, I just came to say I'm sorry for what you have to go through day after day. All the weather, cold stew dribbled down your chin, letting loose on yourself. And everyone talking at you, and I mean everyone, because you can't get away, and they don't have to look you in the eye when they are whispering in your ear.

~*Exseco*~

As far as I know, I am the only one not to return with them. There perhaps are others, yet until I am approached, mayhap given a sign, Ichnabod makes me ponder. I will keep my own council. Except concerning you. I know what you are about. Your coyness will not play on my ignorance. I was one of Thee Lupercalians, now I am *only* a Lupercalian. And as I know you, you already know myself. Half in two and once again, right? Three groups descend on the valley. This is...was our...their annual journey, but those who attend us at our destination do not know it begins with a journey. One group from the North and West to conquer Thee Mountains that contain no rutted passes. They carry the equipment. A dunking machine, nets folded down to 1/32 of their functioning size. Trapeze poles used as braces between beasts burdened with scaffolding, arcade paraphernalia, rides of every want, flat-gravity and vertical, Thee Dodgem, Thee Drop Tower, Thee Pendulum...and they carried trade products as well, occasionally special requests from needful souls. *But not Thee Grand Wheel.* One group

from the East. Passing through Thee Wandering that no one conquered during any other time of the year. They carry the majority of people. Be they dwarves, oddities, high-flyers, barkers, fire-tamers, ghost-speakers, game-runners, exotic chefs...those above driving the caravans. *But not Thee Castrato.* The last group comes from Thee Water. Thee Grand Wheel lays horizontally, doing double duty as the colossal deck. Its struts laying on the backs of a team of elephants who conquer so easily this water that no other craft dares to challenge. Elephants swimming the untouchable Sea. On their backs, atop Thee Wheel are animals and tents of stiff canvas to protect against travail. Horse, wolf, cats of all make, birds to blind the eye, animals they cannot name, unfamiliar to their senses and inadequate historical knowledge. Atop Thee Wheel are spokes that are used as braces for a removable deck. The decking to be used as walls to isolate the beasts once they tote all to the land. No bars here. But this *shore* is no shore. It is mammoth in scope, steep, unscalable black rock in its entire length. Except for a schooner length of sharp scree sunken just below the surface that would rip through any hull. But an elephant's feet are not a hull, they can step heavily to punish what is underneath or they can tread lightly with their will. And lastly, not accompanying the equipment, apart from the essential beings, steering the beasts with a cane strip and bark is Thee Castrato. I might say, Thee Current...and this, my friend, is why I only speak to you in a whisper.

~Fater Nigrescent~

His name *is* Hock, in a schoolyard manner they called him Hunch-Hock. And, not to enable their name calling, but Hock told me he had 'A hunch that it was close to another *special* day.' It had snowed big and heavy for weeks. Transportation is not one of our talents, and certainly with the hard weather, only the essentials of life were attempted. At that time, I had absolute belief that what I provided was the fountainhead of any essential list. And Hock, being a devoted servant, asked no questions. With my belief as his strength, he got out his hand-push plow-cart and cleared the lines. The people poked their heads out the snow tunnels that reintroduced their doorways to the world and asked Hunch why he was 'Working at to clear the way?' Says Hock, 'Because I's got a hunch.' They shook their heads and laughed at the man's ignorant joke, believing he was trying to ingratiate himself to them with his self-deprecating humor. They laughed because his back *was* hunched. The hunch forced his face to always look down. So the people couldn't see the look of faith on his face, the faith in his hunch. With downcast eyes, Hunch-Hock couldn't see that the people had not used his paths. They all had closed their doors. He completed his trek by shaping a basin upon my church's threshold into which all the other paths were funneled. Without lifting his head, says Hunch, 'Fater, now the way is clear for you and yours to come and go, *if* you can believe it.

~Grandfater~

Who's this little fucker holding the bars up in my window? It ain't polite to look down on someone in their trap. Mayhap I'm his unwanted catch. Snare, body-grip, glue, deadfall, if there were ever an unwanted I would always set it free. In fact in my favorite trap, *The Pit*, I once made a near catastrophic bumble. This was in a copse in Thee Wulf's Woods that only had a few tree/crosses. The elms and black oaks were for the most part, still individual from my ancestors' crosses. Well, I was young and heedless in my work. As I preened and strutted while admiring my work, my attention was on my youthful ego, and I ventured too close to my trap. Under my right foot the fresh wall had not yet set, and I went tumbling into my own creation. I cranked my head on a prehistoric, calcified, petrified, ancient tree root that was even older that I am now. The blow put me under for what I later learned was three full days. For three days I was in a dream state. I visioned mythical beasts, bears with wild cat heads, buffalo with snake teeth, horned painted horses muscled with wings that ran so fast embers charred their path, and fish that finally dared to walk upon land. All came and nestled down with me in my trap. And feral pups of a sort I've never witnessed, only a few weeks old and already large enough to give pause to hunting hounds. They stood on the edge of my pit, tilting their curious pup heads inquiring with yips as to what I was doing down at the bottom of this freshly scarred earth with all these beasts. Their sadness at our shared condition was raining down tears in an effort to encourage us to escape. I hallucinated the largest of the litter standing on hind legs and seeming to lean his *arms* on a fence post, as a man will do when discussing crop conditions with another man. The visions stopped when one of my family's heavy iron crosses collapsed. The downpour weakened the pit banks further and barked against my right shin. In inclement weather I still limp to this day. I propped myself up and extricated myself from the hole by using the fallen cross as a ladder. I returned to the pitfall days later to remove the nearest crosses, so this luck that befell me would not repeat itself with one of my future captures. See boy, I can get out of any trap. You think you can save me? An unwanted catch is unwanted for a reason; unwanted begets unwanted.

~Jahbulon~

How many times have I passed you and never spoken a word? I'm here now. I hope you don't think it's only because my feet need a rest. You should have seen my trek today. Six miles isn't too much usually, but today I tried to forge a path that has never been attempted. The scree would bury me up to my ankles, 'Just a taste,' it was saying. What little goat trail I found was soon halted by a ledge that was beyond my footwear's ability.

I retraced and reforged the trail uncountable times. How did this become my lot? As we both know, my service has been in question before. It makes me question my necessity. How many people's shoes have I worn? I once had tried to keep a tally, my hand began to cramp as I was running out of paper. The leather they use these days is quite stiff. Is it inferior, or the cobbler, or probably my aging, arthritic feet? Those first pair of shoes I think back on at times of angst. He wanted them done so his wife would not have an excuse not to dance with him. I ran up and down Jackass Ginnie for a day and a half. The heels aerated the ground so well that next spring grass grew where it never had before. My ankles rolled like Polly's piano. They gave me this job thinking they were doing a favor for me. No one really needs their footwear broken in. Am I not depriving them of these lessons? Still? My arcane past, a failed God once and always. At least I am alleviating them of *some* pain. I bind my own feet, they will never have to know my wounds. Oh, that's right, your wounds could compete with mine. Look at those, isn't that interesting? They covered your stumps with a pair of boots I manipulated. You know if you put them to use I guarantee you wouldn't feel a stone on your path. Not like these clodhoppers; mayhap one more mile in these...and it will be done.

~Jehu~

Women. Don't know their place. We made a place for them, taught them their right way. Then some folks get new thoughts into their heads, think to change the women's place, close it down. They stood on the platform of progress. Let me tell you how slanted their platform is. That Polly girl did not agree with being sent away to her proper place, and then she progressed Ichnabod straight into Thee Bedlam. How's that for free-thinking? What's more, people said she wasn't at fault, that Ichnabod was well on his way without her assistance. Was she at fault when she kept pushing us? Singing songs on her own, never any songs like those here before. Still, she pushed more, pushed her piano up Jackass Ginnie. And her piano pushed back, crushed her as it must have known what she deserved. It is said some people are thicker than wood. Well that piano must have been made of some fairly progressive wood, because it sure knew what's what. She got what was hers, and we'll get ours.

~Jonas Groan, King Of The Underworld~

Mull, my love. You gifted me with this backbone. I can use it as a weapon to fight the beast for these people, to vanquish my Brothers who believe me a fool, or to pierce myself and become an offering for these others while losing you, my love, Mull.

16

~*Linney*~

I know some are predicting and even preternaturally concerned about Thee War. While if they witnessed what I go through daily, they would see now the war has been initiated. I am the General, commanding this one-man army against the niggling shadow tails: squirrels. I shan't fall to them of the under-developed thumb. I see them sending out their scouts to monitor my movements with those dewy, marble eyes. Those seducers of deception that entrance any weak-minded nimrod. I know the youth, for I was of a like kind — naked, toothless, altricial — until I revolted against this governance. I command my own life, and I command you to decamp, secretly. Unceremoniously you will vacate what I have created. A garden of squash, tomatoes, and corns you have invaded for too long a time. And if that is not enough, the seeds and nuts I leave for a fairer species, you horde, and when ready, feast in decadence at your leisure. The fencing I create to deter your interest, you use as an exercise course. I draped netting to block your maneuvering, and you gnaw through, disengaging all connections and removing it to line your hovels of depravity. I engaged endless time and effort into studying chemical compounds in order to conceive a tincture that would destroy you from within. Secreting it within a delicacy no beast could refuse. Of course, no! You must only assault my garden. Your cache of my efforts now outweighs the original garden. You should feel much shame. Again, no! You choose to mock me with cuteness. Adorability as your munitions. Your chirrups are meant to be an offering of affection, pleading for peace, some treaty that we might achieve. But I see the sarcasm and taunts in your semaphoric tails. It would be easier and less fiscally irresponsible to surrender, go to town and purchase prepared fresh fruits and vegetables produced by professionals, and therefore cheaper in the end when measured against time and effort. My ballooning war-time budget could be allocated to areas of higher priorities. A door for the washroom, a pillow for my thick head. But, no! I am old, a prerequisite to that title was, *you must work your own garden.* So I will neglect my medicines that I can no longer afford; I will rally my troop, and this will end one day, either with you displaying my nuts on your mantle carved into the wall of your tree cave, or myself using you as a pillow for my bed.

~*Lucius, King Of The Water*~

These two, ahhh...why am I bound with their buffoonery? Your oily fear that has coagulated and seeped out your pores, the agitation I scrape from your bodies and haul away to be guarded by my subjects forever...well, our pact is not as firm as I implied. I massage the bellies of my baleens as a Mother does her babes, and I encourage them to burp and disgorge your angst. Once there, it evaporates and infuses itself in the sky. My

scheming and influence, unbeknownst to Marcus Aurelius and his subjects. And your dread oozes, dripping through the cracks in the land, absorbing into crevice and tunnel, pooling in the vast caverns. My scheming and influence, unbeknownst to Jonas and his subjects; though, you and I both know that Jonas is oblivious to anything that might be...*untoward*. And this sludge, as you have figured by now, of course crawls atop your fields, seeps into your water for you to soften your masticated nourishment, for you to bathe and christen your children. And for you to drink deep, and replenish the tears for Marcus Aurelius and moreover, cultivate once again on your hollow insides to once again build up, overflow, and return to me. Repeat, repeat, repeat.

~Mahout~

No one knows my secrets. They would never believe that their animal caretaker, protector, and guardian is actually one of the flock. Yes, I am sheepish. I don't want to die from lack of life. So I look and dream, wondering what it would be like to have all these gifts. And I've even entertained the idea of, what if these things are actually meant for myself, Mahout? What if I am not the middle-man? What if I am the end? And this is the test of it all, given to me by Fater. But would I truly want these insignificant baubles that these competitive talkers think of as treasure? A wheelchair stop-peg? Is she telling Ahmen where to stick it? An improperly used cattle-prod? Did he invent that? No wonder He's not returned. I am a shepherd. Does the shepherd evolve or do the sheep? If they see me as their God, that would make any man change.

~Manu~

Exseco ponders at being the only one to escape to this land. Though, Exseco's was not so much of an escape. Mine however...says Exseco, 'Cats of all make.' I was in the small animals that children can handle exhibit. Simple enough to seduce a lonely youth into secreting me into her oversized duffle pocket. I allowed her my companionship as I made myself knowledgeable of the land. I was made in a place far from here, a terrain of rolling softness, you might contrast it as a gentle version of Thee Wandering. I lived with Pharos, I am descended from the first kings. I am Familiars with Thee Three Hunters, though they are apathetic of me. One day that might change. I have spread my seed upon this land, now my line is the only species to inhabit and populate. For the moment we stay quiet, stay in the shadows, conduct our lives in the night. Yet one day I will raise the stakes, adapt to the wars, evolve to conquer, and finally have some...have some what? I suppose peace would be the proper thing to say, to want. Though I am not certain. Whose belongings would I mark with my scents, whose doors would I scratch to make them believe there

is an unknown quantity they should fear? And who would I wake at an ungodly hour so they can discover my devious behaviors that instigate their fears? That is something to think on. There is something fetching about being worshipped, doted on by all, pampered in all manners, fed and even cuddled when I might have the desire. I still visit the descendants of that first youth, let them comfort themselves with my trills. Some of my own line have bedding there. I give them *the long blink*, letting them know that the plan is still on; but for the moment let's continue on this path, weaken their defenses with our charm. For now, I must return to Exseco, who has been sleeping uninterrupted for one and a half hours and certainly wants to be woken and spoon me out a delicacy that I will turn my nose at.

~Marcus Aurelius, King Of The Sky~

I look at those two in wonder and attempt to remember how we came to be in league. The feathers that are drenched with your tears I haul away to the sky, where my subjects roam and keep them safe within their council...well, I know there was a contract that states they will guard your tears forever, yet...this is not completely in my power. Your tears are eventually sent back down to earth when my subjects squeegee the vanes at my behest. Your sadness creating the waters where Lucius believes he reigns. My scheming influence, unbeknownst to Lucius and his subjects. And your melancholia seeps into the land, the osmosis infecting all in its wake. My scheming and influence, unbeknownst to Jonas and his subjects; though, not much is known to Jonas or his pitiful few. And of course, the sorrow returns to you as well. To return to me. Repeat, repeat, repeat.

~Mattie~

You told me yourself, it was not your fault. It were n't. I most likely did something to instigate it. And I should not have let myself fall down the entire length of stairs. But, I'y'm sorry, so let's make it work for us. Everyone feels sorry for a cripple. I could go roll around town with pity smeared on my face and folks would be handing everything over. I'y'll do more than it takes. My arms will be muscle bound. I could arm wrestle men and win us money. Anything to win you. I'y'm undeserving. I feel all I got is to offer you my lap. You're welcome to rest there after your outings, see, it's meant to be. I'y've no feeling, so no matter how heavy a burden you come to be, your weight would never do me harm.

~Mauchline~

I am completely blind. I didn't know until they told me. I thought this is how it is for everyone, I can't wrap my head around the concept of vision,

what everyone else *sees*. I have pictures, images in my head. I build these through touching and smelling and embellish them with imagination. I have skin, but what does it look like? Am I shaded dark like my imaginings? I feel people's hair, they all feel different...and quite a few smell. My hearing is exacerbated — my cane seems to make such a hullaballoo — I wonder how loud it really is to everyone else. I ask and they laugh at me like I'm silly, my friends say that's how they know I am coming. A bull with his bell. This afternoon after we finished lunch, I was leaving and in unison they all sang, 'Ding-Dong, Ding-Dong.' It was cute the first few times. Recently, even they seemed exhausted by the routine. At times I feel their awkwardness in stretching to include me. But this time they laughed and slapped their hands over the noise. They are kind and continue to try. I hear her crying every day. Well...almost every day. Not yesterday. It wasn't silence I heard, it was her presence. I heard it, smelled it, felt it...sensed it. I went to her for the first time ever. We exchanged pleasantries. She seemed more chipper than I anticipated. I have been told I am not shy; I disagree, but I think because I ask to feel a person's face that is a common misconception. She was beautiful. Smooth skin; hollow high cheeks, a dimple on the chin; button nose; and...dry. Says I, 'Is all good?' I heard her nod, 'you'll have to nod louder in the future.' Says she, 'What does that feel like, getting to touch everyone?' I shrugged, having felt this response from unaware people. She got my joke and laughed. I heard her spit. I knew I wasn't that funny. Without asking, she touched my face. It was a piece of linen. She wiped my face. Says she, 'It was a deep red stain of...something?' After a pause, I started to tear. Says she, 'No...no...I didn't...' She was worried she had mentioned a color. 'Here, you keep this, I don't need it anymore.' We touched our goodbyes, made words that we would see each other again, both giggling at the phrase. We both made a new friend. I removed the ribbon from my hair. I wrapped the linen handkerchief around the end of my cane and fastened it there with what I hoped was a bow. I went back to my old friends. With my new gift, I saw them before they saw me.

~Nolan~

I have always carried a handkerchief in my breast pocket, a tradition passed down by the men, proclaiming it as a light burden to carry for being allowed easy entrance into a woman's heart. Forty-nine years and counting, unused. Ironed and cleaned bi-weekly. Awaiting with patience its christening. I was there when Polly rode her piano down Jackass Ginnie. Her trauma was severe. However, it was ill-got and somewhat self-inflicted. My sympathy was untouched. Tucker happened to view the crown of the material as my coat breezed open when I bent to retrieve the purposefully dropped package. Says Tucker, 'That is beautiful, may I?' Tucker interrupted the reach, both of us mirroring the other by laying a hand upon our breasts. I

might have gifted Tucker, but there was a question that went unasked, and if asked, I am not certain if I could have given the desired answer. Cahie approached me, saying she knows about me and the stinginess with my handkerchief. Says Cahie, 'I've got a new use for that, you can tie me and bind me, place it over my eyes...' I walked away from her beguiling sway. I might have fitted it down her throat to stop her from ruining another. I had finished my meal in Thee Square with a gathering of others and their families. I was with them, but alone. I was about to have an after-meal sip. A child ran into me in a sudden dash to stand at her feet. I spilled the wine. I reached to my handkerchief, I had not decided yet if I would use it to wipe the small amount that had spilled on myself, or wipe the child whose face turned on me in dismay at realizing the stickiness in her hair. Then the woman stood on her box, did her thing, and collapsed.

~Numa~

You remember me. I took care of Mister Petr right towards the end. I was just a little thing then, I had no right to be alone with that man. I don't know why his wife, now his Widow — instead of herself —, wanted me to feed and dress him, scrub his gummy-teeth, even wash his body. She was not too much older than myself. She inspected me when I went to her; she said I would do but that she would need to cut my hair short. She did it right there on the front stoop looking over Thee Cloister. It was nice to be outside and look over the fine grounds, especially because I was anxious about getting rid of my hair. And she surprised me twice. First it was not just a *cut*, she shaved my head. I jumped up at the first shear but it was already too late, I couldn't walk about with the divot started in my crown. The second surprise was that I assumed she put us outside so my hair would blow away in the breeze. Not true, she collected all of it inside her apron. She finished the procedure, and she led me back inside to instruct me on all of my responsibilities. As we started up the stairs she reached for the handrail, my hair scattered out of her unmanned apron. She forcibly refused my help. She fell to her knees and began to gather my hair: no broom, no dustpan. She tweezed every strand between her thumb and forefinger, placing all back in her apron. I offered again to assist. She froze in her work and the scare I felt infest the room was beyond enough to remember me my place. The day wore on, and she was still in the early stages of her task. I could hear Mister Petr upstairs fussing. When I tried to make her aware, I could not distract her and that same cold arose. I went upstairs and began to fumble my way through what needed done. The sheets could take no more of his filth...so I began. Bathe, clean, feed...I bumped his soft head, scalded his crepe skin. I stabbed his gums with a spoon. We made it through. As I left she was still employed with my hair. When I returned the next day, she was nowhere about. And I never saw

her again until she passed. Mister Petr and I went along, me continually putting more blankets around the both of us to fight the increasing drafts in the house. Then he died. When I was cleaning his home for the final time I could not put on enough layers to fend the freeze that was now forming in the home. Cleaning out from under his bed, I found the apron with my hair. I was knelt down wondering on it when a slight singing began...I thought to leave. Not as severely, yet once again some of my hair scattered from the apron. The singing stopped; the cold ebbed...then I did more than *think* to leave. I left. Was it childish? Some fears are good. I still shave my head, and every morning I can't be distracted from gathering my hair from its protective arc circling my bed.

~Petr~

My fascination with the trees is limitless. My people thought to husband the forest, erecting imposing yet ornamental iron crosses within the encroaching darkness. They were placed within to ward off the beasts. Not trusting in any Scare... such as yourself, relying on something older...or younger, depending upon your viewpoint. Certainty, superstition, mayhap faith. Our hoard is dying out and I can only find these answers on my own — though I've learned there might be one left —. Was it solely for Wulf? Or was it wildly successful, vanquishing, ancient, mythical terrors and Wulf is only a remaining devolved offspring? It's no concern of mine, only an intrigue. For Wulf has his hackles pointed at yours truly. He's a cock and he is scrapping the ground outside our cloister. He wants me to groan when I hear his scuffing. He is now free of his Woods, though mayhap he always was, only now he is roaming wide. I go to his Woods to skulk and investigate, and I find the umbrage has overwhelmed the totems. For generations they have dropped their progeny upon the floor, letting wind, minor bestiary, and time relocate them in near proximity to each cross to sprout beneath and confront my family's defense. The loam births vines to climb and choke the crosses, injecting their claws to leach out any strength they might contain. From the detritus, the saplings impinge upon a cross' claimed territory, wending between and through the ornaments, eventually swelling to see which obscene weapon might eventually prevail. Among the most senior crosses and trees, only upon close inspection can I decipher where one starts and the other ends. Plodding decades of enveloping limbs have brought a stalemate to the battle. Is this why Wulf has come forth? Are the trees his totems? Mayhap his soldiers? And it could be that he is marching them towards the cloister, to overtake my own gilt-edged security. My family's home. Yes, we came to your land with husbandry in mind, but evil begets evil. My family has petered out, I find your pup's remains in my Grandfater's forgotten traps. I will not beget, but...it is my family's pride. Which of us shall be the last of our kind?

~*Polpot*~

My short pants are not practical when it weathers, yet that is all I can bring myself to don. I have pairs upon pairs of cut and fashioned coverings in leaning piles, setting here, waiting for her injured...well, she knows what they are for. A person pictures himself acting heroically, plays out scenarios in his imagination, hears narration lauded upon him for his fearless feat. I didn't handle myself as I would have hoped to throughout her emergency. We were going to have the most idyllic day. I had rehearsed that in my imaginings as well. Then...I don't know; I hear my memory is worse than hers. I can't recall if it was a storm, if the little mountain gave way, or perhaps Ahmen's hand. And when I finally wobbled down to where she was, blendered in with the dirt, rock, scrub, ivory, wood and wires, *her* hands were all that I could decipher. I grabbed them, obviously not probleming the situation out. I pulled; she screamed. Was the damage from her ride down the hill, from what I had just done, or from what I did next? I am so sorry, it is all my fault. If I could gift her my hands...I only did what my body told me to. I could see the bones were bent just beneath her skin, blood started seeping where one had germinated. I tore my pants above the knee and girded her stumps, I made a corset and bound them as tight as possible. I've heard people speak about how some of the women here used to bind their feet, mayhap that is what my arms were doing to hers. I know my mind was not...it wasn't doing anything. All I ever wanted to do was hold her. Tight, tight, tight.

~*Theodore*~

Us men of Thee Sifto Mine had not seen the sun since...well if them bosses would have rigged up more than one light, the jolt would have forced everyone of us to close our eyes. Lookin' back some joked that maybe we shoulda closed our eyes, takin' what we could get. We had to keep workin' while our luck was runnin' so strong. Workin' even on His birthday. It took three of the line bosses to hang that one light, then the bosses laid down on the *new* wood-floor, boards that were supposed to be bracin' the walls. Engel stood on the box that held the headlamps — they put the box there so we would not steal them headlamps at the end of a shift, but for a joke Olazabel ended up stealing the box itself. What were they thinkin'? We would see in the dark the next shift? — and Engel started pushin' n' pullin' on his accordion. There were no women down in the mine. So all us men danced with one another, you know, takin' what we could get. Restin' our bearded chins on one another's shoulders. Holdin' our calloused hands against another's unwashed hips. The ablutions we neglected down in the darkness were more criminal than any Olazabel jest. The dance lasted longer than all of Mass day itself, but us men couldn't tell because that

singular light we had was no sun. Eventually us men supposed we didn't care if we did waste a day or two of work. We joked about closin' our eyes, but truly we were glad on seein' our dancin' partner. I think we all hoped that our own face looked as wonderful as the one that was jerkin' back and forth in front of our own. See, we had found veritable treasure that day, and from that day forward we wouldn't let Engel do any work that might cause damage to his accordion fingers.

~Tiler~

Was it the first volley in the inevitable war? I once heard of a man killed by a bird who mistook his bald pate for a rock in an attempt to get at a captured turtle's meat by cracking it open. I have never heard of our carrion-birds to behave in this manner. These birds have become somewhat slothful, they know there are plenty other options that could receive their attention if the one in front of them proves too difficult. And besides, if it was the skull of who I think it was then you and I both know there was nothing there for the bird to consume. No, I think it was some bargain he waged with The Avestans. He most likely paid them to train the bird, it would have to take cunning and foresight. They would have needed to separate the fledgling from the parents, hand-feed it to imprint, and earn trust. Worked with it everyday. Using first snail shells to drop upon from the sky, then graduating to cat skulls as it grew in strength. Once it mastered these, a sheep skull would be wielded and then the aim be perfected upon tree stumps camouflaged to appear like my own head. Much like you. Did they ever use you in their artillery barrage? No, no...you would tell me. It didn't kill me. I haven't seen that bird again. Wait, maybe that is part of his battle strategy: to eventually wear me down with a gradual soft bombardment. Yes, I could picture him scheming it all out. Wait, wait, wait, what if he has an entire fleet? Is a dropped skull more fatal than a deer horn to the belly? An axe to an artery? An ulu? He was...no, *is* crafty. Engaging death-birds to bring me down. It's proven to give me a headache just trying to work it out.

~Wulf~

Shall I never discover an ex-voto on my threshold? Scare..., I pin this composition upon thine's breast for all to behold. The morals speaketh from my ancient's misaligned maws, reimagined and questioned; from my neb! Together will we imbibe, or is the terminus nigh, nay, compulsory?

UNREGULATED; ILL-REGULATED, SHALL WE
BE THE WARD? THE VOID'S AEGIS TO THWART

SUPERSTITION, DESPOTISM, ATTACKS OF HUMAN FRAGILITY. DOTH WE SUBJUGATE, DOTH WE CHAIN? WE HAIL BETWEEN THY COLUMNS, YOUR PILLARS OF COGENCY. COMPENSATION UNYENNED: BAR WHAT THY CONTRITION DEEMS OBLIGATORY. IF THY GUILT SUBSUME THEE, OUR LABOR WILL CLEANSE ALL. THERE SHALL BE NO OTHER TO RECEIVE YOUR OBLATION. OF THIS WE CANNOT ACCEDE. ONE GRAIN OF WHEAT WILL BECKON OUR LUST. DEFENDER, ESCORT, WARDEN, CUSTODIAN, SENTINEL, BULWARK; WE ARE ALL. YOU HAVE SIGNED THIS UNKNOWN PACT, WE HOLD YOU ACCOUNTABLE, IGNORANCE SHALL BE INDEFENSIBLE.

Scare..., is this what it has come to? I am the last attendant, my teeth are ground and loosening. I will overlook these continued transgressions, if the only offering proffered is a progeny that might protect us both from our ancestors, moreover from ourselves. I leave it to your communing;

SPEAKETH THY TRUTH!

~yeshua Asher~

When he first came to me I told him how sorry I was for his loss. And then I began to grasp what he was asking. The monuments I normally erected were for the family members to be able to pay their respects and have a place to visit their passed love ones. Of course, only the women are placed with the stone, usually only part of the men's eventual ashes are placed there; the rest are scattered or retained around a neck...so they take up less physical space. But this monument he was wanting was for himself. I first assumed he was being responsible, taking care of all his preparations so his family would be free to grieve. Alas, he said he wasn't sick and had no intention of going anywhere, anytime soon. He wanted it for himself, implying that some of his *friends* had suggested the idea and he only wanted to do right by them. I asked what size he wanted. Says he, 'Well, as big as myself.' Says I, 'So you want a statue of yourself?' Says he, 'No, no, I don't want people to think I'm vain. Just a monument, like you normally do, but larger so everyone can see it.' To be as large as himself above ground I would need to add half as much below in order for it not to topple. He was taken aback when I mentioned this, I felt more at the idea of it falling than the physics of it.

25

He pictured someone purposefully capsizing it and again implied that will never happen, no we can't let that happen. We agreed on the size, then next was the inscription. Says he, 'Just normal, my name, my qualities...let my *friends* do the rest. Yes...I think a good idea would be to leave space so my *friends* can come and write their messages to me: congratulations, comments of praise...you know whatever the occasion calls for. Remember, they're the ones that are asking for it.' I would never say it out loud, but I crafted his *monument to himself*. Out of curiosity I went to visit it sometime afterward. To my amazement, people had written on the monolith. Each and everyone was as he said: high praise and congratulations. Asinine needless comments that in the past would be better left unsaid, or if truly necessary, said directly to the person himself. As I stood in awe, he came out from around the opposite side with a chisel in his hand and dust on his boots. I inquired, saying I could fix anything I might have been at fault for. He only looked at me quizzically, I could tell he was trying to place my face. He stood on a box that he had left there, to do double duty, holding various size chisels that his *friends* could wield according to their style and taste. He began to etch a number just above where the first comment was. He turned proudly and says he, 'That's how many of my friends have been here.' Wondering at the logic of cementing a fluctuating tally, I feigned not to see him hand me a choice of writing implements and circled to the opposite side to politely escape. Upon viewing the back side, my heart lurched at the wound in my stone. I saw fresh trauma. A gouging and hacking that had crudely erased what had once been there. I was curious if the person who left this deleted message was included in his tally...his life's work.

Kinnery of Lupercalia

BUELL LEGION

~Addison~

Jehu crashed his carriage when he was driving home one evening after a night of imbibing. He left it for someone else to deal with. And so my husband did. I had been disappointed with the gifts that Teardrop had given me ever since our first Anniversary together. So, this Anniversary, in a fit of courage, I decided to tell him exactly what I wanted. Says I, 'Teardrop, I want an outside setting place, should be tender leather, and it could have fancy metal trimmings.' On Anniversary morning Teardrop comes up our lane pulling a weight. He was hauling on two brace poles that he had borrowed from the mule's plow. And behind him rolled the back half of Jehu's trashed and discarded carriage that Teardrop had sawed cleanly in half and then reconfigured. Says he, 'Look Addison, I's got you a custom setting seat. Real leather it is, from a real live cow... well, was live. And to protect the cow's skin I attached a whole heap of metal trimmings. A roof even. Keep the hard weather off of the cow while you're still setting *outside*, but you'll be kind of *inside*. And see if it gets too hot you can lever the window with this pulley I made from your Mother's necklace that's just been setting broken and unused. Look there Add, it's got a trunk that we could mayhap put a picnic lunch inside, then you could set yourself on the seat, and just like them beasts from Thee Lupercalia, I could pull you down to the creek-side. There can't be nothing like us eating your kitchen art, hanging over the creek with the light summer breeze blowing through where them front wheels used to be. Why the crying Add? If you like I could paint it up a bit, do a nice flower motif. Just tell me what ya want.' It was such an odd contraption, not what I had envisioned when I told him what I wanted. But, I think he knew what I truly wanted more than I did myself. Says I, 'No, I like it just like this.'

~Archai~

Fater Nigrescent, Exseco: good men both. I never went in for either. You live your life as decent as possible; you have some missteps, of thyself and to others, and still you might try to be honorable. I don't know what I deserve, I never really thought I deserved anything. My store is gone...it's still there, it's just not me sweating about overhead and profit and every other detail even when I was sleeping between the constant grind. I don't have those worries now so I should sleep a bit better. Now, I've a dent in my skull that has taken up the charge to battle against any rest I seek. I never saw the men that night. I probably knew each and every one, but the hoods they fabricated were purposeful and effective for their purpose. Fater Nigrescent said he would pray for me. I've still a dent in my head. Exseco said he would find the men. I've still no ability to revive my livelihood. My

nausea is constant, my vision is reduced to one eye, and any light worth seeing by can be difficult enough to induce vomiting. If I do manage to stand, the ribs that pulled away from my sternum cause me an extreme lean to the East. Said Exseco, once they are apprehended there will be at least some financial accounting. Said Fater Nigrescent, he was canvassing his people to assist in my time of need. *Time of need.* That made me slow even further than my earned lethargy, to smile and think a bit. Is this my time of need? Who can be certain? I think there are others who are more deserving than myself. I thank Fater and Exseco, perhaps I would also thank my assailants. I have a modest savings to nest in. Given enough time in the day, I can still function for myself. And mayhap that is what we all need. Time.

~*Ashmole*~

Thought I'd run this by you. This is the cologne I've been pedaling out of our black back door. It's been said that you cannot enter a relationship expecting to change the other person. Probably sound advice. If it is true love then you should not take issues with hangnails or flatfeet. Mayhap it is wearisome that their hand is clammy every time they grab yours. Might be that you always find some of their hair sticking to the inside of your mouth. If it is love, then it's best to accept these failings and be thankful it's not tuberculosis. Yet, within this sound advice, the issue of scent was never addressed. The smell might be some rutting-season-musk that your partner emitted to seduce you. And they, being bathed in it for all these searching years, they might be oblivious to the rank. But, now that the search is over and they have found you, you should be allowed to address this failing. With what I am touting, you do not need to say *bippity boppity boo,* only spray this mixture on your sleeping partner to change the offending failing. And, who knows, it may influence hangnails and flatfeet. Hopefully it will not promote tuberculosis, Ha!

~*Askew*~

I was Young Askew Dumb when my Fater had given me a plow...I can't even remember how many years back. I knew that my Fater was mocking me for my lazy childish ways. I couldn't accept them furrows that laid across my Fater's forehead, my Fater said I put them there my-own-self. So...I went to work. |*| And as Young Askew Dumb, I learned to keep my hand on the plow. And now, I am Old Askew Dumb. |*| Before I was given this plow, my Fater had lost one of his limbs in *a* accident when he was trying to go against nature, against that tree. So, though my Fater certainly could keep a hand on his own plow, he was unable to do anything else, lest he let his one gripping hand go. |*| But, his son, myself, Old Askew, has two

hands, and while I was learned right by my Fater to grip tight, I also figured it out that there are other things to hold. It might be a picture, might be an old blade. Mayhap even something of the non-physical type, a memory thought. If a person be truly fortunate, another's hand. Truth be told, it's usually a kinda thing a person would love. And probably yous gotta work harder for these things, gots to hold it even tighter than the plow.

~Augie~

I am the *good* cousin, that's what they call me. We were visiting our relations for a few weeks in the warm months. Because of the heat, we were playing inside, then outside when the walls got too close, then back inside when the sun overwhelmed us. A continuous pattern. My eyes were trying to readjust to the dark, then the light. I reached down to show everyone how you could eat a dandelion raw. I didn't want to ruin the prettiness of the flower so I didn't bite down. That was when I felt a scuttling on my tongue. My sun-blind eyes had not seen the bee. Mayhap it was afraid of the dark like I sometimes got. He struck out in fear. The oddest thing was that I didn't scream, so the bee went further down my tongue and then up and out following the only light it could find. My nose! I still feel bad for harming both the dandelion and the bee. My punishment was this guilt that I still carry, though it is not as heavy as it once was, and a swelling that exaggerated my already permanent smile. As we lazed around after dinner, it was suggested that we children go outside and catch lightning bugs inside of the yet unused jars. Of course, after my recent trauma, suggested I instead that the younger children 'Dance your Papa round the pit's coals.' The children beamed and laughed in delight, and for some reason pulled their Papa, my Uncle, upstairs. It seemed through my wounded and swollen tongue the children heard, 'Dress your Papa in Youtsey's clothes.' Youtsey was the live-in maid of our relations. The children finished, then dragged their Papa back downstairs. He was dressed up in Youtsey's Sunday Summer dress and hat. Their Papa looked to heaven, wondering, 'What do these children hold over me?' But, he endured. He was making his children happy. He could see I had a sadness for everything I had done, done to the flower, the bee, and him, my *good* Uncle. At the end of our visit, after my swelling subsided but my guilt had grown, as we were leaving early he told me, 'It's not so miserable, everyone can see that the cut Youtsey wears flatters.' When we returned home, I found that he had put that dress was in my satchel. After I grew into the dress I wore it until it was almost thin enough to suggest what I did not want to suggest. I finally unstitched it and made a pattern that I use to this day to gift dresses to all my cousins.

~Baal~

Ethier and myself be at an age when these bodies be entering the staleness stage. I am cultivating crepe paper where my joints bend. I should say, should bend. Sometimes their swell makes it look like I gots a tree knot growing under my bark. Sometimes it's not underneath but, right on top. There are mornings I will find a miniature carapace upon my back where only a freckle had been. The carbuncles on my thighs are a grotesquery fit for Thee Lupercalia. But, I am still alive, and so is Ethier, my girl. She has walked with me through my trials; I am guilty of her patience. She has made a glutton of myself. Not her fault one bit, it has been only through a severe love. A love in the bedroom and a love in her kitchen. Her joy derived from indulging my appetites is a luck that every man wishes for, yet no man deserves. And now either my wishes have gone dry or whoever decides these things has made a judgement as to what I truly deserve. My previous complaints were minor, now my body is in full revolt. I went to Dr Dolan to obtain some magic of his science, mayhap a shot or a pill to assist me in re-conquering the bedroom, where recently I continue to not bring my hoe to work the furrow. Instead Dr D gave me brain advice, says he, 'Speak with Ethier, the results will be better for you; you're both getting older. Enjoy it, moreover enjoy each other.' Well, that's what I want, you imbecile. Sometimes his science is just plain dumb. So I went to Mahout... he made me a salve from his goats' horns. This past week our wall has become buckled from the insistence of our headboard. But, three days in, my smell quit, which could be a benefit if I were commissioned on Dakhma Island. I am not. But losing smell goes hand in glove with taste, which of course I have also lost. Which means I have deprived Ethier of seeing me pleasured from her love of cooking. I can no longer enjoy her venison, spiced with secrets she purchases once a year. No more appreciative groan after I mop my plate of bacon juice each morning with her warm loaves of kneaded bread. Mahout was right; we've all seen his goat herd grow to excess. Yet, mayhap Dr Dolan was more right; mayhap I should speak with Ethier. We deserve it. She deserves it. I love her and owe her. We know we both always enjoyed the kitchen more. I'll leave it to her, but I am fairly certain we will both love growing to excess.

~Baphomet~

Everyday there is a growing list of words that I am *instructed* never to say again. Sometimes the instruction is told to my bum; which if I were allowed to say it, the words I might use would be **ass, dumper, keister, booteus maximus, poop chute, patootie, fart blaster, double-bubble-trouble**; which really means diarrhea...oh and my favorite is **badonkadonk**.

32

Beardsplitter: that's when a man is with another man and means his hoo-ha.

Fopdoodle: dumba**.

Turtle Humper: just what it sounds like.

Gonsarn: a substitute for Goddamn. Now I need a substitute for that.

Sard: I don't know how my Fater knew that one...well, it's the big one so he would know it.

Suckface: I was told never to say or think it again when once I said goodnight to Mother, says I, 'Should we suckface?' She laughed, Fater did not. She explained it later and said I should save it for someone I think is special, or at least when I'm older.

Bodikins: that's touching your cousin.

Thingumubob: I thought it was when you forget something's name, but it's a man's dangles. Oh...that's one too...

Dangles: a man's thingumubobs.

Addlesaddlebattle: that's an idjit who tries to have it on with a mule.

Fussock: I thought this was a combination of you know what. It's one that Fater laughed at and Mother educated my bum. It's something bad to ladies.

Bull Corn/Anything: says Fater, 'That's pushing it, there are so many words you could use...but don't. And do you really think I don't know what you're doing?' Says I, 'What? We have a bull and sometimes we feed him corn and...' message to bum, 'you can't put them together like that.' He let me up and I walked out of his reach then says, 'So *stick up the bum* is on the list?'

Hump: I can only say it if I am talking about a proper hump-shaped-thing. Wait...so does that mean I can say...

Wumbas? Those are shapes. Like, 'One day I hope to put my **beardsplitter** between a **fussock's wumbas** and squirt my miracle...' Ahh, now I need a proper word for miracle...

~Barruel~

I had empty pockets. I had two bad teeth and couldn't chew what Boucher offered in a kindness: thick meat, good meat. I was too ashamed to tell him I had no manner to cook the gift. It weren't no fair. I was starving. I had done bad things in this life true. Some not this bad...two more so. It didn't matter if it was easy to do or that if I had thought about it at all, I still would have twisted it around inside my head so I could see it as the right thing to do. I was sitting on the back stoop of Thee Church when Cap'n comes out the back door. What he was doing there late on a Sunday night...well, I'll never get a fair shake to ask that question. That is part of the deal. Says he, 'You keep your maw shut,' and he points to the door, 'and we won't drag you in for a proper trial. One where no one who likes your

33

kind will be the judges. We'll just have that trial here and now.' It wasn't an offer, there weren't naught to dicker. Without asking he took the remaining loaf and ripped it in two, told me to go ahead and talk, eating half out of his left hand. I tried to explain my hunger, my teeth, my pockets, life. It will never be possible for people who have always had plenty to understand us who have not. They have chances, education, opportunity...food, shelter... protection. We had naught. He would never protect us, even though he is paid to protect all. I don't want a hand-out, but a hand-up, just once... just once. It woulda been all I...The swing from his club knocked out most of my left side. The second only took a few. He gathered them and put them in my empty pockets. I don't know why he had that plier device on him, but he was slow. I thought he had a gentleness with his touches, I was fogged thick by then and looking back I would guess not. I carry my teeth in my pocket now: this one right here. My breast. And for anyone who might not talk *at* me, but with, it's harder than ever to understand what I might be saying. All I can eat is one thing. I have to let it set in my mouth until it gets all wet and mushed, then it can slide down to my stomach. You're a good talking companion, skinny as me. You panivorous? Here my friend, let's split this.

~Belue~

Our blood is the same color. Yes they are often impolite. They use my surname in place of my given. But I will not hold them in judgement. I do my best to fix most everything here, and when my best is not good enough, I admit it and figure out a solution. I've seen the rabbits battle behind Harris' home. I've seen the birds wobble above, the sun reflecting the hue off their wet beaks. I was there when they returned Polly to town, her trauma trailing me back to her piano where I went in hopes of repairing the culprit, but Polpot had scavenged my thought. When Titus' nose bleed dripped, before it hit the bucket, I witnessed the true tint. But, what he did with the contents of that bucket...it could make a man weep. It was then I knew he would be my guide. I studied him. It wasn't malicious that I could see. He explored all the uses of his own sample. And mine for that matter. He used his standing with the Murphy house. I think he claimed it as a postgraduate study. His creativity is borderless. He went to the other boys there and drew their blue blood. He had me construct a box, an archival structure where he placed the vials stanchioned off with the *donor's* name stamped on the stopper. No one questioned what the *study* was for, but as more people found out about it, they wanted to help the good-hearted scholar. He drew blood from Buells, Dumbs, Toombs, Cannonballs and Loves. None of Thee Undelivered approached him. But, who would blame them? His collection grew. He mixed and experimented, conjuring like some alchemist from Thee Lupercalians' stories. He made a variance out of every single vial. The book he created

was beautiful as well. He showed no one but myself. He taught himself to bind and stamp the leather cover, he cut and stitched the pages himself. But the inside was the treasure. Sheaf after sheaf of singular shades and hues. As I gazed upon them it seemed as if I had developed a new sense. My vision had acceded to a level unknown to humanity. He was an artist. He had taken a part of every individual, no matter their background, intelligence, economics, health…name. He made something beautiful of each stain. I asked what he planned to do. He shook his head, seemingly thinking on it for the first time. Says he, 'I find it…interesting.' He has been around me a bit too much, he is getting my way with words. He is creating his own future. I am proud to have had a small part in that. And our blood is the same color.

~Blucher~

It was always dis way. Sumetimes I look at my 'flection in a bucket of wader, and it looks burned, or like a horse kick to the side of my head. Made a warble cauliflower that close my earhole. But I come out this way. I speak dis way because I mostly have deafness. I choose words that I can say so others understand. I'm not dumb, but I marry one. I read his lips to understand his words. But I can hear his love for me. Mayhap he say, 'I think I'll go outside to - ADORE! - pick three tomatoes for supper.' Once he say, 'Looks like weather - MY GIRL! - leapt Thee Mountains.' When he say the love words for me to hear, he say them with an exclamation point. Just speaking, then, - BAM! - and then he finish his mouth-reading words. When he was a boy he was put into Thee Bedlam. But even the Dumb men realized his sweetness. He just has a knot in his brain. So instead of saying the traditional sentence like others, he goes a diff'rent route, follows the knot. But, he still get to the same end. People say we perfect 'gether. I've seen this said about other peoples, times 'castically. If we were traditional, like others, then they might say it meanly at us, but they've heard and know as well as us it is true love. Says he, 'I don't deserve - TRUE LOVE! - you.'

~Boucher~

You sons of bitches, you're all thicker than any cow I've cleaved. When you call your Fater, 'Father,' that doesn't make him a priest. When a man's name happens to be Mason that does not mean he hews stone. Moreover, my name is Boucher, not Butcher. I don't know which imbecile first mouthed my name as Butcher, but it stuck. It stuck worse than dried offal. I tried to explain it to them, I wrote down my arguments, supported by facts, surrounded by history. Yet, another mistake by me, as if the humps could actually read my words. Their argument back at me was, 'No, them words are writ on butcher paper and the butcher paper is tacked to a butcher's door.' That was the only thing they got right. They're great logicians. By

that time...I had given in. Their faith beat mine. I gut, cut, and carve. I give the bones to Taras Love; at least he's happy. When I scratch and pet him I rub my hand along his back and envy his spine.

~Cahie~

Nothing comes to me, well..nothing that I ever wanted. So, you know what I went and did? I bought my own self a new used buggy. The single axel is warped, you can see the earth through the cracked floorboards. The traces are so extremely knotted that they must have been manipulated by Jehu's hand. And if it is even possible, the reins seem to be inverted, backward, and on the wrong side; and if I could figure them out the leather is so offensive a person's hands would most likely revolt. Under the backside of my mind, I hoped that this invention might entice the young Abun Love down out of those trees. Inside of my new *present* to myself, I laid down to *present* myself to the young Abun Love. Soon I heard footsteps creeping on up...that was when I remembered that nothing ever comes to myself that I want. I should have gone myself to the young Abun Love. Because now I even has a means to get there...but there is the axel and the traces issue, and of course that damnable rein dilemma.

~Cesaré~

I could cool myself if I could dig down into this ground. But, there's nothing to dig with, except this box. If I could squeeze down to infant size I could shelter away from the sun. If I was inside my Mother, would I be cool and safe? I don't remember her, I only remember her through the stories Olazabel tells me. That makes me remember how I did used to fit in this box. Olazabel found me squabbling inside of it, washed up on the shore of Thee Dakhma Island. He had gone there to get *her* body. 'She wasn't dead so why would the birds chew on her?' that is what he asked the Avestans attending there. Olazabel can handle himself, but no one can put off the Avestans; he threatened them, saying, 'I'll be back,' as they shoved him outside they did not close the door. They seemed to leave it open for him as they stared. But, Olazabel turned away to face River Forktine. When he waded in to cross he heard my noise fussing from the bank. He said I was laying there in my box with all these other empties stacked up in neat piles around me. He says I shouldn't ever feel special because there were so many others like me. At least he was leaving that island with a body, even if it wasn't the one he came for. When he was swimming us across Forktine a magpie landed on his head that he was struggling to keep up. The magpie kept pulling his hair between beak and black bird tongue. Olazabel couldn't do a thing about it because he was pushing me and my box in one arm and stroking with the other while trying to keep

his head above water and even more so with the added weight of the bird. Even though birds have hollow bones the weight finally pushed Olazabel under. He should have done that in the first place, because the magpie had no more perch and jumped over to sit with me inside my box. When that magpie eventually passed, Olazabel plucked him and used the feathers to soften my box/crib lining. Olazabel eventually turned over the care of the canaries to me; there were always birds talking to me while they only screamed at Olazabel. Now I'm back where I started, naked and alone, just myself and my box.

~Chesebro~

A numbness came over the land, brought by the summoning of Thee Three Hunters. Of course, these are second-hand stories informed by the winners. They call it human nature: what we create, we destroy. Why go through the motion? If the Wulf was lost, who would be the enemy? So those of us not caught up in the semantics need to pose the difficult questions; the first, as to who they might have been truly hunting. Could they have come for Petr and his people? That old man was perhaps in Thee Bedlam for our protection and not his own. Possibly our fate on Dakhma Island at the heights of Thee Tower Of Astodan. From ourselves and Döder even. A good possibility is for our countless past corruptions. Setting free the women of Thee Prison doesn't mean we removed their walls. It's my own fault, they did not really need a lackey. A filthy scrub to do their bidding while in this land. There are legion, yet I presumed to be all that they required. One to fetch, one to subdue, one to honor and connive a betrayal. Of course I stepped forward, volunteered, no, offered my services. 'Scum myself,' says I. Hopefully the numbness is only within myself, for constantly beating myself up. I fear it is not only the people, but as the story says, *Thee Land*. The people are of their own hand. Thee Land which we love had no part in this, it cannot defend itself...or?

~Chinetel~

You know I have a most nutritious way to influence men with this little device here, passed down from woman to woman in my family. A tool that would make the most industrious squirrel envious. It does not matter what the situation. Be it in happiness or anger, winning or losing an argument. A stranger or kin, a friend or lover. It is always to a person's advantage to intimidate a man, be it for the present or be it for use in the future...
...In full view of the male, softly take a nut in your hand. Place it gently between the pinchers then lock eyes with the male, affect a gentle yet subtle smile. Then force down the pinchers to explode the nut. Pick up the shrapnel. Invert the instrument. Use the converted dentists' pick to

scrape out the innards of the nut. Make certain to rub the pick using heavy pressure against the wall of the nut. Recreate the most abrasive sound possible, nails on chalkboard, metal on metal, tooth on glass. With this first shucked nut you want to place it inside the male's mouth. This should be easy, seeing how the male's jaw should be open wide. In addition, it will confuse the male. Now it is time for your own nut, after repeating the previous steps, place your own nut in your mouth softly. Again lock eyes with the male. Then bite down to pulverize the nut. Afterwards, give the same gentle but subtle smile. Once again confusing the male. Then offer seconds to the male; confusion begets intimidation begets nutrition. Beget, beget, beget — is that all that is required? I require influence.

~Chitty~

My eye had been focused on Archai's space next door for some time. His space was so much more...well, spacious. I had accumulated so much inventory that it was bending the boards that combined to make our wall. I knew I needed more wall to contain all my gatherings. So I spoke with some untoward men. I spoke in extreme quiet, so reticent that not even Ahmen or the men who enforced men's rules would hear. The men did what they were paid to do. Archai's space now stands empty. But now I have regrets about using these men. I think that mayhap I spoke too quiet. The men had done the job well before they were compensated to do it. Now, I can't stand a job going undone, so even though today is Sunday, I know this mass of inventory is going to keep antagonizing my wall-boards. I had timed and planned this event so I would have Archai placed out later in the coming week, so that I would have time to attend Fater Nigrescent's services as I do every Sunday, and in covering that base I would also be able to offer a pre-prayer for anything that might *befall* Archai or his establishment. I know that I am a good soldier for Fater Nigrescent, but I also know that Ahmen and Fater would understand me working on Sundays and mayhaps arriving late. Because Ahmen and Fater both know that there is still a lot of work to do.

~Clough~

They used to put brands on anyone's hand who did something unlawful. Eventually most everyone had a brand and it appeared to be an honor badge, so the practice was quit. Now, I believe I am the only person remaining that employs a brand. But, I keep mine hidden on the palm of my right hand. My younger...I will never again say *little*, my younger sister Gert was put under my maturing guidance for an evening. There had been much talk of me needing to be more responsible, a contributing member of the family. Bossing Gert around for an evening seemed more of a reward of decadence than anything that my parents were wanting to teach me

prior to responsibilities and contributions being accounted for. Gert, of course, wanted to do what she was never allowed to do without parental supervision: make hot cocoa. And her ability to manipulate my immaturity was a testament to her own. Says Gert, 'I thought you were in charge, so why can't we?' Says I, 'Alright then, we make cocoa.' She retrieved the kettle that was a gift on our parents' wedding day, a gift they were wary to make use of. Covering the entirety of the form were motifs and runes of both an artistic and pedantic ilk. The images were our own, yet foreign and unfamiliar. I built the fire, and with water inside, placed the paragon on the grate. As we awaited our indulgence, we prepared a variation of a game taught to us by asher Asher. As I was strategizing my opening salvo, the kettle blew. Gert was up and away, she reached the grate and began to pull the grate with the tongs. She was unused to the unfamiliar weight of the unused kettle and shifted her own weight to readjust the totter. By kneeling, she had over-adjusted, and the kettle began the ponderous slide to her upturned face below. The scream of the kettle had also beckoned me, steps behind Gert. She tipped the scales of justice, then without thinking of my responsibility, I manipulated them back towards myself. The runes embedded themselves in my right palm as I used my left hand to simultaneously grab the tongs, replace the grate, and turn Gert's face away from any harm. To this day her second best trait is her youthful, cherubic face. Her best trait is her faithfulness. She is the only one who knows of my secret. My only secret. It catapulted me into adulthood, both of us in truth. As when I turned her face away, she now takes my right hand in her own and turns it around and around trying to read what the runes might be saying.

~Comen~

The scent seduced me the moment I walked through the doorframe. Half-price, can you believe that? Not too much ever go mine own way. But, now this falling wind. Yes, sir. A dress like no other. They never would say as to why it was marked as such. I'm supposing they knowed my plighting. They like Comen, feel regret that she is placed as such. It certainly does not fit too well. But when I put it on, all will see my gracefulness, my refining manners, and how prettyish I could be. Then they will line up and serve me much of the food, and I will eat it all and swell up — while swelling them up toos —. I'll eat so much I'll fill that dress so well, so well. But, soon enough it will be dropping to the floor in repayment of the meals; so mayhap they won't fully appreciate how magnifical I could be. I don't want them to use me, that would be of unfairness. A hole in the dress? Yes, craft a type of wedding sheet of it. So when we get down to our doing they can all be gratified. And if for some reason the beautification of my plumage does not stun them to my whims, then most certainly the musk wafting from the stitching will seduce them into four seasons of meals.

~Comptorl~

I have no eyelids. They say I was born this way. I carry a pail and syringe about to continually wash my eyes. They assume I will eventually go blind, there is no pail large enough. You might wonder how I sleep. I used to use a bulged mask. The bulge would hold a patch of moss that I would wet. The moistness would transfer to my eyes as I attempted to sleep. I eventually learned it was causing more harm than not. I could never completely clean the grit from the moss, the debris incentivizing my blindness. Now I use no mask and snooze when my body demands it, waking when my body demands to spritz my eyes. The goggles that were assigned me at birth I have commandeered and made a trophy of. The lenses range from clear to dark. On the metal mounts, I have commissioned Teardrop to draw motifs on every pair. I even drew eyes on one clear pair; it obstructs my view but I can hear the exclamations in a person's voice upon them seeing the image for the first time. I have certain pairs a for specific outfits; of course the time of day, year, and weather hold more sway than my need of style. They say I am pretty, like they said I was born this way. I can't get away from seeing myself, and I don't see it. They say my other senses will become enhanced if the blindness ever comes, like they said I was born this way. They try to ease my pain with jests saying I will see what others miss, like they say I was born this way. They tried to comfort my soul, bringing in the clergy to say *you do not need eyes to truly see.* I told you they said I was born this way? I would spit on them all if I only had any moisture to spare. Born this way? While I still have my sight I watch my Fater with his knife. He can carve an ungulate with barley a splatter. A turkey for Thee Fest he turns into a sculpture. A piece of wood becomes a painting's frame, a flute, or even a set of perfect wooden eyes he thought to make a gift of to me. When I catch his eye and he sees me watching him, focused on his works — be it meat, wood, an almond, or a peach — he blanches, trying not to blink and leaves the room. So who was truly born this way, him or myself?

~Copeland~

She say I am lousy with kindness. Though she say - CHERISH! - it in her special way. I used to startle everyone when I spoke. My spasms barraging my attempts at a conversation. Some of my Brothers were guffing me when I met her. I was released from Thee Bedlam, they did not understand why. Sitting on the stoop of Thee Calaboose they wanted me to do it. She passed by as they poked my ribs. Says I, 'I can't just - LOVE YOU! - do it on command.' She stopped and and turned a full half circle, pointing her ear at me, says she, 'Are you talk at me?' She had a peculiar way of speaking. I thought she had been swimming and caught something. Her symptoms seemed to be clogged ears and a swollen tongue. She - MY

LOVE! - caught me then and there. When we are out walking arm in arm, I walk on her left side, next to her flowered ear. I lean and says I whispering into her bud, 'I don't deserve you, I don't deserve you, I don't deserve you, I don't deserve...' Though all she hears is - *true love...true love...true love...true love...* -, it sounds as a far away whisper being spoken from across a field of cropped corn. She has never given me a command, there is no need when there is love.

~Dimmesdale~

On my last birthday I was given a cowboy hat and a vest to match. To embellish my costume I rode a broomstick about. I have ridden the broom and worn the outfit everyday for the past year, subtly reminding my parents of their unspoken promise. What's a cowboy without a horse? I even thought of suggesting to my parents that they could start me off with a small one. Myself and the horse, we could grow into one another. I knew that they would appreciate the smaller cost that would come with the smaller size. I even promised myself to look surprised. But, then all the presents were open and there was no horse to be found. I questioned my parents; they looked at each other; they surprised me, their sweet birthday boy, with a laugh. They said, 'The pet store was all out of ponies, maybe next year.' My parents thought that I understood their joke, because they thought that they heard me laughing. But, that was only the sound that I make to represent my broomstick's whinny. So here I am again, back atop my broomstick, that is how I got back here with you. In fact, in a fashion, I sort of resemble you, both of us stuck to these pieces of wood. Don't worry, I already apologized to my buttocks for what will certainly be only one more year of splinters.

~Durak~

I can tell the season has changed. You know how I can tell? Because it's a different season. Ichnabod was saying how we used to look at a groundhog's buttocks to see if the season had rolled over. Even One-Ear Blucher tilted her head and listened again. We thought mayhap he was having another... *episode*. Didn't faze him whatsoever, our uncertainty about his...how do they put it? *Cognitive abilities*. He's just standing there as if all is normal. He pantomimes one of his delusions, pretends to stick his hand in a tree stump; first off everyone knows they live in the ground, it's in the name. Then he pretends to pull the beast out by its scruff, you seen those teeth? Not likely. Then with the imagined swollen rat held above his head he says they are looking for his shadow. He looks at us and smiles, says he, 'See, if a shadow, BOO...six more weeks...' It must have been a baby dirt swine

he had imagined, because his hands both shot into his pockets when he realized what we were all thinking. *Time to return to Thee Bedlam.* Of course says someone, 'You believe that a shadow controls nature?' He saw where he was headed and did not want to return. Says he, 'No, no, that was joking, I don't believe, I don't think anyone ever believed it, it was just a thing...' Says I, 'Who's anyone, you mean one of us? There's no one else here. Are you saying one of us sees this shadow? Or do you see something we don't?' He was like a scared cornered rat. I like Ichnabod, he's been an, how they put...*an exemplary citizen* since Charon made him straight. He marched on over to me and rubbed his nose on mine. Says he, 'That's how they talk...groundhogs...hello and goodbye. I was just trying to think of a memorable way to say goodbye to you all. So...see you next season... which is tomorrow. See, you can tell if you look at that calendar there nailed to the wall.' Then he slipped out the door. I suppose *an exemplar* can still be a crazy hump. I look forward to rubbing his nose tomorrow, see if he remembers his...*memorable way*. We all like him, he is a sweet, odd duk.

~*Easter*~

I won the Easter pageant for this past year, so yes'm call me Easter...for now. It is an honor, or supposed to be. They don't tell you that you are to remain celibate for the term. Which for myself, I suppose you could say I have been 'Easter' for all my seventeen years. I get to stay in the auxiliary unit that was added to the Church land. It is wonderful, it far surpasses what we have in our own home. I also get to be alone, not needing to share everything with my siblings. Gifted foods, luxury, and the year of reprieve from work was going to be the ultimate prize. I would read, learn piano, then read, scout for an acquaintance, and then read some more. Then my plans stopped once I read the entirety of the suggested guidelines, with the ability for the Church to constantly monitor and remove your title if these are not met to their approval. Apparently Easter is supposed to be an example of excellence for all. So what they propose as a year of reprieve for a life well-lived is a dupe. And they know where to push. Because nothing is demanded, only suggested. Fater Nigrescent influences me with his throat clears and mumbled tuts. The myriad of guilt that has swelled in myself over these months; it has taken me over, the roots have weaved between my ribs gripping me in a way that I will not rid myself of them until my life's end. I have worked harder than all my previous years combined. My knees are bruised from helping Fater Nigrescent, my hands are calloused from setting a daily example of good labor. The last time I had a moment to read was when I was sent to Thee Bedlam to read Fater's book to the patients. The first time I did this I did not enjoy what I was reading and gave only a monotonal performance, so I continue to return to alleviate my guilt. Once this year is endured I can not imagine confronting my celibacy.

The guilt possesses me in my entirety, I know it would let no other take a hold of me. So who is the winner here?

~Ebben~

I had been working for Mister Archai. Then one day the wall was taken down between the two stores, and I was working for Mister Chitty. I went about the work the same way, kept my head down, didn't speak unless spoken to. In the square I ate my lunch in ten minutes and listened to Mishka for just under ten minutes then went back to work. Mister Chitty had cut ten minutes off my lunch as well as wanting me back and ready to go at the end of the twenty. The months had taken a bit of getting used to, Mister Chitty was not very consistent in his wants. He wanted things done in a certain manner, but I found his wants and manners varied upon his mood. If he would have stayed out of my way, then I could have run the place as smoothly as I did with Mister Archai. But he wanted control of something, I suppose because he had no say in a lot of his life. I had done the tallies every night. Mister Chitty was surprised at first and took over the numbers the first week. When the books didn't add properly on Friday closing, he wouldn't let me leave until he figured out what I did incorrectly with the till. As he concentrated over the receipts, I kept my head down and was able to look at the book. I used my own pen and ink that Mister Archai had gifted me and fixed his mangled sums. He found I had tallied the receipts correctly and raised his head in frustration. He saw me set down my pen next to the ink. Grabbing the book, he looked over the numbers, started to blink fast, shaking a little bit, he looked like an almost ready teapot. Yells he, 'Don't ever use red in my store again! Don't you know what that means?' He slammed the book down and grabbed hard right above my elbow in that manner he has. Says he, 'You understand, no red? Now fix this.' He handed me the book and I covered over my corrections in black ink. I know that Thee Shadders use red paint to mark their chosen. But no one knows who Thee Shadders are, so why would little Mister Chitty be wary of that? I remember last year Mister Jehu left out a red tint liquid with his chisels, so when people wrote on his...uh... stone? Sure, stone, then they would fill in their chiseled message in bright red so everyone could see it from far off. The first day of me working for Mister Chitty, Mister Jehu had come in and asked him if he had written on that stone yet. He answered Mister Jehu by holding up his hand and showing him the un-washable tint. Beats me. I'm just keeping my head down and once again doing the books, though now in watery black.

Faribault didn't owe me naught. I had told him that sometimes I missed being down below ground. The grind, complete darkness, coolness if it is warm outside and warmth if the weather is inclement. Even though they did not let me do the work I truly enjoyed any more, wanting to save my fingers for their own enjoy. Says he, 'I am supposed to be held to secrecy...' He tried to explain directions, but without confessing his secret place, he couldn't explain it competently enough to make sense to me. He said he didn't understand how we could dance, and not only dance, but dance with other men. Then he grabbed his kit, dragged me to my place to gather what I would only need, and guided me there. He would hunt while I did what I needed to do. Halfway there my left closure strap snapped. My accordion wheezed every other step as it bounced off my back. I knew what he was thinking, shaking his head. I was going to scare off everything alive. When I started to flip it around so I could brace it closed with my arms, says he, 'No, no, just keep it there, where you're going there's nothing anyhow. And mayhap that honk will bellow to some unknown trophy that has thus far eluded mine eyes.' We continued on. We arrived. He planned to set up camp and then go scout a bit. I lowered myself into the maw. There was an empty crater where the men had pillaged the relics. I was still attuned with the earth's innards. I followed the slight breeze that brushed my neck. I had to remove my tool from my back to squeeze through the hole. I lit my lamp and crawled three feet. No one from the scavenging horde thought to bend over and look into this hole. When I stood, my lamp illumined a great hall, this was not a hole that I was accustomed to. I felt unworthy to witness, the soft lake reflected my light off the chandeliers of architectural rock that hung from the ceiling with their Brethren raised statues from the floor. And the mounds of treasure here could have rebuilt and then rebuilt again the entire town. The quiet inspired awe. My tackle dropped from my hands and yodeled an appreciative 'Ohh.' The short one note lauding echoed and reverberated. The lake riffled and the bones seemed to shift. I picked it up and began. Mayhap this accordion breathed some fresh air into their calcified disbursements, they certainly blew some against my soft skin covering. In what seemed hours my light never guttered. For the first time in my life I was receiving what I desired. And mayhap a man needs to find that on his own. Though, I do not think I was truly alone, the vestiges in there with me were swaying along to this anthem. The lake lapped in time. And even though he said he was going scouting I could hear Faribault dancing his odd clog above our heads. One day I will organize a reunion and gather everyone from the mine, recreate that Mass night as it was meant to be.

~Esme~

It's an old Northrop tradition that during a wake all the looking-glasses in the home are to be turned about to face the wall. The thinking of the practice is that the ghost's image could get caught inside the glass, and then the home, for all of eternity. See, it's supposed that the ghost attends its very own wake. And sure, the Northrops welcome the ghost, but when the wake is over they want the ghost to leave with the other guests. Some people don't want ghosts creeping about. See Scare..., when I was only a child, for my gift one year, I was given the looking-glass that had been passed through generations of our family. Of course I am not a Northrop; I have my own beliefs, my own traditions. See, I had a different idea. I keep my glass turned every day of the year except one. On that one day I turn my family's glass right side front, I hope and pray that my beliefs are and do come true. And if His ghost does return on this day, I would catch Him inside my family's looking-glass that has been entrusted to myself and never let Him leave again.

~Ethier~

The pressure is off. For the first time in both of our lives there is an ease. School, chores, work, church, friends, family, money, then of course my beau — yes, I still say beau, he is old-fashioned and deserves that certain mystique —. He was my main concern and still is, though there is no more concern. Every day was get him up, dressed...I could prattle a list forever. Mainly it was thinking of him before myself. Do not get the wrong idea, this was no enabling or indentured situation. He acted the same towards myself, and to this day he still does. That is one of the main reasons we fit together so well. People blather on about opposites; nonsense. He is a caring man. He cares for me and our family and that makes me want to reciprocate. And even if we did not end up together, whomever we might have ended up with would have still received our same attention, no matter their temperament. All that being said, one of the best ways I knew to show him my love was by devoting myself in the kitchen. I picked up the basics from my family before we were together. Our first indications that there might be something between us was at a communal brunch after church. I did most of the kitchen work for our families' plates. He tasted a few other bowls out of politeness but hovered over mine pretending to serve anyone who wanted some. But in truth, with every scoop he dished out to others, he took two for himself. He wiped our dishes clean with the bread I had kept warm under my linens. Once we both knew what our fates would be, I began to get educated. I culled dishes from everyone willing to share. I did indenture myself under a few *gourmets* as well. Once I felt complete, I experimented and began to concoct my recipes. Ideas no one

had ever tried. Our garden became overrun with unseen fruits, vegetables, and spices that I procured from Thee Lupercalians every year. Some of my sellers attended meals during their stay, and I was not-so-kiddingly offered a compartment to travel with them. I will only be traveling with my beau Baal. When we realized we had to make a choice here towards the latter part of our lives, it alleviated everything. The choice was obvious for us both. And the pressure that was relieved, then relieved pressure in other areas. What we thought we had to give up has actually once again been possible. We offered back the salve to Mahout. I've put even more effort into his last pleasure, experimenting and concocting tastes we never imagined. And from our love, what we thought was no longer possible, is now youthful with vigor. The pressure has been relieved. Well, love and spices.

~Faribault~

It's no secret, they had a perfectly good building. I had been in it a few times and it always held me solid. Fater Nigrescent's building stood across the street, the steeple had been replaced recently, to ben Asher's joy, so mayhap it was a jealousy. I know he was angry when the new steeple was extended and now measured higher than his jail. He thought of his wasted tithing. He could not have planned it out, because he seemed to only think of it when I was just passing time and mentioning what I had found. I was hunting in Thee Mountains, South and West. I started off from my secret spot — no I am not going to tell you where, only one knows, well, two — then pushed down towards Thee Cliffs. I finished dressing the bull-elk and went to hang it even higher in the tree, to be out of reach of any *thieves* in the night. The elk was heftier than I prepared for, so, it was my fault...the branch snapped and the bull crashed to the ground...and then some. He went through the earth-skin and landed down in a depression. I wanted my kill back, so since I stupidly hung onto the rope, I went down to get it. It was rock and stone, it seemed natural. Until it didn't. The bull was atop a pile of bones. Endless bones, ancient, immense, unfamiliar. Some larger than myself, an equal number in repeating images in smaller and smaller increments. Teeth, fangs, horns. Wings and what might have been fins. Spines larger than ten men put together. Unknowable shapes that did unimaginable malice when working. Did they come on their own, were they placed as an effigy? Cap'n had them hauling for weeks. He razed his adequate building. With no design that I could glean, he and his men begin erecting the framework. Mound upon mound of bones and horns and whatever else these baffling myths might be. It was impenetrable in every sense. The walls rose, they changed a cell to circular-like shape to accommodate some antiqued creature's ribs. The floor was waved when the joint of one creature was forced into the jaw of its new and perhaps

original enemy. From myself, Boucher, and Thee Slaughterhouse they collected the bones of familiar beasts. Ground them down to a paste which they applied as caulk, adhesive, and mortar where it would gravitate, mount and anneal forever as equal and compeer. The mating of the bones finally replete when the variations in hue and girth decisively resembled a dissimilar behemoth. Thee Totem can go back to its original intent. Part of which was a sundial, which is now moot due to the shadows from the new steeple and the storied edifice. Both of which contain secrets new and ancient.

~Gad~

I was sent out to get some tinder and kindling. I came to reassure you that we are not coming for you this year. You were probably getting nervous with the flowers popping up and the trees shooting. *I don't know what some of them are so scared of.* We need to safeguard and make certain that all the frost-tide evils have vacated. *Is there something they aren't telling us?* We know that's usually your job, we're not taking over for you. Look, I don't want you to worry. Winter Fete is more of a release. *Did something happen?* We've been wearing layers for months, huddled inside, throwing silent curses, inventing scenes in our heads to harm the person next to us that is always too close. *Only a dead man is safe.* The older children have started building the tower. They've been gathering wood for three days, and all the gimcracks have been collected from anyone who thinks they need a bit more buoyancy. It's already bigger than Thee Totem, it was cold this Winter. The dancing, the music, the food and drink, it's the stuff of drama. *It is a riot of cleansing. The despair.* We won't be able to dance too close around the bale. Everyone donated a bit; Boucher has everything cut. It will be interesting to see how Ethier plans on getting close enough to the fire so she can feed everyone. *I asked when this tradition started.* The clothes they used on the dummy they built were probably meant for you. Again, do not worry. *Why do they seem so worried?* ben Asher said I could watch with him from his tower, it's going to get so hot this year, so that is probably a good idea. *Turn your face away!* Spy down on all the people, peering through the smoke, squinting through the steam from the melting snow, witness them dance it all away in their circle, just to return again next year. Enough is kept out from Thee Mountains, Thee Wulf's Woods, and Thee Wandering...then why? *Keep out the cold.* I can feel the drums starting up. Scare..., I hope you feel better. I know no one really talks to you. I best get back. If you don't mind...I might take a bit of your leg, I think it's just what is needed to get this started. See you next year. *Next year?*

~Gauldim~

I'd rather be forsaken than saved by a failure. I am now in a fierce seclusion. I walk the fields and valleys alone. The foothills of Thee Mountains, the edge of Thee Wulf's Woods, the ebbing skirt of Thee Wandering. I never tap a stick against Petr's fence. The ping would be pleasant to my lonesome ears, yet, the slight possibility of attention is worth depriving my senses. I won't say they forced themselves upon me. Mayhap it was myself who was the aggressor. There were slight suggestions on their part. A promise of a necessity that I did not know I needed. The rigors and rituals were said to be repaid in the end. During the struggle the reward would be self-satisfaction. I have come to the conclusion that that is not how I want to be satisfied. My actions are redeemable. It seems I am able to only satisfy myself. Fater has not given up, but in the same fashion as myself, his path has taken a new direction. And again like myself, his guide above has also chosen to deviate. Those are the failures, if you want to term it that way. Where does it end? Did His mentor tread the same line? If I fail it will be a non-story, one of perpetual unforgettable selfish efforts. Yet, if not, mayhap we will all succeed.

~Gert~

I subjected myself to reading *leaves* again last evening at a simple klatsch. I don't know why I continue to subject myself. They think it's just for a bit of fun. And it is, fun. But, they don't understand how much it consumes my thoughts. I wish I could ask the leaves about myself, the importance. I feigned an interest in pottery only so I might create a singular set of cups and saucers, a set that I envisioned with specific motifs and symbols that would secretly aid me in gleaning these implications. I understand how people might not have much faith in sediment on the bottom of my cups, a canvas for me to interpret. In truth, I am still sussing out the technique. I discovered a horse in Cahie's dregs, and I informed her how she will one day be able to run free, no longer subjected to her traces. I almost saw a tree in Joba's, so I told him he would stand straight, tall, and strong, with his roots growing deep. He saw this, he has too many siblings to count. He equated my interpretation to him holding up his family with his vigor and brawn. People see what they want to see, and I know most of these folks, so...within Tiler's I said I saw a storm, which I can see in most every chaos of sediment. We all know Tiler, and it was simple to play on his mindset. He looked at me with wide eyes and open mouth, he bobbed his head in confirmation. Everyone at the klatsch smiled a bit. It was a proper finale. I feel good being able to entertain and satisfy people. I only stumbled into the truth once before, that secret has kept me silent. I read those runes again and again. I compare and contrast them against what I

have ciphered. There must be more in the meaning, I have witnessed the results. I will darken everyone's teeth until I am sated.

~Halleck~

I had been heavy for as long as I had memories. I was able to comfortably wear my Fater's clothing at an early age. I fashioned a veneer on top of my demeanor that I was proud to be what I was. I began the passive self-shaming, attempting to preempt the soft vitriol. I played off the gibes and acted my part as the dumb oaf. And apparently dumb I continue to be. I saw sickness develop in cattle and hogs, drastically altering their image. It wasn't so much a purposeful tactic yet, it was a slight lack of effort that possibly might show results. I began to undercook my meat. When nothing took, I feigned a love for the sensation of raw, natural nutriment sliding down my gullet. Still, my girth swelled. I monitored the pastures and pens, attempting to glean any insight, while pretending to brush aside the taunts wondering, *if raw wasn't good enough, was I going to consume them where they stood?* I noticed they ate their grub directly out of the muck. I began to only pretend ablutions. Something took. I was certain of the sensation of thousands of minuscule incisors embedding themselves in my intestines, absconding with any new nutrient I added to my gut. It was not sated, it began to harvest my corpulence. It left me fallow and progressed to my organs. I now realized my condition was beyond control, which was all I wanted. I attempted tinctures and laxatives prescribed to all like beasts. Nothing took. I had to rid myself of my apparel and have seen it hanging to scare in many fields. My belt notches have doubled upon themselves. Dr Dolan wrapped his small fingers entirely around my arm and easily pulled me apart from the crowd while quietly confronting me. I didn't attempt to play off anything, I had no need to act dumb. I came clean. Truthful about everything, not only my recent self-alteration, but the entire lot that percolated into my current state. Says Dr D, 'The issue is not here,' pinching my loose flesh in his grip, 'but, it's here,' thunking me atop my head. 'Halleck, I don't like you, but, I do love you.' He came to me again, even quieter than before. Dr Dolan fastened a piece of raw beef with a length of fishing twine. He had me swallow it down while he wrapped the remainder about his slight hand. Before it went too far he pulled hard on the bait. I could feel him playing it up and back down my esophagus in some angling intoxicant of enticement. He thunked my head again, with each attempt I made at a gag. It took. He felt the interest and snagged the barb. I thought to pass out at barely passing oxygen through my nostrils. My tears blurred the sight of the malfeasance withdrawn from myself. Much tears. Dr Dolan comes and visits me often... he just has me call him Dolan now. He doesn't poke or prod me. We just talk, quietly. The talks are nice and surprising. Because, I'm not sure if I like myself either, but, I do love myself. Which is also surprising and nice.

49

~Hallis~

I have not been able to sleep. I miss when my Mother used to force me to nap. The screaming from her pond won't stop. I snuck from my captain's bed and went to investigate. The rumpus was worse outside. At her shale wall I peered over, the light from my lantern was reflected back in countless eyes. I was going to step hell on them. I put my leg on the wall, and they scattered. Sure, the wailing stopped, but when I climbed up the still-needed step ladder to my bed, they started again. I went out in the day to take care of them. Miss Elzey was there lurking around her obnoxious plants, she offered me some water. Sure, it was probably the best water I've ever had, but I was so weary I could not enjoy it. She carried me back to my Mother when I feel asleep on her turf. The next day I waited for her errands. At the pond I couldn't find any of the flirty raconteurs. My Mother taught me that word after I told her why I could not rest. I peed a circle around the spring. I thought this would scare them away, you know, telling them this is my territory, do not even think of coming round. No; still I did not sleep. My Mother worried. She asked Miss Elzey for a visit. She thought Miss Elzey could work miracles and she thought to commandeer her advice on my insomnia; again, Mother. At the beginning of their meeting I went to the spring and began to dig. Discovered! And they were all sleeping. I desperately wanted to wake them but stuck to my plan. I filled both milk buckets full. I balanced the yoke on my shoulders and climbed her hackberry. I almost made the crown, but the buckets started croaking. I stopped and enacted my plan. I threw them one-by-one from the first bucket. I saw them impact on the rough gravel path, explode on the ornamental rocks circling her garden, the tender moss on the shale wall could not cushion the blows. I moved to the second bucket. My quarry was fully awake. There is statuary placed about her garden. I made a sport of it. When my Mother walked Miss Elzey back home, they witnessed my last victim being impaled on some mythological trident. She prodded the corpses with her old Sunday shoe. They looked to the cloudless sky. They glanced at her unpruned hackberry. I could not been seen. I don't know how long their inspection lasted. I fell asleep to the gentle scraping sounds of shovels and the pleasing plop of frog guts sliding to the bottom of a bucket.

~Hammurahi~

It had been my Aunt's...no, no, I'm the Aunt. It had been my Greatgrandmother's, Grandmother's, Mother's, and then mine. I think. I seem to remember it was even a Northrop's. Though...I'm not certain what I remember anymore. I have to find that trunk before anyone

discovers that I lost it. Where could I have put it? Every nook, crevice...I even checked the shed. I woke and was going about my morning when I saw my precious linens and other necessaries folded tightly at the foot of my bed. I could only gape. It looked strange to me. First the folding was crisp and tight, a properness that I have never been able to achieve. Second, I believed that I would not leave them out and unprotected in such a manner. Almost immediately I remembered them inside the trunk. I can't go to Thee Bedlam yet. I am too young, too ambitious, too...socially necessary. The opposite of Seneca and his social impotence. But I think he is on to me. He was downstairs when I came in carrying my haul. He stared at me, dumbfounded. He didn't hear any of my rehearsed explanations. Cleaning, rearranging, donating...he got up and left. His chair back stopped bouncing against the floor as the screen door picked up the chorus with two quick slams as he escaped my pleads. I know he was going to Thee Bedlam, arranging a room, implementing a plan for my extraction. An assault of Attendants to arrest my impending dementia. I searched for two hours, closets, inside other trunks, even lifting the freshly nailed floorboards. I could risk it no longer. I fled before I heard those purposeful footsteps marching across my porch. Victims of his dorsum of rumors. I searched on my journey here. Still no trunk. I'll search the fields and wood next. I know it seems non compo mentis, but I now believe that I can no longer trust myself. But, if I find it...well, then we could laugh off one another's belief. So please...please tell me... plangent is my plea.

~Harris~

Cap'n tell me, it s'ginst the law. Fater says me, it s'ginst His law. But, I seen 'em both behind my house, standing close 'round the rabbit ring, laughing and each enjoying passing money 'round. So says I to both men, 'How can something that makes you feel so good be bad?' Then says Fater, 'That's just it son, something that gives a man this much pleasure must be bad.' I tend to agree. That's when I started fighting my own self. My soul went with Fater, but my living, surviving self went with Cap'n. Cause when Cap'n heard Fater say that, well, Cap'n came closer to my side. He's always up for contrary. He laughed at Fater, telling him to, 'Run back to your mittens.' Me and Cap'n exchanged words I'm sworn to, so to make mine and my family's life here best. But, my soul side is hedging the other way, it truly affected me when Fater pronounced as he tried to return Thee Church to white, 'Your soap is useless, no man here has the courage to make a holy end.' None disagreed. I notice Fater still comes, and he stays to collect his winnings. And every time I hand him his money, he asks me to let him have one of the feet off my best buck if he ever loses.

~Hatshepsut~

It's a perverted sense I suppose. I have to wear my gloves inside out. I had two main jobs. I used to scrub the latrines for Thee Women's Prison. And I worked in the kitchen. We were given water and a small bar of soap made by Boucher that we must make last through the month. The water was always cold. There is warm water these days, but the heat is so close the warm water now seems a flashback to a former punishment. The hose I now use to wash the pens was used in an array of activities in its former occupation. I can see the striations and small splits, and even the brown-black flecks that grew on its surface when it was used as a floppy blackjack. It was more of a multi-tool. I clean all the pens. Admittedly I scrub harder inside pen three. It's curious being back in there. My pallet was in the same corner where the sow's scat accumulates. I don't know if there is anything to read into it, it is a limited space. I used to grip the bars at times, refusing to sleep and eat, holding myself up until both were forced upon me. In the fowl section here they do shove tubes down there throat, but here the sows shove their wet noses through the gaps, chuffing as they do when I approach with the yoke on my shoulders and the two pails of slop swinging to knock my balance awry. Three times I've managed to sneak one out from cell three. I don't mean processed. Every now and again Lessing wants to revenge herself, she takes the workers outside to what used to be the yard. In the pens where the pregnant sows are kept separated, but still a ways from birthing, she chooses one of us in her bellicose manner and wrestles amongst the gestating temperamental sows. The crowd is fixated. I've used this time to accomplish my plotting. I next plan to get a boar out, though I don't work in that sector. It will take some seduction. Though I will never farrow. It would be something to see them running wild over our land. It might just be snacks for The Wulf. Though, is it really any different from what my occupation provides? Now look who is a multi-tool.

~Hellebore~

I never even knew his name, he said it was of no importance. He said he would take me under his wing and show me a thing of beauty. Of course, my first thought was, *run away, he's a creeper*. Then he taught me of kites. He seemed to know who I was. My family. My situation. He let me first try one of his. We understood immediately. From there he thought it best if I created one of my own. We would sit in his outbuilding, he instructing on the possibilities. We thought it best to go with workable material for my first attempt. He gifted me wood of not only light color, but the weight seemed unnatural. He had traded Thee Lupercalians a few of his creations for a bounty of exotic wares. I envied the box, circle, gliders, and the experimental options were tempting; yet, after his lectures

52

I thought it best to start simply. I cut and shaped my dowels, measured my fabric numerous times and then once again. The connection clasps were of his own devising, two rings to attach to the tethers. These allowed a controllable movement and flow that would otherwise be completely dictated by nature. As the glue dried we stood outside to escape the fumes. He subtlety asked me of my life. I think he knew the answers, even if I did not know them myself. Even though he is gone, I've kept up this contentment. I cannot brag on my skills, but Thee Lupercalians have introduced themselves, even though I'm still officially a child. They came when I was working my tethers, straight-backed and at ease, though with bent knees *just in case*. She thought I could not see her off at the edge of the tree line. Even if I would not have seen her I could hear her bird, not cooing as a dove does naturally, but screaming in some sort of tantrum and fit. As they approach over the open grass, she reigned that dove in and ran. And now I understand that his wife is the one to be wary of, the true creeper. Keeping that bird tethered to herself, just sitting and watching me with my only pleasure, alone, but not alone.

~Hendry~

It's been over a week now that she has been threatening me. She never leaves her place. Threatening me with some semaphore message of revenge. How could she know what I did? I was careful. I was quiet. No one saw me. Mayhap she works for him. No, no...he fell for it. It was a woman's skull, but who can tell that? Especially when they're dead. One skull is as good as the next. Why would he want that specific skull anyways? There was no way I could get into Astodan. I couldn't even figure out how to get to Dakhma. Though...there is one way. Mayhap that's what she is flagging out to me. No, no...I am guessing she is just a watcher, she saw me sneaking in, *the morning of*. Now she wants a payoff. But, I've got nothing to give her except what he gave me. I spent most already, and that's all I have. That's why I did it in the first place. Yes, yes...she is wily. The old so and so. How will she do me? Poison? She's too weak to do anything else. Can't lift an axe, a horn, or, ha! A Cannonball. Mayhap that is her grin, that was a woman Cannonball that I delivered. How could she know that? I put everything back better than I found it. The stone is straight. I tamped down the ground. I ruffled the turf and scattered a few leaves and twigs so it didn't look as if someone had recently been there, but not too much so some busy body started snooping. But that's what she is, a snooping busy body. What do I do? What if I took this scarf and stood below her window waving it intimidatingly? Signing that I repudiate her disapproval. But I can't sign, so it would just big a big bluster of arm waving. Might that draw more unwanted attention? I wish I could message like her. Subtlety, but with menace. Not draw any attention.

~Herriot~

I'm sorry I'm not there to whisper in your ear. Nobody else seems to hear my calls, but I am certain you can read my curtain. I've been shaking it for almost a week trying to get anyone's attention. I hear my young cousin creeping in and out of his place across the path. He never looks up. Such a shy boy, a little squirmy, and always staring at the ground. Yes, I tried calling out, but I have no more voice. I was in bed for three days: sick. When I tried getting up to empty into my pan I did as an old lady does... when my wrinkled stilts touched the floorboards my hip wasn't interested. I can feel the crack. I'm not certain if it was from the stand or the fall, but it still is being stubborn. The only fluid I had to drink was from my pan. I thought it would help my throat. It made it worse. It made it all worse. If I wanted to drink more of it the act would be difficult: the pan is dry. The only way I could get a drop is wringing out my sleeping gown. The rash it created from setting upon my skin is my newest ailment. I finally figured how to put the pan to use, that's how I'm speaking to you now. Swinging and waving it with my feeble arms, trying to create a breeze, pleading for assistance. Why won't that boy pay attention? If no one comes soon from seeing my calls of distress, they'll come soon enough from the stink and the impending final stench. I am now a member of the great unwashed.

~Hock~

Elihu and her Brother were there. He wasn't as he is these days, no title. He's Mister So And So these days. But then they were relations. I had memorized their shoes: his were buckles, hers a saddle pattern. These days Mister So And So wears thick hobnail stompers; she has a selection. I am probably the only one to notice her meticulous pattern of loafers, straps, toe boots, and still a version of saddle, and in her subtle ways she also has a woman's version of a buckle. These are for everyday of the week accordingly. The other two days, well...that's her business. One of their little friends was there as well; I can't remember who, one of the Love boys. This was not done as a pernicious prank. The way I was born, I would normally have been left in the woods. And I was, but I was found by a benefactor...you know about that. It's not my place to speak some other's mind. They were trying to do me a kindness. That Love boy took us to a tree in one of their stands, he had it picked out. In tree years it was probably in our same age range. After they helped me...no just Elihu and the Love boy, after they helped me to the said tree they turned my crooked back to touch the tree-skin. My back only made contact directly above my buttocks. The rest of me arced away in its given form. That is until they began to strap me to the tree. We were young; they thought they would help me fit in, and not at an angle. They had a bag full of leather straps

and tack paraphernalia. The first strap was tightened around my waist and buckled down on the backside of the tree. They progressed up my torso in the same manner. I laughed at the grunts and incredulity of their hardship in latching the buckles. They accused me of fighting them, not believing that it was my spine and not my mind galvanizing against their therapy. When they finally attached the belt around my forehead and secured it around the sentinel, all three came around front and inspected me as I inspected them full in the face for the first time ever. The Love boy left no memory, but, I think that is because of the disparity between the looks of Elihu and her brother. Her look was of concern, wondering if they were doing the right thing. His was of an awe, a look beyond our years, a lust and yearning. Says Elihu, 'Take them off, we're hurting him.' I could feel my veins stretching to an unfamiliar strain. I could feel the redness in the reflection of their gaze, my sweat and the strain was aiding the squeaks of the leather. She reached to unfasten the buckles. He stayed her in place. He took the Love boy behind the tree, unfastened one of the straps, and extracted my arms. They tightened the remaining straps another notch. With the removed strap they wrapped it around either wrist, one on the left, one on the right. From behind they pulled the binding with the weight of their bodies. I heard the strain of their efforts: the leather and the tree. Elihu's wide-fearful eyes were the last I ever looked directly upon. The tree exploded. I heard the Love boy's screams as he ran away. I've never seen his face again. Elihu unstrapped me from the shrapnel and guided my once again hooked form away. Her Brother just watched it all. He eventually caught and passed us on the path. Raising my eyes as much as allowed, I could see bouncing across his buttocks with every step the sack of bindings he secured.

~Hurd~

The morning was like any other. The occurrence from the day before could hardly alter me from my incessant routine of life. I went to check if Hallis had found any rest from his insomnia. I had no plan if I would let him rest for love's sake or wake him, also for love's sake. He was not there. I did not want to waste away thought on his actions or where he might be. I only desired that he might have started his chores. Of course, no. My chores would have to wait until I took care of others. That is a Mother's life. Last to feast, last to settle, last to all, and yet, first to rise. I lifted the yoke from the mounts outside the back door. I shuffled to the barn, turned sideways to fit the yoke and pails through the door, squatted on the three-legged stool, and clutched the teats. With both pails brimming I went to the attached shed, attempting to not lose too much of the commodity against my seasonal gait. The bottles replete, I thought to leave them until Hallis' recrudescence. That was my first smile of the morning. I knew my boy

too well and decided to at least get a bottle to Miss Elzey. I installed within the frame of her rear window. I envisaged the sight of the morning sun refracting through the milk would bring an early day delectation. I glanced her spring out of my periphery. I turned home so as not to be tempted by its hypnotic pull, even after the matter of the previous day. A short time later she was knocking at my door. I worried that my boy had antagonized her while in the haze of his current state. She asked for another bottle of milk. I asked her what the issue was. There was none. In fact she would double her order going forward. She said that whatever that boy did to it was magical. I assumed she could use some extended cessation herself. I sipped of the milk. It certainly wasn't one of our few bland spices that we harvest. The salt we mine. It mayhap was from one of the exotic powders brought by Thee Lupercalians. I went to the shed and tested another bottle. The same delight. Was it our beast? The feed they consume, did the boy alter the silage, mayhap he added soybeans? It has only been a few days, he certainly has departed before. I'm none too pleased to still be doing his chores, the most unfavorable aspect is the toting of the beasts' water. It was amiable of Miss Elzey to allow use of her freshly developed spring, the difficulty is traversing around her stacked shale wall. Good fences good neighbors. Nonsense.

~Ichnabod~

I don't know how to explain me. I swear I've witnessed the future. I swear the future brought me to Lupercalia. But, you can't swear here. If you do then you find yourself in Thee Bedlam, in Grandfater's old room. Not only a strange land, but, in a strange body. I was once a man with big upon my big. I would roll my fat underneath my clothes to to make myself look even larger. Then I met Polly. Who hasn't? Now I'm even speaking like some of them. Smitten I was. In my past land my Mother had been an insensitive jokestress. To her friends she would say, 'Look at my little wad, what a hump, such an ich of a bod.' And that was stuck to me. Now Polly worked me so hard, I shrunk down to teenage-girl size. She said she was for that other... one...of whom I don't parlez. But, then I give her that book of music. I thought that might get her. And it did, she was more taken with that book than she was with myself and my non-parlezer. She got it good, from her own piano. She looked like a train run her down afterward. But, I'm not allowed to speak of trains. Dr said to let go of my future fantasy world, or I would find myself returned to Thee Bedlam.

~Ingreds'ole~

Which side is the right side? I was under Lessing, and I was further under Jehu. My days are numbered, but at least those few days will not be spent looking over my shoulder as the two of them will be. The only day that was

bearable was Mass. My silence is not an excuse. There's a prison wall that separates the people the whole year through, even now after that physical wall has fallen. Sometimes it's hard to see who's in or out. But, one day a year, the wall drops. The people go through the songs: — *The Upper Room* — *Angels, From The Realm Of Glory* — *He Died For Me* — ...A soprano comes in high, tenor in, out, bass in, soprano out, mezzo-alto takes the lead. Different people of different groups, forming different groups that form into one group. Some in the groups can not see others in their group through the wall that drops on this day each year. Then, on the last song, they all come in. Or out. Sometimes it's hard to see who's in or out. All groups on both sides thinking that mayhap the other side would be better. At least one day a year, it seems as if everyone is on the same side. I don't deserve to be on any side, my past should not allow it. People are forced to pay in all different manners. For years I had no manners, and I don't feel as if I will ever be able to pay my debt. I am the wrong side.

~*Jacob*~

I no longer abuse myself. I repeat this as I slide her beads through my fingers hidden inside my pocket. My mother watches me from the porch. I no longer sit, never again could I totter with her. Men, boys, no thank you. Women, girls, no thank you. I will do my best to achieve a level of decency in my life. Some would say I have set the bar so low that the challenge is negligible. Yet, I am so far below the bar I will need wings to come even. One day I hope to have songs of my own. I only sing Fater's now, which I do to the best of my abilities, but my abilities hold me back because I know that I do not deserve them. When I try to write and sing a song of my own, the only sound I hear; the beating of a fly's conveyance. I believe this fly to be descended from the same line that I encountered when first deceiving my Fater and vandalizing my Mother. A subsequent egg is laid every time I rub a bead sequestered within my pocket. One day I hope to rub them so thoroughly that my finger-pads kiss one another. The only other kiss I will accept for my remaining years. Sometimes I wonder why they won't just end, having hopes that it is almost over. But, hoping again and again...I don't deserve it...hope or an end. I will do what I can for my people. Levi does not deserve my slothful ways, nor Normal my erratic behavior. I will champion their superstitions, they are naught compared to my beads. I crop my hair, shave my face, flagellate my antagonizing body, douse myself in cured water in a regimented twenty-four hour routine. In a futile but necessary attempt to clean myself of past, present, and future.

~Joba~

We are a band of children, truly we are 'quints.' We are only young people, and as a *group* we formed a band of musicians. I know, it's confusing to us as well. This year we're preparing to perform for the first time in public at Thee Mass Pageant. Jochobed is nervous that his new strings might slip; Joppa continues to spill oil into the wrong hole of his horn; Josephson swims all morning letting water pool inside his ears; making it hard for him to hear, Joseffy keeps applying rosin onto her strings, not her bow, and as for myself I have two split lips, one from blowing too hard on my mouthpiece and the other from worry. We continue to practice, to do our best for the event to come. Because we know that Thee Mass is such a revered day. A good thing about Thee Mass is that it is certain to come again next year. Unlike Ahmen, who this day is celebrating...or hoping or... well, I am not exactly certain. I have asked why and I can't seem to get a conclusive answer. But, maybe He's practicing like us, so as to get it just right.

~Jochobed~

Fater says we are an unbloomed garden. Asks I, 'All of us?' Says he, 'A garden has many components, not all are seen, some are working underground.' Funny thing that he never has set foot in a garden. I was walking through our garden and found a half-coin. Who would do that? It wasn't a clean cut. I've seen Fater bite his hidden coins, he says he is testing them. It looked like a fanged beast had ripped it in half during the test. I brought it to his study. He was out. I left it atop a note I wrote that said,

I found this in the garden,
Love Jochobed.

When I went to lay in bed that night I found it back on my pillow with a note from him,

I think you should keep this close or return it to where you found it,
Love Fater.

I didn't do exactly as he wrote. I fashioned a pouch from a worn apron I found to hold the broken coin and switched a chain from a broken necklace —Faunus gave me a hook to fix it — and wear it around my neck. Everyday,

I walk it through the garden. The garden still seems the same. I was hoping it might be a bit different, because I also collected seeds from everyone I could, all the gardens of Lupercalia. From that same apron I made a like pouch and left it again on his desk. I always hope to catch him planting his seeds. Mayhap he already has and they are unbloomed as well. They are at work down in the darkness.

~Joppa~

I have only been put to bed a few times with the story of Döder. I'm pretty tame compared to my siblings. And quite a bit smarter, I know it's only a bedtime story. But still, the part that sticks out to me the most is the mentioning of the *marks upon the skin*. I know the moral is supposed to be the fearsome bit, but for some reason the marks stick with me. I check my skin every night before sleep, so mayhap the story works in a separate manner on each of us. *Two dots.* That is what they say. They don't answer any of my questions. Are they colored, how big are they, do they overlap, are they freckles, how about moles, are they birthmarks? They only raise their eyebrows in response. When I think I catch them by saying everybody has two marks somewhere, mayhap one is on the nose and one is on the hip. 'See, you could say that everyone is marked.' They answer, 'It goes without saying.' Well, they certainly never say it, so that's true enough. I started inspecting others like I inspect myself. I could get close on my siblings, but other children didn't want to play. Then I saw him. Well, I had seen him everyday. Though, I really *saw* him. He has the roundest eyes, fawn-like. And directly above his left eye were two marks. He's a ginger, so he has a lot of marks all about himself. If you look at the night sky and witness all the stars, and there are those two dominating all the others, well, those are his marks. Now we are friends. Our parents think everything is innocent... he was my first kiss. It wasn't dirty. It was romantic. Not on the lips, and he still hasn't kissed his first kiss. I gave him two kisses, yep, right above his eye.

~Joseffy~

I don't remember being sent away, or even being away. The one Uncle, you know who, told me all about it. He keeps telling me about it too. So do my siblings. When I was born with my four Brothers and Sisters, I came out unpleasant. Sometimes they call them angel kisses. They waited thinking that mayhap I was just lightly bruised while coming out of my Mother. I was the last of the five out so I don't think she had any ability to leave a mark on me. And you can see mine, I mean it covers over half my face. They thought I was defective. They put me in a cart, pulled by my pony Kanthaka; he is as solid as a chank off Thee Cliffs. He pulled me out into Thee Wandering. Everyone had forgotten about us. We were gone almost

six weeks. Thee Lupercalians were on their way here and guided Kanthaka and myself back. My Uncle said that was the only time he ever saw such disappointment. It was from my people towards Thee Lupercalians. All were celebrating their return, and it quickly shifted to mischance when I was unveiled. In the dog-cart Thee Lupercalians had placed grapes for me to rest upon. I was just a baby, naked and alone. Kanthaka is a wonderful ride, but even he could not keep me from crushing the grapes. When I was handed to my defeated parents, it looked as if my birthmark had spread over my entire body. Thee Lupercalian who handed me over demonstrated that they should welcome me with a kiss. My parents repulsed but went through with the action for fear of offending my saviors. They were surprised at the taste. They passed me back and forth between them, and then all around. By the time I got to my Uncle, only my true birthmark remained, and that was all his lips touched. Thee Lupercalians bring me a cart full of grapes every year. They will do this until I learn about seeding. They guided me in an art I know nothing of, informing me that I shall never sneak a taste of my creations. I fear my parents, sometimes my siblings, because they are not, at least for now, allowed to taste the grapes either, and I dread my Uncle. What if they don't return one year? I know they will once again put me in that dog-cart, strap Kanthaka to the traces, and with an unnecessary amount of force, smack us both on our behinds.

~Josephson~

Was it the light, the shadows? The first scar I saw kept drawing my eye. Eventually our eyes caught one another. I think my sisters might know, mayhap my Brothers. I'm not sure if I still know, so is that possible for them to have knowledge? I touched that scar under one of the trees, again with the light filtering through the boughs, a shadow, a shine depending upon the caprices of the breeze. I traced the puckered skin from the lower left chin, the convex of the lips, to just below the eye. My finger brushing those exaggerated lashes. I returned to the lips, though...not with my finger. The pull of my belt was a surprise to both of us. A warning canon shot over our negotiations. I reciprocated, though, with a gentle pull of the worn braces, bringing a cloying compromise back to the table. It only antagonized the situation. I lost the buttons from my shirt, they became shrapnel as it was hectically ripped open and off, becoming a wasted article that could have aided against the cones scattered as our bedding. Was there an anger? I don't think so, at least the way my hope invades my memories. We quickly disrobed one another, my heedfulness with the straps and buckles the antithesis of the assault against my own wardrobe. Laying down. My head was pushed away when I was caught attempting to discreetly inspect the body. I was persistent, gripping wrists, though not too hard, only to convey my want and non-destructive intentions. The scars hidden beneath

the clothing were few though varied. Later it became a myriad cloaked exhibit. I could see them attempting to replicate the original. The length and depth experimented upon every piece. I could see the unsatisfied last stroke within each. Though none matched the primordial stroke, I slowly kissed each one. To this day we enter into the same routine, it takes me so much longer these days as there are…how many more? But, we both enjoy the prolonged anticipation. When one day asked to bind my belt around the wrists, I shook my head, says I, 'I won't contribute to your scarring.' I backtracked a bit, eventually catching up to where my kissing had been interrupted. Laying back, with fingers laced beneath the head and elbows spread akimbo in style, a submitting smile. I became a lamb at his heels.

~Jubal~

Too much falls between my lip and my cup. What is the issue with my cup, you wonder? I am guessing the main impediment is myself, said ego. The bovid was unrecognizable, at least to my untrained eye. What I was doing up Thee Mountains is best left unsaid. The body had reached putrescence, maggots tunneling through the once promising offal. I pried the horns off. I was eager to create an instrument of my own. I came back down Thee Mountains. I went to the public house, in need of food and drink, thinking to sketch out my design for my flute. Through the door I went straight to Glaspell to place my order. He laughed and smiled at my trophy, grabbing it to inspect. When he handed it back, it was full of drink. After the third horn-full was downed, the story they put together was true. Not really known for going outside, I had succeeded on my own. With no weapon I had taken down the beast, fed on the bounty, and returned in triumph. Because I was apparently full from my feast, I could not beg Veda for anything from her kitchen. Three horn-fulls are cataclysmic to insides as forgiving as mine. Now to keep my standing, to never hold the mantle I previously held. I have to tote this around with me wherever I go. I have let the tale grow. Complicit in my silence. The horn's lip is ribbed, uneven, and jagged. I never got to sand and soften the edge, where I once imagined the sound would flow from. My own lip is often wet with blood, which adds to the myth. From the mass quantities that I have had to consume, I have put on weight, resembling the man they think I now am, though much of it spills down my chin to my front. A perpetual stain I am forced to carry.

~Laiben~

I have quite an issue with you at the present. Why do we dress you and take care of you if you are just standing around? Yes, I understand that everyone needs help now and then. We were going to quell our nemesis last week and almost went to war with our Brothers. Spring comes and those damn birds return and try to nest in our roofs. We put the word out

the day before and expected all to show and make an occasion of it. The Dumbs showed up triple armed, each and everyone. Thouar went and applied every accoutrement he could find to the entire clan. The children and seniors and the fighters in between. We were laughing as they strolled up, seeing everything they had on display. The axes and deer-horn pikes, the cat-claws and sledges with spikes. Us Buells had broomsticks and nets. A few of the kids had picked up their kick-rocks to do what frightening they could muster. When asked what they were planning to do to the sparrows, swallows, and other pint-sized invaders, they would not answer. That's when we knew there was about to be some business. Though we were lightly availed we had the numbers and the wits, obviously. One of the mid-youths spoke up, the one without the beard, Jacob. He seems a bit more sensible than the rest, though we have heard stories of a few of his odd behaviors. Says he, 'I've been told to tell you that our people can not accede with your plan.' We did not know what he was referring to. He took me aside and reminded me that they had gone through a hard year, and they would need all the luck they could get. I said we don't touch owls or anything of that sort. He remembered me to his seniors and other *gone-over* kin. Reminding me of their ancient belief that being...pardon my mouth, *shit on*, is good luck. They would not allow us to, 'Cull a one of them.' I could see where this was headed. I made a quick decision, knowing there was not a thing to think on or discuss. They would never change their stubbornness, and we will need them for something more dire in the future. And damn, we can live with a few extra birds. Says I to all, 'Let it be.' The Dumbs stayed and we ate and drank. I spread word round to my people, and eventually everyone thought we could all do with a bit of luck. Mind you, we're not like the Dumbs, we're not going round running underneath an airborne flock. We don't sit our rockers underneath a perched raptor. But, we have relations with them, and we do hope some of their luck rubs off on us. But you Scare... from the look and smell of it you should have plenty to spare. You got to start pulling your weight.

~*Lamar*~

I knew only your eyes would see this as only I see you in mine...

then the rest, a bit private if you don't mind. Such a feminine hand. Who do you think it could be? What I'm more worried about is who is it who knows I've been sneaking around those quince trees? The joy of the jam is my own shameful secret. But, I can't raise one up for the life of me. The seeds won't take. I've asked Thee Lupercalians, as I'm certain they know the secret I lack. They only want the seeds from me. They couldn't lug around a fruit tree, why would they want the seeds? They naught to suck on. Believe me, I've tried. I only get a headache, little upset body. I keep trying

though, mayhap I just haven't ingested enough. Tonight though, could be that it's a setup. I get there and all the Loves surround me, saying they know what I've been up to for years now. Then they lay in on me. I could handle a few of them well enough, sure I can have soft hands when it comes to making preserves. They don't know that my hands can be hard enough when accused of what they will claim. Then again, what if it's one of them Love girls? Not only are they desirable, but also desirous if the quince was telling the truth. But I would get a jam tree out of the deal as well. She could give me pointers, Pellis would deed me my own orchard. There wouldn't be no shame in working with fruit if you own it. But, just to dabble in it...you know, like the Murphy boys say they *experimented in their youth*...It's not really a decision is it? I'll just go with my lot and accept my fate.

~*Leighton*~

My moral, my spiritual value...I seem to lose them in the dark. I answer my own questions with an infuriating vagueness. Is it secrecy for secrecy's sake? Standing upright behind the doors is not diabolical. We have a bounty of paranoia, manufacturing a fearsome affront is effort wasted upon the true battle. I will apply my tools in multiple manners, my jack can level my swaying foundation, and it can be myself acting as my Brothers' steeplejack. I have scaled the outside of the campanile, observing ben Asher wield his vigilance. Pry a shingle, sand and fit it to perfection,   replace it at such an angle that my level can only set in my eye. I looked through the peepholes and witnessed him crying his cries. There is no steeple on Thee Lodge, repair it from within, yet the steeples on the houses have been erected in competition. And they call on me to *jack-them-up*. It will become untenable. While up on high, doing my best to upkeep their roofs while keeping them all on the same level, I look to the setting sun and chant to myself. *Those Are My Mountains*...I can scuttle round to the opposite side of the bulbs and view Eastward. I see Cap'n Constable's new horned and boned monument, the rebus beyond my interest. No onion bulb to mend. I'm on level with the birds from Thee Tower who mange to luff above men. I look down on Thee Totem. I sometimes make myself smile and quiz myself, *where is my spy hole?* I shift my weight to a new hole. The crosses gleam encircling Petr's cloister, as well as the old crosses breeding with the black ash in Thee Wulf's Woods. Thee Wandering acting our ocean as it recedes slightly then ebbs nearer each day. Thee Giant Tree Of Despear... Will it ever be grand enough for our weight? These atrocities are why I look West. The staggering, the unevenness, these are my Brethren. Mirroring myself. I cannot extrapolate, will not tease it out. Plainly, they are like me, imperfect, yet dutiful. Mayhap, eons in the future, when ancient bones struck down by enemies, disease, or ignorance rise again, they shall be leveled. So Mote It Be.

I got my first set of teeth from my Mother. My Fater was gone, his teeth were most likely dropped as shrapnel from from one of the wobble-death-birds. Hers I found in her sewing box kept underneath their bed. I attempted to process her thinking, the images causing me to slam the box shut. I've since repurposed her box. At the end her wandering mind might have hit on something. See, I also got my original teeth from her, meaning they cracked and crumbled and fell from my mouth all within ten months. I got my first *personal* set of teeth within four months, and when not in my mouth, I secure them next to my mother's within that sewing box. I don't bring those first ones out too often. Dr Dolan made them from beaver teeth. Yes, I thought he was joking too when he first told me. I first wondered if my beaver hat was from this same beaver. I would feel a sense a joy at reuniting them. I pictured myself wearing out a bare patch on my chin hair. But, he cleaned and sanitized them and of course shaved those down. The fit was less than ideal. Thinking of them getting fresh with an aspen was also difficult to overcome. He didn't seem to appreciate my attempted jest when says I, 'Do you think Ahmen believes he's a doctor?' No one knows who produced my Mother's. I forced him into a corner when I first asked him. I appreciate his gusto, but even his bedside manner is more advanced than his dentistry. So I turned my joke upon myself and became a new type of artisan. I accepted Doc's idea and experimented with animal teeth. All have more drawbacks than benefits. I first was drawn to cats, yet these are notoriously problematic and moody, I became unpredictable when donning them. My elk teeth whistle, fox are too small, horse teeth are close yet I can never shave them down enough before it looks like eight squat stumps in my mouth. I even tried dog. Mind you these were natural occurrences, I wasn't looking to mount their toothless maws breaking out from my walls. The molars worked almost to perfection, but I could never tame the taste from where they had often ventured. That is when I returned to the beaver. Or at least his relation to forestry. I bit into a beeswax chunk and from there experimented with every wood about, forming my prosthetics into varying shapes and designs. My set from a butternut tree I shaped to faintly resemble their fruit. From cedar I made my mouth appear to be full of dice. My black walnut set I constructed to be oversized and vicious. Unable to close my mouth, I must carry my handkerchief outside my pocket to account for the spittle. From mahogany I etched a scene from Thee Lupercalians procession, mules, and camels, jugglers atop elephants. The hickory I filigreed into shapes I see when I look up through the branches. I have single wear units I create from pine, and in the soft flesh I etch messages of relevance or nonsense, mayhap terror, all dependent upon my mood that particular

day. I scrimshawed in poplar. Teardrop created a design that I mimicked in silver-leaf and embedded in elm. And my Sunday specials: from white oak I molded the most beautifully shaped guerdons my imagination could create. I sanded them smooth and applied the whitest of paint. After the three coats, I added layers of varnish to give them a depth only achieved in nature. Certainly I get a bit lightheaded when flaunting them about, yet so do my admirers.

~Lessing~

Jehu, I'll bring you much in my wake. I strapped on these brown bottle shoes and worked the right for you. You told me to put myself into the cause, then that might give you *cause* to put yourself in me. So I became the Matron of Thee Women's Prison. And I taught 'em, boy I taught 'em hard. You would think that looking at all of them would make me want to be alone. After I shaved their heads, I taught them a lesson for every finger. And if I do say so, them girls that left here played their roles perfectly after they went home. But, one day when I showed for work, I was told that the grounds are now to be used as a beast-ending location. So, now I Matron over them. And I treat 'em just as hard, with my fist of lessons. But once I got bogged down in their mire, and by the time I was able to stand on my own, one of them chewed half my fingers. I'm still waiting to hear from Jehu. I'm thinking that with his silence he is telling me his disappointment in me that now I'm only working half-handed. Half as hard. Sometimes they can be beasts. Men.

~Levi~

I hiked up here to wear myself out. I only slept a few hours again. Thirteen mayhap. I don't know what woke me, usually it be Jacob hacking and hammering away on...well I don't know, I've never looked, no interest. That kid...and yes, he still is a kid, won't even grow a beard. That's our way, don't he know how idiot-like he looks? The ladies don't want no man who is no man. He still just hang around with his tools, those damn books, our Fater's old songs...and Mother. That's not right. He probably read in one his books how the youngest girl has to stay alone and take care of the parents. Jacob...he's a little bitch. Fater gone dead. Mother...Normal and I will put her in Thee Bedlam when we're ready. It's my choice though, at least Normal know that. That kid would go out there and serenade her probably. He up all day and all night I suppose. I never seen him in a bed. Mother say he knows when to use a bed. Was that some snark remark about me not helping Fater pass over? Well...piss her, piss him too. He should make me a bed. I'm the one who deserves. I know the use of a bed. Says he, 'There is corruption in our genes.' I brought it down hard on him

for his smart-sass. He wouldn't even lay in bed after that learning. He just laid on the porch. Normal pulled him over to the side so he didn't have to step over him coming and going from the doorway. He coulda stayed there as long as high water; he wasn't in my way going to the kitchen, nor when I returned to my pallet-bed. Speaking of which...there's Joseffy in that dog-cart, that's better than humping it back home to bed. You know, you could actually come to me instead of me always having to lug it up to wherever you just lounging about.

~Lincoln~

They called us especial. There have been rumors that the names are decided at sunrise. We went together and questioned them on this. Says the one, 'Lo! Who are you to question us?' Of course they knew who we were...are. Says we, 'We're Lincoln, sirs.' They never answered our question exactly, such as professors do. That is when Tosspa's Twin took my arm and had me guide him out of the room. All have kept us separate since. At times when he has anger towards me he lets me know that I am his petulant *umbra*. My parents don't call me especial. My Fater calls at me, 'A special pain in the so and so.' My Mother cuffs him lightly, while looking darkly almost towards me. I am not bad. Well...anyone who is not bad should not have to say it. What I mean is I'm not Döder bad. I do not get into trouble. My interests have been formed by Tosspa's Twin. Everyone else is led by both, but I only see Tosspa in passing; and sometimes when we come close to coming near to one another I see him shove a large figure into the nearest room before I can glean who it is. It is always Tosspa and his ward who scuttles away, as I am always guiding Tosspa's Twin. He towers over my miniature frame, casting me in his perpetual shadow. Why he has me guide him I am not certain. Mayhap his vision has followed his voice. He guides me by pointing at texts which I never see him read. He does scribble notes for me, but I suppose this could be a series of movements he knows by rote. I am the only one who lights a candle when we are submerged in our isolated tutoring. He seems to cower from the act. I used to light more, yet, I can no longer. If it is sympathy for my tutor or a pining for the shade, I cannot say. We do not speak of it. The guiding continues, and we do not speak of it. I now billet in the antechamber of his room, and when I return home, the conversations with my Mother and Fater are succinct. They seem eager for my return to my lone-twin tutor. I continue to guide him through the halls, hoping one day to surprise Tosspa and whatever he is hiding. Tosspa's Twin continues to guide me in his odd ways, and when the light goes out, we do not speak of it.

How many children do I have now? Don't answer. It's just something I do, asking questions. I know exactly how many. I have a coin for each. Not all of them are perfect in shape, a handful are even halved. A display built to my needs, though I don't display it. I have found it is best if I secret it within the hidden panel under my top desk drawer...Along with those seeds. But that boy...so young and asking more questions than I do. What an oddity he is. I would never ask such a thing. I have to say that I had never thought on it until he brought it up. I don't know if what he asked me is actually what he is asking. Even at his age he understands that men don't have headstones. Why would I ever consider what would be inscribed there? He is unpaired. Headmaster has informed me of some of his unorthodox behaviors. If it is possible, he is both younger and older than his age. His youth seems to be waning. I suppose it could be a compliment, but I would leave it up to him to write the words if he wants a plaque to remember me by. Mayhap it is a more advanced question that I thought him capable of. Could he have been prodding myself to think on what I have done with my life, to question the amount of years I have remaining? To ponder, if I passed today would I be at peace with my life?

~Lommett~

Sure they hated one another. Probably they felt that way before they were borned. But, what you think I supposed to do? Sure their boxes are touching, it's just my back was done when I noticed. I can't dig her up now. That would be...irreligious. He should have to dig his woman up. Mine deserve that spot more than his woman do...does. I don't see why being passed first is some reward. She should be punished for weakness. Those two women were always looking wall-eyed at one another. Circling the room, shooting hate out of each of their left eyes. Then mine started goading me to go after him. Why? I've got nothing against him. Except mayhap his poor taste in the opposite gender. Should I dig her up? Give his woman the good view evermore? I'm sure I could find a suitable replacement. I do mean that in all aspects...just glad she's not here to hear that. Kind of glad she's just not here...Well, if I were to move her I'm not dragging her all over and back. I've got my own health to think about. She was constantly at war, now she has one more battle she wants won. Is this the one she was prophesying? Says she, 'It's a War coming, just you wait and see.' So am I supposed to wait and see? I already fired the first shot. Did I just initiate your clairvoyant scheme? If you weren't so big yourself and didn't want the fanciest box — which happens to be the biggest —, I could just put this to rest...Aha! That is the crux. Why is just men in Thee Tower? There is my solution. She always said that even though she ended

up with me she still deserved the best. Well, here goes my best...it's what she deserves. I think she decided this for me before she was borned.

~Lowndes~

We've fought outside before, sometimes there is a romanticism about it. But that night it was just too much, the boys aren't mudders in a trifecta. So when Cap'n suggested Fater Nigrescent's old place I saw the humor immediately. Some would fear entrapment, and Cap'n should be one to fear, but not in this endeavor. The congregants had jested that next they would get rid of the pews. When I walked in, the pine floor had geometry in shadow where the pews used to be positioned. Did they expect everyone to sit on the floor, some masochism of fidelity? No, no, there were two rolling pallets of folding wooden chairs. That seems unsanctioned to my untrained eye. I looked to Cap'n for an explanation. He shook his head, says he, 'They think with these they can hold service outside in fine weather.' Not my concern at that moment. The open space was well ordained for our purpose. I chalked out the twenty square feet of a ring. The corners I cordoned off by ascribing a straight line between correctly spaced apparitions of the removed pews. We wanted nothing to do with the folding atrocities, besides anyone who came to witness would want to be standing at ringside. In the third corner, the one closest to the sacristy, he set down what looked to be the most ornate spit-bucket ever fashioned. From his almost empty satchel, he pulled out an oddly shaped brass or mayhap even gold gilt contraption. He held it outstretched hanging from a chain, and when he swung, making contact with the immovable cross from Fater Nigrescent's days, I knew we even had a bell to commence the fights. I asked where all the new pascal candles and fancy sanctuary lamps had gone. When I says, 'Do you think it's a bit dark?' Says he, 'No, no, it's just right.' I looked again, and I had to agree.

~Ludendorff~

I have revived my youth. When I was younger I was elite at Thee Dry Tine Ditch Jump. They discontinued the practice until recently. Now, if they want to get over it, they just walk. But we used to do it right. I remember fighting for the longest quant from those Dumb boys' Fater's punt. That's where the tradition started. They didn't even ask when I asked them why they did not do it anymore. We've had punters with their quant poles forever. Now they just hit each other with them, which has its amusements as well. Yet, I found a better method. Those old water-logged shafts were good, but I found a way to improve them. Hmm...so mayhap I destroyed the sport. But wait, couldn't they take the poles I made and apply them to

the punts and barges? I don't really know. Pellis was none too pleased to find me filching what I thought were his scraps. Says he, 'There's not a scrap-piece in a tree.' And he demonstrated by taking a switch from a nearby *child* of his and demonstrating his belief on my buttocks. But I then noticed the flex in the switch he used, even better than the pine I was planning on relieving him of. He dropped it after he finished with his point. I picked it up and pushed it against my palm. Says I to him, 'This is perfect!' From that day on I worked in one of his outer groves. I had my pick of the ash tree *scraps*. And I remained undefeated until my life took over and I was replaced by newer and brighter...Then, after years of respite I returned for one more jump. I managed it awkwardly. I found I had missed vaulting more than Manasseh informed me that I did not miss it. I used my wisdom of age...Ha! and a fortuitous event, and I improved the ramp we used to vault over Thee Dry Tine Ditch. Pellis loved this. I repurposed the grand old oak pews that for some unfathomable reason they were removing from Thee Church. I refitted a runway, sanding down the grooves formed by the heavy guilt of past parishioners' buttocks. Feeling the depth of these ruts I don't believe Pellis would have been able to convince them of the certainty of the sun rising and setting even if he used a 2x4 as a switch. The stilts and their braces I reconfigured from the disassembled crosses. Ornamenting the slope and refuse contained within. The wooden filigree once used to cradle the hymnals now holds the participants' poles. We used to guard them jealously, yet none will be able to resist the display. Someone left me the remains of the alter rails. I affixed them to the side of the ramp to accentuate the exhibition. And again our benefactor gifted us the past celebrant's chair. On the seat was left a censer. I stationed this on the far side of Thee Dry Tine, it will be where the eventual victor will reside. And about his...or now her neck, the champion will display the censer while perched in the celebrant's throne. I hope to add to the divots often. Eventually the neglected pews found their way to us as well. We set them up as formally as they had been. It was the only layout that seemed appropriate. This Fall, when Thee Dry Tine Ditch is swollen with detritus, we'll hold a month long tournament on each of the four Sundays. Of course, after we go to the other service first. People will come from every corner, the old as well as the new youth I have enticed after they witnessed the magnificence of the new arena. And for those who arrive by punt, they better make certain to switch out their poles for the proper poles, or else there is no doubt that they will end up in Thee Dry Tine Ditch.

~*Lurline*~

I made a tit of it all. With my *toings* and *froings*. I wanted him terribly. My family did not. He asked me to meet him, a picnic overlooking the coming storm. I could not subject him to my dying peoples' peculiarities. I did not

worry my habits would run him off, his own were serious and charming. But, one sideways look, one inaudible thank you, and they would end him. I ran. I went to Thee Mountains knowing him to be at Thee Cliffs. That was my first *toing*. I ran up the first slight hills, the soft turf with shoots of primrose. I bent to pick a nosegay of crocus. I stopped to rest under a hatch of lindens and mountain ash, adding to the crocus a few of the edelweiss that claimed sanctuary under the slight canopy. From this point I could faintly see Thee Tower. I hoped if I went higher I might even see Thee Cliffs and the storm. I stood and pushed on to the spruce, pine, and larch. What slight trails there were I attempted to follow, yet they were few, and seemed to be going where I had no want to return. And yet I did; return. I viewed the crowns of the elms from above. I hesitated thinking I was descending an unrealized topography. Then the chestnuts appeared, and I found myself once again under the same linden, edelweiss about my ankles. Thee Tower faint to the East. I did not rest this time. I ventured extreme West and slight North. Spruce, pine, and larch. My breath was staggered, I surveyed. It was not Thee Tower, but now when I looked East, I saw the shimmer of the fence surrounding and trapping The Northrop's cloister. Once again I went West. I hoped to eclipse all memory. Passes, hills, valleys. I finally came to the snow line. I put my head down and marched, following hard the sun, certain that I was on my way to achieving his safety. When I lifted my head I saw Thee Sea. To the East were Thee Cliffs, and below the defeated hurricane. If I looked Northeast I could again see Thee Tower. I headed towards this marker, trusting it more than the sun. I was pleased I would get to look upon him again, unpleased at finding that this was no way to come by and no way to go.

~Manasseh~

I discovered where he'd been going. Coming back smelling of nature's pit. I knew he wasn't rutting with some sow like Lessing, he'd never do that to me. When I came out from behind the willow still keeping guard on the lip of the former riverbank, he was standing on what I thought was an alter. And gathered at his feet was a flock of pre-teen disciples. Plumaged in the detritus he insisted on dragging beneath my lintel. I went and sat in the first pew, just before the alter, after all, I was family. He looked at me and shrugged, then went on with his sermon. He spoke of the mechanics, weight distribution, the physics. Where to place the pole depending on the individual. Where to hold chalked hands to best take advantage of each participant's unique anatomy. After the lecture he went up the aisle with one of his *ancient* poles gripped in his woven fingers. He turned and sprinted back in our direction, passing the cheering audience seated in the pews banking his runway. Up the alter's ramp, planting his pole in Thee Dry Tine Ditch...It was glorious! He rose and floated,

pausing in the twilight, gravityless before whipping his middling form into a graceful roll that brought him to a victorious pose before what looked a throne. He brought us to our knees, my Ludendorff, who husbands me with care. I had a gravity, but no longer. He reconfigured one of his ash poles to accommodate my form. Now I fly like one of Thee Lupercalians whose ash is a trapeze. His disciples are adept, they have translated new connotations from his sermons. When Fall arrives we will all deliver our own interpretations. People are eager to once again sit in the removed rows of pews. Fater Nigrescent jokes, 'At least this time they will be paying attention.'

~Manumitt~

I used to frequent it more often, but then it became what it is, and my interest fades as my age grows. I don't go to his house too often. Some are there nightly…and daily. I go in Fall. I love apple flesh, when their skin mimics the the leaves of the season. But, I crave the fading plums, they are slipping into tartness. Eaten straight, the blood slides to the joint of your jaw and forces your eyes to squint in response. He takes these late-season jewels and soaks them in one of those minor evils. I only call them evil because they now govern his house and influence his clientele. In his pans that he prefers to his cups, he smothers them with custard and intense sugar. Then he comes to my table to *put on a show*. And it still gets me. He waves his arm aristocratically, spinning the pan on his finger, strikes a match on his tooth, and blows a flame that ignites my feast. I am not one to succumb to flare, yet he truly is a virtuoso. The crust then caramel, the heat then cool. I am his slave. How many times have I scalded my tongue in impatience? The sugar coats my teeth. The melt down my throat. The brandy is extinct after my assault. I approve of his house, just not what he has done to make it prosper. Yet, I am a glutton, and every Fall I am shovel-ready.

~Maude~

You know what I did to Pollux. It was just an honest effort. I thought we would get on better. And we did, it worked…after a fashion. Fashion… ha…he is the most fashionable thing around; un-thanks to myself. He is a good sport. I thought it only proper to allow him…says I, 'You should do something nonsensical to myself.' I thought he would say, *no, no,* and we would just move on from there. But the so and so took me up on my offer. Our size is about equal, but still, a man getting pinned by a woman. I was thinking his Brothers would shave his beard right off after seeing me take him down hard in the yard. He packed a bindle and went out the

71

door. Did he leave me? Was that how he was getting even? I was pained that I truly hurt him. He returned three days later. Says he, 'You're were right, you said nonsensical. Well, I'm going to knock some sense into you.' I was devastated. I had made a tit of myself. I had never backed down from a fight. But this wasn't a fight; it was a reckoning. I would take what I deserved. He told me to close my eyes. He played it out. Slowly pulling his weapons from his bindle. Pacing measured circles around me, leaning in and blowing on my face. He was nursing this misunderstanding. I heard the canvas of his coat when he cocked his arm. I braced myself, something hit my face as say he, 'You are amazing.' Another hit my face as say he, 'I would never change anything about you.' He repeated this, hitting me in my face with each statement. 'You are perfection.' I open my eyes. Flowers he's softly smacking my face with: a smartweed. 'I wish you loved yourself half as much as I love you.' Flower: sheep sorrel. 'I'll be forever unworthy of you.' Flower: arrow-leaf tearthumb. 'You lift me while I drag you.' Flower: lady's thumb. 'I didn't want to hurt you. This is what you deserve.' He looked up into my eyes and reached to kiss me. He went to every corner to fill his sack. Thee Lupercalians would have paid handsome for this haul: Star-Of Petr, Daisy Fleabane, Yellow Goatsbeard, Orange Hawkweed, Nodding Bur Marigold, every possible Aster...Houndstongue, Viper's Bugloss...He stopped me from ticking them all. He wrapped his fingers as far as possible around my wrist and pulled me upstairs.

~Mishka~

I was released from the left side of Thee Bedlam three years past. They are still weaning me back into their world by giving me something productive to do with myself. The subvention of welfare. I am to be The Town-Crier. We have no written form of distributed information here. It has been attempted on a few occasions, though from lack of paper or lack of reading...or just lack; it has yet to take. So I arrive at break of day, *a term that still affects me*. I sit and wait on my box in the square. When someone has news that they need shared they are to come to me and speak it in my ear, *much like you I've just realized*, and then I stand and cry it out for all who care to hear. At least I am supposed to. I continue to learn on the job. Fater Nigrescent whispers, telling of an incurable situation for a certain someone asking all to keep him in their thoughts. I cry, and I cry, and I cry. ben Asher tells of the beginning of a fault in the town bell, he will miss the evening call while he mends it. I cry, and I cry, and I cry. People now gather to watch me *deliver* the news. They bring their children and picnics, making an event of the situation. They converse as at home, jesting and speaking upon their day, some attempt to include me, offering me my favorite loaf. Then as digestifs are poured, Petr's Widow comes to me. I stand atop my box, the cups are stilled in waiting, the children halt their

after dinner games and gather at my feet. Petr's Widow floats away. I open my mouth, and I cry, and I cry, and I cry. Some stare, uncomprehending. None laugh. Some smile at me and nod. They pack the baskets and the children and head for their homes once again. As I surrender to my box, my hem sopping up the moist dirt around my ankles, someone hands me a handkerchief. I cannot see who through my tears.

~Mulcahy~

We used to swim in Thee Lakes when I was a youth. On the specific day I am thinking we only rode out for the day. My Mother had one pack between the lot of us. Most everyone wore their swimming kit underneath their clothes. I had tried this, but wearing my Brother's hand-me-downs, they were baggy and bunched under my own clothing, aiding my tightening pants in not fitting. I was also a fat child. What adults referred to as husky. What we now call normal. I suppose I am always ahead of my time. I took my kit from the pack and went to change. I couldn't use the tent as all the others did. I could barely get undressed in front of myself. I opted for the only other location that assured privacy. The outhouse. You've seen them, wood box, hole, collects so and so. And if you've seen them, you've tasted them. You would ask, 'Don't you mean smell?' No, no, this was high Summer, we went to Thee Lakes to cool off from the swelter. I held my breath and entered. First I made certain to hook the door behind me. It was quite dark. Boys have been known to fling wide the door to expose another's shame. My eyes already began to sting from the swampiness at closing the door. I de-robed as quickly as possible, again more from fear of intruders than the torture of being in the box. Thinking quickly, staying a step ahead of pranksters, I picked my clothes up off the ground. There was about a three-inch purposeful gap around the base and below the roof that was supposed to aid in airflow and add a little light. It did not offer too much assistance with either. I knew that if I were a mischievous boy I would wait for my shy nemesis to undress, then reach under the gap and flee with his clothes. I put them out of reach from anyone, really the only place, the bench that took up the back part of the tiny shed. Aha...I thought, impressed with my cunning. I had done this numerous times and have a pattern. I set my *to-be* clothes on my left foot, remove the outfit I am wearing and put it on the right foot. I reached and came up empty. I tried again. Nothing. No problem, in my haste not to be seen I must have turned myself around and set my bathing kit on the right. I felt with my right hand. Nothing there. The sun was high and gave no angle to assist the three-inch gaps that were already failing at their tasks. Of course, since I set them there, then I also picked them up with my deposited clothes and placed them on the bench out of the reach of my antagonists. I was so anxious at being discovered that I accomplished all of this in a matter of

moments. I felt where I had placed them. My hand went through the hole in the bench. My heart now began to race. I frantically frisked the bench. Nothing. The floor again, the bench, again and again. I was a fat, naked youth, trapped in a wartime torture of my own creation. I could not bring attention, everyone would come if I yelled. I got down on my hands and knees to peer under the gap, waiting for my Mother. My stomach ground in nervousness. At least I had a place to sit if she took a while.

~Mumphrey~

It would have been easier to burn the fields, but I thought this poetic. It was hard work, but he deserved it. If I would actually work that hard regularly I'd be a different man. It took me seven days to find enough salt, took out three debentures. I waited until I almost smelled rain. I wanted to get it down, but didn't want it to wash away before it took root. *Borrowed* a wagon and two mules. I was practiced and the mid of night proved no obstacle. It was artistry. As if I were Teardrop, painting a white stripe down every row. People have called me a skunk, this looked like all the skunks ever made were lining up head to bum to measure their species. I had to walk backwards and straddle-legged to quickly dump the bags evenly, but I could hear the rabbits skitter away at my approach. Rabbits can be a nuisance, but not even they can breed enough to be a plague. My stance was frozen at an untenable angle. Yet when I had finished my sowing I rolled the hogshead barrels down from the bed of the wagon. I did not have much time before twilight. I did not need to do this deed, the other would be enough, but I thought...Ha! Get this, I've been waiting to say this out loud to somebody, 'It'll be *salt* in the wounds!' I rolled the barrels up to the highest point of his fields. I was done being quiet. I had a hatchet in my hand. That vinegar seeped out and covered the other. Veda would have been jealous of my dessert, it was drizzled chocolate on top of frosting. I took the empty barrels, thought I could resell them to somebody. I needed to start thinking of angles to pay off my new debt. I thought I would leave my hood on until I returned the wagon, then I thought better of it. A little cover-up and I could make this wagon convert. Between it, the broken barrels, and the mules, I would come out ahead. I could do with a new hood though, this one's getting a bit...*ratty*.

~Munly Munly~

Awake! Open right eye, keep dirty eye closed, pattern of three torso touches, then to waist and knee three, stand, right foot first, right hand last to touch bed, collect belongings pattern, rug with right foot first and last, go through first door of the day, if successful open dirty eye — three spins

were the original. Was it my Sister who caught me? — a memory of my Brother popping my arm when he witnessed my dirty eye at work, Sister confronts our Fater *ignore ignore ignore*, to the grass right foot on surface then split with next surface — anxiety about going to bed — school, not as clear, can't touch a myriad of familiar objects, — a memory of a school friend witnessing my face pattern, hearing whispers afterwards but not to my touched face — walk the straight path and do not double back must retrace exactly or must start over...did I sing the correct songs in the correct order? What was my first word? Fater *ignore ignore ignore*, hear him confront Mother, she smiles and says I am such a character and her specialness, inundates with whorehoundish confections, three bites drink two bites drink — anxiety growing about bed — remember the dirty eye, get dressed for post-school activities, left leg out first, right leg follows, once around the torso, same pattern with shirt, and inverse on the dressing, sit to tie shoes/boots left first touch inside sole — what word did I see first today? No it is alright — finish tying, touch right shoe with right hand, back home, three spins before the door right hand to first second then the lock, right foot forward, on the rug then split the rug then through the first jamb, wait for Mother to speak, respond, consume love, pattern of homework... — bed is approaching, *terror terror terror* — Brother slugs, Sister sleuths to find me out, feign ignorance, at table Brother snitches about the whispers, still feign, indulge in corpulence, knock over milk because of dirty eye, disappointments wash over Mother, Brother purposefully knocks his own milk because he actually loves me...Bed! My bed is level...I've measured it with my cable. If I could wear the hoodwink over my dirty eye then I would not have to confront the light. Awake!

~Narghile~

Sometimes I find myself just hitting my anvil with my hammer. Nothing in between. This is what I do all day long, why would I want to go through the motion when my work is complete? I suppose, because my work is never complete. My Fater started me smithing to get my adolescence out. Of course everyone grows out of it, it was just that mine was an aggression of extreme acuity. He found the physicality worked to dull my pugnacity. My tutor taught me to count in a rhythm, so everything was being struck evenly; *one-two, breathe, one-two, breathe*. I have outgrown my tutor — alright, I had a...disagreement with him, and his hands no longer allow him to follow his craft — so I am the only smith. So this is my own fault, bringing everyone's needs on to myself, but, I have my own count now. *One-two*, only went so far. My new coping mechanism is, *Buell-Toombs, Dumb, Buell-Toombs, Dumb, Buell-Toombs, Dumb*! Each and everyone comes to me with suggestions concerning my trade. Demands that they alone believe they are entitled to. There is no manager here, so I must deal with them quick

and hard. It might be interesting if Mumphrey approached me. Arguing with a child is untenable, so as they tantrum their singular rant, I drift into my chant...*Buell-Toombs, Dumb*...I picture convincing them that my anvil is that long searched for pillow...*Buell-Toombs, Dumb*...As they lay down their head, I gently brush their wishing hairs behind the ear...*Buell-Toombs, Dumb*...Says I, whispering into said ear, 'When I finish counting, you will... *one-two, Dumb*!

~*Negral*~

...If it goes without saying then why are you always saying?...We have business...The wind has been sowed, the accounts need tallied. War...

~*Normal*~

Sure, I know it's curious that I only come to you at night. Well...not even night, just before the sun assaults. That's what I have to do though, you know, to survive. Levi lays about perpetually, but his true sleeping is in the mid of night. And the offensiveness that comes from his body is unbearable. Not to be youthful, but I do mean both ends. It is jarring to be near the expired perfumes coming from his room, he says he can't close the door or open a window because he doesn't want to waste the time of either action. And the rasping combined with the dry-gasps are a grind on my ears comparable to Jacob and his songs. Jacob at least lets me make use of his tools. He says he is glad that I put them to use. He doesn't need them in the dark because he is usually off making eyes with someone or other. The ladies and some men both seem to like his beardless face and smooth, roped body. Our stock is now on Levi's schedule as well. I don't know if you can call it mine as it was forced on me by circumstance. The brays at 3:00 A.M. are my cue to do the *midday* feeding. The rooster now goes off when the moon pulls up. The feral cats are irate at this arrangement and have attempted to prowl at noon. Skulking is not particularly effective at this time, and now they mostly laze with Levi which is appropriate as the only real difference between their lifestyle is the bathing and grooming. Jacob does his share; he feeds in the morning, what is now supper, as I am falling to sleep trying to evade Levi's woken bowels. I'm not certain when Jacob beds, I stay out of his business. I love him, but I don't particularly like him. He is foreign to me, says he, 'Corrupt from within.' His weight is pulled, and I appreciate it. I respect his version of normalcy. Which, fittingly enough, is all I desire. Work, rest, and one day mayhap a commonplace family.

~Omie~

We hoped to be taken under their wings one day, just like the Tosspas did with the Lincolns. I was always Marcus Aurelius when we would play as youths. We pretended to go on hunting expeditions. Othar and I would be racing to get ahead of one another while Otho was somewhere far behind us digging in the soil. Then that day came when I was done pretending. Because I was Thee King Of The Sky, I would climb trees and speak down to them from on high. I was in that black ash that sits on the hill overlooking the willows that ride Thee West Bank of Forktine. We had lost interest in repeating our same rote game. I was bored, swinging my legs from a seat in a branch waiting for night. Othar was spitting and sucking it back into his mouth before it hit the ground, even Otho had caught up with us. I didn't bother to see what he was not doing. I heard the chirrups. I climbed higher and found the nest. Five premie-mouse-skinned birds all alone and screaming. Fuzzy, bulging black eyes, and beaks that were so oversized I knew they would never grow into them. I touched one and recoiled at the sensation, it felt like my Grandmother when they were preparing her body to be laid out. I held onto the branch with one hand and grabbed him in full. I let him sit on my hand and try to stand on his wheat-weak legs. He toppled over, unable to catch himself with his bald elbows. I couldn't hear him hit. I only heard Othar say, 'Hey!' I grabbed another, still bracing myself so I would not fall. I tickled him while he wobbled in my palm. I tapped his weighty beak with my extended middle finger. That made him stop squawking for a moment as he unhinged his jaw and tilted back his neck. He didn't get what he wanted and a little so-and-so came out his other end. It icked me out and I launched him from my palm trying to rid myself of his filth. Says Othar, 'Hey!' Even to this day he has that phrase down. I grabbed the other three and started launching them at Othar. When I got down to the ground, Othar was crying. I couldn't tell if it was because I proved myself the best hunter or if it was because Otho was sitting with the broken bodies and deflowering them of their wispy fluff-feathers. He seemed to have trophies of exploded dandelions displayed from each and every one of his button holes.

~Othar~

I believe that I will be hunting for the rest of my days. My neck is at this permanent angle because of my inability to sleep. Since a certain day in my youth, I have been on a quest for a perfect pillow. Anything that is ticked with feathers is incompatible. I have tried the flat earth, I don't believe it is flat enough. I have tried my Mother's discarded dresses. Sheep wool and buffalo locks, even buffalo dung. My tears were a catalyst in reigniting the refuse. Cat, dog, any fur from any beast. I offered some Dumb males

77

to shave their beards. I had begun to test sleeping naked, rolling my own clothes into a form that would enable my discomfiture. I could not even begin the test, my nerves racing in fear that someone would enter and see me in my shame. Before my neck was constantly causing my eyes to view the ground, I used to look up at the clouds and envy their form. A garland of clouds about my neck, folded and halved beneath my skull, combed and brushed over my crown. I would even dream of tearing a handful like a cotton candy so I could nestle it within my sockets, diffusing any light, sopping any...Well, there is nothing up there for me. Omie once thought to bring me a sack full of leaves from an old ash. I don't believe the genus mattered, none sufficed. I see Otho daily on his hands and knees. He doesn't seem to care for Omie or myself. And I do mean not care. No love, no hate, no...nothing. It would be a blessing if he found something while he is doing whatever he does down upon the ground. Though, he would would never think to gift it to me to aid my ailment. I must continue my hunt; there has to be something out there that will let me weep freely but not drown me in my sleep.

~Otho~

It must look as if I am groveling at your feet. But, penance for my lust must be paid in this manner. I don't have a chaos of feelings. My purpose is clear: to crawl this land on hands and knees until my sentence is served. I came out my Mother and was on the right path until I stood, then I began following my Brothers, and even at a distance did I misstep. So I must begin again. Anything to aid my crossing would be anathema: cushion, ointment, clothing, certainly not the luxury of feathers. I have seen Mansard's banks, cut my knees following the scree on the lips of Forktine, balanced on the edge of Thee Cliffs heading West. At the foothills I climbed the lower rolling hills, practicing for the inclines, boulders, and beasts. The months of anfractuous paths, the freeze, the seclusion had only the effect of delectation, knowing I was that scant bit closer to reckoning. This is not a reprieve I am begging from you, spilling my ways out at the foot of your cross. This is an accounting for myself and the others who I would have done harm. If it is said aloud, mayhap those who misunderstand my taciturn ways will hear. It is not for me to redress their ways, at least not until I surpass my own.

~Padraig~

The old carousel is still there. I don't ride it myself anymore. I rode it once when I was a child. It was beautiful, still is really. But only to look at. No one knows who any longer, he probably doesn't want the credit, but it was

carved with meticulous care. The artist recreated every animal brought by Thee Lupercalians. Horse, giraffe, tiger, buffalo, camel, elephant, fox... you get the idea; and they also carved a man standing kind of hunched over, so if you rode him it was like a piggy back at relay day. All these bounced in alternating rhythm mounted to the poles in the roof and floor. There is glass and looking glass to capture and recast the light. When you see it at night for the first time, with lanterns mounted everywhere, you are seeing the unseen and are enchanted. If any care to look, the ceiling and roof, which resembles a tent, has triptychs of Thee Lupercalians. Yet, my favorite display is the rotating image that disguises the center post concealing the inner-workings. It depicts every aspect of our Lupercalia. It also projects the mechanism for propulsion. From the center post, one overlarge horizontal bar extended out past the mounts and their riders. This was where the water-buffalo was harnessed to the bar attached to a yoke. From the yoke, on another extended bar, hanging in front of the beast's head was some type of prize. I have never particularly looked. I suppose it is whatever a water-buffalo craves. Upon my first ride I sat somewhat behind the bar. On the third revolution the music switched to something more jubilant, all the children began screaming in joy, mouths wide in awe. The carousel picked up momentum. The perceived danger enthralled all. We called our calls and hollered our hollers. By the seventh rotation all were covered in buffalo scat. Scat is polite, it was a wet deluge of shrapnel. As I said, my seat was unfortunately positioned. Yet, even if I were on the opposite side, I soon realized that the buffalo had perfected his range through needless practice due to genetics. A water buffalo has such a tail that can launch said projectiles in any direction and in miraculous perfection. His tail is a bat launching these soft bombs. A destruction that must be cleaned and attended to after every ride, which in later years I noticed happened only once a year. I don't mean to be scatological, the children should be warned...And again, as I realized in later years, I am again realizing as I say this out loud, mayhap this was the warning. A, *this is life kid, shut your mouth and take it,* kind of warning.

~Paestum~

I don't know if anyone will ever see or hear this, and a part of me hopes that this is the case. It might bore to distraction. My acquaintance — whom they dub, Ichnabod — brought her to my attention. He, along with many others, was smitten by her charms, as soon was I. My writings had been claimed as genius, though I knew them to be only mediocre for my abilities. I began writing for her, being what I thought was truly unselfish. She played and sang and spoke my new pieces to their fullest potential. In fact she expanded their potentials bounds. The earth hummed its joy and grated its skin with giddiness. Alas, a weak link was exposed, not in

Polly's or my own words...but, her dead wood piano. Though the earth was moving in joy, the piano, being formed by man's hand, had reached its full potential when it was only playing folk songs. It proved itself to not be too weak an instrument for this grand deed. We are cursed with insufficient tools to realize our dreams. My opus' are crushed and lost. Mayhap selfishness was sitting the bottom of the beaker, after all, who do I think would have received the glory? The writer? Even you know the answer to that.

~Pollux~

You probably don't recognize me much, huh? Remember my gingerness? Yeah, that was myself. Sure I had a skunk-like stripe in our clan's plumage. I been chewing leaf since before my beard sprouted: I'm not the carefulest spitter. All the women who had been there always said they enjoys the essence. I did not know I had this quality, which now worries me. Cause, either they all lied, or Maude be lying now. She couldn't hide her pulled face anymore. She intimated that if I want her near my beard, then I would need to give attentions to my foul streak. She made a paste of vinegar and apple, no good. Added lemons, no good. Tried a cut potato. When that don't take she puts them all together, makes a mash in her bowl, weighs down my beard so heavy that I cannot blink. No good. I joked that mayhap she was unwillingly agreeing with my former women, she would like to enhance my essence. Says she, 'No good.' She could have been meaning my beard, them, myself...guess she could be applying it to everything. Thee Lupercalians come, and before they could drive a stake, she drags me down with her and assaults them. Claiming a dire situation we are in. I was standing behind her and wanted to pipe up about her not speaking for me, that apparently the direness was only her own. I thought better on it. One of them steps forward with a straight blade. Now the situation was dire for me. I was no teen in short-pants. I let everyone nearby know of the difficulty they would encounter if such a thing was attempted. They shrugged. Another stepped forward and dragged us to her own trunk. She done just what Maude done, mixed and mashed, but from unknown sources, mortar and pestle as well. It fizzed unfriendly like. I pulled Maude's face. She tamped the fizz down with a hard water. She had me strip my clothes, says I, 'Well, I see where this is going.' Maude's big, I didn't think anyone could smack like her. This lady didn't even spill a drop from her bowl when her palm connected. She smiles bigger than Maude as well. She dunked not only my stain, but all my hairs, eyebrows, chest...you know...*All! My! Hairs!* I am a faded ginger. Purified, Maude likes to joke. I'm afraid to tell her my eyes now always itch. I cannot imagine how she does not feel my burning skin when she is close on my pale beard. No telling what they might concoct. I hope it just might all fade away. Stains gone, gone good.

~*Polly*~

She's my *Second Hurricane*. I love her, I love her, dearly and dearly. I need her hands to help me raise her. We leave most doors open, I can't get in or out without her. Nor would I want to. Our bath is a ritual we both cherish. It is a luxury and indulgence, a therapy of sorts introduced to me by Thee Lupercalians. Polpot, Ichnabod, that wickedness of a child Hallis...I could go on, many have been kind to us; they gift us an inordinate amount of unnecessary items. They say the milk would turn if it was unused. I'm suspicious of their motives, but Pollywog and I bathe bi-weekly. Thee Lupercalians retuned three weeks after the incident: my *First Hurricane*. They rode an elephant to our house, something that has never happened before. Thee Ladies brought with them a copper tub. We gathered in our front room, forming a circle about the tub. No words were passed, not an uncommon occurrence in my prior dealings with any of them. Yet, what they were about I could not guess. I was still on a pain...*supplement* at the time. My stares went unanswered. To my dismay, they disrobed. Pollywog walked the circle, touching each in turn. The shades were of every variation imaginable, each as beautiful and unique as the last. I did not circle with my baby, but I could see what she felt. Supple, pampered, causing a relaxed air in their behaviors and even an alluring hook. Pollywog no longer surprised me. She disrobed and tried to haul herself into the copper container. It was too tall, she retreated and fetched one of the many unused chairs. She sat in the basin, smiling in victory. Thee Ladies had unveiled jar after jar of milk from beneath their robes. I noticed it was *Our* milk within *Our* jars. I didn't know this was a commodity. After the tub was filled to Pollywog's chin, a flame was ignited from the burner underneath. The flame was adjusted until they felt it was appropriate. My wrist was taken in hand, and I was tenderly disrobed as Pollywog splashed in delight. I was was gently born to the tub. When the milk passed where my button should have been, I finally let go. My love and I indulged; my mangled hands were blindly guided to the form of a routine, a ballet that was indoctrinated until it could be done by rote. Thee Lupercalians re-attired themselves and closed the door behind. The lotions, herbs, salts and spices were left on a floating shelf on the lip of our cradling joy. When we became stingy in their use, I found their reserves on our porch and realized a year had passed. We are no longer cheeseparing with the larder. Do I deserve this? No, but, Pollywog does. She aids in my constant need to heal. She is the original balm.When I brush her in passing, set her to bed, bathe her shell with my limp stumps, I feel what I only saw, while she had the courage to engage.

~Pollywog~

I don't understand kick-rock. No, I mean I do understand it; it's just stupid. I guess I won easily. They said they didn't want to play with me anymore, and I was as dirty as my Mother. When I laughed they thought I was doing it at them. No, well...a little bit. But, mostly because my Mother and I bathe so much we can't get away from clean. She calls me her little angel...and her Pollywog. I can swim even better than I can play kick-rock. My Mother says I came that way. I've never met my Fater. When I ask if I ever will, answered she that she 'Truly did not know.' She always answers me, that is nice. I ask, 'Why not?' She answers, 'I suppose that is a copper-bottomed truth.' She always answers, but her talk is Ladyish sometimes. One day I hope I understand the answers. She said once that I was as old as the elephants. Again maybe one day. Everybody tells me how jealous they are of my skin. Mother taught me how not to brag, even to be humble. But, I like my skin, it's not exactly like Mother's but when you touch them both they feel the same. And she doesn't feel like any elephant. I know, because I get to ride one every year they come. It's not like the other rides that they offer to children. Inside and around a tight circle, which I've done but will not again after the rides we take. Some of Thee Lupercalian Ladies take me out late at night, mayhap so we don't make the others jealous, and we ride through Thee Mountains and The Wulf's Wood, where I'm not allowed, and then we go to Thee Lake. We start at Thee Upper Lake, the water coming up to my smooth belly riding on the elephants back. I sometimes get off one, dive below and swim between their legs, but I grab a tail and pull myself back on before we get to the Falls to Thee Lower Lake. I hold onto the ears and then they leap. My belly drops, but not too much. We sail clear of the falling water and starting with Thee First Star, I count as many of the smaller child stars as I can before we barrel into Thee Lower Lake. I ride them all the way to the bottom where they push hard off the rock, and we explode back onto the surface. We break the surface and the splash from our dive is just hitting its highest point, so we get hit with that waterfall and then the natural one when they swim me through to the backside. And we stay back there floating on the backs. We watch the small child stars fade. And when the light from the rising sun comes, we exit the silky view and follow the only other light in the sky. They take me home, following Thee First Star.

~Seneca~

I used to hide in that trunk when I was a little boy. I was so careful getting it out. Creeping through the door that squeaked my arrival, sneaking on my dancer's feet across her freshly nailed floor. Of course the hinge gave salutations as well. I had to open it to remove linens and as-yet-unpacked

blankets. I lifted the trunk and set it by her door. I returned and refolded what I had removed and placed it in the un-dirtied silhouette of where they had been hidden. I was silent in my work, though my heart was pounding a resolute and deafening confession. She still did not wake. I was no Lupercalian elephant, my awkwardness would have been a riot to witness if the situation were not what it was. I finally made it to the field where it happened. I had bought a second-hand saw from Chitty, he only charged a five-piece and a promise to say it wasn't from him. I didn't understand at the time, but now I do. I started sawing, and it did not seem to take. I cut my losses and returned to my own blade. I cut the leg. It started the first incision in a clean line — only a seepage of red arose. I had a serrated section on my blade, but the width was insufficient. I had to choose between neat or fast. I returned to the second-hand saw. The tool seemed practiced at this act, though its grace was akin to myself impersonating a beast of burden. I snapped the tendons with my blade but had to apply the saw to the bone. The wool was ruined. I completed the other appendages in the same sequence, each taking a bit longer than the previous. Removing the head proved the most difficult. My blade initiated the procedure as easily as before. In fact, it was the antithesis of the saw. It seemed to whet itself and relish in the act. My difficulty came when our eyes met. My guilt began to rise, then shortly escaped. It entered the arthritically frozen jaw to cake the swollen dorsum. The repudiation now drowned in my shame. Any semblance of elegance vacated me as well. I hacked. I could not decipher the larynx, the spine, the end...I stopped when I realized I had exhausted the saw's being on the earth's slag. I had my plan committed to memory. I will trust that I completed it. I have no recollection of burying the trunk, bathing in Forktine, or returning home. I retuned to myself when my Aunt came downstairs, dumbfounded yet attempting to disguise her confusion, searching for a place to lay/hide her cradled collection.

~Senatobia~

I never really had to go there when he was there. Thee *Cathedral* I avoided, my Mother always wanted to go. She would do chores for six days as long as she got to have Sunday for that need. Worked out well for me. Then I got a bit curious. Was Mother pulling something over on me? I started skulking around there. I had a lot of time on my six days of freedom. It was difficult to determine the draw of the situation. He was there administering to needful souls constantly. There seemed to be no break. Certainly not for himself, not even close to my six days. Then I noticed that he hung around there late late late, on Saturday nights. I thought that seemed peculiar. Everything was shuttered, the lights were dimmed low. Was he so devoted that he was practicing for his show tomorrow? Do you need to practice

reading someone else's words? That doesn't seem likely. Was this the only time he could manage to be alone? He had to bar the doors and scuttle the beacons so no entitled do-gooder would take advantage of his generosity? I came close and put my ear to the corner stone, most people don't know that is the best place to listen. A high call was almost heard, something that brushed my lobe but would not go inside. My face was chilled for having pressed so hard and long on the granite when I saw them exit. I knew him, I knew his Sister as well. I felt sick. The moon showed me the wet mica flake on his lash. A trusted man, a trusting youth...Fater says, 'I'm done.' I didn't tell on them, but someone must have. That was the last time I ever saw either of them anywhere near there.

~Strabo~

I sent him up there...purposefully. I thought he could go play la-la with Engel. I'd had my suspicions. Thought if I sent him up in Thee Mountains it would take care of itself. Or...that I would take care of it. No one was supposed to know, but, I knew about those caverns. See, I always thought I was good about intuiting secrets; Faribault spilt the location. I had never had reason to go, it was just a thing to hold over Faribault. But now, I would meet them up there...*discovering themselves*. And then he proved me wrong, made me discover something else. He come down Thee Mountains as a man. Little girly Jubal. Not no more he is not. I crawled onto my belly searching for them. When I could stand up, I saw nothing. Of course I thought, they want it dark for their purposes. I ignited everyone of my flares and lanterns, bringing down a celebration like as Thee Totem. And now I discovered...neither of them were there. There was no music... but there was. I saw it all about me, a lake underground, can you believe that? Shapes dripping from the ceiling, they were tears of giants that had walked above. And the tears' echoes rising from the floor, reaching out to their Brethren, in an attempt to make one another whole. I had to submerge into the brilliant blue of the water. I opened my eyes, and from underneath I turned and watched through the warped water. My flares bent the unfamiliar surroundings to a further softness, an altered perfection. I emerged from the lake and found another room of crystals. I placed my flares in the statued web they created. I don't believe in wishes, or...I didn't believe in them. But I now wished Engel and Jubal were both here, to not only witness this miracle, yet, to serenade the architect who crafted such perfection. I've never returned. If what I saw was false, I don't want to know. And if Faribault needs a secret, I don't want to be the one to hold it over him any longer. Jubal and I have a quiet agreement these days. And he's grown so large now I think he would carve me hollow and play me if I broke it.

84

~Tattnall~

The day after my husband passed he came into my life. I was returning from his final procession to Thee Tower. I heard his cry. On the riverbank I turned, from behind Thee Tower the dove bloomed. And just as miraculously it wilted, crashing down in Forktine. The current took hard and pinned it against a boulder in a position of dissection. I jumped into the torrent, my dress sticking to my form and making it impossible to swim. Yet the same water grabbed and hurtled me at the spread-eagled dove. I braced my arms on either side of him, defending against the will of the water until the other mourners pulled us from the cold. He sat in my palm all the way home. We nursed one another back to ourselves. I could never put him in a cage. I had found a piece of driftwood and placed it where I had always wanted my Husband to keep a valet. He began stretching his legs about the house, hurtling himself into the windows. What didn't he understand? To the two rings I attached a chichi chain. The smaller fit about his leg, the other slid perfectly over a broken branch still on the driftwood that was the size of my index. Now when he would try to damage the windows, the perch wobbled slowly and pulled him back down. I don't want him *not* to get outside like he thinks he wants. So...I slip the ring on my finger, and we go for walks when I feel up for it. I had to clip his wings for his safety as well. I didn't want him to pull me up into the air like a miracle. He understands his wings now, he no longer flexes them. He only turns and watches the kite fight the wind in the sky. I wonder if he understands if the wind is as dangerous as the water in Forktine, I can't dive into the air to save him.

~Teardrop~

Our Mother died three weeks after my little Brother was born. My little Brother was and still is different. He did not cry when she passed. He was too young to understand what was happening, but still, any animal would show distress at such a loss. I was six years old, I cried. My Brother still has yet to shed a tear, well...except one time. I cried until I was nine years of age. Then my Fater was done with me crying. When Thee Lupercalia came he took me to one of the men there who knew how to permanently paint on the skin. Thee Luper tapped with a wooden needle dipped in ink and painted a tear on my face. Fater had my little Brother watch the entire process. He grabbed his arm in that controlling manner he wields, says Fater to Brother, 'You don't want this.' Then to me says he, 'Not much of an example for him are you?' Fater did not notice that I did not shed a tear while Thee Luper worked on me. I never forgave my Fater for his lesson. I never had to, because I used it as a weapon. I fell in love with the art. I practiced on gourds then eventually myself. I dabbled in other mediums. I

learned to work wood, altering the ancient trees in Wulf's Woods. I *mastered* painting on animal skins and then on canvas, commissioning myself out to earn a living, and what I eventually found was, unwanted respect for my abilities. Their validity waned when Addison showed them her *new* skin. I still find myself returning to my original love. Or, loves, as it is. I love Addy, what she trusts me to do to her. For her. I love my experiments she tolerates scattered about our property. I already love the children she wants to raise with me. That she loves my little Brother, accepts my Fater. Every night we hold each other smiling, and cry ourselves into sleep.

~*Thouar*~

A bitch of a thing is a cat-claw. I seen it rake a cheek so it's flapping with every dying wheeze. Swinging in close, it's a thing of beauty. Lot of my women likes them. Some of the big, unproven men like the club-hammer, opposite of the claws. It's just plain savage. I call it a smasher. I got different categories I make. The smashers, the staves/poles, the melee, edged, and I suppose the long-range, but I encourage us not to go in for those, they have too much finesse, not a real weapon of terror. I made a mace for Gert that is a thing of wonder. I embedded spikes all around the ball. She's a big girl, I saw her swing it against a tree once. All the sap leaked out of the tree before they could saw the thing down. They had to do that cause she put it in there so deep no one could get it out. I don't know if she could ever use it if she ever had business with anyone, but the trees got plenty to be nervous about. The trees...that reminds me of one of their weapons I seen. They got these cant-dogs that the Loves use in their work. I should make us some of them. Though the Loves themselves prefer anything of all wood and length. Back to those listless things I don't want no part of. They even use bows. Who uses a bow? I suppose I would if I could beat someone with it, but them arrows...You got to catch the birds, straighten the shaft, true the...I don't even have the patience to bitch about it. You wouldn't be able to hear the squelch of your victim, see the misery in their face, smell their last meal as they collapse onto your shoulder. That's how a person fights. It should be a thing of revenge and violence. The despair, angst, panic, awe, dread, and reverence you see in your opponent should be a thing of fortitude and beauty to yourself. I love my job.

~*Tosspa*~

You could rightly refer to our relationship as a muted conversation. Without a roof on the top of a person's mouth, well, that makes it a challenge to be loquacious. But he could tap out a message on your wood and speak to you that way. Etch scribbles in the soil at your base. Lo, no! It is once

again up to me to facilitate this discourse. It will not eventuate into his speaking so I may as well accede and commence. How do we convince the children that there is no prophylactic for what is coming their way? I guide you no further than your teachers who guide you daily. Even prior to ascending to the age of certain harm, I fouled my sibling inside the womb. As we were secreted in her bowels, I hoarded the eu-trophies of our Mother. So, I facilitate my twin. We are an ancient couple these days. We have named every child and their children's children. Our dunking and christening is shadowed with a dread. A knowledge of what is yet to come. Their tender downy heads that we cradle against our crepe forearms, we want to believe are innocent, yet, are they? Might they be stewing with what is yet to come? An unavoidable certainty? Or are we the two who start them on this path? Shaping every turn and cultivating malevolence where none would grow. Is the result their choice or our influence? If we could teach them to flee, we would, though they are also our wards, and we still grasp at the mists of benevolence. To trundle them all beneath our beds and bind their eyes and ears against the atrocities of this land. They are talented acolytes, they soak in our teachings as we bathe in their tears. This is an assiduous mischief.

~Tosspa's Twin~

I know you can't hear me, but can you understand me? Neither has ever occurred between myself and another. One might think that my Brother and I would have concocted an argot within the embryonic fluids of our Mother. Lo, No! Where there is light, a shadow is required. And this world needs light. So, I accept my role. I could not make an argument if I wanted. Most have need of the shadows. They are not solely for nefarious deeds. I have never needed to introduce myself, my Brother assumes that is in his job description. He introduces himself and then with a bow, 'My twin.' We teach the children. We cover all aspects mutually, yet he specializes in light, while I have an affinity for the...*not* as light. People have often wondered our naming process. For some reason the mystery has been a boon to our craft, it was never intentional. When naming day arrives, Tosspa unrolls his school of names, unfurling them to rest before the swing of our Eastern-facing door. I open our door, and we monitor the sunrise. When it bathes the entirety of the scroll, I stand to the side of the open doorway, hold my right arm in the sunlight, and where my shadow rests, that shall be the chosen designation. Be it an agnomen or a cognomen, it is adhered through the submersion. The dousing is when I attempt my first yoking. It was unsuccessful for my Brother and myself, yet, in that same right arm that determined their name, I cradle them beneath the surface and attempt to commune with them through the waters of River Forktine Tippecanoe. I tell them of the wonders of the world, the

goodness, the light. They have been under Forktine for a fretful time by the end of this speech. The parents cock anxious eyes at one another, yet I mutely continue. I then inform them of the malevolence they must confront, the at-times overwhelming darkness. As the Mother and Fater begin to step to the shoreline to intercede, I raise my right arm in triumph. Though, never for what I would hope. There is still not one that has heard or understood. Some have come close, we are stubborn. We will continue until the darkness comes for my Brother and my Brother's Twin. You know, we never named you. I'll come closer, don't be scared.

~Weishaupt~

We had always had that contraption. Usually my Mother used it, but since I had recently become a woman, she wanted me to use it. It helps in easing the soreness from being a woman. I was supposed to empty it every time it was used. I was sleepy, cranky, I didn't have the gumption. I filled the metal drum with the coals. I grasped the long handle and stumbled up the stairs. I did what I did every night: I slid it, squeezing it under my mattress. I remember it was difficult that night, I really had to push to get it under the mattress. I laid down. I thought the excess warmth was from what Mother spoke of. It made me drowse. Then I was asleep, then I wasn't. The smoke is what woke me, or my coughing. I rolled out of bed to the floor. The only thing I could see was my night basin right in front of my face under the bed. I grabbed it and threw it on the growing issue. It only seemed to pester it like a mosquito. The sparks jumped into a flame and sizzled with new life as they dried out the pest I assaulted them with. I was squatting in the corner, using the pan as a shield as the event raged when my parents burst in and and saw the situation. They had to pull me by the enameled keepsake to get me to move. We didn't realize the sun was up. The fire had burned so long and bright. Neighbors brought blankets to cover our modest coverings. The fire wasn't done with its business, but it was now small enough for a few dedicated do-gooders to snoop about. They said it started near my bed. I could see the contraption discarded in a pile after they only glanced at it. They didn't know what it was, no one ever had something so fancy. They used heated bottles or bricks in their own beds. The wooden handle was ashes, gone East by then. The contraption had melted so severely that what was once the lid had waffled and oozed along the side. Certainly to never fit snug again. But, I knew it was me, my laziness that didn't empty it properly. The built-up ashes preventing it from closing properly. I saw them talking to Ulema. I knew her only a little. She was younger than myself, she was *off* in a way. We didn't use all the neighbors' blankets. They swaddled her hard and dragged her...*off*. We used to hear her screaming, you probably heard her from here. Probably, probablies.

~Whitney~

He won't eclipse my memory of him. He was unbearable before...but now he is a hybrid of the hybrid Nuckelavee. I mean he was passable if I were of an average carriage. If I were our clan, Dumb, sure, I suppose I'd be happy to trot him out. Put his bit in his mouth, cinch the bridle, and parade him through the square. Would ben Asher come up with a novel chime? He better, or I would turn my attention to him. Even in the pitch of that night I could imagine his face. He tried to get me to light my candle. Says he wants to look on my beauty. Ha! That tongue of his won't work on me. Well...it did work on me, worked overtime. But even in the darkness I had shut my eyes so hard so I could picture the one I'm meant for. And him, acting the hero to make up for his failings. He is so greedy for me. His so and so Sister came to speak with me. Said she *heard* him saying his heart in his sleep. What was she doing in the the same room where he was abed? Little so and so, trying to undermine our arrangement. I should say our *former* arrangement. Cause there is absolutely no way I could discover enough darkness to tolerate his grotesqueries. Does he think he can melt my heart with his purity? He should hide hisself in the mud from Forktine. Dr Dolan should have put that on him, wouldn't of been any worse than the salve he needlessly slathered all over his warpness. Though I think Dr Dolan couldn't stand to touch him either, he only said he did. Who would be desperate enough to pretend that type of sacrifice? There will never be a hole that I will not utilize to escape his virulent presence, he is the fug in the room. Wulf yowls in dismay, Döder cowers within himself, he harries the dogs, the beasts are held at bay.

~Yancey~

I hadn't seen him for three hours. He swam like a catfish, but I was anxious because he should have already come to get his first and second snacks. I looked around Thee Upper Lake. He never would go to Thee Lower Lake. I checked on the shore-head. When I questioned them, his schoolmates asked me, 'Who?' I checked the changing tent thinking mayhap he was adventurous. I rechecked everywhere again. Nothing. I began to get anxious. I knew he had a nervous stomach and would never use the woods like the other youths. The outhouse was set off away in a small copse of pines, out of consideration for all involved. I saw a bare leg stuck straight out, cracking the door open. Then I recognized it as my own. When I got close enough I saw he was turned with his leg stretched propping the door and looking down the outhouse hole. I was never this strange as a child. Says I, 'Where have you been and what are you doing?' I didn't know he could squeal like that. His leg disappeared and the door slammed on its spring as he hooked it in place. I ripped it open. He didn't have enough

hands to cover his hoo-haa and his little girl breasts. I told him to stop. I'd seen it. He was blubbering too much to fully explain what happened. He reverted to his infant state. While he hid in a shadowed corner, I opened the door wide and saw his clothes and kit floating on the refuse. My eyes started watering as much as his, the tang was officious. I tried to calm him, made a plan and told him to wait. He triggered the hook behind me. I returned with what I had. I told him no one would even notice him. I draped the picnic blanket around his waist. I tried to make him smile by saying something, mayhap something like, 'You look like one of your female schoolmates getting ready for a dance.' The cloth fell when his two hands went to cover his little breasts, then he fumbled with himself realizing he was fully exposed. He locked the hook again. It took awhile, yet I finally found a Mother whose child was not using his kit. He was still young enough to go natural. When I returned, he made me slide it under the gap. After what sounded like a wrestling match he unhooked the door. I only let myself smile in a reassuring way. In the shadow I could still see the outline of his mushrooming waist squeezed into a sausage casing. For being such a big boy he certainly was sensitive. We never mentioned what happened when we returned home. I made one of his favorite dinners for him that evening. But he barely touched it, only the food with color. He never ate meat again. We tried to force him. He put a hook on his mouth that none could rip open. I tried to sit and talk with him, but it was just me talking at him. I think he heard everyone saying, *you're such a pig, look at you, you cow*. He is on his own now. Now his body looks like a prisoner's that was in a detention hotbox. Or mayhap one of his little female schoolmates, but now he is a young version, an unbloomed sapling. When he visits I see it all, after he finally unhooks his coat, committing to stay for a bit.

~Youtsey~

I have access to the children. I never knew the story, but when I was young, just a bit older than the children I began to care for, their parents would tell the story to frighten the children into proper behavior. When they slept I asked the parents if it were true. Says they, 'Of course...' Could be that was when I decided. Could have been decided long ago. When I was in my Mother, Thee Women's Prison...I could keep going. The list is the same as all the others. Now here, hiding in plain view, I seek my reckoning. I have averaged myself up. Plain looks, plain manner, plain clothes. I thoroughly inspect the children and their friends, as well as their non-friends when it is easy. I see the marks on most of them. I work to decipher them. Are they freckles? Could they be a mole, an allergy, could they be a fading birthmark? I found one I thought it was for certain. She had two dots on her left shoulder. They were far apart, tilted. But, a straight line between only two points is still straight. So I convinced myself that my vision was

tilted and she was the one. No, not to be. We discovered a kindness in her that could not be overcome. Next I found the goat. Idiotic say you? Yes, but I was desperate. Two large circle patches on either flank. It was a thing of wonder. I thought, certainly, why not come in this guise? When it allowed itself to be slaughtered, I again realized my error. I saw him first at the picnic after naming day. The sign was a beacon, making me feel a fool for even considering the others. But, I would not be taken in so easily. Mayhap that was part of the test. I watched him grow, attended social circles where young Mothers gathered. His marks remained. I connived the children in my care to befriend him. Play times were arranged, though he could not be befriended. I spoke with his Mother as a confidant. She knew not what to do of his behavior. He came and sat on my lap to get away from the other children, interrupting the meeting between his Mother and myself. She was taken. She offered me his nanny position. I feigned that I could not leave these other banal children. She begged. I strung her along, playing her on my line. I put the hook in her and was living with them the next week, in his company day and night. I spit on my finger and wiped above his eye. The marks remained. Naked in the bath, I inspected his body for any other score. There were none. I pumiced the two signatures, eventually drawing blood. He seemed enticed, smiling slightly. He held my hand with the stone and dug in with an unexpected vigor. We blamed the wound on a particular playmate. The Mother said he no longer had to endure the anxiety of spending time in their company since he was doing so well with me. The scab fell from his brow, the marks remained, for all to see. Though no one did. Two perfect signs resting above his eye and I was the only one to acknowledge them. He seemed appreciative. He has grown dulled to his parents. Most would be alarmed, yet he is occasionally well behaved now and they will accept that as victory. I am the only one he allows to swath him in his bedding at night. Soon I will begin to tell him stories to ease him into slccp...May Döder take revenge for me.

~Zarathustra~

Getting the colors ground down was the hardest of parts to figuring out. I had spied on Thee Lupercalians, watched them creep through our fields and woods, gathering specific flowers and plants...and other essentials. Theys taught me these once they caught me when I got too close. I think they always knowed I was there. They gave me my own mortar and pestle, my main tools, they guided me in building my own set of brushes. That was it though. I hoped they would show me how to use everything once I had maked it. No, no, they just shoved me out their tent flap. The images that come to me are from my imaginings. Some are shapes, some are attempts at things I know, antler, bug...I even tried a person once. I seen her twirling on her skates on top of the hard water. We not allowed to do that, we are

learned that blades are for fighting and such similarities. I worked up the gump to give her after I finish. I knew she would laugh at it, but she held the rock in her palm and stared. Says she, 'Thank you, can I buy...' No one ever say thanks towards me before. Now we good friends. I give her bunches of rock I painted. She planted my designed rocks in the ground, them shapes resemble the paint-rocks themselves. But hers are giant. Her imaginings are like mine, just much more bigger. She first take me up to Thee Wulf's Woods and shows me her designs. I wasn't scared with her, nobody bother us there either. Now we been staying up there for a few days. It's cold, but we mange well. It's adventurous. One of the Murphys came and left a bag for us, don't ask me how he knowed we was there. We got extra clothes, food, and even paper. I never had paper before. I paint them now. I offer Amzie some of my work, she thinks I should keep them and make a book. I did not comprehend her idea. She made a cover from bark she peeled, punched holes through them and the paper, then tied them inside with three ribbons from her hair. A book, imagine that. Me and a book. She likes the way the rocks look after they have banged round inside her pockets. But she says my book would keep my imaginings protected, beautiful, and bright. Then says she, 'Just like you.' And I says back, 'Thank you.' My first one ever.

~Zebulon~

Why did that little pisser come to yours truly? He said he heard I was hard. Hard! Ha! I was of a mind that it was some pranking going on towards me by mine enemies. That he had the gumption to even say something like that to mine own sensitive ears tells me something. But, then that returns me to my philosophies of words being for humps and action is the best orator. *Cut him*, says he. I took my knife out of the Bighorn I'd taken down and turned in stupid-faction. He repeated himself; I heard him right. Then he says more, and I knew not one of mine enemies had the imaginings and wherewithal to concoct such a trial. His weeps assured me of my philosophies. Did he make me go soft? I told him to go to Josephson, Tucker, Ephram. Hell even Boucher would be more sympathetic with his blade than mine own. I won't give Exseco away, he has a decency about hisself, unlike the one presently before your eyes of glass. Then he give me that laugh of his Fater figure, that one that sounds conclusive. 'Ha...' huffs he. I grab him by his lithe little neck. I fold him up and shove him in the cavity of the hanging Bighorn. I wasn't worried about his tendons ripping, the spitter was just a pisser. I took my mattress needle, pierced it with the thick cat-gut from my dressing kit. Yes, I do know how to sew, just ask that little flyer. Give me lip! I am fast too. He kept trying to shove his head out the last bit of hole. I cuffed him proper and he slid down to the empty breast, resting his buttocks on the inside of the hanging sheep. I dropped my knife down to him then closed the Bighorn up. It was a good knife, but worth the...*joke*. He could cut his way out that carcass, cut hisself, both, neither...I left him with a hard choice.

Kinnery of Lupercalia

TOOMBS LEGION

~Abberbock~

I don't have a monopoly on this tree, though I do have a love. I can not deduce if there was an abatement of the sibling, mayhap it was solely apical control of one in power. The bole dives deep with sinker roots, cultivating growth in a time-tested manner. I have fought for my love, the frass I address with salves of my own creation, the base ingredient emanating from the discarded pits. I exercise my resistograph by climbing the scaffolding and listening for the least detrimental location for my intended trauma, then after the surgery I use a brew of sapwood that I harvest from the Northrop's forest to soothe the wound. The severest injury is from the weight of the notes and ribbons that I festoon my love with. I do this for my people. One would not think that a bow could be created by paper and ribbon, yet they are so myriad that I must remove the girdle annually. At this time I begin my yearly three pointed trek. I take the ribbons and paper to each location, at Thee Mountains, Thee Water Cliffs, and Thee Wandering. I leave 1/3 of these wishes in hope that they might be answered. They have their wants...and their own heart rot. My own rot is in my mouth. The doctor said it is too late to operate, in my terms, my guess is I had aged beyond correcting the embedded bark. I will always speak with this whistle and what sounds like a swollen tongue. The pain is only a feeling and is abated by the soft velvet offerings of my love.

~Abun~

I raised these sweets by my own loving hand. I would like to claim that I created them, but the vanity I would never say aloud. Besides, we all know who is their architect. The seeding and laying, crossing and re-re-hybriding...it is my passion. Breeding layer upon layer, always wanting more. The years are countless with more bounty in the future. I have won only once at the fair. That was in the beginning, when I was recycling what had already been produced. Now my efforts are looked on with puzzlement. Yet, they look at me with their own eyes, and that is a wonderful reward. I tried to share this love with another, so someone besides myself could witness and understand the allure. I saw her peering through the fogged glass, walking a circle round the greenhouse. Even though her image was blurred, her pace was leisurely. On her next pass by the door I was waiting with one of my finest specimens in my hand. She stopped and almost smiled. When I handed it to her she kept her eyes on mine and pushed her nose down to smell. Nothing. She looked at it, then back at me, then at it again, then to me. Then she shrugged. When she began plucking the petals I stiffened in horror, or perhaps froze in fright at witnessing this atrocity. Says she, 'He loves me, he loves me not, he loves me, he loves me not, he loves me, he loves me not, he loves me, he loves me not, he loves me, he loves me not, he loves me, he loves me not, he loves me, he loves me not,

he loves me, he loves me not, he lo...really? This is taking too long.' Surrounded by her slow helianthusicide, I fell to my knees. Says she, 'Pleading? You should have started with that.'

~Alazon~

I might have been devious in my scheming. But, I didn't deserve the tricks played on me. I, a lone man, with gobs upon sticky gobs of children. I've been tricked into birthing them repeatedly, every time cause say the woman, 'All women love kids.' But always an unfortune took my kids' Mother's away. So I'm stuck with them, to rear alone. We, a novelty family, exploding ourselves out of my assortment of large, I mean *large*, cannons. So I thought my kids who I's stuck with could do something for me. Get me a new woman, one from Thee Prison. She'd be grateful enough to put up with anything outside them walls. But a joke's been thrown at me. They shut closed Thee Prison, sort of, they now slaughter things there. And my little balls kept having me shoot them over, thinking they might still find me a woman among the swine. And I just might joke them back and accept. It's what I deserve. More than that, it's what they deserve.

~Alge~

She beat at kick-rock on her first try. Me, Alge! I was the champion, didn't she know that? What if I went to her house and beat her at...? Well, whatever girls do. My family laughed because I kept griping about her. Says Alazon, 'You have an unfortune attraction to her. I would say watch out.' Says I, 'Why watch out, just cause you can't keeps no woman?' Says he, 'No, no,...because she has a specialness.' Then he whispers to hisself, 'Sacredness,' but too loud. I hear his breath-talk. All us kids looked at him, confused and angry. Says the family, 'You always says we you special-balls.' He bends and tickles each, but not me myself, he heard me hearing his whisper. If we had to sneak out in my home I would have done. I left late in the night, I would sneak to her and learn the special that surrounds her. No one beats me at kick-rock. When I reached the top of the tree to spy her through her window I saw the back of an elephant come to her front door. Its back disappeared. When it returned she was sitting on the beastie's

neck, holding his ears as reigns. Not so amazing I thinks, I watched some of my youngers siblings ride in the tent in that tiny circle. It was stupid. I say no when it was my turn, I was too old for little games. I jumped out the tree, yes jumped; Alazon teach us all how to land proper from any danger. I run after. Those wobbly gigantics are faster than you would think. When they gots to the foothills of Thee Mountains I had fall way behinds. I see them pause and turn on the top of the last small hill. I worry they see me, but they turn back and proceeds. No one sees Alge! I finally make the hilltop. Dark, dark, I can't not see them no more, I can no even hear them, but I could smell them terribly strong. The hilltop was taller than I thoughts. But then it was not. No, I had sunk into what I thought was the extra tallness. I was back at regular hill height. And I was knee deep in elephant scat. Scat is too polite for it though. I should ask Baphomet for word assistance. There was no getting rid. I rolled in the grass, it pasted harder to me. I try wiping away with my hands, it spread over my body. How did it multiply itself? It was like Alazon and children. Multiplying and a mess. All was ruined. I left everything behind. I strip to nakedness. If I had a cannon I could fly myself over town, hide up in the sky with the faint little stars. But no! I had to sneak through town in my suit. They might have scented me, I was scented for days after. But none saw Alge! I streaked too fast. I made a game of it. I still do. Alge won. Champion! I am a special-ball, you witness the proof.

~Alumbrados~

The darkness was complete. It had been snowing lightly for three days. Not enough time to trust the river, which I would like to teach everyone that they should never trust. The cloud cover diffused the moon. They had only one candle between them. There were twelve of them, but only one went in. I can't tell what I was doing out at that time of night and in that type of weather, mayhap someday. I heard the screams coming from Forktine. Happy and joyous. I remember when I was a child, and even when we attempted to be quiet, our uncontainable excitement turned our hushed whispers into what turned to a screaming competition. The laughter spilled from all. I wanted to warn them that it was not cold enough, yet I also didn't want to be the scourge of our youth. How far had I trudged before the elation in their screams turned? Immediately I knew. There was no sense in attempting to follow my meager path. I had to lift my knees high to make any progress through the drifts. A childlike imitation of the long-legged Birchen peacocking for whomsoever might be watching. The clouds still gave no ground to the moon. I ran into the others who stood in terror on where they thought the shore stood. They pointed to the darkness. As they handed me their only candle, it guttered and failed in the pass. I crabbed out as fast and carefully as warranted. There was

an explosion of a crater in the ice. He had been under for well over three minutes. I felt all around then eventually within, our hands never met. I de-clothed down to my unmentionable layer. The temperatures seemed indistinguishable between the air and water. The eclipse continued below. Forty-five seconds and nothing. I came up for air. And that's when the cold smacked. It took my breath that I had just inhaled. I wasted time filling my lungs, the numbness swarmed my head and pushed on towards my limbs. I dove deep, on the bottom the current grabbed me. Lungs emptied...when I went to take care of them my numb head bounced off the ice. I had lost the hole. I crabbed again, though this time on the under side of the ice. If my hands had any working nerves I would have felt the serrated ice lip attack my palms to the bone. The third dive I went to the bottom and let the current take me. I collided with the boulder, being rolled by the current between the bed and the divot in the rock formed by eons of a hydro-assault. My third roll knocked his limp form free. With no fight in him the undertow pummeled him back into me. As he struck me free I wrapped my arms about him. Somewhere down Forktine the ice had not formed. The snow had failed. A last valiant cloud scudded. I walrused him to the shore. He sank in a snowbank. Once again I pulled him out. I thought the air from my lungs might freeze, shattering his lungs. It did not. I don't count it as my first kiss.

~Amah~

It was before our house was in the air. We were both so young then. Pellis had been on the fiddle for just a bit of time, pulling it day and night. To this day he thinks he still needs to practice, which he does and is something we teach all of our children and grandchildren. Yet he meant it humblish, he is always downplaying his playing. My love was inside practicing, it seemed an early evening. I was tending to some smallish saps when he hit a new line that triggered everything in the copse to take notice. It was then Pellis started to grow. I stood up from the loam and began to dance, right foot, left foot, left foot, right. A gentle breeze came and fluttered their baby hand leaves. But, I was dancing so hard, engrossed in my own world and entranced by this new reel, that at first I didn't notice the flock of butterflies. I soon realized the breeze was coming from inside the cabin, from his bow. And what I thought were the sapling's leaves were members of the butterfly flock alighting on the baby trees. The saplings arched their spines, they began to push themselves up out of the earth as the butterflies pulled encouragingly on their arms. You could hear their skin stretch and answering groans from the old-tree-wood of the cabin. They both leaned to touch one another. The little ones beginning to grip and hold that old wood in comfort. Then the flock did a similar dance with me. I held my head still so I could watch all, but my right foot left foot kept up their

unique paradiddle, and they began to do an air dance all about me, their wings synchronizing with my steps, then taking them over and guiding my once thick clodhopping feet. When Pellis finished they gave me their ticklish kisses all over my skin as a goodbye. I went into the cabin and kissed my love hard. I'm sure it's different members, but that flock comes every year, and they come way up in the now tall trees to kiss us hello and tell Pellis to get his fiddle out. Then they float down to the forest floor, and with the older children guiding the new additions to the family, they all dance, dance, dance.

~Amzie~

I get sick of heel-toeing it. Also sick of Alazon shooting us. That's why it is so nice to be out in this weather with you. Sure I walked across the drifts to see you, but I skated most of the way. What are you doing so far North anyway? It's been three weeks now of River Forktine being hard. I suppose it's always hard in a way, but that's more in a vicious manner. And right before it goes cold hard, in the in-between time, he fell through the ice. He still hasn't been out even though it's safe. I can spin, twirl on my own, and jump to combine all three. The music is always in my head. But, sometimes I just want to move. One day I skated from Thee Falls up to Thee Wulf's Woods. I had to walk on the bank at the chutes, but other than that I got to skate from early morning to late, late, late...Two of my Brothers came to find me. When they were still far away I hoped two fireflies had made it to Winter and were seeking me out. But their lights swayed like a conductor's arm, and as they got closer, I could hear my Brothers whispering their fears just before I could see it on their faces from the cast of their lanterns. I had my hand shielding my candle. I snuffed it as they approached. That's how I learned I could see better without it, mayhap not better, but differently. Instead of seeing my immediate surroundings decently, I could see all around and further, though it was gauzy, which seems appropriate for night skating. I thought they were playing a joke at first when they skated right by me. I had to squint my eyes and turn my face from their lanterns, and I realized what had happened. I still wonder if they were even looking for me, it seemed like they were just going as fast as possible to get it over with. So, of course I followed them...*and did what I did*. I've been hiding from them ever since, no telling what they will do once they get their hands on me.

~Antony~

I got a rabbit foot from Harris. It had fleas. I admire how he has control of rabbits. I thought to do the same for the fleas. Rabbit fights are one

thing, flea fights are not anything. I also admire Thee Lupercalians. So I combine. I mimic their world in flea-size. First I tried a single hair from a horse's tail. The first two heads swelled up then exploded. I learn quick that the finest gold wire is enough to subjugate my pets. I make a mock of all their world. I mock up minis of miniatures. The wagons and carts I attach to the gold wire, and the fleas dressed as elephants, camels, mules... they parade them into the diorama. The tents are erected, yet they are half-tents so we can view into their world. Thee Wheel is erected and spins when I step on my foot pedal pushing air through the connected tube. It is slow, but effective. I believe the fleas enjoy this ride, strapped to their seats they can view the viewers watching them, not having to perform as some of the others do. The tightrope walkers and trapeze flytists are focused on their specific tasks. I have jugglers; the audience cannot decipher that they juggle from their backs only. The band is going through the entire performance. The glue affixing the instruments to their appendages makes them unfortunately a bit uncomfortable, and they gyrate along to the piped music playing overhead. Others are dressed as lions; the tamers wielding the original horsehair as whips, yet no longer around the necks but again adhering to a singular arm. Because I'm a Cannonball I have a certain ingrained knowledge, and even though Thee Lupercalians do not practice this discipline, my children do. A snap cracker imitates the shot and distracts all heads to turn at the sound, while I secretly yank them from the cannon where they fly across the length of the fairgrounds. Even further than they would ever hope to leap were the fiercest of rabbit claws honing in on their camouflaged position. The strong-flea lifting ten times his weight, the conjoined twins which later grew to quintuplets, the merry-go-round riders, the barkers and their shills promoting their untenable enterprises: all perform in the finale...The band turns down the volume, the light begins to fade, I whisper through my bullhorn, acting as the Castrato — no, no, I suppose as Thee Castrato — as he stands on the bull's neck...whispers I, 'I shall sing a note so high and grand that your ears are too big to understand it. It is so wondrous, so magnificent and magical that it brings all who hear it to their knees!' After thirteen seconds of the flea-Castrato singing, a deathly silence to you and me, the fleas all fall as one. The curtains close upon their mass feinting.

~Arras~

How these vermin arrived I cannot say. Yet, they are here, infesting this land with their unique sickness. The grove of macadamia trees have been harvested by my kinnery for generations. Yes, I know our soil is not typical for this tree, the rain is too infrequent, the sun does not penetrate sufficiently. The last two are overcome with only a bit of ingenuity and a lot of muscle. My forefathers had both of these and passed them on to

all who followed, though I do lack in both myself. Overcoming the land though, that is a true challenge for any man. Yet, through persistence, luck, or just thick-headed stubbornness, they learned that the guano from a type of eagle-owl they proclaimed the Damia-Bubo is the elixir that makes our land suitable for our singular crop. Without these birds, we would have no meaning. We have made for ourselves a difficult life. Though the work is fairly easy compared to other crops. The trees were already here, the process perfected. Yet, I sometimes feel I am an ornithologist before I am a farmer. We must ensure that there is always a pair of Damia-Bubos to enrich our lives. This is the only true difficulty in this occupation. Some have heard me droning romanticish ballads in the grove on moon-filled nights. This is not for my amorous benefit. Yet, it has become necessary to induce these birds into action in order for our mutual survival. I have found myself on cold nights breathing my hot air on their neglected eggs. If this is successful, I then need to guess at when to surgically pry the shell open for a proper hatch. Through years of our enabling, the D-Bs have bred out the need of an egg tooth. The relentless chewing, the masticating into an experimental consistency specific to each hatchling, then the spitting gracefully into their unappreciative screaming beaks can be a bit demeaning. They sleep, breed when properly encouraged, and defecate. In fact, they have dropped most of their survival compulsions. And we have taken them up. If you were treated as a king, would you not accede? The hunting can be interesting; we have become expert anglers. Our veterinary skills are supreme compared to most, certainly Stump Love. Why we do not take up one of these other professions has never truly been considered. Most likely thick-headed stubbornness was correct. We are a tough nut to crack.

~Asdrubal~

I am right that I have a son. I saw so and so as they took him from the room. They didn't even let me touch him, not even pass him naturally. They pulled him out of me through a cut in my gut because they thought my hips were too small. My hips are bigger now. He's fifteen today, the same I was when they took him. Of course it's him, no one else in the Murphy house has a naming day today. I was only fourteen when he started inside me but fifteen when he came out. I got to celebrate one naming day with him. I don't know how no one saw. I was so skinny. The withershin weather allowed me a coat, but still? I suppose because it was not even a possibility, something that would never enter anyone's mind. But he knew...he knew it all. And he was at my last celebration. I would catch him eyeing my gut. Staring so hard I finally had to hiss at him a warning to stop. Looking back, it's an insult that no one saw. . I guess everyone was supposed to be looking at me because it was my day. But he was sweating and fish-eyed and gripping

the table until the stain transferred to his fingers. I wonder how old he is now...not truly, I don't have a care for him. I mean it has to be him, right? You have to be fancy to be able to put a boy in the Murphy house. And *he* was fancy. There is that and the naming day. Coincidence still? And of course you can't deny the *look*. He looks like his Fater and myself brewed up equal. But no one sees it now because no one even thought to look then. And, why would someone look for something that is not even conceivable? I've sent him a gift every year. Anonomous...no, anomysly...shoot...He's not sure who is sending them is what I mean. When I shamed my name, my Parents proclaimed I didn't need a celebration because I was too grown up. I miss my special days desperately. I hope these wrapped thoughts of love help him not miss me.

~Augustus~

I always forget my ignorance. The mop needs to be wet before I swish it from side to side. I learned that after Head Nurse was patient with my brilliance. First she showed me the broom. When I started swinging it from side to side, it kept spinning in my hands then cracking against my shins. She smiled and demonstrated that it was a push-broom type and not a swing-back-and-forth type. She is nice to me. She say I have soft eyes. I made her smile again when I lifted up my shirt and with both my hands winked my third eye at her. My softest eye. My bellybutton. My belly is soft. I do a good job with push sweeping the whole left side. I push past each individual room, especially our personal rooms, the ones they call *cells*, which I thought were inside my body, but are right here for me to clean. I finish pushing when I get to the gate of the right side. Mayhap they have someone who does that side. I want to ask if I can do it, but asking is an unspoken tool, which I don't understand. Head says my broom and mop are tools. But she also said tools are words. I will think about it more tonight if I can remember to. Mayhap one day I will make clean the right side. Then I start my mopping. I did not remember if I had made it wet, but I must have because the floor was shiny. I watch myself in the floor when I mop. I make my mop touch my whole softness. I wish I could do that instead of bathing with everybody. I only like Head Nurse to see my softest eye. I could mop all my dirtiness. She says I am the best cleaner ever. She says that everyday. But today she forgot. She unlocked the front door then turned and made a squeak sound like my clean floor, says Head Nurse, 'Oh! that was stupid of me I forgot you were here, you don't make a peep.' Then she close the door quick and lock it so we are safe inside.

My Fater was a ginger-man. When my Fater passed, Pellis was quite kind. From his very own forest where he raised both 'decids' and 'conifs' he gifted me a sapling red maple. Says he, 'If you are able to raise it up well, with nurturing and succor, care for it in its infancy, then one day in the future, when spring arrives, it will remember you to your Fater, and then when fall commences, it will remember your Fater to you. Making both you...' he didn't finish his verbiage. Though its bones had not hardened, I would put some of my Fater's belongings amongst the branches on the anniversary of his birthday. His switch that had been handed down through the men in the family, a lock of his hair from his infancy...odd baubles that for some esoteric reason he alone coveted. As we both grew, one of Pellis' brood became persistent in the act of coming to my rescue. He would happen to stroll by and offer his assistance in raising up the gift from his Fater. He offered impatient techniques of pruning and manipulating that would induce quick growth. And unnatural nourishment that I would need to wear protective clothing to apply. Says I, 'No thanks, I know how to wait.' He became more insistent over the years. It aggravated him that my response remained consistent. There finally comes a time when says he, 'Avesta, this is my last offer. You can come live with me in a tree that is already matured and can shelter us for the rest of our days. This thing won't be ready for that type of life until, well, probably after you are gone and then your children would be left responsible to see to it.' Says I, 'No thanks, I...' he cut me off, as he left, says he, 'yeah, yeah, you know how to wait.' A few years on and the tree does not need me as much as it did in youth. When spring arrives, I appreciate the shade it gives after a day of toil, a shade that grows each year. Pellis has visited a few times. Last visit he asked if it had flowered yet. I shook my head slowly. Says he, 'Well, you've raised it right, it will, it will.' Says I, 'That's alright, I know...' Says he, 'Yeah, yeah, you know how to wait.' We both smiled.

~Battaglia~

My Fater told me to get her body. I was scared and sad. I had loved her. I suppose I still do. I could not disobey his *wish*. I walked up the path to Thee Murphy House, a place I had never attended for a couple of reasons. I reaffirmed the tuck in my shirt. I was friendly with some, but, some others would pounce on any reason for me not to further fit in. Though, I was proud to have a Fater...usually. There were preludial clouds scudding over Thee Mountains. They had contacted us about what some of the boys had come across. How they could tell it was her body, I have no idea. I had grown up with her and couldn't determine hide nor hair of her. Faunus, one of the boys who found her, was squatting by her side, his fist holding

tight to what might have been a chunk of the hair. Then they told me how she had been found. Chopped and laid out in the bottom of the trunk. Their question wondering how we could do such a perverted atrocity. I asked the same, though to myself and to the culprit. They asked if we wanted the trunk returned. That's when, says I, 'That ain't our trunk.' It was too late. I was so ashamed of myself for saying that word. I noticed the Headmaster cast a quick glance at Faunus. Says he, 'I don't know how you imagine you'll carry her back to your Fater.' Says I, 'I ain't going to, she's ruined.' I squatted down. Faunus would not move so I had to inspect her around his pose. She was too far gone. I could not determine how she was killed. Says he, 'You can't expect for us to be responsible for this mess.' Says I, 'Shes ain't the first one we've lost, she has no more use.' Faunus started hauling her somewhere before I corrected myself, 'She is not.' I still go back to their thoughts of us, and I ask the same question: who would stuff a ewe inside a trunk?

~Baugus~

It was only Murphys at the supper. I was surprised almost all of us were there. We were missing six of the nineteen who had been invited. No wives, no children, only those of us who had been raised in the Murphy house. Pelasgus had organized the congregation. Bastards all, of widely varying ages. Our Faters all implanted us there to be educated and taken care of properly, even though we did not come from a family home. Not all the Faters were wealthy, some broke themselves to allow their adulteration the opportunity to rise above themselves. Most of us did not know who our parents were. We referred to one another as Brothers. And what was the need of this bonding moment? We hoped to learn from Pelasgus, he was the first born of our brood and in the majority of cases we differed to his rote knowledge. I sat to Faunus' right, when Pelasgus asked him to pass me the knife so I might carve the fare he feigned deafness and pretended to attend to a malevolent loose cuff. As I stood and reached over his shoulder for the knife, I heard a plinking on the floor. As Faunus was readjusting his cuff, a small pouch had escaped his sleeve. Before sitting myself, I retrieved the black reticule that had fallen at his feet and returned it to Faunus. I don't think anyone would have given it a thought, but his flustered movements drew attention as he hastily attempted to squeeze the clinking bag into a too small breast pocket. He chuckled in some form of defense. Pelasgus, taking the lead, attempted to draw attention away from whatever was confounding Faunus. Always being one to put us younger ones of the *Family* at ease, says Pelasgus, 'Could someone please pass the salt?' All began to look around for the shaker, giving a moment for Faunus to relax. As he rested his arm on the table, his elbow toppled the undiscovered shaker of salt. The spillage magnified Faunus once again as he attempted

to sweep the spillage in his palm. I don't know why he was such a mess of fluster that evening, but as we all began to chuckle, Pelasgus once again averted our lampooning. 'You planning on betraying me?' says he. Faunus did not answer right away, he gave himself a moment to think of a good one. As he tossed the salt from his palm over his shoulder, he handed the shaker to Pelasgus and chuckles again saying, 'You think I would betray blood, Brother?' No one laughed at his attempt at redemption. He had made a mess. But before we could confront Faunus, Pelasgus, being as he is, once again diverted our attention.

~Bel~

It's an anger all my own. I wanted to be one of them. Now, I want to be the best of them. Addy has her body painted. I twisted this around in my head to somehow think it would put me on even footing. It will, it will, there's still time. I could disappear for ten years. Sneak back in with Thee Lupercalians. The trauma will scar over. I'll crop my hair to a men's length and affix the castaways above my heart to camouflage the wounds. It might not be the best plan, but there's lithe men here. Josephson...does he know that some of us know? He could assist me. I tried to convince Alazon to make a Murphy out of me. 'Ha,' says he, and shoves me down his gun. So this is the next best on my list. You want to see? I have to wear this binding, coat it with a salve from Stump. Ha! Appropriate name for my condition. Some of Thee Lupercalians bind their bumps their whole lives. I know I'm young. I wanted to preempt the daily chore. Misinformation travels faster than truth. There's plenty of fool...I'm the only proof, but I still think it will work. Yes, I'm going to leave and return under a guise. I'll stop at home, gather a sackcloth full of belongings, and go. Mayhap, I'll tell Alazon. He's given me a home, it would only be right to let him know there will be room for one more little Cannonball.

~Boethius~

You're looking...like yourself. I haven't come to see you in some time. You know how it is, things get busy...middle age gets heavy. I know I'm not typical middle age. That's kind of why I came to see you again. I've been having these premonitions, and if they are true, then I am actually beyond middle age. Are they signs? Am I just being paranoid? I thought you could mayhap give some advice. I know I have my Brothers, my teachers...a magpie, no, no, no! That is the third one this week. *Good day, Mr Magpie, kindness to your Lady-bird.* It hasn't seemed to work yet. What did I do to deserve this? Anything you can offer me...sparrows! What are they doing? Have you ever seen that? No, no, stop it. Stop it now! They murdered

him. What does that mean? Seven sparrows...one dead magpie? Why does everything happen to me?

~Buboes~

We had done for years, then we stopped, thinking that things has changed. Have they? Not fast enough for some. She came at me complaining that things not fair. Why could she not be a man? I told her the old stories, says she, 'Do it to me.' And that was that. She didn't have to beg or plead with me. I pull Alazon aside to speak of it. Get his blessing? Not sure, but he said it was none his concern and something about business. So, at midnight we woke...no, we were both awake, anxious. We went to the kitchen. Suspended above the fire, I hung the layers of leaves to the side, upon a containing rock I set the iron. As they gathered heat I handed her the mini-wooden rolling pin. We barely used it anymore. It was for squashing single plums; these were then layered in a thin cylinder, soaked with a brandy, then chilled for a dessert. She laid on the bench, put it in her teeth, and bit down. With my tongs I placed the first leaf on her budding breasts. The tears sprinted down her cheeks and flowed into the gaps in the sides of her mouth where the pin propped it open. She did not scream. She nodded. I nodded in return. I layered the rest of the leaves. The only light was from fire, yet I'm certain I could see the redness claiming her body. After the leaves were applied I grabbed the iron and went to work. It ran over the leaves smoothly. For the first week that we did this I could feel the two small bumps fight the iron upon every pass. The next week I began to feel the ribs above her heart. It would work. A washboard path that would lead to her future.

~Bussey~

We were sent to measure Thee Wandering. By that I mean its constantly fluctuating border, for the most part hawing and rarely hemming. He was a Buell. Sometimes we did not speak, more out of indoctrination than want. He had been fasting over the prior week, of course I didn't know this then. Three days into our survey he fell. Said he, 'It's just exhaust...' When he woke the next day he opened his eyes to the bottom of the tarp I had erected from the kit. I thought the shade would be a boon, he immediately claimed/cursed the brightness. There is no way to measure if one was greater than the other. I thought he would be revived after the rest. I realized he had not only fallen, but fallen ill. He refused the food I prepared. Said he, 'You know why.' I certainly did not. He would not take the water I offered. I was mystified. Then I was woken that midnight by his mumbling and genuflections over the cup I had left by my jacket that I had

placed underneath his lolling head. He took down what he could, the rest spilling down his chin to his bare chest and pooling in the furrows between his ribs. He fell back to my jacket. Dipping his fingers in the shallow ditches of his ribs, he moved his dripping fingers to different stations on his body, mumbling incoherently. That was finally when I began to understand the direness of the situation. I told him I was leaving for help. 'No,' says he, smiling and rocking his head once to my right then once to my left sleeve, unable to repeat the action. Another day, I began to fast out of guilt. He took no water. We both squeezed under the tarp, avoiding the beat of the brightening light as much as possible. With our shoulders rubbing, hoping to stay within the safety of the dark, I would feel his hand grabbing weak handfuls of Thee Wandering, letting it slide through his fingers creating a mist of film on my left and his right leg. The motes of dust floating into the brightness outside the insufficient covering. I don't know what night it was, but when he woke me he seemed somewhat lucid. He handed me the cup. It was half emptied of the water I provided and formed into some compound he created from the slough of Thee Wandering. He lamely waved his right hand at me, a magisterial benediction. He would not answer my pleas. I don't know if he was able. I should have asked more questions during our surveys. I dipped my fingers and moved my hand around in an amateurish approximation. I think he might have been gone by then. There was still a sludge on the bottom of the cup. I slathered it on his face, he looked a warrior going to a battle none of us know. He had a lucent sheen when I ripped down the tarp. I wrapped him within, and with my stained hands I grabbed the arches of his feet and pulled him for days until we reached Dakhma Island. There I left him. I rinsed the cup in River Forktine and drank once again, hoping to wash away the guilt. Can I be forgiven?

~Cabot~

So far I've broken forty-nine bones. Alazon was going to shoot me into Thee Wandering, but then Jeansomme told me that I looked her in the eyes and she demurred. Says he, 'None of my concern, it's yours now.' Where others' eyes are white, mine are tinted blue. For awhile I didn't understand how I made it out of my Mother. I mean without the ordeal killing me. And Jeansomme told me I didn't come out through the hole, because that surely would have crushed my birdish bones. Mayhap my Mother knew this already about me, because, when the time came she refused to push. It turned into a battle between Mother, midwife, and eventually they even called for Dr Dolan. I was the armament she would not fire. Dr Dolan finally had to cut her open. It seemed I had already combusted. I left a swamp of shrapnel behind. I had seven bones broken when I was done being scrubbed down. Either from nine months of my

Mother shifting, Dr Dolan pulling, or the midwife toweling. Alazon has only looked on me a few times. I would catch him glaring at me every now and again, the look he gives me makes me think he wants to hear my vitric bones after launching me through the air. He was caught in the act once... he was trying to put me into a barrel, but even after my bowlegs cracked I still would not fit. I was pulled out, and say he to my siblings something such as, 'I suppose I could shoot you all through his legs...I'll give you points for grace, points for execution...and bonus points for chiming his bells as you're coming out the other side.'

~Caliph~

About three miles down past Thee Tower Of Astodan, you know Dakhma Island, lady Polk lived alone in a clapboard farmhouse. Once a week my Mother would send me down to keep her from her aloneness. She had the biggest dining room table surrounded by countless empty chairs. I asked 'Why?' Says she, 'For all my friends.' Then she proclaimed a little blue tin one to be mine, just for me. Through all the years of visiting, my chair was the only one that moved. Lady Polk once told me that all the artists got it wrong, every picture of Ahmen surrounded by his cohorts while eating at that extended table was incorrect. Because in *those* days, from when the picture was imagined, folks would only eat laying down. She just liked to point out when people got stuff wrong. She didn't want to be compared to Ahmen or anything, that's why she had all them chairs. So her friends would be in comfort...and now Scare..., because you've been as you are to me, I bring you this same chair so you can offer it to your friends. I hope that it doesn't stay as empty as lady Polk's lot, but, this ain't *those* times, and I know you wouldn't take your friends lying down.

~Camila~

Layer upon layer, an onion is a miserable fruit to eat. Yes, I know what it is and is not; it just sounds better that way in my mouth. It might be the shape of my hips. I would never live in Thee Tower, vulgarly shaped, a man's place until the end. I built a spiral staircase to enter the opening, and once I entered I wanted for nothing. No pillow, no blanket. I was cradled snugly in this reimagined womb. Once I closed the hatch I could sleep in any position, as if gravity had no pull. I had finally achieved...something. And of course I infested it with an unnecessary, a luxury of vice. I invited him over and something in his clothes, his breath, or bubbling up from inside infested my onion-dome-home. I could taste, smell, and feel it. He had left...something there I needed to rid myself of. Because they had done the refurbish themselves, expanded their own house, I went and

108

asked Veda and Glaspell for advice. He heard my first few words and said that was Veda's expertise. I was surprised. I had heard that he initiated the hustle. He spat at me to buy something or go. She said it sounded like eelworms, nothing to do but burn them out. He had infested my reprieve with parasitic nematodes. My home would soon be crusted with rust. It would swell and crack, smut oozing out of the fissures. There was only one cure. *Cure* is again an inappropriate signature. Apparently the land could not be used again for years. The rot would be dwelling in the ground until it passed on with nothing to consume. It kindled slowly. A simmer on the ground floor. What paint I had applied began to bubble. My eyes watered from the gases. The stem took light, traveling up the spiral. I was outside watching now. Trying to stand downwind. The onion turned yellow then transferred to brown. Out of the stem the flame burst. In the morning it collapsed in on itself. Veda and Glaspell came, said they were about to go to sleep for the night — my morning — and saw the flames out their open window. She asked what I was going to do now. I had not thought that far ahead. Says she, 'There's good living in gardening for a woman.' And I just might, she gave me some advice on some land she knows since mine has all gone to pot.

~Cap'n Constable~

They're trying their best, yet, their best is stacked against his righteousness. And their taste is guided by baubles that transfix with weight and shine. No one is going to question me going into a place, late on the night. Nigrescent used to do that as routine. These new...replacements...let's call them, stopgaps, would never roam these halls out of hours. Where they collected the bric-a-brac from I won't begin to guess. If they weren't the artisans themselves...well, it goes to show that art shouldn't be an open competition. I'm not certain whose taste is worse: the creator, or the people that bought it. Either way, it needed to be dealt with. They will probably expunge the heavy worn oak pews, replace them with thrones of gilt for glory or three-legged stools for penance. If that happens, mayhap a blaze of effigy will be appropriate. Until then I'll continue to gather and loose the paraphernalia they assault the walls with. I'll let you watch over them for me, just don't tell anyone I'm breaking the law. Though in this offense I believe I have a case. So...I bury this treasure at your feet, good sir. Ha! What no laugh? First we have the sanctuary light, sixteen tapered candles set in brass ostentation. This ambo encrusted with mock-up jewels; the modest ash one was more than appropriate. Three mirrors surrounded with tackier frames; a mirror in a church? Why would these people want to witness their faces? The paten that takes three boys to wield. I left the old...traditional...appropriate instruments in the rectory. They will be fine. Here is the new, braggadocio they brandish; the chalice, pall, ciborium, cruets...I've never seen so much

shine. That place should be dark and austere. However, I do like their censers. I took a few for my new Calaboose, cut the reek from the nefarious nimrods I collect. Lastly, the pascal candles and the ambry. This over-sized pyx, we got that many sick? It's mine too...that's going to make a fine spit-bucket. Scare..., I don't even know whose field this is. Do you? Ha! When harvest comes they'll have a generational crop.

~Charon~

Three days ago was my first official day at Thee Bedlam. What? Oh not like that. I receive people, workers and patients who arrive. I am supposed to patrol the middle, between right and left. The right side is for the ones who have been graced with physical challenges. The left is for those who have been judged unable to function, you know, someone who needs some assistance getting their thoughts in order. I have questions now but was too timid to ask when says The Head, 'If you have any questions for me, this will be your only chance.' I wanted to make a good impression. Her look was opposite of her words. My Fater got me placed there: *The Doctor*. He wants something for me. He expects more from me than other Faters of their Daughters, ever. He is a leader in this place, his thinking is original. I can't let him down. I suspect he thinks that I might abandon my duty, imprison him on the left side when my patience ebbs, even put him on the right side through a frustration of violence. Again, with my patience... but what qualifications do I have to keep these people from passing to the other side? Being the Daughter of *The Doctor* does nothing for my abilities, knowledge is not transferred at birth. What if there is a person who falls into both categories? Say, my head is busy receiving someone, and out of nowhere what if a senior-looking person starts circling around me and babbling in some invented language that only he knows? Where do I put him? Right physical deficiencies or left incapable mentally? I won't be able to ask anyone where he goes because of the looks I will get and everyone wondering why *The Doctor's* Daughter is an imbecile. Says The Head, 'One of our main purposes is to put all The Residents at peace so that they may return...' She didn't finish her instructions, she removed the keys from around her neck and crowned me with their heft. Then she exited the front entrance: the only entrance or escape. She didn't return the rest of the day or the days after. I would have seen her. Despite my fear of my incompetence being discovered, I was going to ask questions. I've been anxiously standing under the lintel, waiting upon her return. The pressure is overwhelming, and I fret that it will put me inside a cell on the left side of the building.

The most intoxicating aspect? Mayhap the yellow cast to her skin. Crepuscular light reverberated from her being. The scent that preceded her arrival infused with every fabric so you might not be too overly remiss at her departure. She was...is an intoxicant. Our kissing was small, it had a childhood gravity. I was eager to not push her, she had chosen a path. I did not want to sway her direction but join her in her desired pursuit. The initial irritation was only a feather's weight. I blamed the storming pollen, gathering and assaulting me in a continued affront. It seemed I had taken on more syndromes than past seasons. I bathed my cats in a battle of stubbornness, their dander would be doused. Their claws introduced me to my numerous rashes. I knew they were there, yet had avoided them by rolling my sleeves. A cat's claw raked through a dermatitis patch would look like a hurricane through an algae bloom. The topicals I slathered on only stained my sleeves. The patches extended to my torso, sloughing southerly to unknown lands when the bleeding began. Nose bleeds were common in my youth. Some males are taught to wear handkerchiefs to offer gallantly. I carried them shredded in my breast pocket, loaded and ready to be stuffed into battle. I apologize for my speech. She made a romantic out of my most confused, beating heart. The blood flowed... how? Glowingly? Alluringly? Gracefu...? No, no, I suppose that is the issue, blood rarely flows in any kind manner. Any I might mention would find me a dreadful creep and leave me to nurse my wounds alone for my remaining life. I know I dripped on her clothing, but because we were always kissing in the dark, she would only return the next day to exult to me what she thought were interesting patterns created by her osmotic skin. And she was right to be proud, they were beautiful. So, I suppose we both should be proud. It never could have lasted. As I said, I did not want to deprive her of her wants. I wanted to enjoin her with my passion in a positive fashion. But, I would have bled out before I won her, and if I might have survived, then upon the next anniversary she would have been bathed in a substance that no mere handkerchief could staunch.

It's comfortable. It functions for my employ. Dress it up, dress it down. I had been getting guff from others for quite a bit. Lots of men used to wear them regular. Now it is considered...erm...I suppose it's not considered. The jests flew: *Fancy Boy, Compton The Captivating, The Wind Is Blowing Batten It Down, Comto Me Sweetly*...also, *Come And Deliver Me*...whatever they might be asking, *Real Men Don't Wear Nothing Underneath*. This was the last one thrown down. We were in back the club and drinking, as does happen there. Of course it was late, my inhibitions had surrendered. I still don't

properly know who said it, and it doesn't matter, they've all said it, or something equally inept. So, says I, 'We could ask your woman what I wear underneath.' They took up my gauntlet, or more accurately, their drink did. I wasn't the only one who didn't know the perpetrator, so ten wives/friends/comforts were either volunteered or volunteered of their own volition. They laid on the ground in a line of a totem, the bottom head touching the next person's feet, and so on up the line. Some of these women are big, it was a long line. I was given a free drink, but only if I finished it by the time I passed over the last totem head. Of course I had to accept. Of course they went to the locked case and pulled out the largest trophy inside. Why these were there, no one alive knew, probably won by men who used to dress like myself. They had to smash the glass for want of a key. My arms were sore carrying the talisman. My cup did runneth...As I progressed, straddling over my recumbent ladder of inquisition, many of the women got wet. Even towards the end when my cup was nearly done. Now whoever thought it would be funny to place Mauchline in the row had their plans stymied when some women got vinegary. Mauchline has heightened senses and all, and when I went over her I could feel a grasping of understanding that I didn't receive from the others. But, the others were having none of it. Saying, 'That's not fair, she's a good girl and all, but she's blind.' So I soon realized the bottom of the totem had gotten up, run around, laid down again with her feet at Mauchline's head. And again and again, so on up the line. The totem ladder would shorten then extend itself until some of the perpetrators got a bit touchy with their wives/friends/comforts. I got a free drink that night. I got to keep the trophy. The next morning when I woke, yes, a bit dazed, I found ten ribbons inside the memento. So no, I suppose they were right. I'm not a real man, every night I untie my undergarment and put it back in my gargantuan................... cup.

~Coptic~

We have two quince trees in our Southern orchard. The quince...well, I'm mixed on it. I suppose it's fine in a jam. But the tree dangles some enviable ornaments. A pale pink can be a fine thing, but carving on a flower petal proves difficult when up against my penknife. Pellis had an arrangement with different people during this season, her time was the next morning. She could fill one creel of quince. The amount is appropriate, they can be overwhelming if used by a heavy hand. I only assume her hand is not. I have yet to touch it. But, everyone's tastes vary. I took a pome in my hand and as femininely as I was able, I scratched my message. It was much tougher than what I had practiced in my head. The flesh opened. The fine hair highlighted my words of devotion, exacerbating the fine divots with a subtle shadow. I'm no artist, my standards are low. She would have to twist

both her head and wrist to decipher it in full, probably squint a bit as well. I set it carefully within the catch I had devised. An inverse trap of sorts. I stretched a simple snare and string across the pathway. When her ankle struck it in the morning the quince would be released from the cradle and roll to her feet. This was more intensive than the original carving plan. I'll wait for her late this evening. Let her come in the dark of night. I know it would be best to start in the open, let all know my intentions, it should always be level. But I am only thinking of her, if she is hesitant, her family disapproves, mayhap she only wants the fruit.

~Copus~

We can't figure out where they came from. As Headmaster I thought I would distribute them to my favorites. I have access to all their dorm rooms. While they were attending a double block I removed their worn and soiled pillowcases; oily, stained, and ignored, a prerequisite for being a young man. I stuffed their pillows inside these endowments. They appeared to be cut and re-patterned from a woman's dress. There was an inkling in my head to disregard them, fretting that some of the older boys might view them in a...carnal manner. Though, I went forward with my plan, concluding that most would find comfort in the smell and feel of the objects, equating them with the matriarchs who brought them into this world. As they went to sleep that night I don't believe anyone of them noticed the gifts. However, in the morning, the sickness could not go ignored. Each and everyone. My list of fears began with typhoid, then cholera, and hepatitis. And concerning past events with that Halleck boy my mind jumped to helminthes. When Dr Dolan was finished with his exams he informed me that we must have improperly prepared our meals. Salmonella seemed to be the antagonist. A good cleaning of the kitchen, lecturing the staff, and leaving buckets by the boys' beds should eradicate the offense. All this was done immediately. I refrained from telling Dr Dolan of the gifted pillowcases. I stripped them and added them to the the barrels that held the leaves for the annual fall kickoff. I thought it best not to create any scandal. Most of the townspeople come to celebrate the season, symbolically burning away the sins of the past year. I had kept this tradition going smoothly since I became Head, any distraction might put an unnecessary pall on the celebration. I certainly wanted to keep my hands clean.

~Curtius~

I goes to class blocks with all my Brothers, but I's not give attention. '*I am very special.*' That is one of the note in my pocket saying. Times Headmaster

makes my own special blocks, has me helps clean and pick grasses. This is special work that only I can do. Usually he leave me alone, and I walk round and play kick-rock alone, and I walk to Forktine alone, and I try to play shoulder-fight so I can practice so me and Custus can beats Faunus, and I don't member his Brother partner, but I can't not ever practice because alone. I seed them man and woman in the middle swimming hard like they were running from terrors. She don't swim good, I do. He try to pull her and the sacks and the bags they have. Then he don't swim too good cause he worn from swimming all of it. Says I, 'Blo!' He look at me with scared rabbit look. Says I, 'Ti, to ta toota, blo!' He swim at me, hold finger over face's hole that mean quiet. Says he whispered, 'Help...' I good helper. Special helper. I grabs bags, heavy, and start to swim for them. Says he, 'Boat?' I run down bank. Return on water of Forktine. No boat, canoe. He roll pretty girl in. She make wet smacking sound and I giggle. He fingered over his face-hole. Bags in, then him. I turn canoe back downwards. He shake head in worry and point up. I turn round, though I think it is not a special idea to go the hard way. When I start going again Forktine starts to come inside canoe. He looks at me. He throws most the heavy bags in Forktine. Water don't come in. I row and row and row. How long? You guess! Pass Jackass Ginnie, The Loves, Petr's Cloister, and when we get to Thee Wulf's Woods he pulls me over. He gets out, says he, 'I'm Neimiah, this is Lurline. You never saw us please?' Then he do the finger again but I know it can also mean secret. I do same back, so excited! They walk bagless into Wulf's Woods. Those woods are the hard way. I go home and think special thoughts all the way. You know's what I do now Scare...? You cant's tell, just you and I please? I bring them bags of loot. I fill bags of food, clothes, tools, and...everything's I can get secretly. I tie them in the trees where they had turned and both covered their face-holes then wave big bye. The bags are empty when I return. Now I have another note in my pocket. It's from Neimiah and pretty Lurline. It's a whole hand over face secret. 'Blo!'

~Custus~

I don't think Curtius will be one of the future leaders of Lupercalia. But, whoever our Fater is, he wanted him to go to The Murphy House. It's not part of my curriculum, though part of my work here is to watch over my twin, as it will be for the rest of our lives. He still soils his clothes. I do my best to cover this transgression, which I feel is also due to his medication. This morning, well before meeting in the dining hall, I went to check on the state of his pants. They were surprisingly clean. I need to investigate his pockets to make certain he does not have anything that will put either of us in detention. His left had a frog, still alive. He was saving it for either Ichnabod or Faunus. I set it on the open sill. His other pocket had his note from Headmaster; it was worn from his constant reassuring rubs. Headmaster would need to draw up a new

one. There was also a list of items. Certainly not in his hand; it was legible. It was on the headmaster's stationary, though it wasn't his writing either.

Potatoes
Any Available Seed
Hammer
Two Cups
Cold Weather Caps
Needle And Thread
More Paper
New Hand Saw (The Other Looked Dull From A Bone)
Chisel
Mortar And Pestle
Your Smile

At first I suspected one of the proctors had him running personal errands, using my Brother's kindhearted nature to his own benefit. He is ductile. Then I found the third note. It was the least worn, obviously he had recently received it. My mind went racing. I thought I would be watching over him forevermore. Listening to his same few jokes day after day after day after day after day...Now, I am not so certain. Is he in trouble? I don't think so. He shuts down when admonished. Of late he has seemed exceedingly enraptured. Actually he has enlightened the house. My other thought is perhaps he knows our parents. He can be militant with keeping a secret. One day when I am cleaning up after him, pleading with Headmaster, bargaining with our Brothers for an unintended transgression, scrubbing his soiled trousers...he will whisper in my ear the author of his notes...mayhap even, the author of our, well, his happiness.

You're OUR special one!

~Dagobert~

I keep peeing in my bed. I don't know why, no control Alazon say. I even tried to stop drinking anything, that just made me sick and veiny. Mister Stump hooked a drip to my arm that night, it's frightening to have a needle in my arm. I keeps waking me up, checking on it to see if it had killed me. The last time it woked me I realized I had to let loose. So mayhap that's what it's really for, I suppose Mister Stump is a good Vet after all. I didn't like cleaning the pot under my bed, so I went to the porch. I like peeing there, tell Taras, '*This my porch!*' Not really. I love Taras. I like the sound my water makes dripping between the slats. It was so dark. Good thing I knew where it was, or I wouldn't have been able to find it; I was pinching my

hoo-haa, about to pull it out when they come marching up the path. Not soldier march, it was all quiet, like a funeral procession for a Mother. Their hoods were darker than the dark. They slid out of the black and seemed to float by me with their robes hiding their feet and sweeping the dirt. My hand down my sleeping pants, all I could do was hold on. A frozed fawn. Was there something in Mister Stump's drip to make my head funny? Was I still upstairs? Was the sound of them kicking in the neighboring door just me falling out of my bed? And that was my last night I had an incident. It's only been a fortnight, but I have not once let loose in my bed. Sure... once in my pants, but, I don't think I should take the blame. They scared it out of me.

~Eiron~

Jumping the ditch. He wanted to be the best ever at it. Now he just skulks around. Angry, sullen; yes he is becoming a young man, and I am trying to give him space. He was so good at the ditch. Gravityless in his jump. Where is he going when night falls? Why won't his Fater say so and so? As if he is complicit, they seem to be involved in an unannounced pitched battle against me, who loves the both of them; usually. He grabs his satchel and slams the door. He was so sweet. His moods swing so hard I don't know to cuff him or hug him. He still comes to me, but he always makes certain we are alone. No more games with the well-kept Murphy boys. No attempt to get a little girl's ribbon. Hopefully it's just some filthy weather. He nurses everything: his pride, hate, and yes, still love. His Fater has to keep warning me off him. It just gives me an attack of the sads. He returns in the mornings, and I can feel the both of us mentally apologizing. And the other morning, I'm certain he stalled until his Fater was gone. He comes down with that satchel and hands it to me. Inside was his soiled linen. Think I, what in the what? He hasn't done this, well ever that I recall. He broke right then and there. But we both mentally agreed, it truly was not about the muss. Says he weepily, 'Did Döder make me do it?' I wanted to hold him, but I restrained myself and lightly held a handful of his night clothes. From what little he tells me I never expected him to behave in this manner. Says I, 'No, no, you're too good for that.' I don't want him to grow too fast. I can't expect him to behave constantly, but I hope he is beyond that type of influence.

~Eliphas~

We would go there every chance we could in warm weather. Cold as well, but those chances were much fewer. Our cabin was on the South end of the top lake. Fishing never interested me. Listening to stories about fishing did, the speaker always made it sound romantic. That might be telling of

my life of bachelorhood. I would swim the miles of Thee Upper Lake daily, then dive down to the cool bottom. Hoping not to disturb a snapper, I would palm and scoop the muddied bottom, repulsed both at the feel and my need to touch it. Towards the North end it was only a foot of lake. A haven for carp, frogs, and lillypads coated with alge. When Petr's people redirected River Forktine they thought the lake would dry. They still dug. But, it turned out it was fed by a spring under our lake. I think that was why I used to dive to the bottom, hoping to find it. Putting my finger in it and eventually draining both Thee Upper and Lower lakes. Then I'd be able to compete with the romanticism of the anglers, canoeing a few hours before the sun fell. No one talks about that light. Mayhap it is my peculiar eyes, but I can see clearest then. People's stories only speak of the set and rise of the sun. I was expertly quiet with the oar, sneaking up on beavers scuttling to and fro in their work. Catching them floating and watching the sky, I mirrored them in my craft and understood. Of course I was young, and a few times the Döder in me would smack the water with my oar, and the usually graceful-when-in-water beasts would flip and flail back into a position of high alertness. They soon saw me floating feet from them, and their tail hit the water harder than I even could have in a story. And the lake at night. My Fater would go out and night-fish. I went once. I enjoyed waking in the mid of night, laying in my cot on the screen porch and watching the the lake lap, listening to the frogs who had ventured from their Northern pads and the raccoons prying shells on the shore. And rolling on my back, tilting my head to peer out under the eaves to watch the same spot of sky that the beaver and I had watched in that perfect light of day. You would think it would put me gently to sleep. No, no, it was too important. I knew I would sleep during the day, underneath the shadow of the willow patch where my Fater was content with me, done trying to convince me in joining him in his *sport*. Later I would lay on the flat granite rocks that an ancient behemoth had dredged and arranged into an unknown effigy and were now the backdrop to the falls that fell into Thee Lower Lake, where I rarely went as a youth. Now I go to neither. Our cabin has most likely been razed. Think I, *not by the waterfall artist*. Only certain entities have the lakes now. Though they have their own spring to give them life, they seem to be dying. We have been told we are no longer allowed, it is no longer safe. Mayhap I was unaware, yet there is a shade that now looms there.

~Elzey~

I wasn't wielding a divining rod. It was my right Sunday shoe. Before service I was in my back garden pottering about. I spied an unknown shoot and went to bend and excavate the foreign intruder. I stopped my action. I couldn't arrive with soiled hands. Using my toe I attempted to disgorge the

rock and soil about the protuberance. One particular rock proved difficult. I re-lived my days from playing kick-rock and swung away. I antiqued my shoe. I popped it out, getting good distance, the rock resting against my stacked shale wall. I heard a release of breath and stepped back. A supple shoot of water came forth from the ground. It was down a slight slope from the house and in a bit of a divot. I had no worries and went to service; well I did worry about the scuff in my shoe. I absorbed a handful of raised eyebrows and scolding tuts. I did not feel completely cleansed, but it was mid-Summer, a scourge, and people's ire and Fater's lack of effort could be forgiven. I made myself a pleasant brunch of Spring lettuce, summer squash, and mustard paste. My depth perception is always testing me. I knocked my water glass over to spill across the table and drip upon the floor. I had removed my marked shoe, so with my bare foot I pushed a small rug over the spill. This is how I clean my floor between intrusions from visitors. I went to refill my water from the pitcher on the counter, I looked out my kitchen window as I was about to pour. Of course you see where this is going...I bypassed the crushed gravel path and walked my bare feet through the turf. I now had my own spring that had formed a modest pond. It's not my bailiwick, though I now consider myself an adequate aqua-gardener. I have water plants, an array of new lilies, frogs, deer that share my spring at dusk, and a gift of what are named koi-fish brought to me by a Métis from Thee Lupercalia. I never had a chance to ask her how she knew of the well. I saw her standing there one sunrise. We spoke, says she, 'You have a Lotus.' It had been there since the beginning and was the only one. I was proud to give it to that broken-backed boy, he could use a miracle.

~*Ephram*~

Never straighten me out will they? I am so sorry...I can't bring myself to face him and tell him. I can't tell anybody anything. How could I expect myself to be able to tell him that? I avoid him, in a military style. I am perpetually looking for him, which doubles my dilemma as Josephson and I always have to be looking over one another's shoulder. The mark on my face reminds me of his back. Jagged and puckered, evil and mocking. I have tried to stop my hand. But my hand is all that alleviates my guilt. No, not alleviates...seduces? Fulfills might be getting close. There is always a word. I just need to find it one day. I think it is hiding within me. Burrowed underneath my skin. Brewing in the marrow of my bones. When I die will someone carve my bone into a soft *lullybying* flute or into a weapon to bring another's death? I try to perfect his back, etch the malignancy into my skin. Tracing and re-tracing until the canvas becomes logged. Then I have to prepare a new tarp until my excessive study heals thyself. If I sit in the sunlight to attack my next effort, I chance getting caught from a wandering

do-gooder. Sitting in the shadow only leaves me blind, my eventual efforts a waste of my limited material. So I sit under the tree where Josephson and I first...it is just downhill from the sight of the detonation. I look like one of Thee Lupercalians, bobbing and swaying in some hocus trance, but I am only trying to hold the light in place that is dappling through the boughs. I cut and carve. Do I put Boucher to shame? I think not. I only put my family to shame, my *love* to shame, myself to shame. I need to straighten this out. Make myself as straight as this blade, invent a new word for it. Knowing me, when I do, I'll probably paint it on my chest.

~Etienne~

Forktine can be unforgiving in certain sections. That was my first mistake. *My first mistake*; that could be a thesis all on its own. I chose that quiet oxbow where I've passed so many peaceful hours. Picnics, reading,...watching. The water is so calm there, you can only tell it is moving if there is a leaf to verify the state. It's as if someone is gently pulling the water instead of it being shoved from behind in a torrent to reach Thee Falls. I wore my apron, the one with the pockets. I left my shoes on, it seemed proper in some fashion. I ebbed into the water. I was so looking forward to the feeling of freedom I enjoy every time, but it was disagreeable. As it always is when water gets in your shoes. I stopped my march, wondering if I should turn around and take my shoes off, mayhap keep going because I supposed it should be uncomfortable. My shadow didn't mimic me as it normally does. It wavered on top of Forktine, which is always moving even when you can not see it. And it got taller as I stood statued in my wet brogans. That's when my apron made a decision. It snapped from the weight of the rocks and dove into the water. Why I didn't tie a Cannonball around my neck I don't know, there is always some miserable Brother who has a death wish. So, things had taken an unexpected turn. I could figure out this temporary setback. Though the apron would not be held in judgement of the weights. It popped up to the surface and floated away downstream, again proving gravity and will are able to work in conjunction. That was my favorite apron. It would be nice to see it again.

~Eustache~

We had snail trails under both our noses. Why did he make us go to find her? Pitch dark and freezing. Yes, we love her. She was actually a good Sister, just in Winter she goes messing around on the river, and after what happened a few weeks ago and Alumbrados having the other accident... well, I guess Alazon was trying to be extra vigilant. We put on every layer we had, wearing the cloth of our land. Our heated water bottles were bound tight against our ribs. We were sweating before we got outside,

which of course froze as we opened the door and put us in more of a mood than we already were feeling. Lugar wanted to only use candles, he said our eyes will work better with less light. Says I, 'You ever hear of Thee Wulf's Woods?' I shoved a large lantern at him. We backtracked to Thee Tower then turned around and began our rescue for real. The snow had passed, the cold wind bit us as we headed North. What unmans me? That night. We passed the shadow of Jackass Ginnie, through the Love's copse, into the cloister. We even sidetracked to check Thee Duk Pond. Nothing. I worry that she went through the ice somewhere and had passed under us going back South with the current. I think if Lugar and I together did not pass through then her lithe littleness didn't either. At Thee Wulf's Woods we stopped. She would not have gone into there to mix with the breeding trees and crosses. For almost five minutes we shout-whispered for her. That's when the first rocks started landing on the ice. They sounded a dull thud with a muffled echo from the water beneath. Two skidded and pinged as they each hit one of our blades. We both picked up the shrapnel. The painted imagery on them looked ancient, from some ungodly horde that once hunted and now haunts this land. I lifted my lantern and two glowing eyes peered from behind a tree. We sprinted towards home, a laughter of supreme menace that turned to anguish at our backs. Our whispers failed, our hunt failed, we are rebuilding our nerves to inform Alazon. Mayhap the rocks in our pockets will prove that she is gone.

~Evatt~

Thee Lupercalians have a sort of sacrificial lamb. I have *volunteered* twice. I was a *clean* girl. I had made twenty years and had yet to find a suitable mate. That's an odd term. I had not found a mate nor looked too strenuously. I have never been piqued. The parameters are unwed, not virginal specifically, I am unique in my circumstance. Thee Lupercalians deem this lamb to be doused in spice upon every fifth name-day. The spice is meant to entice, attract, mayhap overcome a mate. It's also a moment of levity for all, both Lupercalians and Thee Lupercalians. I am proud to be that person, in fact it might be the only thing that does pique me. My first year was cinnamon. I was put on the the riser in the center of the ring. A Death-Harlequin entered the ring with me. His, or hers? I couldn't tell. The large shoes, baggy and disheveled plumage was counterbalanced with the black mask and fearsome paint. My nerves rose when we met eyes, and I suddenly became wary. So when the spray bottle came out and doused me in water, there was laughter all around. The bags of cinnamon, having been handed out to all upon entry to the tent, showered down. That kicked off the end of Lupercalia for the year. A time of release, absurdity, and if all lines up correctly, posterity. I sneezed cinnamon for two weeks. I had to cut my hair to a Prison shave. I loved the scent and so did others, though in neither

enough to halt the spicing. When Massday came around I was invited to an inordinate amount of events. I feel as if I were a light shade of red for some while. When I mentioned this to others, says they, 'Yes, they go light on you the first time.' I only understood what they implied when at twenty five, I was still unwed. Of course I *volunteered* again. I had a wonderful five years. I was independent, employed, young, and happy. There were two Death-Harlequins this year, I expected water from bottles again. The eggs they had in every hidden pocket were myriad. I hypothesized that it might at least be good for my full head of hair. From underneath their hats, they both added a batter of some ancient chemistry. They massaged it into my pores. I prepared myself for another cropping and months of chills. But it certainly got all excited about the event. Turmeric that year. You would think the scent would become tiresome. Not at all. I had never had such blissful rest. I dreamt of pleasantness, sweetness. Every far-fetched fantasy I daydreamed as a little girl now invaded my sleep. It was wonderful. A certain man loved the taste. I would let him kiss me in the dark. Was it the fact that they were only kisses or that in the daylight I cast a jaundiced visage? Either way, it was another magnificent five years. When they return in a few months, I am hoping for blue-spice-basil.

~Exousia~

Fall was official that day. Or that night; it is dependent on how a person measures such things. I heard the first holler as we were crossing Forktine. It came from behind the Murphy House campus, it would have carried well even without the aid of the river. It was a Buell holler. I didn't recognize it down to the individual, but it was familiar enough, and I knew it was not one of ours. There would be plenty more before the evening was through. There were still some leaves hanging on to the tree limbs, but the barrels had been filled and already started baking. They started them early that morning, sort of a holler of their own, telling everyone that the celebration was beginning this evening. The scent of the burning leaves signifying the start of Fall. It wafted up and down the land, faint and compelling on the fringes and dominant once you reach the campus. Underneath you could smell cider and the base notes of the full apples as people bit into them. Of course the heart notes were rising from the pumpkins and their brethren gourds displayed about the event. We reached the campus quad, had been fraternizing with others not seen since Spring and knew we would not see again until Mass. They brought out the thirteenth barrel. After the new batch of leaves had been smoldering for a few minutes, with people bathing in the camphor, a top note fugged the air. Noses were scalded with the sulphuric haze. Headmaster tripped over the bales and bowled over his disciples in costumes to get to the tempest. He grabbed mugs and attempted to douse the smoldering leaves. The fetor of urine erupted, the

barrel expelling it like a cannonball. The swill in our mugs was a catalyst for this terror. Whatever sins were being burnt away must have been extreme. We weren't there for the absolving. We began to leave. Back at the river, approaching us, Tushka and Comen were crossing together. We warned them off of the debacle. Together they let loose a call or a holler that pained all our senses. They moved up the hill towards the barrel, chanting; if I didn't know better it sounded of collapse, failure, holocaust... not a sound I wanted to sense when casting off old sins and welcoming the season.

~Faunus~

Headmaster says I have a kink in my brain. I smarted him back that a kink there would kill me. He agreed, says, 'Mayhap it will.' So I was correct yet again. Then he says it's not a physical type of kink. What the so and so was he speaking? He tried to demonstrate with a picture. Lecturing, the thoughts inside my head are not straight. He showed me a hook. He thought he had me. I went into one of my, as they call them, *trances*. But, he's never about when I fall into them. He thinks that I am entranced by his wisdom. No, no, it's the hook. The anatomy of it takes me. The eye at the crest, the length of the shaft, the barbs...one at the crux of the bend, the other to enhance the tip. Genius in the simplicity. Jochobed is not supposed to know of me, but...we found one another. She might not *know* of me...I have never revealed our Fater's secret. But she revealed all of his. The one describing the coins is my favorite. Does he have one for me and the other mutts? Well, now I've begun my own collection. Something I can plant in my heart and nurture in my silence. I first stole from the anglers casting from the shore. I spied on Mahout, his hook obscene and ostentatious. It is now hidden in a false door I made within my wardrobe. It is blunt, but will be appropriate in certain circumstances. Mahout will *gift* himself another. I hope to apprentice under Belue or one of his ilk. Learn how to create my own darlings. Wear them around my neck covered by my blouse, beneath my gloves affixed to my fingertips, a different size and shape organized on the inside of my buttoned jacket, each close at hand for their specific purpose. Baugus will rue his barbs. I have one set aside for Jochobed, should the need ever arise. I shall have one for all. Allow them to see the light when they are ready to one day bloom.

~Fichte~

I can't seem to wrap my head around tithings. Specifically the ones from my chest. I'm not understanding as to why I now hand them to Jehu, Chitty, and strangely enough, Cap'n Constable. There are rafts of rumors. I was never completely happy with handing that portion over to Fater

Nigrescent, but he was a good man...Is, I mean, is a good man. Before he...opted out...I spoke with him about my condition. In private, so as not to shame my family. And he kept it that way. We came to an agreement, no, no, I did...I offered him a spiritual dilemma; could I not offer ten-percent of my soul? Says he, 'This is not something I ever demanded, what a person can, or cannot do is accepted.' I asked him if he accepts. I started working on his building, up-keeping. He suggested that I spread my gaze. I began to assist those in need across this land. I spoke with Fater again, telling him that after doing these deeds I now felt guilt. I felt as if I were paying myself when these emotions I received flooded my being. These three did expose my secret, well aware of my situation, proclaimed my failings to my family, the town, and the land. And even though I now must conceive a way to pay a financial tithe to this new trinity, I continue to perform these acts.

~*Frye*~

It was the last operation of my remaining life. Plus it was unofficial, non-authorized. So I'm not certain if that makes it magical imbecilic, which are often times bedfellows. I was withering. So much of my intestine had been removed, I believe I was about seven pounds lighter just from that. In addition, all the food I could no longer consume because there was no place for it to go, so I lost additional weight as well. I most likely only had a half pound of intestine remaining. Because I was officially retired from surgery, I went the unofficial route, to Stump Love. As I said...though I probably should have placed imbecilic in front of magical. He did what he could. And here I am, look at this here. He tried to sew me up, but his entrance wound was so grievous that it wouldn't hold. And my body is so weak anymore the skin disintegrates when pierced with sutures. I have an open wound that can't heal over. Which is fascinating in some respects. I can clearly hear my stomach moaning when it wants fed, which is often these days. But my stomach is not my heart, and it's just not that interested. I worry when I go through the motions of sitting or standing, my insides that remain in my employ will eventually slide out the hole in a fit of jealousy towards their departed Brethren. So I mostly sit still in my remaking time. One reason being is when I do move it jostles my organs and causes the noxious fumes to vent out of the hole. This can be hard on my family nearby. They are patient and dishonest. It's right below my nose, they are deceitful when saying they notice nothing. It can be blinding in its terror. And when I sit still, I also find myself looking inside my hole. Has man not always yearned to understand his inner workings? The temptation to extend my finger to my kidney is treacherous. The wound suppurates, and I am forevermore holstered with a weapon against spillage. If I can keep myself from peeling back the aperture further, from turning the chink into a chasm, I might finally find out what I am made of.

~Furtippet~

You might catch me dancing around a pine blaze; that is if you ever thought to follow me. Though no one follows. When I implanted my thin, scalloped blade to the beast's groin, I flensed my secret free. The stench consumed the valley, pushing back the approaching storm. Thieves rode the thermals. Cats skulked the understory of bladdernut and spice bush. I like to think they judged me not, for they were most likely envious of my accoutrements, my tools specific to my needs. While I was jealous of theirs and the multi-use they 'suffer.' In fact, I would later collect their personal baubles and wear them as trophies when performing my secrecies. Buffalo offal stuck to my boots, leaving a trail of where I had been, marking the thresholds of your stores. And yet, still no one followed me. When I enter Boucher's establishment, I finally blend in. So much more than himself, the thought makes me wonder if he has a secret as well. I am about to ask when he touches the knife I thought I had secreted on my hip. We laugh it off, though the new wariness won't succumb to humor, I will need to keep my eye on him. If they ever caught me in my cape, my totem would be razed, but Boucher would only wonder...I want and need this land to survive. For them all, and mayhap for myself. Can I ruin a species on my own? I truly hope not. When I return to town after my sojourns I pray that I have scraped all the indigo from my skin, scrubbed the malodor from the folds in my flesh. In my stiff oak chair, I sit not touching the back, proper in my place of persuasion. They follow the others who only use others' words, they are only guessing, even hoping, at belief. I don't want to knock down others. I want to raise all, but only after I raise myself. One day they might concede to follow me. Follow, yes. But, never catch.

~Gabby~

Sealed in wax. If I were able to feel anger that might be what I felt. But once I thought about it I had to agree. I am sealed tight. They both know themselves to an extent that I am not even close to learning. I have tried. My efforts always come up too short. I will go extreme one way, drink let's say, then I will stop before I lose control of myself. A boy, again I can flirt and entice, yet when he touched me I ran. My horn fails me, it does not have that within itself. Nor do I. They are both on the far lengths of their personage. One takes of Fater, lily white with the accompanying attributes. The other is Mother, darkness all around, physically and spiritually. And not a negative shade, yet mysterious, the type that draws others to investigate and piques their interest with a flex of a dimple. Then there is me: wax. You know another way to describe wax? Blah...medium skin, hair, eyes... personality. I find myself borrowing everything, I stay inside to avoid the

sun and my skin turns a sickly pale, no flowered tint anywhere. My Mother sends me out to get some air, my skin blossoms with red patches and uneven freckles. Again, no flowers, the red patches look like algae on Thee Lakes. My horn is dull, both sight and sound. They have tried to teach me, but again, my horn doesn't have that note.

~Gaspee~

I suppose I gots what I deserved. I was the one who pull the first prank on Alazon. I whisper in all the children ear of the plan. I was oldest, but you don't have to be old to be mean. They bought in. We thought the pigs funny, could have been our age. Other day one the children come in says, 'Women Prison is back open.' Everyone all together look at me. Because I am oldest, I am going to Women's Prison first. Even though I play tough sometimes I still a little girl. I start to cry, cry, and cry some more. I don't want to go. Alazon turn his back and his shoulders start to shake. He cry, cry too. I feel so sad that I run to him and hug him from behind. Then I feel his cry cry is really a laugh. I let him go. He turn around. When he see I have more *disappointedment* from his laughing than I do for Women's Prison, he puts his arms about me, his fiery Cannonball. Says he, 'I'm sorry, my Gaspee.' Now we both cry. Then all the children in perfect Cannonball synchronization fall down flat on the ground. They so amaze at seeing me, Gaspee, and Alazon touch that they succumbed. Us two know not what to do. Did we just kill all? We almost start crying again...then all together the children laugh. They had double-prank both Alazon and me, Gaspee. He had put them up to the prison prank at me. They pretend to go along, but all along are finished with the animus and made insincere their final fall. It was...A Mass Feinting.

~Gebchka~

One has been referred to as *sealed in wax*, about another, *she is about to give everyone a headache*, as for myself I have been called *a riot of sunshine*. Our Fater fashioned our horns on his own. They were only supposed to be for decoration, he felt they were apt gifts for his similar daughters. After we were done using them as toy canes, swords, and spyglasses, we put them to our lips. Says Fater, 'No! Not becoming.' Then we blew, and our lives changed. As it is not Fater's job to craft, it is not any of ours to play these horns. It is a hobby for all of us, mayhap a better verbiage is a passion; somewhat similar to how Fater views us. What we produce is not what the ear is prepared for, the sound is *unconventional* and eventually overwhelming. There have been cases of siblings inventing their own language. This is what has happened with my Sisters and our horns. We can play in a birth and play out a life. We can split your frontispiece. We have summoned Thee

Three Hunters and warded off the Wulf. We stand at the gates of Thee Bedlam and play The Mass for all inside; is it a reward or a punishment? Our knuckles are swollen above where a ring might be placed. Cheilitis overwhelms our lips due to the metal our Fater uses in his hobbies, which is exacerbated for a few hours after we play due to the occupational atrophy. Through all this joy we bring, we still represent a disappointment for most. We have yet to beckon Thee Lupercalia. We can't beg out of the continued requests. And did they ever conclude that us being the masters of these horns, possibly we don't want to signal them? A sign is not for us to gift. Ichnabod's proclamations might bear truth. Mayhap we are only sounding another of Ahmen's shrugs. The mirrors we have broken are no longer tallied. This life blows hard.

~Glaspell~

I can not think of a worst thing I might want to do with my life. But she drove me to it. Says she wanted time with me. She never liked me too much; it was just a life routine we were dragged into. Everyone kept gathering at our place. I'm just too friendly, I could never say no. I hated it more than she did. But says she, 'You might as well charge them for your company.' She said it thinking it would get me to finally say, *sorry, not tonight*. But, just to spite her that's what I did. Added on to the main floor, built an open space centered around a river rock fire place. It spits out so much heat that when we finally sleep our windows upstairs are wide to the night air. The bar on one side, the kitchen on the other. I put more spit in the drinks as the night progresses. These unappreciative so and sos are entitled and pushy now that they must pay. Hard on the furniture that they did not craft. Unable to close the door on the way in or out. I fell sick from overwork, she caught me coughing into the unwashed cups. Later that evening I found the plums that she uses to make our now *famous* plum brandy dessert, resting in our bed pan to cure. She grabbed the pan from me in shame. I looked at her. I stepped close, loudly gathered up my flem, then I leaned and spat. It mimicked the custard to perfection. After years of familial expectations, months of spite, we laughed. We now pass each other looks that we never threw when courting. She brushes my arm when I pull a draft, setting it down in front of the patron so it appears an accident that I splashed his sleeve. We clip one tine on each fork, comparing notes on who we saw pull a splinter from their gum as we bed down each early morning after dousing the fire and barring hard the door.

~Guare~

I hate my job. If we must be prepared, I will do my best. We would rather the children not be involved, but our children are stubborn. If they want to be

126

of this land in the future, then they must be of it now. The blowguns I have prepared for them can devastate. They can attack in a swarm, or if imbibed with a contagion, they can be used singularly. Though we fear for the child who cast this dart if they ever laid eyes on the putrescence of their victim. I have adopted a bow and arrow from a game I studied performed by Thee Lupercalians. The less physical interaction we have with the foe, the better chance of our success. I have seen the terror in the eyes of a man with a crushed right side, an exposed lung, a slowing heart. Success can also be won for most not to see their destruction inches from themselves. Yet, that is also a reality, and for those instances I have made an object of horror. I watched the fishermen, the power generated in their strokes. I replicated a shortened form of their oars in my lathe. The Loves provided me with a small supply of verawood. In these short oars I encased perfect shards of obsidian. The weight along with the texture will leave the wielder wanting for the putrescence from a dipped dart. But, those who must do this work understand the levity of the situation, coming to terms with the horror they will inflict before the first assault. I make lengthened staves, elegant in their destruction. Bolas to entangle and trap, an attempt to convince an assailant without lethality. Ulus to use in a last desperate situation, when your antlered spear has severed and the wounded is set on finality. One catastrophe we will not inflict: the tool of my Fater. And Alazon agrees, he was the one to convince the Legion to not convert the cannons into an oppression of carnage. We want to defeat, we do not want to exterminate. There are some of us who would like to be one. I love my people.

~Gweilo~

I went to get money from him and I wasn't allowed to see him. They said he was dying. I asked of what, and they said he might have eaten some bad meat. Well, I ate the half-dinner that was mine in the first place and he overcharged me for, and I am just fine. They said he cut up dear Enbarr and fit what he could of him in his cold box. That love did everything for me. He pulled my cart when he deserved to be fighting in great battles. Plowed my fields when he should have been studding in luxury. He endured cruel tack and crueler children and did not blame me afterwards when he could be roaming naked to explore the unknown. I would pat him down in the evenings, a treat of a quince, a carrot. He offered back appreciative noises and gently pushed his muzzle into me while blowing his soft air on my neck. I rode him to the Summer dance, we had matching ribbons he secretly adored. He waited patiently at the gate as the couples entered, giving a wall eye to the men's corsages. When I retired the dance, my 'date' let him snack the delight from his chest. Enbarr nudged him encouraging his acceptance. I waited for the same and he feigned ignorance until I gave in and presented him my nosegay. He carried us double to both of our homes, watching protectively as I was pecked upon my cheek before the

'date' dismounted. When all others walk through their own muck, he left his apples in one corner of the corral. I believe it was for both our sakes. Even though his hoofs could split a man's skull, he did not want to stain them, and he knew the ease it created for myself when shoveling. Every evening he stood with his chest pressed hard against his stall, his head pushed forward and ears perked listening to my routine. As I extinguished my last lamp he softly drummed his cannon twice against his door sending his love to me. I hope someone finally knocks on Cowan's door. Some bad meat...Ha! He's some bad meat, just like all the Northrops. Well, good riddance to the last of the Northrop stain.

~Harpe~

You never knew they called it a White Mass because of me, did you? I know I shouldn't be smoking around you...but, if you want my companionship, well, sorry for the occupational hazard. I have learned that I receive my affections in a different manner than others receive their affections. For the majority of people, an over abundance of tartrate leads only to a slight case of the shakes. Yet, the overabundance of tartrate for myself led to the loss of seeing colors. Everyday of the year things are shadowy and dark, including myself. Except for one day. On that day there is a whiteness that overshadows the dark. From what's left over of my upbringing in the umbra of Fater Nigrescent's former ways, I light a cigarette as a form of offering. An appreciation. I know what happens when I leave a room. I hear people whisper, 'What's with her?' The dullness in my eyes still makes out their shaking heads. Except on that one day. I appreciate the whiteness that shows those same shaking people the possible beauty of this day. The people are thankful as well, in appreciation of my *gift*. I share and they share, and they light one up with me. Can anything or anyone truly be *only* black or white? Mayhap the smoke, their modern day censer, is a more apt explanation. At least it can bring happiness. And at least on that day, so do I.

~Hesther~

Fall's coming, your fields are all shorn. You can see well out here. Quite a view. I'm not normally awake right now, but I wanted to come out here and see it before the snow hits. And of course it wouldn't be the same if I came to look in on you in the dark with only one of my lamps to see by. Still humorous to me that I am the lamplighter. No one else wanted to do it. The pay is what it is, the benefits are why I do it. Please don't let on to anyone my true reason for working the lamps through the night. They would take it from me. They were startled enough to hear a woman had interest in skulking about in the depths of the dark. Their trust is on a short

leash, not that they are tethered to said truth. I was doing it on my own, just on a small scale around my porch and well. I had lamps lit all over. My neighbors were worried I had a fear that they did not know of. They would probably have their own fear at what they might find in my lights. I collect bugs, insects. They are drawn to my beacons. Now I have them all over town and further. I invented my own trap. I say it is on level with any from Petr's Grandfater. At first I found all my interests had set themselves alight. To circumvent this, behind my lamps I suspend a rope. On this I drape old handkerchiefs that my Fater left me. Most land on the vertical or horizontal drape; I found it is dependent on the individual beastie, not the species or genus. My collection has grown tremendously since beginning my new sub-career. Ladies think that I am covertly taking in sewing in the evening to earn extra. The amount of pins I consume surpasses all. I truly enjoy each and everyone of my captures. Jarring, subduing, and pinning them to my wax displays. They all give some bit I was missing. Yet, my favorites are the moths. I like sugaring for them as well; it keeps off some of the repeat species and has drawn Lepidoptera I have seen only in image. Goldcap Moss Eater, Maple Seedminer, Leafcutter and Miner, of course the tobacco moth, and longhorn. The Skeletonizer does not bring guilt when I crucify him and his brethren. One who is like-minded of Thee Lupercalians brought me an Atlas Moth. I was amazed and humbled, but I returned it, only feeling proper if I harvested it naturally. After they departed that year my collection expanded, not by much quantity, but quality. I only found one of each: a Lime Hawk, Twin-spotted Sphinx, Garden Tiger, Cecropia, Luna, the very mannered Rothschildia Aurota, and the owlet Noctuidae. I am holding out hope in the darkness for one unseen; my ultimate laurel, Hesperia Busiris. I am nervous I will never find it before my time is up. My wicks are shortening, my wax is melting, my sugar is running low; though this might be my own fault, my sweet-tooth is never satiated.

~Hickey~

I miss the person my younger Brother was. Not the one he became and subsequently failed to become, as my peers were outside wiling away the time of youth. In one another's constant companionship, I was watching over him. There was an *accidental* gap between my younger Brother and his older siblings. I am the youngest of the oldest. I was in his position of envy until he arrived. The other older siblings had progressed with their lives, while I was just entering that first phase of the downhill trend of childhood. He smelled of milk: all stages, fresh from the teat or ripe with age. I loved smelling his downy hair when giving him his bottle that he would suckle even after it drained, until he finally slept. Or when he would for no reason I could see, just lean on me and create a suction of sweat. On the evening our Mother and Fater went to speak with my professor, — nothing amiss,

only trimester accountings — we fell asleep together at the foot of my bed. My room was in the attic with the moths and their dandruff wings, and their own unique smell that warred against his milk. It was warm up under the eaves. There was a small six-inch high window that was at your feet if you stood. We were touching shoulders, his was wetting mine, and watching the last light from the fallen sun. I woke to darkness. My shoulder was dry. However, my back was drenched, my neck was moist. I felt his little weight. He had moved to my back while we napped. What new mothers call cat moves. I slowly turned my head. I could see nothing though I knew he was there, feeling his feet flexing against my lower back, and I could feel the crown of his head cradled contentedly in the nape of my neck. I lay motionless and watched the stars by only shifting my eyes. My parents returned home. I wanted them to see our bond, see what a good son I was, so I did not move. He heard them creak the stairs and leapt off me fully alert and ran to the landing to greet them. I stood, said goodnight to all, and went to sleep. In the morning my Mother passed behind me at table. She stopped and fingered my neck, calling my Fater over. On one hand they were disappointed, thinking I had neglected my younger Brother. On the other, my professor spoke fondly, and they were relieved I had the courage to not only speak with a girl but initiate with one. These days, with him passed on, I feel like the youngest again. I don't know if I have, but he changed, and he certainly left a mark. He took my original name. I hope it is a comfort to him...wherever he might be.

~Iahu~

Can I speak honestly? I truly do not know. Why must that be a preface to most peoples' proclamations? Obviously that implies their usual speech is...as they say, to be, *taken with a grain of salt*. My pockets sway when I walk. My gait is unladylike. Too much salt can be poisonous, as I have learned. Yet, one grain...*I want to tell the truth*, they say, 'Go ahead,' says I. *I deserve a thank you*, anyone who wants a thank you should have already received one; it is most likely not deserved. *I tell it like it is*, if so then you shouldn't have to tell people that you do. *No offense but...I mean this in the nicest way...I don't mean it as an insult...I apologize if I made you feel that way...*I will stop, this will go on and on. I just need to improve myself. No one can judge another... now wait, I just did it. And that is not true, I can judge another perfectly well, especially if said other is a jackass. I just hope people do not judge me to harshly when I reach into my pocket before they speak to me. But, with these people, mayhap a grain will not be sufficient. A pinch, an eventual overdose...and finally I will be released.

Who does he think he is? Who does he think she is?..Was? My Wife was up there alone, where she always wanted to be, probably the best view in all the land. His Wife used to go up there too, when they were both living. It was a wonderful spectacle...they would circle the tree staring at one another, claiming the ground as their own while invoking their inherited chants. He and I would stand at the bottom of the hill chuckling at their chicken dance. I went up there to visit her grave...well, and to see if he had moved his wreck of a Wife somewhere proper. And I discover he had. In fact, he is such a slothful beast he did not even recover my Wife's bejeweled box. I could see by the divots scarred in the earth that he had drug her off by himself. Good, I thought, that is deserving. Then of course my overthinking crept up, and I began to ponder if he might have found a superior location. I followed his Wife's path. Not too far away I found her empty box. He had discarded it. The same box as my Wife's, yet with gaudy baubles displaying her taste. However, there was still a path to follow. She was a large woman, he is a lazy man. He had dragged her as he did her box. Her heels left a similar map that had been outlined by her box. All the way to Thee Tower I went. Can you imagine? What right did she have to be up there when my Wife was stuck in that hole? I have since remedied the situation. Under cover of night, I relocated her. The Avestans will wake to find her all prepared. They will need do nothing except bring in the birds then light the bones. She will certainly proceed his Wife, he most likely left her in a pile beneath the stairs in the foyer. I also didn't leave her box to perish. I plan to gift it to Lowin; I'm always supporting a hopeless cause.

~Ignatius~

It was my time to walk. We started on Upper Field, following the path past the Art Barn and the shed, past the other outbuildings, and finally we commenced on the Headmaster's Lawn. I walked in the center; my ten Brothers formed a large rectangle around myself, leaving enough space for each to swing their fireball. All had adorned the thick white gloves, these were used in ritual as well as protection from the heat of the chains. The balls were dipped and lit, the march began. I had never participated in a walk, yet I could tell that no other light was needed. The ten swinging balls mirrored the gloves in both beauty and fierceness. Our shadows battled all around us, one overtaking another only to be trampled to extinction, then reborn to fall again. A new battlefield dictating the rules of warfare according the the hill we climbed or the ditch we traversed. These could be transfixing satellites to induce a young couple or ancient weapons of trepidity. The whooshing hum overhead eventually began to emit a high

whine, a whistle to an unknown beast as the tinder withered in size to create an ever changing wind-hole. These shrinking cinders began to project, pioneering ahead, bouncing upon the path and forging our way. Exploding in fits of tiny terror to our flanks and rear, keeping any would be antagonists at bay. I deduced what was inevitable moments before the first ember brushed my robe. One of my proceeding Brothers launched a weighted volley, when it struck my forehead the blood only covered my left eye. I was stunned but continued on, waiting for my Brothers to come to my aid. The lighter embers floated in a slow tease of dread, softly swaying in the night then quickly darting on an unseen draft. With my swimming head from the strike and my dulled vision from the blood, I could only feel my robe falling away. It did not flare-up and engulf me in flames. I was stupefied that I had not peed myself, then I was angry that I had not. As I concentrated my will and began to extinguish mine enemy, I found my robe was worried off. I had burnt a regrettably written letter late one night, to not wake anyone. I had to keep the burn to a soft, small glow, just crawling along the unfortunate text. I imagined that as my fallen robe. When we arrived at the Headmasters lawn, I was naked except for the urine. Now is when they would notice the accident; they would dramatically drop their destructive chains and come to my aid, lauding me for my silent stoicism. Headmaster handed me my scroll, it was wrapped in a cloth chamois. As I used it to cleanse myself, they left me to find my way back in the dark. Walking back to my room, unrolling my lambskin to cover what was possible, I realized none of the robes of my Brothers had succumbed.

~Iman~

I have a fading dimple. I used to be adorable. Saddle shoes, knee stockings I wore just under the knee, an array of dresses, matching bows to hold my flowing dark hair, matching eyes, straight white teeth, and my hypnotic dimple. Now I age in my sleep. I saw a dream in our home. Shadows, rolled furniture, meek Fater,...and Mother. I went with boys on cart rides. My card was always the first to be filled while dancing. I once went to Thee Lake late in the night. The boy, I won't say his name, wanted to take me in his boat. I found them uncomfortable but enjoyed the possibilities. Now I only have the third best smile. I once held my Fater's hand, no longer. I once was held by my Grandmama, I'll never again know her lap, the cuddle of her bosom. My cat will no longer be a kitten for me to dote upon, he will be the lonely petulant creature he was bred to be. I will attempt to look my Mother in the eye, though both of us will never again hold a gaze. Certainly not one another's while our eyes are always cutting to the corners of the room. I no longer will use Summerish speech. I saw the sheep massed in the field, the mosquitoes gather and swarm, the smell of panicky rabbits, and a flea walking across my lashes. My shame tucked

between my kidneys. I endured the anthology of shame and touches. Shadders. They came for me for the first time the other night. I now know what to call them.

~Jeansomme~

Says he, '...Yours now.' Well, I made him mine. We all have brown eyes, olives complete. Yet, his olives were floating in an angel-blue pool. I understand what Alazon is feeling, he has no more Wife to...I want hold them both. During our first swaddle I broke his sweet clavicle. It sounded like a jar that doesn't shatter, but just cracks slowly. You watch it progress from the very bottom to the top, purposefully altering its path over imperfections, purposeful abrasions, or prunts. I finally perfected the coddling about his imperfections. When he still needed me to clean him, bathe him, well, I loved seeing his naked self. I could see his hollow bones right beneath his veins and skin. I would worry that his veins would pull too hard, that his skin would stretch too tightly and snap his breast in a disturbing melodic arrangement. His delicate pea-size marble, an unattainable elegance for most male Cannonballs. I feel a fervor for him I don't believe is common in life, a passion I never thought capable. He deserves it, mayhap not all do... but...I'll take care of Alazon after I take care of his son. I could never bow my legs as perfectly as he. The grace, and with such execution.

~Jeremiad~

I'm still uncertain of my growing feelings. Apparently she is as well. She never came to bed, and I still have not seen her since I finished. It was a lot of work picking and hoeing and then hauling those rocks. Then they were apparently of a stubborn breed of rock. They went and broke out of the wagon and planted themselves in the garden again. They might have a mind of their own. They might understand the greater scheme of things and knew how necessary it was for them to return to their resting place. It might be a conspiracy conducted by her. The rock-wagon was sitting on that little hump that overlooked the place where I pulled them up from. And when I looked at it in the morning the wagon tail was busted open. Conspiracy would say she took an axe to it and flooded the rocks back into their original pose. Either way, I am certain she wants me to once again, *rock the garden*. Could be she's not coming back until I repeat this and haul them and the now broken wagon afar. She's most likely sitting with Miss Missal, foraging in her kitchen and laughing at me through the drapes. That's why I have done naught yet. Could be I give her time to cool, she can be stone stubborn. Mayhap this will convince her that we can get all our vegetables gratis from the Miss Missals of the land, there is no need for us to labor and toil in a waste of sustenance garden. Now, if she wants me

to turn it into some sitting place, put a fountain, a bath for birds, a bench where we could sit and watch the sunset on the day and our years, even have a late dinner eating other peoples' food, well, we could talk on that. I think it would make a grand place to finally rest.

~*Josias*~

I witness the rust already spreading on her plate. I see the shading of the land. Thee Mountains are fading to gray. Thee Lakes have gone still. Jackass Ginnie is collapsing on herself. Thee Wandering is crawling closer, invading with a meticulousness only achieved in nature. This end is unnatural. Exotic and deserving. I smell the tang from Wulf's Woods, the fetid air tilting the Loves' loved trees. Thee Tower could soon be full, only none will bring the bodies. They will litter the land, enriching the future with their entrails. The sun and the shade summoning all to war.

~*Josua*~

It was a brilliance of nuance. Everything. Us coming down the slope from the North. We were on par with the tallest onioned-dome, sandwiched between the stars overhead and from our view, distant stars below. We paused, prolonging our disbelief at being balanced between worlds.
Magic lantern. Dance with paper lanterns outside. The sound of the push-pull Engel worked was like a siren. Others joined in his call. Strings, delicate brass, and woods antiqued from the moistness of lips and fingers alike. From my eye the floor they put down was 50x50. As we drew nearer you could see it appeared to be levitating, though the mechanism by how this was achieved was hidden to the eye. From under the raised platform were lights emanating from small holes bored in the ground. We tried to decipher the pattern of the paper lanterns hung above the 50x50 floor. After our failed analysis, we realized they had been draped singularly, as a tree at Mass is decorated, and the pattern they configured was determined by the observer who wasted such time trying to find meaning in joy. I stepped onto the stage, turned and offered my hand to her. We paused again, my right foot between her feet, my hand on the visually imperceptible swell of her hip, our opposite hands entwined...and we danced. Were there others? We never had to dodge or deke. We might have been selfish and commanded the entire space. Our feet swept a a baritone oomph that carried out and up from all four sides of the platform. We had only stared at one another through the night, yet when two lights crossbeamed through our path we looked up. Two white sheets, crisp with starch, had been placed opposite one another. And upon them the end results of these crossbeams displayed. We did not stop our procession, yet on each pass we viewed the contraptions. A small lantern within, throwing an inverted image through

a concave mirror. Some were other dancers, beasts, and landscapes; our favorites were those that were brethren to the hanging lights. They had no specific shape, only a purpose. We would move through these and our shadows would create a perfect form, then move on to eradicate it just as quickly. Our bliss formed and gifted only to us. The push-pull had stopped breathing hours past, yet we moved to the light breeze, the crickets brushing softly on themselves, and the gentle notes of owls that later passed off to morning blackbirds, robins, and chaffinch. Our breath slowed and our dance came to a standstill. We returned to our original pose, staring again at one another. The boards no longer baritoned, the lights winding down their day. They guttered out softly. It was kind of the lanterns, as if they had a conscience and respect for the sunrise.

~Lent~

It might be something I need to suss out. She finally spoke with me again. She had started her own food patch. She knew what she was doing. Fruit and vegetables, even flowers to appease the eye. People had always cut or picked flowers, usually in the foothills or on a difficult-to-reach mountainside. She was the first to dedicate some of her land to this discipline. Others had a difficulty in grasping the concept. Yet, after her displays were seen in a few prominent windows, it graduated from a whimsy into a tradition. When Veda came to her and said she wanted to buy all her fruit and vegetables, she agreed. I arrived as she was crating the first delivery. I saw what she did. I've been unfairly accused. It's not my place to tell. Not that she would deny her deed, she understands that in whole. Yet, no matter how many people believe, *despite what you have done you are decent*, it can never be wholly true until you believe yourself. I brushed her arm that held the last crate. She bowed her head in...something...I might equate it to shame. We unpacked the crates, burned them and their spoiled goods. We filled new bins and delivered them in full. Though unasked for, she included a bouquet that she has never been fully able to replicate. And she does try to outdo herself when she makes her deliveries. Veda has pleaded, Glaspell has tried to slip us something for them. No, no...we don't need...something. We return home to do some night gardening. We don't need a fire to see our way around. We are able to do everything by feel. It's my job to keep the weeds and worms at bay.

~Leptus~

It's an anemic sinecure. I did beg the position, this is not a whinging discourse. Every class has a valedictorian, yet there also needs to be the one who pridefully exudes the contrary role. I have prophesied my future. My Fater put me here out of love. He will not allow me to fail. He has the

means and the guilt to afford me a life of leisure. I coast, as Headmaster would say if he were not intimidated by my benefactor. I pass my lessons... and am satisfied. No more. I spend my study hall reading stories. I feign the need for the washroom and pull a book out that I hide beneath my tucked shirt. Actually, that's no longer the case. I am now so brazen and uncaring that the books no longer rest against my ribs. Again, not completely true. Often I fall asleep while reading in bed, and a book will droop from my hand and laze upon my bare-chest, naked because putting on my sleeping kit seems unnecessary. Is it truly any dissimilar than the path you have taken. We both do not do much, yet we get the job done. Our roles could effortlessly be interchanged, though I don't believe I could read with my arms held like yours. In fact, that's quite apathetic. You refuse to hold your arms yourself, leaving them to be nailed into the proper position. Mayhap if I ever get truly indifferent to reading, my Fater will secure me in your position. Though that might impede my machinations to write. All this reading of others, I could rearrange and improve their words. Yes one day I will write...or not.

~Libanus~

I finally lost all my teeth. Linus had lost all of his. I didn't understand why my twin Brother would be ahead of me when I am older than him. Seven minutes can be a long time. I'm a fraction taller than him. A bit heavier. We all know I'm sharper as well. And this proves it. Everybody knows that after you collect all your fallen teeth, you throw them on the roof that very night for the good future luck. And if they make it through the night, then your adult teeth will grow straight and strong and good fortune will follow. All the boys have done it, my Brothers, not like Linus, my Murphy Brothers. Not all their teeth are perfect, and not everything is wonderful, but I think those things come in grown-up life. And honestly they were all too cool to take it seriously. All the boys were excited for the event and watched one another until it got dull and routine for everyone, and only a few might watch a closer Brother. They lazily tossed their teeth and strutted off pretending boredom. So I wonder if all their teeth made it way up to the roof, and if they did who checks to see if they made it through the night? So, right when my last one fell, I went to my drawer for my tin of teeth. Linus was the only one that showed any interest. We went out, and I took my time — tested the wind, practiced with some rocks, and when I was prepared, I hucked them all in perfection. We heard the tink of the shrapnel cascade and settle. I prepared for bed, proud that I had leaped this obstacle. I was that much closer to manhood. But, I couldn't close my eyes hard enough to sleep. I worried myself awake, concerned that my last remnants of childhood were being carried off by a greedy spider, or mayhap a colony of ants would use them to make a castle wall to keep out

that spider. That's when we heard the tumbling crash. That's how I know, everyone knows, I'm sharper than Linus. Of course your leg will break if you try to climb out of the attic window. He said he wasn't trying to climb out. I didn't try to get any sleep. I went with Linus to have Dr Dolan set his break. The sun would rise in two hours, then I would be a man. And a man should share his fortune with his Brother.

~Lincoln~

I thought that was a strange word they called us, like one of Thee Lupercalians called us special. When we were still allowed to see each other we went to kindly ask them about all the gossiping. I did not want that, yet, Lincoln did. I did what he said. Says the one, 'Lo!..' They speak in their own way. And that's when Tosspa and I were left in that room. I used to think I could hear him speaking low. I don't think that any longer. Every time I think I might hear their shuffling steps, Tosspa feigns as if I misbehaved and shoves me into an impromptu lesson. But, couldn't be, everyone knows I don't misbehave…well…I want to fit in and say that I do have behavior issues, but we all know that I am not capable. At least not yet. Mayhap Tosspa will teach me one day. When he pretends to scold me he calls me his penumbra. My parents have pet names for me as well. They are silly; if the other boys heard them they would grief me. But I love to hear them every morning as they send me off to Tosspa for the day. They are wise enough not to say them out loud where others might hear. They whisper them in my ear before they reluctantly open our front door so I can go to learn from my tutor. When I return to them nightly we sit and talk and discuss their day. We speak of my day as well, yet there are some things that Tosspa has intimated that I might not want to share. This deception is difficult, though my parents have repeated their want for me to follow Tosspa *somewhat* blindly because, says they, 'He's so bright.' And I agree. Though he is old and already shrinking, I almost can see him eye to eye. And 'times I feel I have to turn away and shake my head at his thorough teaching, but his gaze holds me in its shimmering aura. On warm days…well, even if there is a chill, but mainly if the sun is working, we do our exercises outside. Our voices eventually growing so loud in their excitement that we drown the birds calling out their lusts from the shaded branches of the trees. We are both rue to end the lessons but are eager for the next day. He leads me to his door where I listen for Lincoln. I hope to hear him again one day.

~Linus~

They thought I was climbing out. I was coming back in. Then the last time I would do this, I fell. I didn't scream. I remember telling myself not to

make a sound as I was falling or somebody would hear. I was planning to land, probably take a moment to get my wind back because I would lose it on contact. Then I would quietly go back inside and crawl in bed and in the morning make up some story about the bruises and cuts. Mayhap Döder. Though my leg went and hit the second floor sill, it crashed the window. That's not when my leg broke. The sill flipped my body into a somersault, so instead of landing on my side and only losing my breath like I had planned, my body behaved like a bolide and gracelessly collided with terra firma. Crack, snap, crush, all manner of breakage in my leg. I had two of his teeth in a pocket I had sewn in my nightshirt. I've got them with me now, along with all the others. How many mouths? How many teeth? You don't know do you? I do. I kept them all in my pocket and fingered them everyday, my own rosary, praying for my last tooth to fall. I needed all their good luck and coming fortune. I only took two teeth from every boy, they would have plenty enough of luck with the others, they could spare what I needed. A long time before Dr Dolan set my leg, he told me my last tooth was embedded sideways. My grownup tooth would pass it by, yet my infant tooth would never come out of its own volition. So when Libanus saw my last tooth pushed through my gum, I played it cool and told everyone I'd already threw my teeth, only a child needs to attention himself to everyone. I brought these teeth to you for safekeeping. I need you to hold onto my rosary for me. I grew out of my nightshirt with the secret pocket, which is usually fine, but we have inspection tonight. If I got caught with their prayers, I would feel...I don't know, I guess like a little boy who did bad.

~Llewelyn~

I originally was making it for Jacob's Mother. They had done me a kindness that day. I was only wanting to repay it. But, Jacob was having none of it. Says he, 'No other man will ever touch my Mother's bed.' We have not spoken since, not much lost for either of us. I heard of the disruption at Ulema's house, she was always a sweet little girl. I never had one myself, but if I did, she is what I would want. Or...she was what I would have wanted. I have a soft spot for her but not a dumb spot. I think she has herself a soft spot in her head. I originally thought she had something against my re-gift, but...how many beds has she burned? At least one too many that I know of. But, it wasn't personal. She went after Weishaupt as well. I didn't have any spot for her. We weren't close in age, but she was too close to my age for it to not be creepish if I gave her any attention. I twisted it around in my head, that what I did next was not giving her attention, but, doing like The Dumbs gave me that once and I gave her a kindness. Though, I suppose you could twist it back in my head and say, 'Well, Llewelyn, isn't giving a teenage girl a bed creepish?' So, yes, I could see that side of it as

well. Unlike Ulema, I was overthinking it. I refurbished that re-gift. She deserved it. It wasn't her fault that my soft spot went hard at her. Burned down her house she did. I try not to give her attention, but when I see her and look at her from under my brow, I can see she looks good. No, again, I don't mean that in the manner you keep taking it. I mean that I can tell she is resting well. She deserves it. I'm sure she gets so much comfort when she's in my bed...ah, no...erm...I give up, maybe kindness isn't for me.

~Loton~

So, he came and spilt out his plan to me. My fields that had been looked over by generations of my family, says he, 'They need proper management.' I understand how he might have thought I was slow, I mean, I was just standing there with my mouth hanging open after his little speech. I did a full circle, looking for the jokester who was hiding nearby. Mayhap I am too polite as my Wife often says, though she is the one always apologizing for me, so her argument is made of thin netting. It would have been nice if she were there to apologize for me then. I was about to punch this man in the neck. He got a little ferrety, he had stepped extremely close by the time my circle ended. I looked at the congealed product he collected in his thinning hair. I could see the sun burning his pasty scalp. He spoke to my chin. Says he, 'Every place of commerce has a guiding hand. I could be the secret to your children's future.' I lightly put the toe of my boot on top of his shoe. He gave no sign of noticing. Then I saw I would have to wipe my boot hard before I went in my Wife's home. The black of his brogans could never again be total; they were too worn and could only be ephemeral. He was going on about some of the shops, he mentioned some names. Then when says he, '...Chitty...' I grabbed his scruff, caught some of his lank hair, and dragged him off my land. Says I, 'I think we can manage on our own.' I went back to speak with my Wife, cool off a bit, see if she needed to apologize for me again. My anger swelled again when I looked at my hand and realized I would need to wash that hard too. His shoe polish was not only for his feet.

~Lowin~

Yes, I am a Love girl, but it doesn't seem to be in my future. Love. And I accept that. I've had three attempted suitors. I thought the first would stick, love is love, are there varying degrees? That does not sound like a Love thing to say, not one of our chants, calls, or hollers. He went to Thee Tower. My second swooped in with the first birds. Those same birds soon met him at Thee Tower. The third waited a year, my black wardrobe had been downgraded to grey. The birds had their fill with him. The trinity all passed within my bed. As I watched the smoke from this last man's bones

rise from Thee Tower, I decided three was enough. I'm fairly certain there is no curse, but it seems that, again, *only a dead man is safe.* You only pass this place once, and I don't want to foreshorten that for anymore. So, I didn't ask the reasoning, but when Ibold gifted me her old box, I gladly accepted. Not that I deserve it, yet it was nice to have something go my way. I asked if he would return it to the hole, so I might know where it is when the time is nigh. The time was the first night and everyone after until there are none. I went up to that hole the first night. I laid in the box and watched the stars pass through the branches of the giant ash. And I closed my eyes. When I woke, I was alone and none had passed, which is how it should be. In Fall the stars took the place of the diving leaves. In Winter I raised a tarp. I angled it so the snow slid to the ground and so it still afforded a glimpse of the clouds that were hiding the stars behind. In Spring I dodged the hailstones that competed against the stars for my attention. It has been almost a year. My clothes are still black, but that is only from being outside, sleeping in a box in the ground. I might graduate to a dark grey if the Summer stars combine with the ash tree, combine with rain, and wash this coat from me.

~*Luce*~

My birthday — as well as Luxe's — falls upon Dec.25. This is one thing I will always have in common with Him. I want more. I've heard often that He suffered. Now, I don't know if I actually want that. However, I am suffering at the moment. I wonder if His friends dragged Him to Scare...'s field on His birthday? I wondered if Marcus, Lucius, or Jonas made Him listen to their songs on His own day. Then again, the more I think upon it, those three Nimrods don't seem to have many talents outside of...let us just say that they are single-minded. Well, my friends are just trying to be nice, and truly, in the only manner that they know how. But, I can't stop my head from wandering...maybe if I stoned him he would stop singing. Oh Luce, just be nice, you can tell Luxe at home. Ahmen, that is a humorous vision. I wonder if He ever joked. Oh no Luxe, now they're singing a song about you, they wish you could be here. I suppose it could be worse. To suffer a stoning or a song? My thoughts can't combat that kindness. So for all of our birthdays, I'll try. In fact listen to this, I suppose we've been practicing for reason. I'll make their charitable bewailing decent. After all, I don't want to make anyone suffer. Scare... I'm glad you're here to listen.

~*Lugar*~

Well, Amzie is back. Says Alazon, 'It's not a hill I'm willing to die on, you all stop the fuss.' I thought it was a bit funny. Eustache won't speak with her. Amzie has anger at him, but she also feels bad. She even removed the rocks

she put in his shoes. She is still too nice sometimes. I met her new friend. The three of us have grown closer, not Eustache. I like Amzie's friend, she is a bit older than I am. Though it seems like we are of a same age. She is not dumb...she is a Dumb...but she is just different. Mayhap if Amzie was raised in her environs the one would be the other. She showed me the rocks she had thrown to scare us...oh, that's right, so she never told Eustache that was her. If she ever gets an apology she said she might let him in on it. He thinks he deserves an apology as well. I will learn from Alazon here and stay out of it. I am happy she is returned and that I met her friend. We have had artists in our clan, yet, it was always art for promotion. Telling people when and where in ostentatious colors and fictional realisms that could never be achieved. Her pictures are subtle. They seem archaic to me, at least what I imagine ancient story tellers might have worked in conjunction with, an embellishment for their failed words. She says she has those. I don't agree. She does not speak as we do, but she gets her point across; the words are only different. She thinks she doesn't have a point. If she does, she does not know what it is. So she is trying to find it with her pictures. I've had enough of Forktine for a bit. Though, when Spring fully arrives and we have the miniature midnight boat festival I'll participate. No one had ever added a sail to their models before. Mayhap people thought it would just burn from the candles mounted in the boats. I had a new idea. If I placed the candle aft at an angle of the mid-mast sail, the heat would work to push and propel the craft. What about the imbalance you might ask? Well, I was thinking, is that one of the things her rocks could be for? I will put a mid-size one in the hull of the bow, finding a perfect one to counterbalance the physics. But, I think they are all perfect, so no matter what happens I know it will be not only the best looking model but also the best intentioned. I told Amzie's friend of my plan then asked if I could buy a picture from her. Says she, 'Thank You,' and she blushed a subdued red. I hope she uses that color on the sail.

~*Luxe*~

He used to let me into his building every Saturday night. All services were long over, so it was empty. He said it did not bother anyone. We started singing so early. I think we spoke to one another in a secret twin language before we actually spoke. But, it was obvious to both of us when I began to surpass her. We never spoke of that either. I could hit all the up notes that she could only graze. She would slide to them then fall away. I would stand up straight and tall to them. Other boys heard me sing one time, and out of uncertainty and fear they attempted to chastise. And out of fear and uncertainty I said to all that I quit. That's when Fater said I could use his building. Because what I had is not something you are able to quit. So every Saturday I had Thee Cathedral and its sky-touching ceiling to myself, and of course Fater was there. He remained out of sight. I suppose

he was in his sacristy sitting and enduring my needs. Knowing, because of his chosen life, this was something he could not abandon himself of either. As we left every evening I was certain I saw upon his cheeks, wetness flash like mica from the moonlight. I would not look him in the face. I had no chapel to offer him. And he no longer has one to offer me. After that last Saturday that happened to fall on our birthday, says he, 'I'm done.' I had overtaxed him. I had put him through too much. Neither of us have ever returned. Neither of us has since wielded our craft.

~Mansard~

There are hunters, bakers, farmers, doctors, shepherds...I myself am a banker. The noisomeness has got to be confronted. My first trough I placed North to South in town. The next I positioned horizontally three quarters way above the Southern end. Everyone could get to one of the positions relatively easily from wherever they happened to be hauling their excreta. I dug a foot down, though only in the center, along the sides I patted with the flat back of my blade, creating the gentlest slope ever made by hand. Banker. To alls' relief. The cistern I created at the base of the inverted cross also needed to be dealt with. My second solution. I offered it to the gardeners and farmers. For a fee, I would construct a similar slighter system around Thee Land. I had deduced a recipe to convert the feculence into future wants. With my additives mixed in the proper ratio *the waste* was now a need. I maintain the banks; all my clients clean after themselves by scraping my ditches and cisterns dry. They come to me for my alchemy and reverse out my door backwards and bowing in gratitude. I have two tools, one's replaceable, my shovel and my heart.

~Marcinkus~

I apologize that I have been sitting here and have yet to speak. Sometimes it's just nice to be....I was about to say I don't know why I did it, but, I do know. He talked and talked, and I could only listen to so much. He just wouldn't let it be. Some of it is my fault, I should have stopped it immediately or found a way to be more understanding. Though we are not supposed to know them, I had accidentally learned who his Fater was...is. And he seemed ashamed. I had met the man. I actually enjoyed his quiet company when we both happened to be sitting in the foyer of Dr Dolan's place. Miss Moriah had tried to harm herself somehow. We didn't find out, the Doctor came out of his pass-through and was saying how *it was personal* when my Fater walked in. We are not supposed to know one another. He started speaking as he does, and I just nodded at him and walked out, Nilus' Fater leaving on my heels. As he shut the door we could hear my

Fater's voice get sucked into a vacuum. It was nice and quiet beyond his door. His Fater went his way, and I walked, as I do. I often find myself walking to Thee Wandering. I will start going from South to North with only my right foot in Thee Wandering and my left in our land. Or if I feel like it, I will do the opposite, start by Thee Wulf's Woods and go South until I hit Thee Cliffs, straddling my gate between both lands. I've never gone too far in. The sun, the heat, the slow scorching terror. It would be a hard end...I'm just going to sit here for a bit. I don't feel as if I am quite ready to depart.

~Marduk~

I won't tell you her name. That just wouldn't be appropriate. I don't want to put our future in jeopardy. We went to Thee Lake late that night. I was going to take our family's skiff out and...well, kind of go from there. She held my hand all the way there. The path came in from the Northwest. I wanted to take that one, it followed my favorite willow patch. Underneath the weepers she smiled at the turf, which was natural but looked manicured by a premeditative scallion's hand. The moon dappled through the hanging branches, creating a translucent tent. I felt her grip tighten. I was so naive that I could not determine if the squeeze was a warning or an invitation. My nerves behaved per usual, erring on the side of cordiality. Thinking that if she accepted the boat ride, well, then that would be a certain sign of her wants. If for some reason I misinterpreted then mayhap we would have an accident and my humiliating rejection would be submerged. Our modest dock was just South of the copse. The larger path that carts use arrived from that sparser direction. There was a film of moisture between our hands; she still held on. Yet, I as well still held onto the uncertainty of my position with her. The frogs were barking from the pickerelweeds. When our steps echoed in the space between the dock and the water, a family of water birds shifted in the sedges and rushes. I've seen the duck potato plants there in the daylight so I am assuming it was the family of canvasbacks. We never saw them, yet I could feel their initial shifting freeze into a spring shaped tenseness, ready to burst to safety from the nocturnal unknowns. Our hands made a soft kissing noise when I released her hand in disappointed dismay. The skiff was gone. Was there another brute circumventing my cunning plan? She grabbed my hand; it felt protective. Did she think I feared what lurked in the shore-weeds? The soft, slow splash came from somewhere out in the darkness of Thee Lake. It was no goose or beaver tail, not catfish escaping the sloughed depths. Something had eased into the wet. I tried to listen, and though there was not another splash, I thought I could hear the drip of water from an oar in respite. Then the distinctive squeal of our un-oiled left oarlock began a rhythm. I had attempted to quiet it in various manners. But the gunnel

seemed to be the issue. She began pulling me off the dock. I was ready to confront my antagonist and pulled loose with a moist suck. She persisted. She ducked us inside the camouflage. We were soon insulated in the coverings of one of the willows. We still gripped one another. The moon illumined all; I thought we would be seen and at the moment had no need to fear. I wanted that boat. Then...The blackness never totally released the five forms. Two rowed, two perched in the bow, and a cox balanced on the transom knee in the stern. We unconsciously slide deeper in the hide. They took the same path we had entered on. As they passed soundlessly by our naked veil, I could not differentiate the forms underneath the black draping robes and pointed black hoods.

~Matrie~

Fairly certain that I have all the calls down. AHHAAHE... That's the one to call our beasts in. They are not too intelligent so we don't have to have separate calls for each. OEOphEI... Get inside. LaLiphaliaLaLIphI... Of course that is my favorite, supper. Hey, do you know these? Wait, do you have your own calls? Oh...you should, but instead of calling beasts like us, you could call them away. You could use ours, but mayhap backwards. EHAAHHA... That sounds neat. Go on, try it... ...Don't be intimidated. I know I sound good, but I'm just a little kid. If I can do it you can... EHA... Alright, how about this. I started with hollers, with a lot of them you just answer me back. This is me asking if you are coming; KaLINGKaLANGka... ... ... Erm...I guess you're not coming. So, just to make clear, YOU ANSWER MY HOLLER... Good thing the Cannonballs aren't teaching you their chants, they'd set you alight for not being witchy. uuUUURRRRMMMMMUUUURRruu... Don't know what that one was, do you? That's one I just made up especial, and it's just for you. What do you have to say to that? ... That's right, just what I thought. I'll come back everyday and curse you if you cross me. You'd better keep your mouth shut, or you'll never make it in this place.

~Meigs~

I'm a lost marker in this contest. Not a thing to redress. I've been eclipsed by your memory. When I was a little boy I went to Thee Giant Tree Of Despear with my boyfriends. We wanted to get high. If we went to the Love Forest there was a good chance of climbing into one of their houses, so to Despear we went. As used to be the case I was first. I climbed past the wound where most others stop. It was early in the year, the branches weren't bowed. I could see the crown. I marked out my last path ahead. But, my foot did not see the path that I was still on. On my first step my foot caught in a ribbon. The hopes, even wishes of others. The fall was fascinating. I

was falling with my back to the ground. It seemed ponderous. I remember thinking that I could still grab the wish that tripped me up, it was right there behind the scudding clouds, that one cloud the shape of a panicky rabbit. Then another branch met my spine. The time I had gained in the leisurely prelude was soon lost. There was a chaos that slammed into an abrupt coda. I will never again bound as a roebuck. Most bodies fail with age, I only have my mind to war against me. That was my first procession. My boyfriends lifted me on an unused door they had found somewhere nearby. I don't remember, being early within my daze. My first true memory of this new life was wondering why they were carrying me raised above their heads. A stretcher configuration seemed natural. Yet, mayhap without me to lead that was their first instinct. They carried me in relief. As we neared town I could hear the crowd grow. I could feel nothing when I rolled my eyes to watch the hands from the swelling audience brush my skin in beatification. The flowers thrown upon my steadfast form smelled of lilies and roses, accompanied by a lone lotus. I could shift my eyes to the left and right; I could glimpse the scalps of the aging men, an occasional ribboned bow of a larger woman. My other senses would grow with the loss of one. The ritual parade was followed by every voice I had ever known. It was a reverential hum that accompanied our march. I drew even with the branches of the olive trees. We were at the North end of town. When they first attempted to bring me into Dr Dolan's surgery they were made aware of the odd manner in which they bore me. My plinth smacked his lintel. They soon realized their mistake. It's not put to too much practice. I begged and pleaded; they looked down upon me the entire journey we made to you.

~Missal~

Her face run out of room. She smile so big. She no know what had happen yet. I no know either. She holler me over, and I come see her dug up patch of land. She could not garden ever because of rock. Her Jerimiad dig it all cause says she, 'Dig it all.' And he did…dig it all. All the big, medium, and smallish rocks he pull out. Long, hard work. He hate the garden. Always has. That why the rocks lounge inside it so long. Says he, 'Everyone has a garden. They can't give enough of enough away, it makes no sense.' Now the wagon sits there, full of rock, overlooking her garden. Says she, 'Now if he would only take that wagon away.' She want to work that patch too where the rock-wagon sits. But she so happy, she start working the soil as she showing me. She work into sunset, the wagon full of rock casting nice cool shade from up high on the hill. It so cool in the shadows she keep working into night. Her bright teeth shine in joy and show her where to spade. I leaving. I remember waking in the middle of night. *Boom, Boom!* I think Alazon is shooting his little Cannonballs. I went back to sleep, thinking tomorrow be long. Why do people say, *sleep like log*, not, *rock*?

~Moriah~

Neither of them ever truly caught me. Both of them, always and forever, have been jealous of the other's bump. The bumps they shoved in me. Now they are going to go and end it all. It seems as if they are the two feuding Brothers, not their sons. Dueling over a Mother's love. *He got a bigger piece...You always take his side...I always get blamed...It's his fault...*One of them dulled me into submission with his verbiage. I wanted to do anything to get him out of there quickish, putting my mouth on his unmentionable to end the process. The other dulled me into the same submission with his spectacular dullness. Again, mouth, tongue, over and done. But, it has never been over with either of them. Both kept trying to catch what can't be caught. Skulking around, then seeing the other doing likewise the peacocking starts. I should have walked into Thee Wandering and put an end to it all. It might be that this is all my fault. At least half...is that the math? There are two boys and two men, but one Mother...I don't even know the boys, yet if they are anything like their Faters...Well this land has had it. I might remove all my clothes. I've never been truly naked. I could go sit in the snow, dull myself down into listlessness, finally catch my death.

~Muff~

I'm going to kill him. I'm not going to say sorry. A deer horn? I know it's going to be unnatural, as he has done to my Husband. No, no, a deer horn is too kind, too quick. I can't defile a beast that way. A blade, a hatchet? They will probably rust through...wait...we suspected him right off, but when he returned to our land in the guise of selling us used barrels, we knew for certain. My Husband even bought them, trying to one-up the little coney. So that is it, there is my plan. I will nap him with a deceit, bring him to our land. It won't take much, but knock him dull with a hatchet butt. Stuff him in one of the barrels. And here it is...Ha! Ready? Fill it with his *assault* of choice. Thank you. We've had two men drown in a silo. This will be an encore. I'll tilt his head back just so, leaving only his face to know the air. From his thinning widow's peak to his ferret chin will be an imperfect circle of white. The only imperfection due to himself. I'll take my table spoon and start feeding him. Feeding him and feeding him and feeding him. Of course a bit of sauce on top to wet it down. I don't want him to dry out too quickly. Mayhap, I will have the barrel situated on the same hill from where he made his final assault. It's a good view, a good, good hill. If he is somehow able to speak he could say he was *willing to die for that hill*. Then I will say, *you are correct, but I'm not.*

~Mull~

My fingernails are all gone, I wadded them up and left them with Mahout. Everyone up there would eye-hump me. Yes, I'y'm a bit twitchy, but I have good reason. There's not much choice for one such as me up there, get sent away, submit...so I went underground. I'y've dug tunnels everywhere under this land. Certainly I go up every now and again, some people are even friendly towards me. Boucher leaves scraps of the high-brows scraps out for me, no offal. But, mostly I find everything I need when I dig. Slag and dross and much that comforts me. It is fascinating what people think they have hidden by disposing of it. I'y'm keeping that cant dog until I find whose hand it is from. But the most amazing thing I found in my home underground is this other *person*, Jonas Groan. He be a Hunter. I give him one of my best prizes: the backbone of a hellhound. Thinking, *here 's' one who understands*. I still keep faith toward him, though I had much disappointment when he double-crossed me and re-gifted my gift by giving it to the humps above ground. They are the ideal of cowardice. And...I should know.

~Negus~

We found out that Solomon had recently found an apron floating on the river. Why can't I have that luck? I deduced there must be ladies stripping down to, if not nakedness, at least their unmentionables. During a period of free blocks myself and some Brothers went to the river in hopes of having some prosperity, skulking in the bushes to spy the bathing nymphs. That would be worth any treasure. I mean who really wants a piece of the covering when you can witness what it is supposed to be covering? It was myself, the twins Curtius and Custus, and Faunus. It was all bumph talk while getting to the shore. Faunus and I broke away so we might not be subjected to twin traits. He's quiet, which at that moment was what was wanted. We hunted the shore, skulking North and then South. No ladies, nymphs, or teasing garments. We got the twins to stop nattering so we might listen for any seducing chorus. Still nothing. Faunus told us of how he would watch Solomon fishing, he showed us an assorted pocketful of hooks he had retrieved from snags that fishermen through the years had left to rust. The twins grew bored and were soon in the water wrestling. Faunus put me on his shoulders, and we were soon joined in battle against Curtius and Custus. We put the best game of kick-rock to shame. The wooden chest bobbed and dunked as we ourselves did. My straddling legs felt the slow turn of Faunus' head as he stopped the game to follow this phenomenon. The upper combatants dismounted. It took all of us to tote it to the Western shore. It was unwieldy, partially full of water, and another weight we soon discovered. Opening the trunk, the stench made us retreat

in hilarity, daring one another to investigate. We went as one, though Faunus was the first and only one to touch it. He pulled out offal and a sodden body that was unrecognizable to any of us. If death occurred prior to its being interred we could not tell. It could have passed just as easily from basic lack of oxygen, either from the closed lid or the water. It was only of interest to Faunus. He prodded and poked at the desecration. His distraction was total. The twins and myself saw our opportunity. It was a free block at the river, the ladies and their garments never showed. But, we could use this. We would put kick-rock and chicken wars to rest forever with this new foray. The acrid filth was booty to our young noses. We battled to command the trunk, two ships fought to dethrone who would be the new King! As I was fending off the attack of the twins I saw Faunus attempt to cradle what he could in his arms. He departed, oblivious to us now, enthralled by this intoxicant.

~Neimiah~

It was legion; I stood on Thee Cliffs and witnessed in awe. I watched the naturalness of the outer world, the perfection in the storm, come to do battle with our seemingly unnatural bulwark. I witnessed Polly. Was it a hurricane? I think not. It was singular. As I gazed down upon this colossus I was reminded of Polly's descent, a gradual momentum that accelerated into an impending holocaust. The bulbous clouds shifted from light charcoal in hue to a hybrid of glass corn, and of course climaxed within a species of black tourmaline. They looked a Calvary tightly circling their General, who was calm yet encouraging while rousing them for the battle to come. If I leaned a bit over the edge I thought I might hear the hulking waves of foot soldiers slamming and testing the defenses. Though, I was not certain. My ears were then assaulted by a gang of house sparrows. With their monochrome, infantry dullness they were fast upon a single bluebird, evicting him from his rightful home for no other reason than to push history backwards. I felt a bit of breeze then, from the hurricane avalanching below. The thirty-two sparrow wings, mayhap my own sigh at knowing my safety was assured as up on high upon Thee Cliffs I remained, to not leap into the battle below with the expendable hoplites. Though we live overlooking Thee Sea, no storm can touch us. I was only alone, in that I stood apart. It is a holiday of sorts for a crowd to gather. Packing a picnic, reacquaint with lost ones, and if a bachelor might be a plunger, a reckless bettor, bring a first-date. The holiday ends when the faintest mist rises to kiss the hem of the dresses and the waxed toes of the boots. I don't know why I thought that day might end on a different note. This was myself, with an unbroken basket lid. The storm foolishly gathered all of the gusto it could muster, slamming headlong into the wall. I leaned and wiped the fresh dew off my boot, pleased at seeing it was so insignificant that my

boots would be fine with their monthly care and polish. Unpleased at once again finding that this was no way to come by, and no way go.

~Nephthali~

It was my fault. I admit this much to you. When they brought him in it was chaotic. Dr Dolan was with the child so they brought him to me for some reason. Come think of it, I remember them saying they saw the candlelight from my window. So my candle...I warm him as best I could. Crack off his frozen clothes. Got him to take down hot water. Buried him under blankets in the bed with three heated bricks. He made it through the night. He asked about the boy when he first exhumed himself from the cocoon. Through the week he could not get sufficiently heated. He came to me once again, and at the same time they had dragged him in, thinking this was my chosen normal. I asked why he didn't go to Dr Dolan, he pointed to my candle that drew him. The look on his face befuddled at my asking. He had a severe cold. He had difficulty hearing my hushed late night voice. He mentioned ear discomfort; he would never acknowledge pain. We aren't the Dumbs, but we have some techniques I have seen work wonders. Until he could see the Doctor in the light of morning, I would try and draw his ailment out. He again laid in my bed. Once propped on his side, held upright and fortified in a wall of bedding, I slid the tapered candle in his ear. I didn't slide this insert through a dish or cup, I knew I could clip it. He watched the flame with his walleye. I reached for my knife so I could trim the candle, not wanting it to drip hot wax on him. I was in my nightgown, my knife was hanging in its sheath on the far wall. His one eye saw this in the low light. He is politeness. He went to hand me his knife. As he shifted to reach the knife under his opposite hip the pooling wax spilled from the candle. It hit his hair and the obnoxious smell was instant. He tried to calmly right himself. He was so methodical in his carefulness that I panicked and reached for the tipping candle. My flailing grasp snapped it in his canal. The remaining lit shrapnel landed in his framework cocoon. I attempted to extinguish him with other bedding, it was just as combustible. He fought me off, outwitted his blindness to find the door, and submerged himself outside in a bank of snow. Once again he was dragged through the night. Dr Dolan extracted the offending stump from his ear. He salvaged what he could of the skin. One side of his head looks as a frozen, blistered, red flow of magma. He can hide his other attacks under his unmentionables, no one would ever see them. Mayhap he could wear feathers in his hair, mimic one of the long-legged Birchen he loves.

~*Nestor*~

That child, he has no idea how many others have beads wallowing away in their pockets. He thinks that if he wears through them it will all be gone, his hatred will be completed. No, no, I have a small chest filled with more and more. He will come to make certain his penance is complete, that there are no more prayers to be said. I wish I could give him a different answer. I can't judge his judgments upon himself. It might turn out well in the end. The Dumbs could have themselves a reasonable liaison between us and their archaic superstitions. I still call him child, no, no, I just always remember him as sitting on the porch with them, always ebbing closer to his Mother. Mayhap I am to blame. I never spoke up, believing it was not my place to intercede. Now he sometimes follows me around, at my heels like a puppy at the age I will always remember him at. I don't know what he's told you, hopefully something. He has strained to speak with me, made his fingers bleed for squeezing them so. But then he runs. I have heard him up on my house in the middle of the night. When I asked what he was about, says he, 'Just inspecting the worthiness of your roof.' He returns often. The first time was the next day, he repatched my entire roof. He sang low and sad all through the labor. I know his affection for words, the book I gave him would assist. Now when I hear him sitting and rocking on my new roof, he is chanting those words in a perpetual repeat. Inches above my body finding reprieve on the bed he delivered to me. I try to chant with him, to guide him. But then I always hear a drone and hum. At first I thought he was complete. No, no, I tell myself. And I always drift off to sleep, praying I remember to leave my swatter in the eaves for when he returns. My memory is slipping.

~*Nilus*~

In the snow he tried to drown me. I knew who his Fater was, he knew mine as not an antagonist, but *The Antagonist*. Brothers will fight, we were that and more. We did that and more. We spoke no more words. He's not as loquacious as his Brothers. I wasn't speaking to him, though I made certain he could hear. My Brothers around me smiled nervously. His Brothers did the same. When he finally looked my way is when I smiled. That might have done it. He came over to me, and I don't remember what I tried to say, he open-palmed me with such severity my stomach drowned out my speech. He dragged me outside and commenced my submersion. I remember being under and giggling at how abnormal the situation was. *Who fights someone by dunking them in snow?* I thought, *is this even a thing, is it possible?* I soon found that it was effective. Dangerous on multiple levels. He was relentless in his force. The crystals covered my nose, then my panicked breath melted so the liquid begin to enter where it began to

150

freeze from the extreme temperature. I opened my mouth to scream and the same experiment in chemistry engaged my throat. Any noise I made was muffled by the deepening drift that he was exploring with my face. I passed out. I truly do not remember anything afterwards. I know it's hard to believe when people say I'm being honest, but...*I'm being honest*. I know we are supposed to fight our own battles. And I will once my wounds heal. None of our Brothers interfered before or after, frostbite, hypothermia, concussion from the initial hit. My Fater, — whom I'm not supposed to know — interrogated me. So I was almost as honest with him. He said he would *take account*. That's his way of speaking, sometimes I am truly grateful to be here. Honest, I am.

~*Nola*~

I had to watch him do it. No one has ever loved me like that, and I wanted to witness what pushed him. He would have had better luck pushing a boulder. He borrowed a wagon to get it out there. At first I didn't understand why he unloaded. I wondered at his sending the cart away, and why he would not put it to work. I eventually understood. Now I don't. He unscrewed the one-inch wheels that were affixed. Put his shoulder against the profile of the piano. I thought he was resting before he began, mayhap he was whispering a prayer into filigreed embellishments. Then it budged. He is not the biggest man, his traits did not lend themselves to this endeavor. Most would say he is panicky, even twitchy. I could not hear the discussion from my hiding place when Polly arrived. They were both yelling in a whisper with clenched teeth and set jaws. He spread his arms wide so she could not grab the flank. She went up to the forging flank and attempted to kick away the gathering rocks. It was a futile. As he continued his flagellation she rounded from uphill, as he passed she depressed eight C notes until he drew even with her. She brushed his shoulder as he pushed, that was all the reassurance he needed. He loved her unconditionally, still does. And she had enough kindness to let him face this task. The clouds grew with the gathering crowd. All wanting to bear witness upon this oddity. Faribault said the swath behind him appeared to be from a panicked stampede from the hunted. The swollen clouds were reflecting the arrayed light from the sun falling behind Thee Mountains. Polly walked through the crowd — she had left at lunchtime — and began hiking up Jackass Ginnie. Her smooth-bottomed performing shoes slipping on the sleek path he left in his wake. Her stool upended, balancing on her head, its wheels increasing their spin from the building wind. She passed him. She set her stool down, then herself, on the crested lip at the peak. He positioned the pedals to her waiting, soiled feet. The first note fell in a perfect synchronicity with the first drop that kissed the scar of Jackass Ginnie.

~Okhrana~

Finally I no longer need to fret about my health. Nineteen years they gave me to brood over my head. The tenterhooks seemed to be pulling at me from inside that hole. When I was born I had a hole in my head. Not a hole like Mister Frye has, mine was because my skull would not fuse. I squirmed out of my prudish Mother and my head was a form of new geometry. But I had the fortune of Youtsey. She showed her love to me before she moved on to that other. She fed me from her own breast and manipulated my head into an acceptable shape. No one knows of this. She informed me after she installed herself elsewhere. She molded my soft head, giving me high cheekbones, a button of a nose, eyes aligned to visual perfection. But she could never cover the hole in my head. The hole could not be permanently addressed until my body stopped growing. I had to wear headgear until last month. Helmets that hid my faultlessness from Youtsey's hand. Because none saw my supposed beauty, including myself, Youtsey instructed me on my behavior. Kindness and humility I wield swordlike underneath my helm. The rules were myriad, and I obeyed all demurely. A strong wind could eclipse my life. No walking under trees, pinecones would be a deadly shrapnel. No kick-rock, an errant kick, a high flying rock would certainly seek my soft spot. Swimming, dancing, even laughing with too much vigor were anathema. But nineteen years and my penance is complete. They affixed the plate to my head, brushed my purposeful long locks over the fortifying talisman, and now I am my complete self. I have stood on the side and observed how all live their life. Or, in most instances, don't live. I will perfect this as well. I will speak with the boys. Swim with Nilus. I will dance under the trees with Marcinkus. I will repay Youtsey, she seems so overwhelmed. I will aid her in her work. I will show Josias my shield, and he will be happy for the future. I will let Pael tap and rub my triple-lamina, luck and good fortune for all. This life is about to truly begin. I march off to explore this land, my destiny is certain.

~Olazabel~

A friend is giving. Always thinking of others well being before his own. Memorizes and lives the shalt nots. Which could really be one shalt not, which is, *one shalt not be bad, but good*. Which is not me. I'y've done too much bad in my life, my failings is many, too many for myself, Olazabel, to even try to form a friendship. The effort would be futile. And frankly the philosophy, tradition, and gall of the practice are grating. I'y've found people who want to inflict me with their friendship. I always let them grind away at their half of the task, then...well...let us say we both begin to search for a superior partner. I'y've been called crass and lazy. After tallying my accomplishments, I call it cunning. It is true where I do

152

not have to sweat, I do not, I say, 'Let your friends work for the privilege.' — Ah...I'y'm so worn from talking. I'y'm turning it over to my...*friend*.

~*Pael*~

I rang the doom when I tapped her plate. I feel it in the hum of Thee Mountains. I walk round Thee Lakes and slog through the now-muddied and broken shore. When I touch the skin of the trees, I feel Thee Wandering's heat warping them. Below my bare feet the grasses are singed. The flowers I woo with encouraging strokes have wilted to a limp. Jackass Ginnie quaked at my contact. I taste the bile in Forktine; the new gravity of Thee Falls insistent in my demise. This wounded land is throbbing a rhythm summoning all to war.

~*Pelasgus*~

Custus believes he watches over him. He does, for incidental daily occurrences. However, in my position, I must oversee him in a more... esoteric manner. As with all the Brothers, there just has not been one like him before. Him, with his *factual* sounds. He is socially impotent, but when he interacts it is a charm offensive, the sense of levity lightened beyond the arc of normalcy. Our house has an ebb and flow that is paramount to it revolving as a true wheel. Though it was pleasing when he created this titillation, the downy strands on my neck rose. I began to monitor his behavior with persistent tenacity. I spoke with the Headmaster and was given permission to observe him from the slated view of the shed. His gathering was thorough. I had my own studies and other Brothers to attend, so I am certain there was and still is a bounty that I am purposefully ignorant of. His demeanor, inanities, and mental encumbrances disarmed all. His smile would be the envy of any double agent. Though his is genuine. Nothing was reported missing. I educated myself on his ways. His booty was peculiar. My imaginings moved from innocence to diabolical. He would vanish for a full day, my own life impeding on my care for him. I inspected his room. As I inspected his trousers I found the cuffs wet with the perfume of Forktine. He shared a room with Custus who woke abruptly and pulled the trousers from my hand, pleads he, 'Please don't tell, he can't control himself.' I let him believe that this fell back to his incidental daily occurrences. But, I had all I needed. I left the murder hole of the shed and sequestered myself on Forktine's shore. I thought mayhap I was incorrect, then I saw him straining upriver, a stuffed sack as his companion. I knew he loved the water. I had no chance of matching him in a water vessel, and his swimming put his paddling to shame. I returned to the the shed's big brother. The barn; the former dining hall. There I mounted Enbarr's dam. I rode her hard, cutting across the upper field, finding the causeway

and halting upriver gambling that Custus might travel this far. He traveled excessively further. After spending the day falling behind, dodging copses, sprinting ahead to wait at a known oxbow, he finally ended his journey at Thee Wulf's Woods. He removed the sack, lugged it into the second level of trees, the first one I could see that had bred bred with a cross. There he climbed and suspended the sack, beyond most known creatures' reach. He returned to his canoe, smiling and babbling one of his faultless melodies. I remained to surveil the act. Hour by hour by hour by...I went to check the sack. I attempted to climb, and it was my last laughable remembrance. On my back. Back on the ground, I saw the left hand shadow. This shadow split in two. I retreated slowly. To my right, an even larger shade. It remained as one, a rose on a tree, posing in a silhouette, making certain that it allowed me to witness its presence. I crab-walked in horror. I found Enbarr's dam huffing and rolling her eyes, attempting to release her reigns from the sapling I made her millstone. We fled. Hour by hour by...this is why I am here with you. The dam needs a blow. My mind needs one as well. I cannot piece together his purpose. Can I save him from this? Is it in my purview? He is a good boy, do I trust his innocence, weigh it against our bias of knowledge? His Brother would deduce this is simply for Mahout. No, no, this is not incidental. If he is aiding a human stain, I fear for him. If he is courting the Wulf, I fear for him; and for us, one and all.

~Pellis~

I am way beyond twelve year old. My life love, who was once two years younger than myself, seems as if she has passed me in age. I'y've finally got a knowledge of my fiddle, yet, a funny thing is that by the time I stuck my head back out the doors — because I determined myself not to leave until me and my fiddle had come to an understanding — well our house was floating up in the air. It seems I took longer than I thought I might. Meantime the trees come up out of the ground carrying our house on their shoulders. Well, truthfully, it has turned out fine. Me and my love got romantic about the view and held one another even harder. And that is nice. Now we got little Loves monkeying around through the trees' arms. I had the genes that expected me to be a wrong type person, but my Loves have forced me otherwise. So I teach what I know. I tell of the bad I once was made for, then teach talk of other choices. I'y've teached music and steps, words and philosophies, giving each the knowledge and ability to at least think they can have a choice.

~Petr's Widow~

Some say he took advantage of me. I say, some say too much. Sometimes I feel I should say more and tell these folks there is no afterlife. But, then again, I am the only ghost here. I married Petr, then next day I'y'm alone. Now I think about it, I still am. See, Petr and his family had this idea that if no one is here to guard the family home and land, then the Wulf, or worse, would squat down and make it their own. Petr's family felt that they fought hard for this land and will take on any comers who think they can fight harder and make it their own family's. So even though I was fifteen, my bones were so sick they made me look as if I was as old as Petr. He said he would cure me if I liked. I said I would give my life and more to be able to stand up straight. So he took me up on it. He made me this contraption that he calls only a cane, but if u've seen it you know it would bowl over any cane. And because he kept his word I'y'll keep mine. I lived there all my living life, keeping away everything, and now in my dead life I do the same. I keep away everything by singing. I hear people say the place is haunted. I'y'm only singing, and I sure have seen no other ghosties here or anywhere. Do not tell me it is haunted. That brings up another matter of philosophical believing, if I have not met let alone seen another ghost being, then am I an anomaly? Did I throw my whole afterlife away because we all fear something we don't not know?

~Polk~

There's always a rug in the room. Nice to get out of it though, so, thank you for that. Why don't you ever sit? I mean I know you got's a job to do but...Is that my chair? No, no...I'll just sit myself down and keep you from feeling loneliness. I sures like talking to you. Look at your hat, it's all marbled with sweat. You know you're not going to keep any friends around if you don't take proper care. I got this girl who comes to me because she just can't figure out how to wield her social graces. So I's showing her. She's harrying the dogs, says I conspiratorially to you my friend; sotto voce sotto voce. I should get back to her, the poor thing...she's due back anytime and I know she would crumble if I weren't there. I'm having a tough go looking at you; that is some failed hat. Has your friends never said? Well, I says it now. If I had the room I'd 'vite you over for the dinner. It will be grande. I should have thought on you earlier, some of these staple-headed folk do not deserve my hospitalities. Oh, I see that makes wide your eyes. Jealousy? Not a admirable quality, sir. You would fit in well with this lot. But, I'd need to wipe you down a bit, you look like you've been invested in a dust-bath. I wouldn't want you shaming yourself in front of the company. I mean, they probably all twist their clothes to dry them, you know my meaning. Yes, I best get back. The place must be filling up, bumbling around their

ignorance without me there to show them the manner of things. Say, since you's obviously not using it, it would be proper of you to offer me this here chair I'm keeping warm for you. You know, in case I get some unexpected trespasser or someone I forgot that I had extended an invitation to, I at least want to show them I'm proper. They all want to take a drink, take a break, take a meal, take a seat; I can't stand while people are lying down.

~Rafe~

She ate everything in sight, which was an interesting change. She had railed against me for years that I ate too much, that she would have to take on additional work. My Mother used to treat me with much love, the majority came in the form of *ingestables*. The whole family was large. But I took the challenge of *improving* on my siblings, having more *success* than my parents. Yet, I also wondered at people who were thin, jealous of their heredity and being able to wear clothing that fit. The guilt from my Mother was a hinderance, my self-will was not an option. But, finally when there was no crutch in front of me, I began to walk. As she swelled I mimicked her; in reverse. I deflated. I did not realize this was happening. I was working so hard, earning more and more to keep her content that I didn't even think to look for my crutch. When people saw me for the first time after this began   they asked of my health. I thought to myself, odd question, why not ask about my pregnant wife? I was in charge of the washing during the time, I worried she would swing one of her moods at me because the clothes were no longer fitting correctly. When she eventually asked if I was feeling unwell, she cut off my answer by showing me her stretch marks. She broke into her tears. I mimicked my Mother and brought her much love. I took a long hard look at myself...After the birth she took to a quiet mood, said she didn't think I would ever want to touch her again. I had always made certain it was dark before, yet I de-robed in the light. Then I did the same to her. I took her hand, and we stood side by side in front of the looking glass. We took a long hard look at ourselves. When I lay on top of her, our scars mimic one another. Lining up and touching in imperfect perfection.

~Regius~

I shan't tell you who is my Fater, my benefactor. He is a clean man. He once was a man of the people...I believe. The purest this place knows. He had one black mark, myself. I have vowed to redeem him. I will have no black mark. My purity will buoy his one failing. His deep well of faith I draw from. From this well, I gather the unadulterated milk that cleanses me. What be the meal bears no consequence. I will only drink my milk. Water, wine, brandy: these are vanities that I will never imbibe. As a shepherd

carries a crook, a blacksmith carries a hammer, a fisher a rod, I carry a glass-blown jar containing my milk. The taste matters not. Only the result. I need no flagellating cane or whip. My succor will one day bring peace, yet with it also comes payment. The hives that mount my body are quick and fierce. My lips swell, my eyes close. The single small red bumps gather and amass into large weals of penance. No, no, I will have no black marks. The white on my lip will cover and quell any affront. It will drown, cleanse, then rebirth any attempt by darkness to influence this land and the people herein. All man's sins are his own. And because I will have none I am capable to stand against them. It might be a task I am unworthy of. Yet, I will quest to purify all.

~Rujo~

So she blackmail him. We barley even fly no more. Said she would leave if she didn't not get her way. I couldn't hear their *discussing*, but, I saw her bag. I had to shimmy to fit correctly. I hide in the deep parts of the cannon, and sounds always have an odd cast when I am in there. They would pass in and out of my round little view. I heard her tones and nothing from Alazon. As always. Then I saw her fly through the air, real quick, from one side of my view to the other. Then he walked real slow through that same path. I hear her clothes ripping, and he laughs. Well...as *he* laughs. More of a conclusion. Asks he, 'Hurt?' She don't respond. I hear him grunt and think, no, no, I must stop this mal-ness. I don't know what my little boy body could do, but mayhap an interruption would be enough. I start to crawl from the depths when I discover his sexing noises are him lifting and shoving her into the cannon. She slide down and landed on my head with no shimmy. She stuck me there. He concludes again. 'Ha...' laughs he. Saying no ramrod necessary, no lightening the load, no grease to fly, fly, fly. 'It's yours if you want it.' So now she have my job that I deserve. Says she, 'I'll be the best you've ever seen.' She blocks my view so I don't see him leave, I thought I hear his boots scuff off. But it was hard to hear with her start to cry. Her tears rolled down the length and cause she freezes my head I could not move when they flow into my mouth. Guess I might just have to cut off my little balls to get anywhere.

~Saugus~

One life was all that I desired. And that was all I took. Though it was the wrong one. Or was it? I thought by running Aristides into that ash I would quickly end it all. I did not, and it was not quick. Aristides was so devoted that he absorbed the majority of the impact of my demise. A broken clavicle, a concussion, cuts and scrapes were all that I could inflict upon myself while my steed assaulted the ash with the flat of his forehead,

splitting both it and the tree. His crest compacted into his withers, his chin groove un-grooved and folded back upon itself. The cannon of his front left leg snapped and flopped at me in farewell. The collision was such that as we both lay on the ground, the leaves from the ash were shocked into freedom, to float down to our positions and mop up the blood seeping from either his split head or flowing nostrils; the point being moot as the blood was doing no good where it was flowing, no matter its path. Laying next to Aristides, his breathing slowed, it reminded me of watching children in town play in the leaf piles with their siblings. I never saw the appeal. After Dr Dolan's examination, he looked at me as Aristides did, with one side-eye. Was it because I was unsuccessful, because I sacrificed such a faithful friend, or because I might do it all again? Well...It's what I deserve. There is a part of me that twists it around. Is it possible that this is what Aristides desired? Did he manipulate me? He might have been bullied at the barn, forced to eat alone, shunned by his Fater who I know he never knew. Mayhap they spit in the trough from where he was meant to drink, left their feces in his stall, hiding it under the hay so he only discovered it after a vicious night of no rest. Was he exhausted by it all and weary of attempting to calculate how much more time he had to endure?

~leumhS~

.hgin si elttab eht nehw ycamolpid esu ot yrt ylbaborp lliw ssApmuHregniG ehT .yalpsid edalb toy sih ni meht tnuom lliw I fi ro emoh ruo fo llaw eht ni spmuLraguS sih dna mih esacne lliw I fi si dediced eb ot sah taht llA .denimretederp si tI .daeheroFpalFhsaG sih tsniaga tohsgnils eht deppans I elihw sllab-elbram sih htiw eloHnigriV yreve gulp dna tsehc talf sih no tis dluow I dnA .sedalb fo yalpsid sih ni tsellud ot tseprahs morf gnivom ,sreyal ni niks sih snelF .setaks eht htiw mih ffo stiTehTkciK .ecno ta lla gnisu yb mih elzzad dluow I .tuo em kaerb ot mih rof sekat ti tahw si taht fI .enif neht ,yarra sih esu ot stnaw tnuCAfOsllaB taht fi ,tuB .eert a nwod ekat dluow taht ecam a dnA .nairtsedep leef I fi god-tnac A .sworra htiw wob hcnuMyssuP a tog neve ev'I .sekip dna sevats ehT .sremmah-bulc dna swalc-tac ehT .stab hguoht decreip slian dna ,sekip dna ,sexa era erehT .sniahc dna spihw ,solos ,sulu ehT .ereht kool ot kniht reve dluow eno on ,llaw eht dniheb meht dih I .yromra ym fo gnihton swonk eH ?eciohc fo snopaew eht no em gnirutcel ereht nwod s'eH ?kcirPgiB siht enorhted ot stnaw rehtorBkcoCelttiL ?stnaw eh raw ti sI .dnuorg daohCsAefaS eht no nwod morf em tnuat dna emoC ?foorp-htaed s'eh kniht eH .od ot gniog ma kcuFnmaD I tahw s'tahT ?drawkcab m'I em lleT .esuoh eht ni enola erew ew tnemom eht mih ffo I taht meht dlot I !nruBnruBnruB ti tel neht sserttam reh ni reh ffuts d'I reh no sdnah ym teg reve I fI .pu ti tuhs ot amelU hctiBAfOhctiBgnikcuFrehtoM taht rof detiaw I...eracS

~Simeon~

You probably don't recognize me, eh? Just kidding, oh...sorry, I shouldn't be slapping your back unless I want to get splashed, huh? No sense to come out of the rain? I'm outside as much as you...No, no, when the sun goes down I'm usually someplace with a roof. Alright, I am at Glaspell's and Veda's place. So we were only on our second cup, still polite, just a little loose. Everyone had de-coated, the fire was built up for the evening. They started in on me about my toils with some of the available young women. It was soon agreed on by all that my lip hair was the offending trait of my trials. By the fourth cup I was convinced of their logic. *You can't get the stink out-you ever kiss a girl with a mustache, it's repulsive-you have pulverized peas still in their from your toothless years-the freeze thaw cycle in there is a barometer all on its own-wait, you have had a girl like that so you do know the repugnance-aren't you ashamed that hers was even thicker than that worm?-* By the fifth drink I was leaning back in a chair and...well, someone I suppose, was having at it. I had been sporting it since I was first able. It was my half-life, a marker they just erased. I had seen them perform practical jokes on my peers. I was proud to be included. Those occasions were joined by continual laughter, guffaws, and barbs. When they brought me a looking glass they were all biting their lips, sounding like they were holding back sneezes. It seems they felt sorry for me. I looked at my image and saw a stark white shadow where once had been my courage. You see it on people's bodies at the beginning of Summer, but opposite, they are dark down their arms and the light is hidden under clothing. Plus it is nowhere near as lily-colored as my lip that had been in hibernation since I was a youth. When I realized that I could not possibly even speak to a woman for who knows how long, they all erupted. It was grand. The house had never heard a chorus like that. I was bought...well, I suppose many more cups. I don't know how I made it up here in this state and through the dark. Though my lip did light the way. Tomorrow mayhap I'll get out my shoe polish, dab a bit on, make them laugh even harder. Probably get me some more bought cups, I hope the drinks are cold even though I've naught to keep me warm.

~Solomon~

You ever been damned...just kidding, I've been waiting to say that...oh wait I need to tell you the rest for it to work. See I was out in Forktine watching the fish rise as I mended my line. Then I became a dam. I thought there was a brookie with a suicidal wish. I was feeling a kiss on my leg. Looking down I saw a woman's unmentionable enveloping my straddle. My mind immediately flowed with jealousy. Who was the fortunate son who removed these? Why was I always alone holding my rod? Ha! I didn't have to plan that one out, it just came to me. Then my mind jumped to a worst case.

What if this was a nefarious act? Whoever removed these was forceful, even not in their right mind. Before it pulled me down I raised it from the water. A talisman I held spread before the falling day. It was an apron. I had seen the men at Lodge rolling them into their telescoping containers. One day I hope to have one of my own. I thought I would try this one on to see how it felt. Squeezing my pole under my pit, trying to wend my line and still tease my fly, I fumbled the lambskin placeholder around my waist. It felt natural. The falling light was absorbed within then bearded outward out to illuminate about me. And I got a strike, playing it in I realized I didn't bring my creel. I stood in Forktine, wondering how to cure this temporary problem. Landed. I no longer tote a creel in my kit. The pocketed apron is more practical for my needs. I fear what a person might say if they witnessed me in the water. The girls and boys would jeer me once again. A woman would most likely retreat from the sight, her look accusing me of a forcible removal. The men would not offer me *to be one*. Maybe I have been damned.

~Solon~

If she were our Mother she would have been screaming his middle name. Mad was she. My Brother and I had a special place on Forktine, well on the bank I did; his was in it. He had gone earlier in the day. I had some *business* to finish before I could go. She was out in the current with him. I thought she was a starved hussy. Trying to pull his clothes off, so famished she was. I sat on the bank and got comfortable, settling in to watch this odd hippopotamic foreplay, an attempt at violence perpetrated by pacifists. When they attempted a prolonged double baptism I had to intercede. I walked down the steep Eastern slope, too steep, I slipped. In a trifecta we rose from the water. Their exchanged glances exposed a sudden a guilt that what they had done underwater produced another life. Their child spoke, 'Solomon, I've beaten you up our entire life, and if *you* are at best pulling even with him, then I know neither of you should be fighting.' My Brother stepped towards me in the East. She looked at myself, and then Solomon, and then myself, Solomon, and finally myself. From that day forward she would never look away. The yoke-neck dress she wore would soon be balled in my corner. She told Solomon to take the apron, she didn't need it any longer. He hauled himself up the darkening Eastern shore. My sweet and I paced gracefully up the gradual Western shore, slowly emerging onto the soft line and into the setting sun.

~Soufia~

I've chewed leaf my whole life. It soothes my empty belly, sometimes so much in a day that my mouth is numb. And, yeah, mayhap my head. When that son of a...I can't say that, I remember his Mother. When he said he wasn't going to pay me, there really isn't much someone like myself can do. I could go to Cap'n, he wouldn't even put me in cuffs knowing they would slip off my wrists. Fater Nigrescent, he would have brung us in for a sit-down-talk-it-through. His irrational thoughts had put him in such a windup he would have never sit still, especially after I did the only thing in my power. After he was done with his rant and walking away; from the back of my throat I let the wettest, heavy glob of muck go. Smack! I crowned him right on his bald, pink head. It wasn't all pink anymore. My sputum was brown-red, even with a mix of the *poor man's walleye*, yellow perch. I am guessing that yellow was from my years of chewing the leaf, whatever is gathering on the walls of my chest. I thought that was it, we both *said* our bit. That was half-a-year back. Then three months ago I see him again in town. I was up on the balcony and he was walking below. No, he was hobbling. Then I saw he hadn't wiped off my soft-bomb. Imagine that, half a year and no bath. It had aged a bit, grown reddish brown with a layer of fleshy crust. He took forever to walk on by. I thought mayhap he was taunting me into another spat. When I saw Dr Dolan race out and take his arm to help him gimp up those two feeble steps, well, I swallowed my words and spit both. When I hadn't seen him around again I went and asked Doc about it. He said saddish that he couldn't disclose that information to me. I made a joke by saying he seen me plenty times dis-clothed. I knew it was wrong the moment it left my mouth. Says Doc, 'You might want to consider giving up the leaf.' He still said it sad but with a little malignancy as well. I've gained a little weight, my gums aren't always numb. My chest feels lighter, but when I might cough I make certain to cover my mouth.

~Stump~

The funny thing is, she ain't none too good at the writin'. But her Ma never did get it. Her family had a tradition of givin' three gifts when one of the daughters declared their intentions. I was her intended. Her Ma was from a different time when daughters were not allowed to declare nothin'. She wore her dresses in a country manner and was not used to her daughters' loose way of speakin'. She did all of her own speakin' onto paper..
Her first gift was the man gift Me- it was a light made from Claudius. Claudius had been their best old percheron years back, he worked hard, touched mares, sired a dependable family line that is still paying off. He

161

had a commendable life, then he broke down in the pasture and the family turned him into a light. She told me to burn that light in times of darkness and Claudius would show me how *it's* done. I didn't get it...........................

The second gift was the woman gift -Daughter- it was a steel-hard shoe. She said it come from the wise old-wrinkle-lady of Thee Lupercalia. The woman told her of the greatness of the females in her line, and it was due to the tradition of this shoe. The women had to bind and bend their feet, then jam them into the shoe. The reformation was s'possed to make the woman more appealing. She told her Daughter that she couldn't force her, but, she should at least hang the shoe above her headboard as a reminder. Her Daughter didn't get it..

The third gift -Us- was that red book. She said when winter sets into our togetherness that we should write our complaints on the inside paper. She said that she understood that we were young and forward thinkin', that these days men were allowed to be womanly with their talk, not only the Daughter has to speak on paper. Then after the book is full up and we've stumbled out of love, to bring the book and ourselves to her so she could highlight our failings then learn us how to stay together, out of love, forever. Her intentions, we did not get...

        1. I didn't trip in the pasture
        2. We were both satisfied with her feet
        3. Neither of us carried a writin' tool

We sent the book back to her, without ourselves: empty. We included the hangin' shoe and Claudius' tallow. Maybe idyllic, maybe out of sass, not sure of our own intentions..

The three pieces were delayed in their return on account of Winter settin' in. So's when they did arrive here Ma didn't think on them none. All that was on her mind was Winter, she grabbed Claudius and turned that dead horse on. She crammed her foot in the foreign piece and balanced above Claudius' light. Her plan was to treat her own self like a fryin' pan, warm up the metal, which would then spread to her old, perpetually-chilled body, bringing her cold self back to normalcy. But the heat snuck up on her, Winter did an about face. She tried to push the foreign piece off her foot by using her other foot as a prybar. But, because the heat expanded the metal, her pryin' foot slipped in the new space, jamming inside the foreign hangin shoe with her other foot. Unable to run away or to really function at all, she tumbled over sideways. In that position she could see the metal shoe now glowin' red. The red shoe reminded her of the book. She rolled to the empty book and waved it at her stuck feet in an attempt to cool down the red-hot shoe. Her actions only fanned Claudius' flame, he jumped 'crost the room and mounted her country dress. Makin' her wear it in a different manner. A dead manner...

That's not a funny thing, and mayhap her not bein' good at the writin' ain't funny either. Maybe I should burn it all?

162

As you know, my parents passed awhile back. I've just gotten around to going through their secondary documents. Though, only because I found them hidden within a wall that had begun to crumble. And what I found should have been in the primaries or burned, or even never documented. I've been an only child my entire life. Officially this is incorrect. A score of days before I was brought into the world, I had a thirteen-year-old Brother who was taken to Thee Bedlam. He was never mentioned within my hearing. From the decision I would assume that he was never mentioned at all. He was deposited and forgotten, except for the proof on this paper. Why did they save it? In case I did not meet their standards? So they might start a collection of receipts until they were satisfied with one of us? I remembered the tale of Petr and his Grandfater. And that is what I have decided to do. Diplomacy has never been a function of that institute. If I went and showed them the certificate and proclaimed him as my own they would most likely place me in the room adjacent to his. I have already been on a reconnaissance mission. It was not exactly what I had hoped for. Though I won't commit the same transgression as our parents; I am lacking in qualities. I will not judge him solely on our first meeting. I have taken possession of our parent's bedroom. I have remade mine own to be his. He outdistances me by a decade, but from our first interaction I am left to assume that he has missed out on his youth. So, I thought to bless him with one; or...even mine. I have left him my old ice skates so he can enjoy Forktine in Winter. My collection of knives in their display; I never took them out of their container as other children did, mumblety-peg is a game for bores. I will show him the beauty is in their bone handles and pearling. Of course, I will gift him my marbles and slingshot. I had always enjoyed the two individually, until I realized together they conformed into a formidable weapon. Mayhap I will relive my childhood with him, follow him like a true little Brother, deep in his shadow.

~Tanach~

Nothing much like good game of the kick-rock. When I find good rock, I kick it good. Sometime, other join in. They kick my rock as well, sometime they kick they own rock. Good thing is to pick a non-cannonball rock. Cannonball-rock not good for this game. Some people kick Cannonballs, but that is other game; at least to them, to Cannonball Clan it is not so much a game. If this game continue then all sos-and-sos break...out. Times I practice on my own. I invent new game of kick-rock version. Alazon discard old net so we don't die when we land from Cannonball practice. I take old net and secure to two tree. Larch and cork oak. Now are goals. I kick-rock. It goes through net holes and it makes no fun. Like Alazon I

discard old net and new version. Goals, bad idea. I return to classic kick-rock. I kick, kick, kick, and then I kick some more. Good game; kick-rock.

~Taras~

At least they never developed this divot scar around their necks. The three of them working together were able to pull the stake out of the ground. I was out with Neimiah, he had me scenting out who had been scratching pictures into the pines. They were interesting. Were they malicious? We still don't know. The blame probably starts with me...Neimiah had me breed with an unknown quantity. Her keeper gave Neimiah these three as some sort of payment, and the rest of my offspring were retained by the unknown's keeper. I had difficulty controlling them. And I heard Neimiah saying to Pellis and Amah that he thought he was doing a favor, he didn't want any payment. So, between the two of us there was not too much desire...effort...We were two copses distant, but I could hear the unexpected hunt. Neimiah was still unaware. I of course could not control my bestial senses. He didn't have a good grip on my chain, and I was able to slip it. I bolted to my boys. I discovered them running towards me on Thee North hauling trail. They were being chased by the unknown's keeper. I'm sure you heard all the hubbub from here. He was screaming nonsense and throwing rocks as missiles hitting my boys in their retreating rumps. If it wasn't so real it might have been humorous. He was a mastiff of a man. He had winded himself getting through his front gate, by the time I arrived the chase had turned to him hobbling and huffing, leaning his girth on his knees between steps. My boys would stop and wait for him to catch his breath. They didn't understand this plodding game, they could have easily escaped. But the act had gone complete, so mayhap they understood more than myself. I could see the blood and offal coating their brindled fur. The mats in their muzzles were dark and wet. When they broke their chains, some might think it was romantic, going back to their Mother. But they did what a young group of untrained males often does, they worked each other up inside the newfound freedom. The keeper was raising their siblings to work as herding dogs for his new sheep. The keeper had no idea what he was doing. They were all living in a pen as some sort of family. It was only a fenced pen with a flimsy gird. If they could break out of the slip chains this unpracticed colonnade would pose no problem. When they got in they could not control their natural lust. Seven sheep and all the siblings before the keeper hefted himself to the pen. The keeper is as equally young as my offspring were. He'll learn to choose the right tools: that you can't keep the herders in the pen with the captives, that the pen needs to be a cage, impenetrable whichever side you are on. But, he doesn't need to learn about cleaning up after a mistake. After I gathered everyone together, Neimiah and I showed him how. Neimiah took the first

one, I took the next, after understanding what he was to do, the keeper at last took down the the third and last of my sons.

~Taxil~

I'm not particularly incentivized by money. Shelter, food; that's about it for myself. And not so much the latter. Bread and water are normally my fare. I walk the land, finding and subsisting...living. I can't say I'm searching. Only walking, thinking, passing my time. Our time here. Observing, enjoying this life. I bury my face in the nosegay of this land. Find that shelter, find that food, and that's about it. I'll trade my cache with Mull if she deems to trust me on that day. She never truly needs anything I might bring her, yet neither do I. So I play her game, pretend to be offended at the offer. She returns the favor in kind and allows me to only take little in return. I believe she is hoarding the abundance in her depths, guarding her adit until return. I noticed the spray of blood splayed on the turf and the base of the oak. The pattern was unnatural. It had been completed on a hill sprinkled with protruding boulders who were disguising their girth in the underworld. The hast was unnerving. The remains were not about. Though a faint trail seduced my perpetual curiosity. I was disappointed by the lack of a quest. Near the base of the slope, in the copse to the Northwest, the disheveled ground was comical in its attempt at concealment. My boot was enough of a tool to unearth the trunk. What booty was this? My *dumbfoundness* outweighed any anticipation of forthcoming ease. I easily excavated the container. My bread and water had a companion that day. It's not a skilled hunter who dresses a body in this manner. I had to carve delicately to find something salvageable. From the corpse I scavenged anything of value that Mull might crave. And for myself, well, meat is meat. I made a stew of wild shoots and this bounty, cradling it inside a bowl of bread. I managed the trunk down to Forktine. I washed it thoroughly, lined it with turf and my remaining shoots. I normally wake early, yet when I emerged from the trunk I was birthed into midday. I thought to bring the find to her tunnels. Yet, I thought this phenomenon might have a greater purpose. I retrieved the rest of the petrifying carcass. Placing it gently atop my bedding, I placed it on the river's surface and softly pushed it into the current.

~Thee Assumption Chorus (Athelstan)~

I'm Athel...Athelstan if you need it formal. They don't really let me sing for them, so at least I'll talk for them. We were told we have a job to do, asked I, 'What's the pay?' The others in the chorus turned on me and told me to shut-n-up. Like always. See, them Hunters come, and that *Marks A Realist* say when they were working in Greece they had these Chorus' there that

went round and looked on everything. Though no one else asked it, we all thought it and of course I misstepped and asked, 'What's a Greece?' He didn't answer. He said we should do that here, cause not all the people read or write, so we would have to put our history to memory. The easiest way is through song. So that is what we do. We watched when The Shadders came for Lochobie, when Polly got pushed...Some participate more than others, and I participate more than those some. That's part of my anger, I'm always working and still they don't consider me a *Full-Pledged* member. So when I'm the only one at a new history, I return and turn the story round. I make it untrue. Said they, 'We don't need your opinion, just your hands.' Now they got both.

~ Titus ~

My interest was piqued when I had received a paintbrush on my last name day. We were discreet about individual celebrations. Since my secret birth I had received an anonymous gift every year. I told him I wanted to repay the Murphy house for all they have given me. The Headmaster said it was demeaning work. He practiced no social grace, he said it directly in front of Belue. Belue blinked slowly, the Headmaster saw that as him being named appropriately, Belue Dumb. I saw it as a slow patience, an aggressive obliviousness that one must endure to practice his trade. I told him I was ahead in all my lessons and would like to learn something physical. He said it was nonsensical, I was placed here with a purpose and would have no need of this in the future. He checked with my tutors. It seemed I had surpassed the majority of them, and they would like a break from my pedantic overshadowing of their lectures. The Headmaster finally assented. I was ready to study a book and then come to Belue with my questions, where he could respond with a lecture. Not the case. Belue taught me in a manner I had never experienced. First he showed me the preparation, I equated this to an outline or a first draft; he then took my brush, inspected it, and he showed me. He looked at me and smiled and shrugged. No words. I kept close and worked close to him, mimicking his technique. He would step back and watch me and either nod or grab my wrist and guide me in a more sophisticated stroke. I eventually ventured away from him, feeling a bit more aggressive in this new landscape. I would return to him and ask quick questions. Trim, drippage, sags, bleeding, seeds, runs, and the first one I committed and my favorite: orange peel. He succinctly instructed me every time. All he had been hired to do was clean and touch up, put on a light coat of the same paint. A few days in and we were almost finished and well ahead of schedule. The Headmaster inspected it and shrugged his approval. Belue blinked a long slow blink, his nostrils flared to accommodate his deep breath. Belue said it was time for a break. We walked to the square, sat on the fountain's lip, and took

a lunch. He asked me a few questions, I answered and asked similar ones in return. We slipped into an easy silence. He nodded to a man walking distractedly by, the man veered closer to say hello to Belue. Belue attempted to introduce us. We began to extend our hands in greeting when the man's eyes gaped, and he dunked both of his hands in the fountain. He said he really had come over to wash off the grim. I was not certain of what I had done to put him off. We all pretended to ignore the gracelessness. As I watched his ablutions I saw his hands were stained, the color of the stain was dark. The color of the water was deep blue, and the sunlight that illumined his weaving hands enlightened my future. The color was singular. I discreetly nodded to Belue so that he might be made aware of the unique communion. He would not look, he was shifting his gaze between myself and this stranger. He is still a stranger. We waited there patiently, myself hoping to grip his hand and amend for whatever were my transgressions. But, he continued to wash, looking at us and smiling, pushing his hands deeper, obviously wanting to be alone. We three nodded our goodbyes. I was too distracted by my thoughts to give much thought to the man's peculiar manner. Walking back, I lectured Belue on my idea. He clapped his hands with an affirmative nod. That evening I trialed in the laboratory and then the shed. Two days later we finished. We stood back and looked upon the new Murphy house. The Headmaster saw us from his window and soon was marching across the lawn. 'You said you would be done two days ago, and here you are on another break!' When he registered our ignoring stances he turned. Belue quickly explained what I had done. The Headmaster responded, taking our stance, 'It was not what I asked for...however, it is more than I could ever ask for. Yes, perfect.' He turned on me and handed me a box from his pocket. The same wrapping I had received for fifteen years. I had been too preoccupied to remember my naming day. I gripped both of their hands, wanting to be alone with this offering. My elation blinded my hearing, I had to stop and ask him to repeat himself, 'You graduated.' They both smiled and nodded. I left to discover my present.

~Tombaugh~

It's not fair. Everything. My age, my size, my parents...most of all, *him*. We weren't even playing kick-rock. She gifted me that ballon! Her whisper in my ear was private. When she was done with my ear, says she, 'Remember, it's private.' Then she turned around and raised her eyebrows at *him* while he was staring at us. I've been practicing on how to do that ever since. When I do it I don't look sassy, but more kind of afraid, and I have to squeeze my mouth so it doesn't open. Because the sun only had a little bit left we all went home to supper. *He* tried to walk with her but I saw her run a bit ahead and go inside their home first, even before de-shoeing.

Our home was just across the path. When I went up to my room to write what she told me to write, I could see him still outside their house looking up at my window. Even if the falling sun weren't in his eyes, I know he couldn't see me right then. I knew because I had tested all times of day. I liked being able to watch out but not have anyone be able to watch in. One time as punishment I had to wash all the windows. By the time I got to our second level I was getting angry with my punishment, and finally when I got to my room I just smeared the soapy water on the window and was done with it. I went downstairs to tell Mother and Fater I finished. I was sent to my room for the rest of the evening and realized I could not see out my window. My parents think the lesson was not very good because now I volunteer to wash the windows weekly. And when I come to my window, I figured out with a little less water added I could see out but it made a kind of mirror on the outside, so a person who might try to look in only saw themselves. I just leave the *dirty* film there and I can watch all in secret. I finished scrawling the message she said to write and tied it to the ribbon she attached to the ballon. The dark was dropped hard. Then I realized that once I lit the candle in the basket that floats the ballon — I'm not supposed to have matches — and opened my window that person could see what I was doing. Then I realized that was what she wanted, she wanted to witness me do what she asked. I let the ballon with the message go. It was floating to her over the path when I heard the snap of a sling followed by the pop of the ballon. I heard *his* boots walk and step off their porch. The candle was in that little jar so it didn't gutter when the ballon dropped. I could now see *his* shadow lean down and pick up the crash. He held the candle close to his face, when he was done glaring at my open window he spat in the candle jar. I couldn't see his shadow no more. But one day when I'm older and bigger and not living under my parents I'll walk across that path myself. Just you watch me.

~*Tucker*~

Some might say they made the choice. For myself I say the choice made me. My sister who was fermenting with me inside our Mother now lives inside me. I absorbed her, I didn't need to form her as a Golem of immortal clay for her to live. She is insentient in our one soul. We have both a right and left slant to our writing, depending on our needs and wants. Thee Lupercalia have approached us for the past two seasons. They have one like me, though he/she is almost extinguished. They have tempted me with baubles of uncommon make, trinkets and treasures never seen before in this land. Much like myself I believe. Never before in this land. My parents love is unconditional, mine is not. My self-hatred dictates our daily activities. If I could only speak with the he/she, ask questions, and calculate if that life could be for me. But, that is a condition of Thee Lupercalia,

that I can't interact with the he/she prior to any decision to accept or reject this life. I have tooth-cropped nails due to my anxiety, if I could only speak with someone. I put up a fierce facade, yet when I dance in front of the mirror I see my truth cleaving to my reflection. I wanted to speak with Ichnabod about a sign I had witnessed, in the midst of one dance session the Blowhard Sisters blew and shattered my image, pinging and tinging upon my floor, though I could not violate my parents unconditional love. They have never asked me, though I know they feel it is best to stay in the shadows. It is a poverty of choices. If there were two of myself then that would alleviate and aid this life. So, I will ask you, do you tuck or untuck?

~Tushka~

If I could boil myself I would. Of course I don't have the heart, soul, nerve, gumption, wherewithal, follow through...odd I mention heart? It is beyond the ken. Every year I devolve. I tell myself I am a good person, but, if you're a good person do you really need to say it? He says he tries to improve himself every day, month, and year. Certainly after rebuffing me he has his quota set for a generation. I was a scattergood in my preparing. This dress cost me...so much. Of course the bank was there, I watched the Banker gouge it through the spine of the street. And me trying to be elegant and nonchalant in the step, well, my feet forgot which one was supposed to go first...I was so slow in my roll. Refined and dignified after my second circle I found myself in the five-inches between the banks. Quite calm, I composed myself, then I saw his handkerchief-ensconced hand somewhat offered. I extended my ungloved hand so he might pull me from the filth. He dropped his square back between the banks as he walked me home before the evening even began. He was concerned I would draw ill if I did not immediately rectify my current standing. I understood him to have an insinuation on his tongue. I flicked and pulled the refuse from buttonholes, some shrapnel flew across the room and sounded wetly a few inches from his shoes. I stood naked before him, except for what had seeped through the dress and began to ossify in arbitrary patterns on my body. I had a copper-lined tub as part of my dowry, I told him it fit two...I still see him in the street now and again. He is quickly kind, he is better everyday. I boiled that dress and returned to the store. Says I, 'No, no, of course I never wore it.' It is five years later, I still don't feel clean; so yes, if I could only boil myself.

~Ty~

The redemption I never sought has found me. Should there not be more to redemption than conquering my vices? I crave more. Which is why my knees are bruised daily despite the calluses. I want a reward for my

redemption. All I have is a wanting of past days. An insatiable craving that my renewed taste buds activated. A cognitive memory of past glories that were easily fogged over in my self-inflicted destruction. It is such a mediocre story, *man is falling, finds glory, conquers vices;* end of story. But, I don't want this to be the end, there has to be more. I put in the sacrifice and now must endure this boredom until my end. I should be some leader, a great man, someone others want to be for all I endured. No one else could have survived my self-destruction. You wanted me to feel bad, I wanted me to feel bad. Once you *cure yourself* shouldn't I have something to believe in? They said, 'Believe in yourself and your path will present itself.' And, alright, *that* path presented itself...then it came to an end. Now I am aware of my miserable life, boredom and dullness engulf me. Is there no more path? How could so many succumb? What if a man completes his life before his living is over? There was no premonitory allusion to this ennui and despair. I attempt to make it interesting; I tried kneeling on uncooked beans, flagellate my mid-aged husk, attesting to discomfort with any lame plan. These were only weak efforts to return to my gratifying, destructive, ancient life. Some say gambling is a vice. Could I outmaneuver the grand scheme if I doubled down? Then I might have a new scourge to evince. And if I am successful at this next deed would my life finally be complete, maybe even hopefully over? Now that I can always think clearly, I certainly don't feel redeemed.

~*Ukilus*~

I had never been one for Dumb girls. Yet, it was late in the season, even later in the evening. She offered for me to purchase her, *a sit down meal*, was how she said it. And I did, I suppose that I had plenty of stipend that I needed to get through before the next outlay. Verecund she is not. I suggested an aperitif, she seemed to hang her mouth open waiting for me to pour it in. And after that she was off. She took every suggestion I put forth. She shoveled her plate in a state of reverie, openly touching my shirted arm, then even to the bare skin of my hand. It took on an odd scientific turn as I could no longer eat, consumed with observing her behavior outside of her natural surroundings. When finished with her venison, she held my hand in what felt like a restraint, and she cleared my peppered duck with pea and wild mushroom ragout. She was enthralled with Glaspell's display, the plum brandy was inhaled first with her eyes before she set it to stewing in her bowels. She spoke again, *now we going*, was how she said it. Great I thought, I wanted to get home and write down my findings on her. Not to be...I am ashamed to admit it, mayhap because of the darkness, probably because it was so odd it was not something I would even think to look for. She eagerly pulled me along, leading down the street. As we passed a lamplight I saw a hole in the back of her dress. I felt terrible for

her but thought it best to let her know. After I passed on the intelligence she turned around and said, *yeah, one in front too, up to you*. I was still trying to process her proclamation when I found myself thrust into her home. She locked the door behind me. As she brushed by me I caught me first true whiff of her. I had taken in hints of it earlier, yet I presumed Veda had been experimenting with a new recipe, something with overripe ingredients. She stood in front of me and stared with her mouth open again. I raised my eyebrows in uncertainty. With both her right and left hands she grabbed her homemade holes and went a little bow-legged when she raised her eyebrows at me in return. I did not want to engage her insinuating that I was the idiot here, but of course I could not help myself and informed her of the giant hole. She informed me that it actually came with the dress. I responded that it could function in much the same manner and there was no need for her to cut holes. Then she had a bit of wetness in her eyes. I turned and unlocked the door. I now try to force myself into sleep, my head unrestful on my crisp clean pillowcase. Even while my eyes are open I still see her standing in her doorframe, silhouetted in that bag of an outfit, holding the unlocked bolt with both hands, and tears in both our eyes. I keep trying to convince myself that they were from the reek she can't fully get out.

~Ulema~

Scare..., can you hear me from here? Probably, problies. If I keep yelling the disputants will tie me in the jacket again. Bad enough I don't have a bed to couple with, but laying on the floor in the buckles and straps...I am stuck in place not able to wiggle even my nose until they come and release me. There is still a stain on the wall from where I did what I do to the last one. Headmistress Charon said it will remind me of my Döder and assist me when I am feeling urges of weakness. Probably, problies. There was no stain on the wall from my first bed. They drugged it outsiden to burn after I got it wetted too many times. It was so wet it didn't catch proper. The black floated up to the sky, calling everyone for miles. They sat through the stink, enduring as he poured a liquid from the lamp onto my wetness. That got the thing going. Blacker still, but now doing what they wanted. The stench was amazing. And everyone was tearing up for poor Ulema, feeling bad I would have no mattress. So when Llewelyn brought a new bed the next week my family disputants reluctantly puts it back in my room for me to sleeps on. And sleep did I. Probably, problies. When I woke just before dawn I had anointed my new bed brilliantly. And I remembered I liked that feeling so much when everyone was crying for poor Ulema that I wanted that savor again. I went down the stairs and got the embers from the fireplace. I throwed them on my bed and tucked them in tight. I stays in the corner, watching the sun hit Thee Mountains, waiting for the people

to start crying. And then they come, it was only my family disputants, the main one easily putted out the cinders. The mattress was a mess, but not destroyed. How would the people cry for me? He took my mattress and mattress-holder backs to Llewelyn. I slept on the floor. Crying. Few months passed, Winter come. I saw a same smoke calling everyone that looked just like the first one. I went to the call. Whole entire house burned down to the ground. Asks disputants, 'You do this?' 'Probably problies,' says I laughing at their crazy. That's when I finds myself under locks in here.

~Unknown~

Hope you don't mind me coming to you in the dark like this. I think my cover is necessary for both our sakes. I think you understand how difficult it is to breathe in this thing, the only holes in the hood are for my eyes and in reality they are only wide enough for my ears. Why must they be so small? Hopefully I will get used to the plumage. This was my first time...*Passing Through*, as they say. I'm not allowed to speak to anyone about it so I don't know if they are all like this. I would guess not, otherwise...what are we meant to do? It was just to grab Youtsey. *Speak* with her, again as they say. I stumbled up the path. They put me in the middle to guide and keep an eye over me. I guess they can see out their hoods better than I can. I couldn't even see my nose, and I was trying not to hyperventilate. I was so eager to impress that I was making myself light-headed between my eagerness and close-fitted fabric. I only realized we were there when I heard the door kick in. I heard a scuffle and tried to participate. I was ashamed to learn I had grabbed one of Thee Shadders after he shoved his fingers in my eyeholes and set them straight. So when I could finally see, the boy was standing on the landing naked. I've heard of adults and mayhap newborns sleeping in this fashion, but it seemed inappropriate for someone our age...I mean... his age. He had both his arms spread taught to either banister. From what little I had been told, they were not supposed to react in this manner. It was expected that all behave. He made me feel like what I thought we were supposed to make him feel. Behind him, at the top of the stairwell stood Youtsey. I didn't know what the pause was for. I supposed it was to put the hell in them, build-up the dread. Sure I had what some would say, *The Fear*, but with my eyes finally set straight, I was anxious to set an example. I went a half step and was halted by another grabbing a handful of my loose robe. I was guided over the fallen door backwards. We went back down the path, empty handed. I saw that little Dagobert sprat with his hand down his pants, the urine stain swelling through his night pants. I guess he had also met with that little one next door.

~Veda~

We don't have time any longer for a garden. He expanded and covered it right over, which makes me nervous. My whole life our family had a garden, a large amount of my chores were carried out within that square. Then we got married and I recreated my family's garden in the new patch. Every one of our meals was either based around or embellished by our garden. No longer. Now we buy in bulk from others. We've done the calculus, and it is actually less expensive doing it this way than when we were supplying ourselves. But, how can we trust these people? Who knows what odd behaviors they might practice? That habit of spitting tobacco overflow on young vegetables. Emptying their child's cloth diapers under the wide leaves. What are these fools doing with their eggshells? What if someone were to bite into that and split their lip or cut open their tongue? And the sloths who are too lazy to bend over, instead using vinegar on the weeds. I've heard rumors that some spray cat urine up and down the rows to deter raccoons. Urine! Can you imagine? What am I to do but just have faith our patrons are honest gardeners? I walk out of my kitchen, displaying his meal like a grandee. It shows me his own dependence when I say I would never do anything to his food that I take pains to create daily. He smiles, takes my cup, and refills it from behind his bar.

~Zuleika~

These finger-tip-scars, I'm alright with them now. Remember thinking I, 'What is this weight in my hands?' It made my arms sore to lug it about, to hold it correctly. In the beginning my youthful, hungry eyes had misjudged its girth, I cracked my forehead against its side again and again. I could not *refrain my first refrain*. Tehehe, I am silly, my Sisters don't appreciate my clean anecdotes. It made my hands rough and my fingers tips man-like. The thing growled and barked if I touched it awkwardly. Yet now there are no more bumbling touches. I have come to terms with these finger-tip-scars. The bruises on my forehead have faded. My arms no longer ache. Today, I realize that this weight I carry about; it is a present.

...War. We have sowed the wind. I hope he doesn't think he can talk his way out of this. It has gone on too long. There is no way I can be deterred any longer. Since our Grandfaters were children has this steeped. I can explain to you. I can't understand it for you, though I do offer my brilliance. I offer him nothing. We cannot suss this out. There are no more undescended tears. His Legion is failing; his clan is voiceless. I am shovel-ready while he is cowering behind his fearful blue-lipped offspring. His garden grows one thing only, and it keeps him from becoming too thoughtful. His repulsive signature has impregnated the land. He will not pervert my senses; I am tethered to the truth. Our plumage will be draped upon our girded armor. He nurses a misunderstanding that he would never be able to pronounce. They must all die a death, though they have been warned off. It is an anger all his own that stays his words. A persecution complex is no excuse for unwarranted reactions. It will not be a democratic battle. All this should go without saying. He is a... SonOfATitHumpingHumpWhoTicklesABastardsDickHeadAnd DrinksHisAssSweatThroughAPrickStrawThatIsMadeOfCrapFromASon OfAWhoreSlutWithABloodyVulvaDripToBoot...

These following pages were transcribed from papers found within the breast pocket of a coat believed to have once been worn by Scare...

Scare...This is a note to yourself-myself, to try and keep straight the Imbeciles, Nimrods, and Gods. Though is there really any difference? They drive me mad at times. No, no. No judgements here. I wasn't designed for this, but it's flattering that they would come and whisper in my ear. So, I will at least try and do a decent job with their confessions.

Undelivered Legion

Ahmen-Deity; <u>Confession</u>-I've never met a more woe filled specimen of his ilk-journey to land by any means, frets; will people believe?

asher Asher-Young Male; Orphan; <u>Confession</u>-Apprenticed to Astodan to work in Thee Tower, cleans bird area and bodies away, starts collecting pieces of bones, later discovers that skull/skulls are missing.

ben AsherYoung-Male; Orphan; <u>Confession</u>-He liked the height of Thee Tower Of Astodan, wanting something similar, he went to live in Thee Church Tower, he rang the bell when Thee Lupercalians were arriving and now that is his job.

Bird Northrop-<u>Confession</u>-Trapped by Petr, escapes, wants to be my friend.

Cat Northrop-<u>Confession</u>-Rambles about his every day, sleeping much, waking Petr, antagonizing Duk, rutting, peeing on everything ˟ including myself -, concludes day by sleeping on Petr˟s face.

Cowan Northrop-Male; Very old, cannot remember if he is some relation to Grandfater; <u>Confession</u>-Takes hidden teeth from me, ruins ladies day, gives horse teeth back to me.

Döder-?; <u>Confession</u>-Once a so and so; always a so and so.

Dr Dolan-Male; Father of Charon; <u>Confession</u>-Conducts Thee Mass Chorus, had arms held out when wind blew out most light and made him appear as a miracle-vision to all.

Duk-?; <u>Confession</u>-Perpetually scared, does not like the open, thinks he will be safe if he's inside Wulf.

Elihu-Female; Twin to Jehu; <u>Confession</u>-Tied to Thee Totem while the new jail is being built. What did she do to anger her Brother? If anything, did she not have to go to his prison, did she go and he made it easy for her so Lessing and all are angry and Jehu is angry for looking weak?

Exseco-?; <u>Confession</u>-Of the coming of Thee Lupercalians and how Exseco only whispers so none will piece together the escape of Thee

Former Castrato.

Fater Nigrescent-Male; Has left the church; <u>Confession</u>-Of Hock and his Hunchback clearing a path in deep snow for his flock.

Grandfater Northrop-Old Male; Dead; <u>Confession</u>-In Thee Bedlam, Petr-his Grandson-watches him, remembers when Wulf saved him from his own trap, thinks he can escape on his own.

Jahbulon-?; Mayhap an old God; <u>Confession</u>-Breaks in shoes for others by walking the paths, wonders if he is depriving them of the experience.

Jehu-Male; Twin to Elihu; <u>Confession</u>-Angry at not having Thee Women's Prison any longer, where he was the head guard, believes Polly got what she deserved, makes some wonder if he had a hand in the accident.

Linney-Male; Older male; <u>Confession</u>-Squirrel war, has diatribes in my ear threatening his enemy.

Mahout-Male; Shepherd; <u>Confession</u>-Wonders if these offerings might be for him, he could be a future God.

Manu-Male; Cat; Derived from the first kings of cats; <u>Confession</u>-Escaped from Thee Lupercalians and now lives in Lupercalia where he is biding his time until he conquers the land after the human wars, he knows who Exseco is, has changing thoughts if he wants to give up on humans.

Mattie-Female; <u>Confession</u>-Seems she was pushed down the stairs and crippled and placed in her wheelchair, believes it was her fault.

Mauchline-Female; Blind; <u>Confession</u>-Is disturbed about a lunch with friends, meets Mishka, Mishka wipes food from her face that her friends did not tell her was there, she cries, is given the handkerchief.

Nolan-Male; <u>Confession</u>-Handkerchief, carries it daily to assist people, has never used it, until he handed it to Mishka the town crier.

Numa-Female; <u>Confession</u>-Takes care of Petr, is haunted by Petr's widow, still spreads her cut hair to distract the ghost at night.

Petr Northrop-Male; Now dead; <u>Confession</u>-Of his coming battle with Wulf.

Polpot-Male; Loves Polly; <u>Confession</u>-Was on Jackass Ginnie with Polly, did not react well, ripped his pants to make tourniquets for her hands, wonders if he destroyed her hands or if the crash did, now only wears short pants.

Scare...-?; <u>Confession</u>-Me complaining to myself of being a confessing pole, I wonder about Ahmen and self, consider Wulf.

Thee Three Wise Hunters-Males; <u>Confessions</u>-Marcus Aurelias, feels he controls other two, Lucius also feels he controls other two, Jonas Groan does not care, he only thinks of his love for Mull.

Theodore-Male, Mine worker, <u>Confession</u>-Of the Mass Day dance and dancing with only men, of Engel playing accordion and being protected from hard jobs from then on.

Tiler Northrop-Old Male; In some unknown battle with another; <u>Confession</u>-Hit on head with adversary's skull, the battle is old but, he thinks still continuing even after one's death.

Wulf-?; <u>Confession</u>-Of the fact that it might be the last of its kind, will forget all trespass if someone will deliver a child/pup, leaves the note pinned to me myself.

yeshua Asher-Male; Orphan; <u>Confession</u>-Usually builds headstones, Jehu asks him to build a giant monument to himself-he does not seem to understand, nor do any of us

Buell Legion

Addison Buell-Female; Wife Of Teardrop; <u>Confession</u>-Teardrop made a gift out of Jehu's destroyed wagon.

Archai Buell-Male; <u>Confession</u>-Former store owner whose head was cracked by Chitty so he could get the place.

Ashmole Buell-Male; <u>Confession</u>-Makes a perfume to cover foulness.

Askew Dumb-Old Male; <u>Confession</u>-About his one arm Fater who told him to keep his hand on the plow.

Augie Buell-Female; <u>Confession</u>-Youtsey is her relations maid, has a good Uncle, she is the good cousin, stung by bee, has Youtsey's old dress that Uncle gifted her.

Baal Dumb-Older Male; Married to Ethier; <u>Confession</u>-Has sex problems, goes to Doc D who offers mental advice, then Mahout for a concoction for his member. Loses his sense of taste and leaves the decision of food or sex to Ethier who he loves dearly.

Baphomet Dumb-Young Male; <u>Confession</u>-List of bad words.

Barruel Dumb-Female; <u>Confession</u>-Stole bread, Cap'n smacked her. Boucher is kind to her. She can only eat bread now with no teeth. What was Cap'n doing in The Church so late?

Belue Dumb-Male; Handyman; apprentices Titus; <u>Confession</u>-Discovers Titus is using peoples' blood to create new stains.

Blucher Dumb-Female; Married to Copeland; <u>Confession</u>-Has only one ear, other is cauliflowered, almost deaf, she only hears Copeland's tics of love.

Boucher Buell-Male; Butcher; <u>Confession</u>-All seemed to have his name confused, though I think they might be having their way with him.

Cahie Buell-Female; <u>Confession</u>-Buys buggy to seduce Abun Love. Very nervous, full of procrastinations.

Cesaré Buell-Teenage Male; Olazabel's apprentice, <u>Confession</u>-

As infant was placed in a box and floated down Forktine to Dakhma Island, Olazabel stole him because he wanted her body. He alluded to me that women were secretly being burned in Thee Tower when before they were buried by their loved ones.

Chesebro Buell-Male; Confession-Assisted Thee Three Hunters, did not get much out of it and feels guilt.

Chitty Buell-Male; Confession-Storeowner, greedy, has something happen to Archai next door and takes over his space, concerned at missing church but knows that they will understand because there is still a lot of work to do.

Chinetel Buell-Female; Confession-Nutcracker.

Clough Buell-Male; Brother to Gert; Confession-Has scar on hand from when babysitting Gert, he saved her from boiling teapot, only Gert knows his secret, hides it from all in shame and because all bad people used to be marked.

Comen Dumb-Female; Confession-Buys Tushka's old dress, plans to seduce people, reluctant to remove it, so she decides to cut a wedding-hole into it, she is also seduced by the musk that cannot be removed.

Comptorl-Female; Confession-No eyelids, suspects her Fater might have done this because he is so good with a knife. I am still uncertain of her Fater.

Copeland Dumb-Male; Married to Blucher; Confession-Has a tic that manifests as terms of endearment, had difficulty until he found Blucher who is mostly deaf and can only hear his loud proclamations of love.

Dimmesdale Buell-Young Male; Confession-Broomstick, wants a pony to match outfit, mayhap next birthday.

Durek Dumb-Male; Confession-Of Ichnabod telling the history of something called Groundhog Day, no one has any idea what Ichnabod was speaking of, think he might be delusional again, though most care for Ichnabod and see no harm in him.

Easter Buell-Teenage Female; Confession-She was looking forward to a year of freedom and feels duped to being worked so hard. Will have guilt for life. I think this might be their plan.

Ebben Buell-Male; Confession-Worked for Archai then the same job for Chitty, Chitty yelled at him for using red ink once when he corrected the books, now he only writes in black.

Engel Buell-Male; Once worked in the mine, plays accordion; Confession-Faribault guides him to the pit where he found the bones for the new jail, he takes his accordion and plays in an unexplored cavern that is wondrous and feels transcendent.

Esme Buell-Female; Confession-Gifted family mirror, inverts Northrop fear of funerals and mirrors, wants to trap Ahmen if He comes.

Ethier Dumb-Old Female; Married to Baal; Confession-Food and Baal are her life, Baal can no longer be aroused without an aid, aid negates his taste, she decides she would rather have him taste his food than be aroused, they have grown large in old age and expanded their love.

Faribault Buell-Male; Hunter; Confession-Found ancient bones while hunting, Cap'n used them to build his new jail.

Gad Buell-Female; Confession-Of Thee Winter Fete, thinks there might be more to the idea of a bale fire than just burning off steam, tells of the huge fire, food, and drink, reassures me that I will not be harmed, takes a bit of me as kindling to start the fire.

Gauldim Buell-Female; Confession-She alludes to something bad that she was the cause of or it just happened to her, or a mix, now walks alone trying to find...

Gert Buell-Female; Brother to Clough; Very big physically, Confession-Sweet natured, reads tea leaves because of incident of Clough burning his hand, she is the only one to know his secret, still searching for answer to why it happened to him and not herself.

Halleck Buell-Male; Confession-Fat as youth, ingested tapeworm, Dr D got it out, friends and at peace.

Hallis Buell-Male; Son to Hurd; Confession-Is perpetually woken by frogs from Miss Elzey's pond, kills frogs by raining them down from the tree, finally falls asleep in tree as his Mother and Miss Elzey clean the mess up, does not properly clean the buckets that contained the frogs.

Hammurahi Buell-Female; Aunt to Senaca; Confession-Wakes to find her trunk missing, worried she is deranged, wants to find where she put the trunk before Senaca puts her in Thee Bedlam.

Hatshepsut Dumb-Female; Confession-Works in the slaughterhouse, sets pigs free from the same cell she was kept in while she was in Thee Women's Prison.

Harris Buell-Male; Confession-The Rabbit King, breeds and fights them, talks to Cap'n and has an agreement, but is torn about Fater N.

Hellebore Dumb-Male; Confession-Taught to make and fly kites by Tattanall's husband, now he sees her sneak and spy on him while she is out walking with her dove.

Hendry Buell-Male; Confession-Has stolen a skull for someone, though he cheated and unburied a different skull that was not asked for, thinks the woman next door knows his secret, she keeps shaking her curtain in a threat to him, he doesn't want the attention.

Herriot Buell-Female; Confession-Falls out of bed, is immobilized, attempts to get attention by waving the curtain with her bed pan.

Hock Dumb-Male; Hunchbacked; Confession-How Elihu, Jehu, and

a Love Boy-Ephram-tried to straighten his back, favorite of Fater N.

Hurd Buell-Female; Mother to Hallis; <u>Confession</u>-Needs to do Hallis' chores after he disappears, the milk is wonderful, the beasts have been drinking from the spring where the frogs live which Hallis has killed, is it the water or frogs or muck in the buckets

Ichnabod Buell-Male; <u>Confession</u>-Speaks of things I've never witnessed, thinks he might be from another land, thinks he used to be fat, met Polly and became thin, was put in Thee Bedlam, threatened to return unless he quits with his lies...french, trains...other world...

Ingreds'ole Dumb-Female; <u>Confession</u>-Of singers one day a year at Mass, ashamed of working at prison, tries to be good though feels she can not make up for past deeds.

Jacob Dumb-Male; Youngest Brother to Levi and Normal; <u>Confession</u>-Has freed himself of all sins, still does not feel it is enough, has committed himself to self-abnegation.

Joba Buell-Young Male; Quintuplet; Fater is Lochobie; <u>Confession</u>-Of being a quintuplet band and needing more practice just like Ahmen.

Jochobed Buell-Female; Quintuplet; Fater is Lochobie; Half-Sister to Faunus. Vows to find her Fater's killer. <u>Confession</u>-Finds a half coin in the garden, gives it to her Fater Lochobie, he returns it, she carries it through the garden daily, gives him seeds hoping he will take interest in the garden.

Joppa Buell-Female; Quintuplet; <u>Confession</u>-About Döder and her interest in the mark on the skin, kisses a boy with two distinct marks just above his eye.

Josephson Buell-Male; Quintuplet; Gay; Lover to Ephram; <u>Confession</u>-First experience with Ephram, speaking of his scar and his worry of Ephram's continuing scarification.

Joseffy Buell-Male; Quintuplet; <u>Confession</u>-Is put into a cart at birth due to a birthmark on his face, is brought back with the returning Lupercalians, they show him how to make wine for the others, they bring him grapes annually, he will not learn to plant seeds until puberty, he is worried they will not return one year and he will again be banished.

Jubal Dumb-Male; <u>Confession</u>-Finds a bovine horn and plans to make a flute, has a misunderstanding and now must use it to drink from because everyone believes he viciously killed this animal.

Laiben Buell-Male; <u>Confession</u>-Is about to quell the birds that annually nest in their roofs, Dumbs come and will fight them if they do, they believe being...dropped...on is good luck.

Lamar Buell-Male; <u>Confession</u>-Finds the scratched quince left by Coptic Love, worries that someone has discovered he steals them to make jam, worries it might be a Love girl, allusions of sexuality is not a choice.

Leighton Buell-Male; Confession-Steeplejack, looks out over Lupercalia while maintaining the steeples, loves to look West, Those Are My Mountains.

Leonidas Buell-Male; Confession-Found Mother's dentures, because he has the same bad teeth he now creates his own from animal and wood, considers himself an artist.

Lessing-Female; Confession-Once loved Jehu, worked at Thee Prison as The Matron; uses fists to teach women and beasts, she now works at slaughterhouse, gets trapped in mud, pig eats fingers, mad at Jehu and all men, everything.

Levi Dumb-Male; Oldest Brother to Normal and Jacob; Confession-He is slothful, comes and speaks to me only because he was awoken by noise that he didn't even bother to check, seems to hate Jacob.

Lincoln Buell-Male; Confession-He was named on the day of an eclipse, it was a double shadow cast upon his name, Lincoln was also christened as Lincoln Toombs, they are kept separate, Buell with Tosspa's Twin learning his ways, mayhap they are being groomed to take over for Tosspa and Tosspa's Twin who are aging out, he is dark and at times called the umbra.

Lochobie Buell-Male; Fater to quintuplets Joba, Jochobed...; Fater to Faunus; Confession-Tells of Faunus asking him what he would want written on his tombstone, men are taken to Thee Tower so he ponders why his son would ask, eventually killed.

Lommett Dumb-Male; Confession-Buries wife right next to someone she hates, Ibold's passed Wife, plans to move her to Thee Tower where women are not allowed, is firing the first shot in Thee War with this new competition.

Lowndes Buell-Male; Confession-Because all the old artifacts from the church had been removed, and the new hideous ones by Cap'n, he sets up a fight inside the open space of Thee Church due to a storm outside.

Ludendorff Buell-Male; Husband to Manasseh; Confession-Pole vaulting over Ahmen's Ditch, refurbishes it up from the furnishings of the gutted Church.

Lurline Buell-Female; Mate to Neimiah; Confession-Has a date with Neimiah, tries to run away over Thee Mountains so her family will not harm him, cannot escape Lupercalia, returns in defeat.

Manasseh Buell-Female; Wife to Ludendorff; Confession-Follows Ludendorff to Ahmen's Ditch, where he takes her in and teaches her to leap it.

Manumitt Buell-Male; Confession-Used to like the public house, now only goes for a decadence he cannot resist, plum brandy.

Maude Dumb-Female; Companion to Pollux; Confession-Self-conscience of her size, feels bad for bleaching Pollux's hair, tells him

to do something to her to get even, he leaves, returns and feigns to harm her before hitting her with flowers while speaking loving words to her.

Mishka Dumb-Female; <u>Confession</u>-Released from Bedlam, is now the town crier, does not know who handed her a handkerchief.

Mulcahy Buell-Male; Son to Yancey; <u>Confession</u>-Tells of being a fat shy youth who accidentally drops his clothes down the outhouse hole and is trapped.

Mumphrey Dumb-Male; <u>Confession</u>-Returns to Loton's land and ruins it with salt and vinegar.

Munly Munly Buell-Male; <u>Confession</u>-Trying to get through the day as a youth.

Narghile Dumb-Male; <u>Confession</u>-Becomes a smith because of anger, now is stuck in his life and has fantasies about harming his own people.

Nergal Dumb-Male; Fater to Nilus Murphy with Moriah; <u>Confession</u>-Interrupts Molay's tirade, is taciturn in accepting the declaration of war, one of the instigators of Thee War.

Normal Dumb-Male; Middle Brother to Levi and Jacob; <u>Confession</u>-Can only work at night because Levi disrupts what could be a normal routine, appreciates Jacob just does not understand him, wants a normal life.

Omie Buell-Male; Triplet with Othar and Otho; <u>Confession</u>-How they used to play at being Thee Hunters in youth, he was the first to kill, Othar cried and Otho plucked the budding feathers of the newborn birds.

Othar Buell-Male; Triplet with Omie And Otho; <u>Confession</u>-Traumatized from when Omie assailed him with baby birds, injured neck from not being able to use traditional pillow, now on a quest for a perfect pillow without feathers, one where he can weep but not drown.

Otho Buell-Male; Triplet with Omie and Othar; <u>Confession</u>-Performs a penance of crawling over the land, feels he needs to pay for the lust he felt when he plucked the feathers of the dead baby birds.

Padraig Buell-Male; <u>Confession</u>-Of the carousel ride he took as a child, wants to warn the children, then wonders if the ride was the warning.

Paestum Buell-Female; <u>Confession</u>-Quiet girl who eventually befriends Ichnabod after Polly's neglect, writes music, Polly improves her music, all lost.

Pollux Dumb-Male; Coupled with Maude; <u>Confession</u>-Wants to get rid of tobacco stain in his beard, one of Thee Lupercalians bleaches all his hair evenly, he thinks it is worth it.

Polly Buell-Female; Mother to Pollywog <u>Confession</u>-Injured in piano accident, adored by many men, milk-bath, is gifted a copper tub by Thee Lupercalians, feels it is an indulgence but keeps it for her Daughter Pollywog.

Pollywog Buell-Female; Daughter to Polly; Unknown Fater; Confession-Taken by Thee Lupercalian Ladies annually for a late night elephant ride all over the land, at sunrise they follow Thee First Star home.

Senaca Buell-Male; Nephew to Hammurahi; Confession-Steals Aunt's trunk, takes it to a field, cuts up a body and stuffs inside the trunk.

Senatobia Buell-Female; Confession-Seems lazy, only works one day a week so her Mother can attend Thee Church on Sunday, starts to worry she is missing something, spies on Fater, did she catch him and Luxe doing something inappropriate...

Strabo Buell-Male; Confession-Sends Jubal to Thee Mountains to teach him a lesson, goes up there to catch Jubal and Engel, they are not there and he goes into the caverns, finally discovering beauty.

Tattnall Buell-Female; Story, husband passed, saves a dove from drowning, ties a chain 'round its leg and takes it for walks.

Teardrop Buell-Male; Married to Addison; Confession-Has Brother whose birth eventually killed their Mother, cried as child, Fater sick of it took him to get a tattoo, now loves art and invented new techniques for tattooing, loves Addy, vows to be good person and parent.

Thouar Dumb-Male; Confession-Weapon maker, hates anything new, just likes the terror and destruction they can cause.

Tosspa Buell-Old Male; Twin with Tosspa's Twin; Confession-Names all children with help of Brother, his body harmed his Brother's in the womb.

Tosspa's Twin Buell-Old Male; Twin with Tosspa; Confession-No cleft, mute, is worried that he has inhibited his Brother's life, thinks he is the darkness in teaching the children.

Weishaupt Buell-Female; Confession-Accidentally burned down house, let Ulema be blamed and taken to Thee Bedlam, eventually gets re-furnished bed from Llewelyn.

Whitney Buell-Female; Confession-Leading Alumbrados astray, she thinks she deserves better, now she is completely repulsed by him.

Yancey Buell-Female; Mother to Mulcahy; Confession-Of finding Mulcahy naked in the outhouse, and how she brought him two inappropriate replacements for clothes, and how he is now thin.

Youtsey Buell-Female; Confession-Her dress was taken when she was younger now the pattern is what all the females prefer, is a live-in maid for many families, is always looking for the Döder sign, takes care of children as a profession to inspect them, finally believes she has found one with the mark, manipulates to be his nanny, will soon begin to tell him stories...

Zarathustra Dumb-Female; Confession-She is the rock painter, makes friends with Amzie, now hiding together after her Brothers did

not find her, they take one of Curtius' bags, she keeps the paper to make a book of her usual rock paintings.

Zebulon Buell-Male; Confession-Rujo comes to him asking to cut off his testicles, he shoves him in the sheep he is cleaning and sews him inside, leaving his knife so he can cut whatever he likes...

Toombs Legion

Abberbock Toombs-Male; Confession-In charge of The Des-pear Tree, affixes peoples wants to tree, men=paper, female=ribbons, takes them down annually so not to injure the tree, which he loves, has an issue with his mouth that causes a whistle.

Abun Love-Male; Confession-Cahie Buell wants to seduce, created a flower with myriad petals, gave it to someone lurking around his greenhouse, she pulls off the petals and becomes angry at how long it takes and gives up.

Alazon Cannonball-Male; Head of family, Confession-Gets shot over wall, shoots kids over wall hoping for wife, it is slaughterhouse now, they play a joke, he threatens that he still might accept.

Alge Cannonball-Male; Confession-Mad he was beaten at kick-rock by Pollywog, steps in elephant dung, must strip naked to return home, now makes a game of streaking.

Alumbrados Cannonball-Male; Confession-Is out in the middle of a freezing night, thinks I don't know about W B, children have snuck out to play on a frozen Forktine, a child falls through and he rescues him.

Amah Love-Female; Wife of Pellis; Confession-About how she first danced when Pellis played, butterfly flock, trees began to rise, butterflies return annually and dance with the new children.

Amzie Cannonball-Female; Confession-Went for a skate by herself, Brothers came to find her, passed right by and she followed, at Thee Wulf's Woods she passes them and from the woods throws some painted rocks.

Antony Cannonball-Male; Confession-Catches fleas from Harris' rabbit foot, makes a flea circus that replicates Thee Lupercalia.

Arras Toombs-Male; Confession-Runs macadamia crop, uses bird guano from a bird his family bred specifically because the guano is good for the nuts, stubborn about his family tradition.

Asdrubal Love-Female; Confession-Was seduced, had a child at a very young age, was taken away at birth, she never learned what happened but has deduced that it is Titus and sends him a gift every year on his name day.

Athelstan Toombs-Male; Thee Assumption Chorus, Confession-Wants to be a full member of Thee Chorus, changes many stories because

of younger age and bitterness at not being taken seriously.

Augustus Murphy-Male; Confession-Lives in Thee Bedlam, left side, cleans diligently, does not truly comprehend that he is committed, lacking intelligence, very big heart.

Avesta Toombs-Female; Confession-Her Fater passes and Pellis gives her a tree to raise, one of his sons wants her, she is not ready, she knows how to wait.

Battaglia Toombs-Male; Confession-Thinks I don't know who his Fater is, Fater makes him go retrieve the body of a ewe, it was the body stuffed inside the trunk found by Faunus and others, he leaves without the body or trunk.

Baugus Murphy-Male; Confession-The last supper, wonders why Faunus is acting strange.

Bel Cannonball-Female; Confession-Irons down her budding breasts, wants a different chance in life, has a plan to hide in the wilderness for a few years then return as a male, will go home first to gather her things, I wonder if she has been harmed.

Boethius Murphy-Male; Confession-Feels there is a hex, sees a magpie killed by seven sparrows.

Buboes Cannonball-Female; Confession-Irons Bel's breasts down so she can pass as a man, or maybe not be molested, she is uncertain of Bel's motives.

Bussey Toombs-Male; Confession-Goes to survey Thee Wandering with a Buell, Buell has been fasting and falls ill, wants Bussey to give Extreme Unction, he does his best but has tremendous guilt at what he feels are failures, failures of man, himself, nature, all.

Cabot Cannonball-Male; Confession-Has osteogenesis imperfecta, kills Mother in birth, Alazon disowns him, Jeansomme take him in.

Caliph Toombs-Female; Confession-Has kept Polk company since she was little, Polk gave her one of her many unused chairs, Caliph re-gifts it to myself, don't take your friends lying down.

Camila Cannonball-Female; Confession-Sleeps in her onion dome on her house, invites Lent Love home, burns it down after a...I don't know what to call it, these are just notes not judgements...but, stupidity...

Cap'n Constable-Male; Law of the land; Confession-Removes all the new doodads out of Fater Nigrescent's old church, buries them with myself Scare..., except the censers which he keeps and the pyx he will give to the boxers as a spit-bucket.

Charon Toombs-Female; Daughter of Dr Dolan; Confession-Her Fater gets her a job at Thee Bedlam, the first day the Head nurse shows her around and then leaves never to return, leaving her to eventually take that role.

Chenery Love-Male; Confession-Courted Evatt Toombs, became

allergic to her spice, discovered that overdosing on ginger can cause excessive bleeding and skin sores.

Compton Toombs-Male; Confession-Wears a kilt, walks over women in bar game, wins a trophy, receives ribbons from women, real men don't wear anything underneath.

Copus Murphy-Male; Headmaster of Thee Murphy House; Confession-Receives Tushka's and Comen's old dress she cut up into pillowcases after her humiliation with Ukilis, all the boys get sick, he puts them in the barrels to burn at the Fall festival.

Coptic Love-Male; Confession-Scratches a message into a quince for a girl he somewhat admires.

Curtius Murphy-Male; Twin of Custus; Confession-Mentalish, finds Neimiah and Lurline escaping, helped them get to Thee Wulf's Woods, now brings them bags of help.

Custus Murphy-Male; Twin to Curtius; Confession-Must take care of his Brother, finds the notes in his pocket from Neimiah and Lurline.

Dagobert Cannonball-Male; Confession-Is a bed wetter, wakes to pee outside and sees Thee Shadders for the first time, that is the last time he has an accident anywhere.

Eiron Toombs-Female; Mother to Issachar; Confession-Confused about her son, does not know he is now a Shadder, he pees her bed after his first Pass Through, breaks down in front of his Mother.

Eliphas Toombs-Male; Confession-Of how in his youth he went to the lake, never fished, enjoyed it in other ways, he no longer goes as no one is allowed.

Elzey Toombs-Female; Confession-A spring welled in her backyard, a Métis told her she had a lotus, she gave it to Meigs as he was being processioned through town.

Ephram Love-Male; Lover of Josephson; Confession-Participates in attempting to straighten Hock's back, gets a scar from the snapped strap, thinks he is soft and scarifies himself because of his interaction with Hock as a youth and his sexuality and relationship with Josephson.

Etienne Cannonball-Female; Confession-Attempts to kill herself in Forktine, puts rocks in her apron, apron snaps and floats away, would like to see it again.

Eustache Cannonball-Male; Confession-He and Lugar are sent to find Amzie who went skating alone, they do not find her, she plays a trick on them by throwing painted rocks at them to scare them, they leave fearing she is dead, she hides fearing their wrath for playing a joke on them.

Evatt Toombs-Female; Confession-Bathed in spice every five years due to being unwed.

Exousia Cannonball-Female; Confession-Goes to the Murphy

House Fall Celebration, smells the stink from Tushka's and Comen's old dress, thinks it is a dark premonition of the past and future.

Faunus Murphy-Young Male; Son of Lochobie; Unknown Mother; Half-Brother of Jochobed and Quints; Confession-Tells how he knows who Jochobed is, learned of his Fater's coin collection, begins to collect hooks after Headmaster says he has a hook-like kink in his brain, accidentally kills Castrato, eventually kills again.

Fichte Toombs-Male; Confession-Of tithings, his former agreement with Fater Nigrescent, and his confusion at having to pay a new tithing even though Fater is no longer involved.

Frye Toombs-Male; Confession-Has most of intestines removed, now has a permanent hole in his torso that is unable to heal because he is so sick.

Furtippett Toombs-Male; Confession-Has secret double life, hunting for something, involves killing, has connection with Boucher, is confused by Jehu's totems but still plays the game, mayhap one day he will lead.

Gabby Love-Female; One of three Blowhard Sisters; Confession-Is the middle sister in every way.

Gaspee Cannonball-Female; Confession-Was the instigator in playing the pig prank on Alazon, is retaliated against first by Alazon who recruited the other children to say she had to go to Thee Women's Prison, then they double pranked them both and pretended a mass feinting when they touched.

Gebchkha Love-Female; One of three Blowhard Sisters; Confession-Given horns as toys, learned to play them, wants more from the horns such as beckoning Thee Lupercalia, can break mirrors, this life blows hard.

Glaspell Tombs-Male; Married to Veda; Confession-Turns home into public house to spite wife, they both begin nefarious acts against the patrons, they finally enjoy one another.

Guare Cannonball-Female; Confession-Weapon maker, hates her job but loves her people. Has a new way of looking at battle.

Gweilo Cannonball-Female; Confession-Had day ruined by Cowan, the last of The Northrop Stain, Enbarr is her horse who was killed by a tree meant for Cowan, love for Enbarr, remembrances of him, disgust with Cowan.

Harpe Love-Female; Confession-Lifelong smoker, colorblind, usually shunned except on Mass Day when the people share a smoke with her.

Hesther Toombs-Female; Lamplighter; Confession-Takes lamplighter job so she can collect bugs through the night.

Hickey Love-Male; Confession-About a Brother who probably passed away in later years, as a youth he was close to his then infant

Brother who laid on his back and suckled himself to sleep, leaving the mark for his name.

Iahu Toombs-Female; Confession-Wonders if she can tell the truth, sick of peoples' ways, carries salt to give to them before they speak so she can stomach their ways.

Ibold Buell-Male; Confession-Is in a feud with Lommett, removes his Wife's box from the grave and mimics Lommett by taking her to Thee Tower, gifts his Wife's old casket to Lowin.

Ignatius Murphy-Male; Confession-Swinging fireballs, robe ignited, graduating alone and naked.

Iman Toombs-Female; Confession-Feels like she used to be adorable, then she was visited by Thee Shadders.

Jeansomme Cannonball-Female; Confession-Takes care of Cabot after Alazon disowns him, loves him dearly, might take care of Alazon after Cabot is grown.

Jerimiad Toombs-Male; Confession-Of his Wife making him clear the rocks for a garden, he does, he puts the rocks in a wagon and they spill in the night, he sees the mess says he would rather have a resting area there than useless garden, does not seem to realize what he did to his Wife.

Josias Toombs-Male; Confession-He senses the coming of Thee War.

Josua Love-Male; Confession-Dancing through the night at an outside scene.

Lent Love-Male; Confession-Partnered with Camila Cannonball once, reunites with Camila, convinces her not to seek vengeance on Veda.

Leptus Murphy-Male; Confession-Satisfied with being the bottom of his class and coasting through life, having everything handed to him, he reads and will one day write.

Libanus Murphy-Male; Twin to Linus; Confession-Last to lose his teeth, throws them on roof for good luck, Linus breaks his leg stealing teeth.

Lincoln Toombs-Male; Confession-Was named on the day of an eclipse, it was a double shadow cast upon his name, Lincoln was also christened as Lincoln Buell, they are kept separate, Toombs with Tosspa learning his ways, mayhap they are being groomed to take over for Tosspa and Tosspa's Twin who are aging out, he is light and at times called the penumbra.

Linus Murphy-Male; Twin to Libanus; Confession-Didn't really lose all his teeth, stole the other boys' teeth from the roof as good luck, gives them to me for safekeeping because he doesn't want to get caught.

Llewelyn Toombs-Male; Confession-Was originally making a bed for Jacob's Mother, but Jacob makes it for her after making the bed

for his dying Fater, makes bed for Ulema, gives the refurbished bed to Weishaupt who burned down her own house which Ulema was blamed for.

Loton Toombs-Male; Husband to Muff; Confession-Runs Mumphrey Dumb off his land who is trying to strong-arm him, convince him that he needs a manager.

Lowin Love-Female; Confession-Gifted an old casket that is a catalyst for Thee War, vows to be alone for her life after three suitors died in her bed, sleeps in casket under the giant ash tree.

Luce Toombs-Female; Twin with Luxe; Confession-She thinks she is mean, dragged by her friends on her birthday to sing to me, is suffering and unhappy at being there and hearing the bad voices, wants to talk to Luxe, eventually succumbs to their kindness, does not want anyone to suffer.

Lugar Cannonball-Male; Confession-Goes out with Eustache to find Amzie, later when she returns he is happy, likes Zarathustra, asks to use one of her pictures and a rock on his model for the midnight Spring festival, she blushes a red he loves.

Luxe Toombs-Male; Twin to Luce; Confession-Fater Nigrescent used to let him sing in Thee Cathedral on Saturday nights, Fater stopped practicing after one Saturday night that fell on Luxe's birthday, December 25, intimating that perfection was found.

Mansard Toombs-Male; Confession-He built a type of sewer system, invented a recipe that recycles it to be used as an additive to crops, they buy it from him, thereby cleaning the sewers, he considers himself a banker.

Marcinkus Murphy-Male; Son to Molay; Unknown Mother is Moriah; Unknown Half-Brother to Nilus; Confession-Tells of why he might have tried to drown his Brother, of how he sat quietly with Nilus' Fater when Moriah had tried to take her life, how he walks with one leg in and one leg out of Thee Wandering.

Marduk Love-Male; Confession-Takes a girl to Thee Lake and wants to go on a midnight boat ride, someone has taken his boat, he wants to confront them, the girl pulls him into a tree to hide, sees five figures in robes and hoods.

Matrie Toombs-Female; Confession-Young girl that just learned hollers and calls, tries to teach them to me, then threatens me with her own curse.

Meigs Toombs-Male; Confession-Fell out of Thee Despear Tree, paraplegic, carried in what seemed a processional manner, now when they deem to carry him somewhere he is low down by their waists where they can look down on him.

Missal Cannonball-Female; Confession-Neighbor's excitement that her husband Jerimiad finally cleared her garden patch of rocks, she gardens all night, she wishes he would take wagon of rocks away so she could garden where it sits as well.

Molay Toombs-Male; Fater to Marcinkus with Moriah; Confession-One of the instigators of Thee War, lists grievances towards the land and Nergal who eventually interrupts his tirade.

Moriah Toombs-Female; Unknown Mother to Marcinkus and Nilus; Confession-Tells of meeting Molay and Nergal, they were always adversaries, does not know the boys Marcinkus and Nilus, is exhausted, thinks to die in Thee Wandering or the snow.

Muff Love-Female; Wife to Loton; Confession-How she is going to kill Mumphrey Dumb because he ruined their land.

Mull Toombs-Female; Confession-Was banished, lives in her tunnels underground, gave a backbone to Jonas, she {likes} him, she thinks she is cowardly, why...

Negus Murphy-Male; Confession-Wants to find a treasure like Solomon found his apron, goes to river with Faunus, Curtius, and Custus, finds trunk, Faunus is enthralled with the body inside, he and the twins battle for supremacy over the trunk.

Neimiah Love-Male; Mate to Lurline; Confession-Watches a hurricane from atop Thee Cliff, it smashes and dissolves against the wall, disappointed once again that this is no way to come or go.

Nephthali Cannonball-Female; Confession-Alumbrados is brought to her for treatment, she gets him warm for the night, he returns feeling ill, she treats him with an ear candle and catches him alight.

Nestor Love-Female; Confession-Gives Jacob a rosary, Jacob sits on her roof in anguish, she is hesitant to intercede because she knows it will never end, he fixes her roof and makes her a bed, she tries to sing rosaries with him and then can only hear flies, she always forgets to leave a swatter for him so he would be a little less miserable.

Nilus Murphy-Male; Son to Nergal; Unknown Mother Moriah; Unknown Half-Brother to Marcinkus; Confession-Gets beat up by Marcinkus, tells his Fater, part catalyst to Thee War.

Nola Love-Female; Confession-Witnesses Polpot pushing Polly's piano up Jackass Ginnie.

Okhrana Toombs-Female; Confession-Born with a hole in her head, helped by Youtsey, when done growing has plate put over soft skull, finally able to live her life, but her good fortunes seem to foretell of the coming War.

Olazabal Love-Male; Confession-Only Love who is mean, lives alone in the mine, sent Cesaré off to Thee Wandering, he knows he is bad, wants to be alone.

Pael Toombs-Male; Confession-Foretells the impending war, has a connection with the land.

Pelasgus Murphy-Male; First born; Confession-Watches over his Murphy Brothers, worries about Curtius, follows and finds him

leaving a sack in the Wulf's Woods.

Pellis Love-Older Male; Husband of Amah; Patron of all Loves; Confession-Selfishly taught self fiddle, trees grew up around house, most Loves live in the forest trees, is very kind, teaches about art and love to all.

Petr's Widow Northrop-Toombs-Female; Ghost; Confession-She was offered to Petr when very young because she looked old, he fixed her ailment and she kept her word to guard the cloister which she now haunts.

Polk Love-Older Female; Confession-Scares people off with her bullishness, rants at me, then discovers her chair though does not realize it is hers that was re-gifted by Caliph, takes it back because she might need it for her never attended party, insults everyone.

Rafe Toombs-Male; Confession-Tells of his and Wife's stretch marks, hers from pregnancy, his from weight loss because he had no food when she was pregnant.

Regius Murphy-Male; Confession-Fater is insinuated to be Fater Nigrescent, though he is extremely allergic he only drinks milk thinking it will make him pure enough to cleanse his Fater and this land.

Rujo Cannonball-Male; Confession-Is hiding in a cannon when Bel comes home to get her bag to leave, Alazon rips her clothing and sees what she has done to her breasts, Rujo thinks it sounds like a rape which is what some girls do to prevent rape, not Cannonball, they do it to fly, he shoves her into the cannon and she flirts easily, Rujo is upset she took his job.

Saugus Murphy-Male; Confession-Attempted suicide by running his horse into a tree, only his horse passes.

Shmuel Toombs-Male; Brother to Tamsen; Confession-Locked in Thee Bedlam before Tamsen was born, he speaks of Tamsen coming to release him, shows why he was put in Thee Bedlam, seems to be extremely violent, parents thought he was backward.

Simeon Toombs-Male; Confession-Has social troubles, people convince him to shave his mustache, it looks very odd but he is happy to be included.

Solomon Toombs-Male; Twin to Solon; Confession-Fishing, finds apron, uses it as a creel.

Solon Toombs-Female; Twin to Solomon; Lover with Etienne; Confession-Finds her Brother and Etienne in the river fighting, Etienne is trying to get her apron back, Solon breaks up the fight, she and Etienne connect, Solomon gets to keep the apron.

Soufia Cannonball-Female; Allusions to whoredom; Confession-Working woman, chews leaf, was not paid for a job so she did all she thought she could do and spits on his bald head, he eventually gets cancer in the shape of the spit, she wonders what happens to him, Dr D

tells her to stop chewing, she is trying to rectify her ways.

Stump Love-Male; Veterinarian; <u>Confession</u>-About as smart as myself, Petr brings Bird asks about losing feathers, his Mother in law marrying him to her daughter, three gifts they send back and the Mother dies.

Tamsen Toombs-Male; Brother to Shmuel; <u>Confession</u>-Discovers Shmuel is his Brother locked in Thee Bedlam before he was born, does not know why, plans to break him out and give him a childhood.

Tanach Cannonball-Female; <u>Confession</u>-Her love of kick-rock, she invents new version with goals, does not like it, returns to classic kick-rock.

Taras Love-Male Dog; <u>Confession</u>-Boucher gives him bones, sheep and sibling killing.

Taxil Toombs-Male; <u>Confession</u>-Wanderer, finds the trunk with the sheep body, eats what he can, sleeps in the trunk, places the remaining body inside and sets them in River Forktine.

Thee Assumption Chorus (Athelstan)-?; <u>Confession</u>-Only Toombs are in Thee Chorus because they are winning history, Athelstan is not a full member, but because he works harder than the others he sometimes changes the accounts.

Titus Murphy-Male; though he is not supposed to know parents his Mother is probably Asdrubal; <u>Confession</u>-Excellent student, helps paint Murphy house, meets a man at the town fountain, man won't shake hands pretending to wash the stain off, Titus invents new color and stain technique inspired by the mans hand-washing, receives annual mystery present on naming day.

Tombaugh Toombs-Young Male; <u>Confession</u>-Given ballon by girl neighbor, she told him to write message, her Fater shot it out of sky, he wants revenge.

Tucker Toombs-Youngish Male/Female; A He/She; <u>Confession</u>-Confused about self, Thee Lupercalians have offered to take he/she as new one because theirs is dying.

Tushka Toombs-Female; <u>Confession</u>-Falls into the sewer on a first date that she hoped would be a last date, tries to seduce him anyways, he declines, she returns the ruined dress and feels miserable about everything.

Ty Toombs-Male; <u>Confession</u>-Used to drink excessively, was very happy, conquered vice and now unhappy, does not feel redeemed, just waiting out his life.

Ukilis Murphy-Male; <u>Confession</u>-Takes Comen out to eat in her soiled dress, is stymied by the holes, she offers herself, he leaves and wants to believe her tears are from the stink in the dress.

Ulema Toombs-Female; <u>Confession</u>-Locked in Thee Bedlam, bedwetter, bed-burner, accused of another person's house burning that started in their bed.

Unknown-?; <u>Confession</u>-One of The Shadders first Passing Through, goes to get Youtsey, they leave when confronted by a boy, passes Dagobert who pees his night pants.

Veda Toombs-Female; Married to Glaspell; <u>Confession</u>-Is terrified that she has to use other people's food to make their own meals because they covered over their own garden to make space for their public house, determines that she will just have to trust others to do a good job.

Zulieka Love-Female; One of three Blowhard Sisters; <u>Confession</u>-Finger-tip-scars, she likes them, thought it was curse, now thinks everything including trials are a gift.

~ S C A C U N I N C **W O R D S** ~
Denver, Colorado + Lexington, Kentucky
2021